"Oh. Wow."

Jesse felt stunned.. 1
the shape of their baby: the outline of the head
and the body, even the skinny little legs and arms,
and—most awesome and overwhelming—the
rapid beating of the heart inside the chest.

He had some experience with ultrasounds—
mostly with respect to equine fetuses. But this was
completely outside his realm of experience. This
was an actual human baby—his and Maggie's
baby. He knew that he'd done very little to help
grow this miracle inside her. Yes, he'd contributed
half of the baby's DNA, but since then, he'd done
nothing. She was the one who was giving their
baby everything he or she needed, the only one
who could.

He wanted to say something to express the awe
and gratitude that filled his heart, but his throat
was suddenly tight.

***

Montana Mavericks:
20 Years in the Saddle!

THE MAVERICK'S THANKSGIVING BABY

BY
BRENDA HARLEN

Published in Great Britain 2014
by Mills & Boon, an imprint of Harlequin (UK) Limited,
Eton House, 18-24 Paradise Road, Richmond, Surrey, TW9 1SR

© 2014 Harlequin Books S.A.

Special thanks and acknowledgement to Brenda Harlen for her contribution to the MONTANA MAVERICKS: 20 YEARS IN THE SADDLE! series.

ISBN: 978-0-263-91331-6

23-1114

Harlequin (UK) Limited's policy is to use papers that are natural, renewable and recyclable products and made from wood grown in sustainable forests. The logging and manufacturing processes conform to the legal environmental regulations of the country of origin.

Printed and bound in Spain
by CPI, Barcelona

Brenda Harlen is a former family law attorney turned work-at-home mum and national bestselling author who has written more than twenty books for Mills & Boon. Her work has been validated by industry awards (including an RWA Golden Heart® Award and the *RT Book Reviews* Reviewers' Choice Award) and by the fact that her kids think it's cool that she's "a real author."

Brenda lives in southern Ontario with her husband and two sons. When she isn't at the computer working on her next book, she can probably be found at the arena, watching a hockey game. Keep up to date with Brenda on Facebook, follow her on Twitter, at @BrendaHarlen, or send her an e-mail at brendaharlen@yahoo.com.

For Leanne Banks,
who shared some honest truths about cowboys…
and other subjects :)
XO

Chapter One

July

Jesse Crawford was an idiot. A completely smitten and tongue-tied idiot.

But far worse than that indisputable fact was that Maggie Roarke now knew it, too.

What had ever possessed him to approach her? What had made him think he could introduce himself and have an actual conversation with a woman like her?

While he'd never been as smooth with women as any of his three brothers, he'd never been so embarrassingly inept, either. But being in close proximity to Maggie seemed to rattle his brain as completely as if he'd been thrown from the back of a horse—and that hadn't happened to him in more than fifteen years.

The first time he saw her, even before he knew her name, he'd been mesmerized. She was tall and willowy with subtle but distinctly feminine curves. Her blond hair spilled onto her shoulders like golden silk and her deep brown eyes could shine with humor or warm with compassion. And her smile—there was just something about her smile that seemed to reach right inside his chest and wrap around his heart. A ridiculously fanciful and foolish idea, of course, and one that he wouldn't dare acknowledge to anyone else.

It was no mystery to Jesse why a man would be attracted to her, but he was still a little mystified by the intensity of *his* reaction to her—especially when he didn't know the first thing about her. The discovery that she was a successful attorney in Los Angeles should have put an end to his ridiculous crush. Experience had proven to him that city girls didn't adapt well to the country, and there was no way a lawyer—from Hollywood of all places—would be interested in a small-town rancher. But still his long-guarded heart refused to be dissuaded.

He'd come to the official opening of the Grace Traub Community Center today because he knew she would be there, because he couldn't resist the opportunity to see her again, even from a distance. It had taken the better part of an hour for him to finally summon the courage to introduce himself. And when he did, without muttering or stumbling over words, he felt reassured that things weren't going too badly.

She offered her hand and, in that brief moment of contact, he'd been certain that he felt a real connection with her. And then she smiled at him, and all his carefully rehearsed words slid back down his throat, leaving him awestruck and tongue-tied and destroying any hope he had of making a good first impression.

He'd almost been grateful that Arthur Swinton intruded on the moment, whisking her away for a private word. Jesse had stood there for another minute, watching her with the older man and wondering if she might come back to finish the conversation they hadn't even started. But Arthur had no sooner turned away when another man stepped into her path: Jared Winfree—also known as the Romeo of Rust Creek Falls.

The cowboy tipped his head down to talk to her. Maggie smiled at him, though Jesse noticed that her smile didn't seem to have the same debilitating effect on the other man, who leaned closer for a more intimate discussion. Jesse finally unglued his feet from the floor and walked out of the community center, berating himself for his awkwardness.

His cell phone started ringing before he'd hit the bottom step, and he pulled it out to answer the call. At this point, he didn't even care who was on the other end of the line—he was grateful for any distraction.

After a brief conversation with Brett Gable, he was feeling marginally better. The local rancher was having trouble with an ornery stallion and wondered if Jesse could take a look at him and let the owner know if he was wasting his time trying to tame the animal or if he just needed to adjust his tactics. Jesse promised that he'd go out to the Gable ranch the next day.

As he tucked his phone away again, he resolved to keep his focus on four-legged creatures and forget about women. Because while horses might not look as good or smell as pretty, they were a lot easier to understand and a lot less likely to trample all over his heart.

Or throw themselves into his arms?

"Whoa." Jesse caught her gently as she bounced off his chest.

Maggie's wide, startled gaze locked with his. "I'm so sorry," she said breathlessly.

"Everything okay?"

She shook her head, an introspective look now competing with the panic in her dark chocolate-colored eyes. "Are you married?"

"What?" He had no idea what thought process had precipitated the question, but he immediately shook his head. "No."

"Engaged? Involved?"

"No and no," he said, just a little warily.

"Then I'll apologize now and explain later," she told him. "Apol—"

He'd intended to ask what she thought she needed to apologize for, but that was as far as he got before she lifted her hands to his shoulders and pressed her lips to his.

To say that he was stunned would have been an understatement. But the initial shock was quickly supplanted by other stronger emotions: pleasure, happiness, desire.

He wanted this. He wanted *her*. As if of their own volition, his arms wrapped around her, pulling her against him as he kissed her back.

Somewhere in a part of his brain that was still capable of registering anything beyond the heavenly feel of this woman in his arms, he heard the crunch of gravel beneath heavy, impatient footsteps and a frustrated voice muttering, "Where on earth could she have... Maggie?"

The woman in question eased her mouth from his.

There was desire in her eyes—he wasn't mistaken in that. But there was something else, too—a silent plea?

A plea for what, he didn't know and didn't care. Right now, he would have promised her anything. Everything.

She finally turned to look at the other man, and Jesse did the same.

Jared Winfree's brows were drawn together, his expression dark as he glanced from Maggie to Jesse. "Are you making a move on my woman?"

Since Jesse had no idea how to respond to that question, he was glad that Maggie spoke up.

"I'm not—and never have been—your woman," she told the Romeo.

But Jared continued to scowl. "We were supposed to be going to grab a bite to eat."

"No—you offered to take me for a bite to eat and I told you that I already had plans."

"With this guy?" His tone was skeptical.

She took Jesse's hand and lied without compunction. "We've been dating for the past several months."

"Then how come I've never seen you with him before?" Jared challenged.

"We've been trying to keep a low profile and avoid being the topic of gossip," she said easily.

It was obvious by the stormy look in the other guy's eyes that he wanted to challenge the claim, but with Maggie's hand linked with Jesse's and her lipstick on his mouth, the evidence was pretty convincing.

"When you decide you want a real cowboy, give me a call," Jared told her, and stormed off in the direction from which he'd come.

Maggie blew out a breath. "Thank goodness." She released the hand that she'd been holding on to as if it was a lifeline and turned to him. "And thank *you*."

"No need to thank me for something that was very much my pleasure," he assured her.

And the big-city lawyer with the razor-sharp mind and persuasive tongue actually blushed when his gaze dropped to linger on the sweet curve of her lips.

"Do you want me to explain now?" she asked.

"Only if you want to."

"I feel as if I owe you at least that much."

Half an hour earlier, he'd barely been able to say two words to her, but locking lips seemed to have loosened his, and he couldn't resist teasing her a little. "Or you could just kiss me again and we'll call it even."

Her mouth curved as she held his gaze, and he knew she was giving his offer serious consideration. "I think, for now, we'll go with the explanation."

"Your choice," he said.

"I met him at the Ace in the Hole a few months back,"

she began. "I was there to have lunch with my cousin, Lissa, but before we even had a chance to order, Lissa got called away. I decided to stay and at least finish my coffee, and he slid into the empty seat and introduced himself. He seemed friendly and we chatted for a while, but when he asked for my number, I told him I wasn't interested in starting anything up with someone in Rust Creek Falls because my life was in Los Angeles."

Which, Jesse reminded himself, was a fact he'd be wise to remember.

"He seemed to accept that easily enough and said maybe he'd see me around the next time I was in town. And I know Rust Creek Falls isn't a big city, but every single time I've been back since then, I've run into him. And every single time, he asks me to go out with him."

"So why didn't you just tell him you had a boyfriend in Los Angeles? I got the impression he would have believed that more readily than he believed you were with me."

"I don't think he would've believed anything without proof—which you're still wearing," she said, and lifted a hand to rub her lipstick off the corner of his mouth with her thumb.

And he felt it again—the sizzle and crackle of awareness when she touched him. And when her gaze locked on his, he knew that he wasn't the only one who had felt it.

"He hit on Lissa, too, when she first came to Rust Creek Falls," Maggie told him. "Apparently he even started a bar fight with some other guy who asked her to dance."

"I don't pay much attention to the gossip around town," Jesse said. "But I remember hearing about that—both the sheriff and his deputy got punched and two guys got arrested."

Maggie smiled. "Lissa insisted it wasn't her fault, but

Gage said something about beautiful women being the cause of most trouble at the Ace in the Hole."

"Then you better stay away from the bar or you might incite a riot."

Her cheeks colored prettily, as if she hadn't heard the same thing a thousand times before. And if she hadn't, he figured there was something seriously wrong with the guys in LA, because Maggie Roarke was a definite knockout.

"So why aren't you involved with anyone back home?" he asked now.

"How do you know I'm not?" she asked.

"You didn't kiss me until you'd confirmed that I wasn't seeing anyone, and I can't imagine you'd be any less respectful of your own relationship."

"You're right," she acknowledged. "As for not being involved—I guess I've just been too busy to do much dating."

"Until me," he teased.

She laughed. "Until you."

The magical sound of her soft laughter filled his heart, and the sparkle in her eyes took his breath away. He didn't know what else to say—or if he should say anything else at all. Maybe he should just walk away while she was smiling and hopefully not thinking that he was an idiot.

"I really do appreciate your cooperation," she told him. "If there's anything I can do to possibly repay the favor, I hope you'll ask."

"Well, I was planning to grab a burger at the Ace in the Hole," he admitted. "And despite the sheriff's warning to your cousin, I'd be willing to take the risk if you wanted to join me."

"Are you inviting me to have dinner with you?"

"It would substantiate your claim that we're dating."

"The Ace in the Hole?" she said dubiously.

He shrugged. "Since this isn't your first visit to Rust Creek Falls, you know that our options here are limited."

Still she hesitated, and Jesse began to suspect that her gratitude didn't actually extend to the point where she wanted to be seen in public with him. And that was okay. He understood what she'd been saying about small-town gossip, and he really didn't want to be put under the microscope any more than she did. But damn, he really did want to spend more time with her.

"I could do better than a burger," she finally said. "I could make dinner."

"You'd cook for me?"

"Which part surprises you the most—that I *can* cook or that I'm offering to cook for you?"

"I'm not sure," he admitted.

She laughed again. "At least you're honest."

"I guess I just thought, with you being a busy lawyer and all…"

"Lawyers have to eat on occasion, too," she said, when his explanation ran out.

"Yeah, but I would figure you've got a lot of dining options in LA."

"We do," she agreed. "But as it turns out, I like to cook. It helps me unwind at the end of the day. So what do you say—are you going to let me make you dinner?"

He was beginning to suspect that he would let Maggie Roarke do absolutely anything she wanted, but he figured dinner was a good start.

"An offer I can't refuse," he told her.

Maggie prided herself on the fact that she was an intelligent, educated woman. She'd graduated summa cum laude from Stanford Law School and was establishing a reputation for herself at Alliston & Blake—a prominent

Los Angeles law firm. She'd gone toe-to-toe with formidable opponents in the courtroom, she'd held her ground in front of arrogant judges and she'd refused to be impressed or intimidated by powerful clients. One of her greatest assets was her ability to remain calm and cool whatever the circumstances. She simply didn't get flustered.

But as Jesse followed her into Gage and Lissa's kitchen, she was definitely feeling flustered. There was just something about this shy, sexy cowboy that had her heart jumping around in her chest. She opened the refrigerator, peered inside.

"What do you like?" she asked.

He looked at her blankly.

"For dinner," she clarified.

He flashed a quick smile. "Sorry, I guess my mind wandered. As for food—I'm not fussy. I'll eat whatever you want to make."

"Chicken and pasta okay?" she asked him.

"Sure."

She took a package of chicken breasts out of the fridge, then rummaged for some other ingredients. She found green peppers in the crisper, onions in the pantry and a bowl of ripe tomatoes on the counter. But what she really needed was fresh basil, and Lissa didn't have any.

"Do you know if they carry fresh herbs at the General Store?"

"I doubt it," Jesse said. "You'd probably have to go into Kalispell for something like that."

"I can use dried," she admitted. "But fresh basil leaves would add a lot more visual appeal to the dish."

"I'm going to have dinner with a beautiful woman," he said. "That's enough visual appeal that I wouldn't mind if you made macaroni and cheese from a box."

She felt her cheeks heat. She'd received more effusive

compliments, but none had ever sounded as sincere. No one had looked at her the way he looked at her.

"Even without fresh basil, I do think this will be a step up from boxed mac and cheese."

She filled a pot with water and set it on the back burner, then drizzled some oil into a deep frying pan. While the oil heated, she sliced the chicken into strips and tossed them into the pan. As the chicken was cooking, she chopped up peppers and onions, then added those, too.

"Can I do anything to help?"

"You could open the wine," she suggested. "There's a bottle of Riesling in the fridge and glasses in the cupboard above."

He uncorked the bottle and poured the wine into two crystal goblets.

She dumped the pasta into the boiling water and set the timer, then took the glass he offered.

"To new friendships," he said, lifting his glass in a toast.

"To new friendships," she agreed. "And first dates."

"Is this a date?"

"Of course. Otherwise, I would have lied to Jared."

"We wouldn't want that," he teased.

She added the tomatoes to the frying pan, sprinkled in some of this and that, gave it a stir. Her movements were smooth and effortless, confirming her claim that she enjoyed cooking. Which was convenient, because he enjoyed eating.

Ten minutes later, he was sitting down to a steaming plate of penne pasta with chicken and peppers.

"This is really good," he told her.

"Better than mac and cheese from a box?"

"Much better."

They chatted while they ate, about anything and everything. She learned that he worked at his family's ranch, The

Shooting Star, but had his own house on the property, and that he was close to his siblings but was frequently baffled and frustrated by them. She confided that she sometimes felt smothered by her brothers, who tended to be a little overprotective, and admitted that she could have gone to work at Roarke & Associates—her parents' law firm— but wanted to establish her own reputation in the field.

She had a second glass of wine while he had a second serving of pasta, and they lingered at the table. He was easy to talk to, and he actually listened to what she was saying. As a result, she found herself telling him things she'd never told anyone else, such as her concern that she'd been so focused on her career that she hadn't given much thought to anything else, and she was starting to wonder if she'd ever find the time to get married and have a family.

Not that she was in any hurry to do so, she hastened to explain. After all, she was only twenty-eight years old. But she was admittedly worried that if she continued on the same course, she might be so focused on her billable hours that she wouldn't even hear her biological clock when it started ticking.

Jesse told her that he'd gone to Montana State University to study Animal Science, graduating with a four-year degree. As for dating, he confided that he hadn't done much of that, either, claiming that most of the women in town had gone out with one or more of his brothers and he had no intention of trying to live up to their reputations.

After the meal was finished, he insisted on helping with the cleanup. While she put the dishes into the dishwasher, he washed the pans.

She'd enjoyed spending time with Jesse, and she wasn't eager for the night to end. He was smart and interesting and definitely easy to look at, and despite the underlying hum of attraction, she felt comfortable with him—or at least she did until he turned to reach for a towel at the same moment that she straightened up to close the door of the dishwasher and the back of his hand inadvertently brushed the side of her breast.

She sucked in a breath; he snatched his hand back.

"I'm so sorry."

"No, it was my fault."

But fault was irrelevant. What mattered was that the air was fairly crackling and sizzling with awareness now. And the way he looked at her—his gaze heated and focused— she was certain he felt it, too.

She barely knew him. But she knew she'd never felt the same immediacy and intensity of connection that she felt the minute he'd taken her hand inside the community center only a few hours earlier. But she was a Los Angeles attorney and he was a Rust Creek cowboy, and she knew that chemistry—as compelling as it might be—could not bridge the gap between them.

And Jesse had obviously come to the same conclusion, because he took a deliberate step back, breaking the threads of the seductive web that had spun around them. "I should probably be on my way."

"Oh." She forced a smile and tried to ignore the sense of disappointment that spread through her. "Okay."

She followed him to the door.

He paused against the open portal. "Thanks again for dinner."

"You're welcome," she said. "And if you ever need a fictional girlfriend to get you out of a tight spot, feel free to give me a call."

He lifted a hand and touched her cheek, the stroke of his fingertips over her skin making her shiver. "I don't want a fictional girlfriend, but I do want to kiss you for real."

She wasn't sure if he was stating a fact or asking permission, but before she could respond, he'd lowered his head and covered her mouth with his.

She might have caught him off guard when she'd pressed her lips to his outside of the community center, but it hadn't taken him long to respond, to take control of the kiss. This time, he was in control right from the beginning—she didn't have a chance to think about what he was doing or brace herself against the wave of emotions that washed over her.

For a man who claimed he didn't do a lot of dating, he sure knew how to kiss. His mouth was warm and firm as it moved over hers, masterfully persuasive and seductive. Never before had she been kissed with such patient thoroughness. His hands were big and strong, but infinitely gentle as they slid up her back, burning her skin through the silky fabric of her blouse as he urged her closer. Her breasts were crushed against the solid wall of his chest, and her nipples immediately responded to the contact, tightening into rigid peaks.

She wanted him to touch her—she wanted those callused hands on her bare skin, and the fierceness of the want was shocking. Equally strong was the desire to touch him—to let her hands roam over his rock-hard body, exploring and savoring every inch of him. He was so completely and undeniably male, and he made everything that was female inside of her quiver with excitement.

Eventually, reluctantly, he eased his mouth from hers. But he kept his arms around her, as if he couldn't bear to let her go. "I should probably be on my way before the sheriff gets home."

"He won't be home tonight," she admitted. "He and Lissa went to Bozeman for the weekend."

He frowned at that. "You're going to be alone here to-night?"

She held his gaze steadily. "I hope not."

He closed the door and turned the lock.

Chapter Two

November

Jesse had tossed the last bag of broodmare supplement into the back of his truck when he saw a pair of shiny, high-heeled boots stop beside the vehicle. He wiped the back of his hand over his brow and lifted his head to find Lissa Christensen, Maggie's cousin and also the sheriff's wife, standing there.

He touched a hand to the brim of his hat. "Mrs. Christensen," he said politely.

"It's Lissa," she told him, and offered a smile that was both warm and apologetic.

He wondered what she felt she had to apologize for. Maggie had told him that Lissa wasn't just her cousin—she was her best friend—and he would bet that whatever Maggie's reasons for ending their relationship before it had really even begun, she would have confided in the other woman. No doubt Lissa knew more than he wanted her to, but she didn't need to know—he wouldn't let her see—how hurt he'd been by Maggie's decision.

"Is there something I can help you with, ma'am?"

"Actually, I'm here to help you."

"While I appreciate the offer, I'm already finished," he said, deliberately misunderstanding her.

She shook her head, clearly exasperated with him. "Have you talked to Maggie recently?"

"Can't say that I have," he said, his tone carefully neutral.

"You need to talk to her," Lissa insisted. "Sooner rather than later."

And though Jesse's heart urged him to reach out to her once again, Maggie had trampled on it once already and he wasn't eager to give her another chance. Maybe pride was cold comfort without the warmth of the woman in his arms, but it was all he had left, and that pride wouldn't let him continue to chase after a woman who had made it clear she wasn't interested.

"If your cousin wants to talk, she knows where to find me," he countered.

Lissa huffed out a breath. "If nothing else, the two of you have obstinacy in common."

He closed the tailgate of his truck. "If that's all you wanted to say, I need to get back to Traub Stables."

"There's plenty more to say," she told him. "But it's not for me to say it."

He lifted his brows in response to that cryptic comment as he moved to the driver's-side door.

"Please talk to her," Lissa urged again.

He slid behind the wheel and drove away, but her insistence nagged at the back of his mind all the way back to Traub Stables. Lissa had to know that he'd been out of touch with her cousin for a while, so why was she all fired up about him needing to talk to Maggie? Why now?

Oddly enough, he'd got a phone call—out of the blue—just a few days earlier from his former fiancée. Shaelyn had said she wanted to talk, so he'd told her to talk. Then she'd said she wanted to see him, but he hadn't thought there was any point in that. Now he was wondering why the women from his past, who had already tossed him aside, had suddenly decided he was worthy of their attention.

He continued to puzzle over his recent conversation with Lissa as he worked with a spirited yearling. And because he was thinking about her cousin, when he got the feeling that someone was watching him, he instinctively knew that someone was Maggie.

He hadn't seen her since July, and the passing of time was evidenced by the changing of the season. When he'd met her the day of the community center opening, she'd been wearing a slim-fitting skirt and high-heeled sandals that showed her long, slender legs to full advantage along with a sleeveless silky blouse that highlighted her feminine curves. Today she was bundled up in a long winter coat that he'd bet she'd borrowed from her cousin since she wouldn't have much use for one in Los Angeles. In addition to the coat, she was wearing a red knitted hat with a pom-pom and matching red mittens, and even from a distance, he could see that her cheeks were pink from the cold.

Her choice to stand outside, he decided. And though it was obvious to both of them that she was waiting for him, he refused to cut the yearling's workout short. He wasn't being paid to slack off, and he wasn't going to let her distract him from his job. Even when she hadn't been there, she'd been too much of a distraction over the past several months.

While he continued to work with the filly, he cautioned himself against speculating on the purpose of her visit. He didn't know why she was there or how long she planned to stay this time, but he knew it would be foolish to expect anything from her. He finished running the young horse through her exercises before he passed her off to one of the stable hands for cooldown and grooming and finally turned his attention to Maggie.

"Hello, Jesse."

She looked good. Better than good. She looked like everything he'd ever wanted in a woman, and he knew that she was. He also knew that she was definitely out of his reach.

He nodded in acknowledgment of her greeting. "When did you get back into town?" he asked, his tone polite but cool.

"Last night."

Which confirmed that she'd already been in Rust Creek Falls when he ran into her cousin at the feed store—suggesting that Lissa's appearance there had not been a coincidence. "More of Arthur Swinton's business?"

She shook her head. "I came to see you."

And damn if his heart didn't kick against his ribs like an ornery stallion trying to break out of its stall. Because he was feeling more than he wanted to feel, more than he intended to admit, the single word was harsh when he asked, "Why?"

"I need to talk to you."

"Isn't that what we're doing now?"

"Please, Jesse. Can we go somewhere a little more private?"

He wanted to refuse. He definitely didn't want to be alone with her, because that would undoubtedly remind him of the last time he'd been alone with her—the night they'd made love.

"I wouldn't be asking if it wasn't important," she said.

"Do you know where The Shooting Star is?" he asked, naming his family's ranch.

She nodded.

"My house is the first one on the left, after the driveway splits. Can you meet me there in an hour?"

She nodded without hesitation. "That would be good."

No, good would've been if she'd come back three months sooner and asked to be alone with him. Then he would have been sure that they both wanted the same thing. Now, after so much time had passed, he had no idea what she wanted, what she thought they needed to talk about.

But he knew she'd been gone 119 days, and wasn't that pathetic? He'd actually been counting the days. At first, he'd been counting in anticipation of her return. More recently, he'd been counting in the hope that with each day that passed he would be one day closer to forgetting about her.

And he'd been certain he was getting there—but only five minutes in her company had him all churned up inside again, wanting what he knew he couldn't have.

What was she going to do for an hour?

She slid behind the wheel of her rental car and considered her options. She was less than five minutes away from Gage and Lissa's house, but she didn't want to go back there. Her cousin hadn't stopped nagging her since she'd got into town the night before. Not that Lissa had said anything Maggie hadn't already thought herself.

She pulled out of the parking lot and back onto the road, heading toward town. She drove down Falls Street, turned onto Sawmill, crossing over the bridge without any destination in mind. She was only killing time, watching the minutes tick away until the allotted hour had passed.

Her phone buzzed to indicate receipt of a text message, so she turned onto Main and pulled into an empty parking spot by Crawford's General Store to dig her phone out of her purse.

Have you seen him yet?

The message, not surprisingly, was from Lissa.

Mtg him at SS @ 4, she texted back.

Good luck! her cousin replied.

Maggie was afraid she was going to need it.

Since she had her phone in hand, she decided to check her email from work. There wasn't anything urgent, but responding to the messages helped her kill some more time.

She knew that she was stalling, thinking about anything but the imminent conversation with Jesse. Now that there were less than twenty minutes before their scheduled meeting, she should be focused on that, thinking about what she was going to say, how to share her news.

She'd hoped to take her cue from him—but the few words that they'd exchanged at Traub Stables hadn't given her a hint about what he was thinking. His gaze had been shuttered, but the coolness of his tone had been a strong indication that he was finished with her. It wasn't even that he was over her—it was as if they'd never been.

Maybe she shouldn't have come back. Maybe this was a monumental mistake. It was obvious that he felt nothing for her—maybe he never had. Maybe the magic of that night had only ever existed in her imagination.

But she didn't really believe that. She certainly hadn't imagined the numerous phone calls, text messages and emails they'd exchanged every single day for the first couple of weeks. And during those early weeks, he'd seemed eager for her to come back to Rust Creek Falls, as anxious to be with her again as she was to be with him.

She'd originally planned to return in the middle of August, but only two days before her scheduled trip one of the senior partners had asked for her help with an emergency injunction for an important client threatened by a hostile takeover. Of course, that injunction had only been the first step in a long process of corporate restructuring, and Maggie had been tapped for assistance every step of the way.

She'd enjoyed the challenge and the work and knew it had been good for her career. Unfortunately, it had consumed almost every waking minute and had signaled the beginning of the end of her relationship with Jesse. Four months was a long time to be apart, and he'd obviously moved on.

She rubbed a hand over her chest, where her heart was beating dully against her breastbone. The possibility that their passionate lovemaking could have been so readily forgotten cut her to the quick. Maybe it was irrational and unreasonable, but she'd started to fall in love with him that night. Even when she'd said goodbye to him the next day, she didn't think it was the end of their relationship but only the beginning.

Of course, her emotions were her responsibility. He'd never made her any promises; he'd certainly never said that he was in love with her. But the way he'd kissed her and touched her and loved her—with his body if not his heart—she'd been certain there was something special between them, something more than a one-night affair. She didn't think she'd imagined that, but even if the connection had been real, it was obviously gone now, and the pain of that loss made her eyes fill with tears.

Blinking them away, she pulled from the curb and headed toward The Shooting Star.

Jesse's house was a beautiful if modest two-story with white siding, a wide front porch and lots of windows flanked by deep green shutters.

His truck in the driveway confirmed that he was home, and he opened the door before she even had a chance to knock.

"You're punctual," he said, stepping back so that she could enter.

"I appreciate you making the time to see me."

He shrugged. "You said it was important."

"It is," she confirmed.

She continued to stand just inside the door, looking at him, wanting to memorize all the little details she was afraid she might have forgotten over the past four months.

The breadth of his shoulders beneath the flannel shirt he wore, the rippling strength of his abdominal muscles, the strength of those wide-palmed hands. The way his mouth curved just a little higher on the left side when he smiled; the almost-imperceptible scar on his chin, the result of a misstep as he'd climbed over a fence when he was eight years old. His hair was damp, as if he'd recently stepped out of the shower, and his jaw was freshly shaven, tempting her to reach up and touch the smooth skin.

"Do you want to take your coat off?"

"Sure." But she pulled off her mittens and hat first, tucking them into the pockets of the long coat she'd borrowed from her cousin. When she finally stripped off the heavy garment, he took it from her, hanging it on a hook by the door, beside his Sherpa-lined leather jacket.

"Keep your boots on," he said when she reached down to untie them. "The floor's probably cold."

It might have been true, but the abruptness of his tone suggested that he didn't want her to get too comfortable or stay for too long. She kept her boots on, but wiped them carefully on the mat before stepping off it.

The main floor plan was open, with a dining area on one side and a living room on the other. The furniture was distressed leather with nail-head trim, oversize and masculine in design but perfect for the open space. Flames were crackling inside the river-rock fireplace, providing the room with both warmth and ambience. Jesse had moved to the kitchen, separated from the dining room by a long, granite-topped counter.

"Do you want a cup of tea?" he asked, already filling the kettle.

"That would be nice, thank you."

Even she winced at the cool politeness of their conversation. It was as if they were strangers meeting for the first time rather than lovers who had spent hours naked together. Yes, it had only been one night, but it had been the most incredible night of her life. The way he'd touched her, with his hands and his lips and his body, had introduced her to heights of pleasure she'd never imagined.

Even now, the memories of that night made her cheeks flush and her heart pound. Though it took a determined effort, she pushed them aside and forced herself to focus on the here and now.

"You've lost weight," he noted, his gaze skimming over her.

"A few pounds," she admitted. Actually, she'd been down nine pounds a couple of months earlier, but she'd managed to gain six of them back.

Jesse studied her carefully, noting the bony outline of her shoulders in the oversize sweater she wore over slim-fitting jeans, and guessed that she'd lost more than a few pounds. She was pale, too, and those beautiful brown eyes that had haunted his dreams looked even bigger and darker than he remembered.

The last time they'd spoken on the phone, she'd told him that she'd been feeling unwell, fighting some kind of virus. He'd thought it was just the latest in a long line of excuses for why she'd chosen not to return to Rust Creek Falls. It seemed apparent now that there had been at least some truth in her explanation.

He poured the boiling water into a mug, over a bag of peppermint tea. The day that she'd made him dinner, she'd told him it was her favorite flavor. And, sap that he was, he'd not only remembered but had bought a box so that he'd have it on hand when she came to visit.

The box had sat, unopened, in his cupboard for almost four months. Now, finally, she was going to have a cup—and the other eleven bags would probably sit in the box in his cupboard for another four months before he finally tossed them in the trash.

"Are you feeling okay?" he asked.

She looked up, as if startled by the question.

"You said that you'd been fighting some kind of virus," he reminded her. "I just wondered if you've fully recovered from whatever it was you had."

She wrapped her hands around the warm mug. "I'm feeling much better, thanks."

"It must have been quite a bug, to have laid you up for so long," he commented.

"It wasn't a bug." She lifted her gaze to his. "It was—*is*—a baby."

Jesse stared at her for a long minute, certain he couldn't have heard her correctly.

"A baby?" he finally echoed.

She nodded. "I'm pregnant."

He hated to ask, but he hadn't seen her since July and he knew he'd be a fool if he didn't. "Is it…mine?"

He held his breath, waiting for her response, not sure if he wanted it to be yes or no. Not sure how he would feel either way.

She winced at the question. "Yes, it's yours."

"I'm sorry," he said automatically.

"That it's yours?"

"That I had to ask," he clarified.

But she shook her head. "I knew you would. If you were one of my clients, I'd insist that you get proof," she admitted. "And if you want a DNA test, I'll give it to you, but there isn't any other possibility. I haven't been with anyone else in more than two years."

"You're pregnant with my child," he said, as if repeating the words might somehow help them to make sense.

His thoughts were as jumbled as his emotions. Joy warred with panic inside of him as he realized that he was going to be a father—a prospect that was as terrifying as it was exciting.

"I'm not here because I want or expect anything from you," she explained. "I just thought you should know about the baby."

Irritation bubbled to the surface. "I don't know which part of that outrageous statement to deal with first."

"Excuse me?"

"We made that baby together," he reminded her. "So you should want and expect plenty.

"As for letting me know—should I thank you for finally, in the fourth month of pregnancy, telling me that you're going to have my child?"

She winced at the harsh accusation in his tone. "It's not as if I was deliberately keeping my pregnancy a secret."

"You were accidentally keeping it a secret?"

"I didn't know."

He stared at her in disbelief. "You didn't know?"

"I didn't," she insisted.

"I'm sure you didn't figure it out yesterday."

"No," she admitted. "But for the first few weeks after I returned to LA, I was so busy with work that I thought the fatigue and nausea were symptoms of my erratic schedule and not sleeping well or eating properly. Even when I missed my first period—" her cheeks flushed, as if she was uncomfortable talking about her monthly cycle despite the intimacies they'd shared "—I didn't think anything of it. I've skipped periods before, usually when I'm stressed."

He scowled but couldn't dispute her claim. Instead he asked, "So when did you first suspect you might be pregnant?"

"Mid-September. And even then, it was my mother who brought up the possibility. Which I didn't think was a possibility, because we were careful both times."

Both times. He didn't carry condoms in his wallet anymore, and she'd only had two in her makeup case. So they'd done all kinds of things to pleasure one another but they'd only made love twice.

And both times had felt like heaven on earth—the merging of their bodies had been so perfect, so right—

He severed the unwelcome memory.

"So I took a home pregnancy test." She continued her explanation. "And even when it showed a positive result, I wasn't sure I believed it. The next day, my doctor confirmed the result."

"This was mid-September?" he prompted.

She nodded again.

"So you've known for six weeks, and you only decided to tell me now?"

"I didn't know how to tell you," she admitted. "It wasn't the kind of news I wanted to share over the phone, and my doctor advised me not to travel until the morning sickness was under control."

"Did you ever think to invite me to come out to LA to see you?"

She blinked, confirming his suspicion that she had not.

That the possibility of reaching out to him had not once entered her mind. "You never showed any interest in making a trip to California."

"If you'd asked, if you'd said that you needed to see me, I would have come." And he would have been glad to do so, overjoyed by the prospect of seeing her again.

"I'm sorry," she said. "I never thought… And when I called to tell you that my planned visit to Rust Creek Falls was further delayed, you sounded as if you'd already written me off. And that's okay," she hastened to assure him. "I know neither of us expected that one night together would have such long-lasting repercussions."

"I didn't think it was going to be only one night," he told her.

"I bet you didn't think you'd end up having this conversation four months later, either," she said.

"No," he agreed.

"I know you've only had a few minutes to think about this, but I wanted you to know that I'm planning to keep the baby."

He scowled, because it hadn't occurred to him that she might want to do anything else. "You thought about giving away our baby?"

"There were a few moments—especially in the beginning—when I wasn't sure what I would do," she admitted. "I was stunned and scared—having a baby at this stage of my life wasn't anywhere in my plans."

"You don't just give away a baby because it wasn't in your plans," he told her.

"Some people do," she told him.

Only then did he remember that she was adopted, given up by her sixteen-year-old birth mother when she was only a few days old.

While he was busy trying to extract his foot from his

mouth, she continued, "And not necessarily because it's the easy choice. I don't know whether my birth mother wanted to keep me or not—Christa and Gavin always told me that she recognized that she couldn't give me the kind of life that I had with my parents, and I've always been grateful to her for that. So yes, I thought about giving up my baby, because I know that's sometimes the best option.

"But," she continued before he could protest, "I don't think it is for my baby. And maybe it's maternal instinct or maybe it's because I was adopted, but I felt an immediate bond with this baby who shares my DNA, and I can't even imagine letting him or her go."

"The baby shares half of your DNA," he pointed out. "The other half is mine."

She nodded. "And if you want to be part of our baby's life, I'd be happy to accommodate whatever kind of visitation you—"

"Visitation?" he interrupted, his voice dangerously soft.

She eyed him warily. "If that's what you want."

"It's not."

"Oh. Okay. In that case, I'll have papers drawn up—"

He interrupted her again. "The only paper we're going to need is a marriage license."

Chapter Three

Maggie stared at him, certain she couldn't have heard him correctly. "Excuse me?"

"We're having a baby together, which means we should get married to raise that child together." His tone was implacable.

"You can't be serious."

"Of course I'm serious. I'm not going to shirk my responsibilities."

"There's a lot of ground between shirking responsibility and marriage," she said, determined to remain calm and reasonable despite the outrageousness of his proposition.

"I want to be a father to my child."

"You are the baby's father."

"I want the baby to have my name."

She'd been so apprehensive about this meeting—worried about how he'd respond to the news of her pregnancy. Obviously she knew he'd be surprised, and she'd prepared herself for the possibility that he might deny paternity. But in all of the scenarios that she'd envisioned, she'd never once considered that he might propose marriage. And while she'd feared that he might reject both her and the baby, his grim determination to do "the right thing" was somehow worse.

This wasn't at all how she'd planned things to happen in her life. Yes, she wanted to get married someday. Her parents had given all of their children the wonderful example of a true partnership, and Maggie wanted to find the same forever kind of love someday. And when she did, she would get married and *then* have a baby. So while she hadn't planned to get pregnant just yet, she didn't intend to change anything aside from the order of things. She would be the best mother she could be to her child, but she wasn't going to settle for a loveless marriage with a stubborn cowboy—even if his kisses had the power to make her lose all sense and reason.

If Jesse had been offering her something more... If he'd given any indication that he'd been genuinely happy to see her, if he'd wrapped his arms around her and kissed her with even half of the passion and enthusiasm she knew he was capable of, she might have ignored all of her questions and doubts and followed him to the nearest wedding chapel. But the coolness of his initial response to her return to Rust Creek Falls proved that he didn't want her—he only wanted to ensure the legitimacy of his child.

"We don't have to get married for your name to go on the baby's birth certificate," she told him. "I would never deny my child's paternity."

"*Our* child," he reminded her. "And it's about more than just a name. It's about giving our baby the family he or she deserves."

"What about what *we* deserve?" she challenged. "Don't you want to fall in love and exchange vows with someone you really want to be with instead of someone you inadvertently got pregnant?"

"What I want—what you want—isn't as important as what our baby needs," he insisted stubbornly.

She blew out a breath. "I don't think our baby needs to be raised by two parents trapped in a loveless marriage."

"You don't have to make it sound so dire. If we want to, we can make this work."

"What if I don't want to?"

He ignored her question as if she hadn't even spoken. "We should be able to make all of the necessary arrangements for a wedding within a couple of weeks."

"Did you get kicked in the head by a horse? I am *not* marrying you."

The lift of his brows was the only indication that he'd heard her this time, as he steamrollered over her protest. "We can have a quick courthouse ceremony here or a more traditional wedding in LA, if you prefer."

"So I *do* have some say in this?"

"The details," he agreed. "I don't care about the where and when so long as it's legal."

There was something about his determination to make her his wife that thrilled her even as it infuriated her. And she suspected that, deep in her heart, she wanted what he was offering: to get married and raise their baby together.

But she didn't want a marriage on the terms he was offering. She didn't want a legal union for the sake of their baby but a commitment based on mutual respect and affection. Unfortunately, that offer wasn't on the table. And even if it was, there were other obstacles to consider.

"What about the detail also known as my job?" she challenged.

"What about it?"

"How am I going to represent my clients in Los Angeles if I'm living in Rust Creek Falls? Or am I supposed to happily sacrifice all of my career ambitions for the pleasure of becoming Mrs. Jesse Crawford?"

His only response was a scowl that proved he hadn't given much thought to the distance that separated them geographically.

"I'm sure you can find a job in Rust Creek Falls, if you want to keep working."

"Or maybe you could find work in Los Angeles," she countered.

"Now you're just being ridiculous."

"And you're being completely unreasonable."

"It's not unreasonable to want our child to be raised by two parents."

"Look at us, Jesse. We can't even have a simple conversation without fighting and you want us to get married?"

"Yes, I do," he said again.

She shook her head. "Obviously we have a fundamental difference of opinion."

"I don't recall there being any differences of opinion when we were in bed together."

And with those words, the air was suddenly charged with electricity.

The heat in his gaze spread warmth through her veins, from her belly to her breasts, throbbing between her thighs. He wasn't even touching her—and she was fairly quivering with desire.

No one had ever affected her the way this man did. No one had ever made her feel the way she felt when she was with him. But even more unnerving than the wanting of her body was the yearning of her heart.

She pushed away from the breakfast bar and carried her empty mug to the sink. She had to leave, to give them both some time and space to think about how they should proceed.

"Maggie."

She looked up, and he was there. Close enough that she couldn't breathe without inhaling his clean, masculine scent. Close enough that he had to hear her heart pounding. And although his eyes never left hers, she felt the heat of his gaze everywhere.

He lifted a hand to touch her hair, his fingers skimming over the silky tresses to cradle the back of her head. Then his mouth was on hers, his lips warm and firm and sure, and she melted against him.

She'd forgotten how strong he was, how solid every inch of his body was. Hard and unyielding. And yet, for all of his strength, he was incredibly gentle. It was that unadulterated masculine strength combined with his inherently gentle nature that had appealed to her from the first.

His hands slid down her back, inched up beneath the hem of her sweater. Then those wide, callused palms were on her skin, sliding up her torso to cup her breasts. Her blood pulsed in her veins, hot and demanding. His thumbs brushed over her nipples through the delicate lace, and she actually whimpered.

He nibbled on her lips. Teasing, tasting, tempting.

"I want you, Maggie."

She wanted him, too. And though she knew it might be a mistake to let herself succumb to that desire while there was still so much unresolved between them, that knowledge didn't dampen her need.

"Tell me you feel the same," he urged.

"I do," she admitted. "But—"

She forgot the rest of what she'd intended to say when he lifted her off her feet and into his arms.

He carried her up the stairs and down a short hallway to his bedroom with effortless ease. When he set her on her feet beside the bed, she knew that if she was going to protest, now was the time to do so. Then he kissed her again, and any thought of protest flew out of her mind.

Her mouth parted beneath the pressure of his, and his tongue swept inside, teasing the soft inside of her lips. His hands slid down her back, over the curve of her buttocks, pulling her close. The evidence of his arousal fueled her own. Blood pulsed in her veins, pooled low in her belly, making her want so much that she actually ached.

She lifted her hands to the buttons of his shirt and began

to unfasten them. She wanted to touch him, to feel the warmth of his bare skin beneath her palms. But the cotton T-shirt under the flannel impeded her efforts. With a frustrated sigh, she tugged the T-shirt out of his jeans and shoved her hands beneath it.

Jesse chuckled softly. "I didn't realize this was a race."

"I want to feel your body against mine," she confessed.

He released her long enough to get rid of his clothes. She sat on the edge of the bed, intending to do the same, but she was still struggling with her boots when his jeans hit the floor. As he kicked them away, she couldn't help but admire the knit boxer briefs that molded to the firm muscles of his buttocks and thighs at the back and did absolutely nothing to hide the obvious evidence of his arousal at the front.

Her mouth went dry and her fingers froze on the knotted laces. He knelt beside her and efficiently untied the boots and pulled them from her feet. Then he unfastened her jeans and pushed them over her hips, down her legs, finally stripping them away along with her socks.

"Your feet are cold," he realized, warming them between his palms. "You need thicker socks."

Not in California, she thought, but didn't say it aloud. She didn't want to speak of the distance that separated their lives; she didn't want anything to take away from the here and now.

"Or I could get under the covers," she suggested.

"That's a better plan," he agreed.

But first, he lifted her sweater over her head and tossed it aside, leaving her clad in only a lace demi-cup bra and matching bikini panties. He sat back on his haunches, the heat in his gaze roaming over her as tangible as a caress, making her nipples tighten and her thighs quiver.

"You absolutely take my breath away," he told her.

She tugged the covers down and rolled over the bed to

snuggle beneath them. Jesse immediately slid in beside her, his hands skimming over her, tracing her curves. He lowered his head to nuzzle the tender skin at the base of her throat, making her shiver.

He glanced up. "Are you still cold?"

She shook her head; he smiled slightly before he lowered his head again, his lips skimming across her collarbone, then tracing the lacy edge of her bra. She could feel his breath, warm on her skin, as his mouth hovered above her breast. Her hand lifted to his head, silently urging him closer. He willingly acquiesced to her direction, laving her nipple with his tongue. The sensation of hot, wet heat through the silky fabric made her gasp, then his lips closed over the lace-covered peak, sending fiery spears of pleasure arrowing to her core.

He found the center clasp of her bra and released it, peeling the fabric aside so he could suckle her bare flesh, making her groan. He tugged the straps down her arms, dropped the garment to the floor. His hands stroked down her torso, his fingers hooking in her panties and dragging them down her legs and away, so that she was completely naked. All the while, his hands and his lips moved over her, teasing and tempting, until her body was fairly quivering with wanting.

Genetics had blessed her with a naturally slim build and the loss of those few pounds had pushed her from slender toward skinny, but she knew that was only a temporary state. Because although her hip bones and ribs were visible now, there was also a subtle roundness to her belly— evidence of the baby she carried.

He splayed his hand over the curve, his wide palm covering her almost from hip bone to hip bone, as if cradling their child, and the sweetness of the gesture made tears fill her eyes.

"Everyone says that a baby is a miracle," he said. "But

the idea of you growing our baby inside of you is every bit as miraculous."

"You call it *miraculous* now. In a few more months, you'll be calling it *fat*."

She'd been teasing, attempting to lighten the mood, but as soon as she spoke the words, she wished she could take them back. Talking about the future as if they would be together was a mistake, even if it was—deep in her heart—what she wanted.

But he shook his head. "You'll always be beautiful to me—the most beautiful woman I've ever known."

Which might have sounded like a well-rehearsed line from another man, but the sincerity in his tone made her heart swell inside her chest.

"I want to be with you through every step of your pregnancy," he continued. "I want to see the changes in your body as our baby grows. I want to be the one who runs to the grocery store in the middle of the night when you have a sudden craving for ice cream."

"I didn't think the store in Rust Creek Falls was open in the middle of the night."

"Lucky for you, I have a key."

"That is lucky," she agreed. "But I don't want to worry about the future right now."

"What do you want?"

She lifted her arms to link them behind his neck. "You. I only want you."

"Well, that's convenient," he said. "Because I want you, too."

Then he captured her mouth in a long, slow kiss that went on and on until her head was actually spinning. The hand that was on her belly inched lower. His fingers sifted through the soft curls at the apex of her thighs and her hips automatically lifted off the bed, wordlessly encouraging his exploration. He parted the slick folds and dipped inside. She didn't know if it was the pregnancy hormones or Jesse, but all it took was that one stroke, deep inside, and she flew apart.

He continued to stroke her while the convulsions rippled through her body. Her hands fisted in the sheet, as she tried to anchor herself against the onslaught of sensations. "Jesse, please."

He leaned forward to reach into the drawer beside his bed and pulled out a small square packet.

Though she was reassured by this evidence of what was obviously a long-ingrained habit, she had to smile. "Isn't that a little like closing the barn door after the horse is out?"

"I guess it is," he agreed. "Although there are more reasons than pregnancy for using protection."

"Oh." She blushed. "Of course."

"But there's been no one since you," he said sincerely. "And no one for more than six months before that."

She took the square packet out of his hand. "Then we don't need this," she said, and set it on the bedside table.

He parted her legs and settled between them, burying himself deep in one thrust as she arched up to meet him.

He groaned in appreciation as she wrapped her legs around his hips. "You feel...so...good."

"You make me feel good," she told him.

He smiled at that and lowered his head to kiss her, long and slow and deep, as he moved inside her.

Maggie had never thought of herself as a particularly sensual woman. She certainly wasn't the type to get carried away by passion. She'd always thought sex was enjoyable, if unremarkable, but that was before she'd had sex with Jesse.

Over the past few months, she'd decided that her memories of the one night they'd spent together had been exaggerated by her imagination. It wasn't really possible that just standing close to him had made her knees weak, that breathing in his unique scent could make her insides quiver, that the touch of his mouth against her was enough to make her bones melt. Of course it wasn't. For some reason, she'd romanticized the memory, turned their one-night affair into something it never was and was never meant to be.

And then she'd seen him again, and her knees had gone weak. He'd stepped closer to her, and her insides had quivered. It didn't matter that his gaze had been guarded and his tone had been cool. All that mattered was he was there, and every nerve ending in her body was suddenly and acutely aware of him, aching for him.

Then, finally, he'd touched her. Just a brush of his hand over her hair, but that was enough to have her heart hammering inside of her chest. And then he kissed her, and not just her bones but everything inside of her had melted into a puddle of need. There was no thought or reason, there was only want. Hot and sharp and desperate.

As he moved inside of her now, she felt the connection between them. Not just the physical mating of their bodies but the joining of their souls. Maybe it was fantastical, but it was how she felt. She couldn't think of anything but Jesse, didn't want anyone but him.

The delicious friction between their bodies was every bit as incredible as she'd remembered—maybe even more. Every stroke, every thrust, sent little shock waves zinging through her blood. She could feel the anticipation building inside of her. Her body arched and strained, meeting him willingly, eagerly, aching for the ecstasy and fulfillment she'd only ever found in his arms.

Her hands gripped his shoulders, her fingers digging into his muscles, her nails scoring his skin. Her breath came in quick, shallow gasps as he drove her higher and higher to the pinnacle of their mutual pleasure.

Yes.

Please.

More.

And he gave her more. With his hands and his lips and his body, he gave and he gave until it was more than she could take. Pleasure poured through her, over her, a tidal wave of sensation that was so intense it stole her breath, her thoughts, her vision. There was nothing but bliss... and Jesse.

He was everything.

With a last thrust and a shudder, he collapsed on top of her, his face buried in the pillow beside her head.

She lifted a hand to his shoulder, let it trail down his back. His deliciously sculpted and tightly muscled body was truly a woman's fantasy—and he'd proven more than capable of satisfying every one of her fantasies, even the ones she hadn't realized that she had.

He lifted his weight off her, shifted so that he was beside her. But he kept his arm around her, holding her close. "Are you okay?" he asked.

Her lips curved. "I'm very okay."

He pulled her closer, so that her back was snug against his front and her head was tucked beneath his chin. "I almost forgot how good it was between us."

"I tried to convince myself it couldn't have been as good as I remembered." It was somehow easier to make the admission without looking at him. "But I was wrong."

"I missed you, Maggie."

"I missed you, too. But this...chemistry," she decided, for lack of a better term, "between us doesn't really change anything."

"You don't think so?"

"Wanting you—and wanting to be with you—doesn't alter the fact that our lives are twelve hundred miles apart."

"We'll figure it out," he told her.

He made it sound so easy, but Maggie knew there wasn't a simple answer. His suggestion that they should get married and raise their baby together wasn't a viable one. She couldn't—wouldn't—give up her career and her life in LA simply because he wanted to be a hands-on parent to their child. She admired his willingness to step up and respected his commitment to his ideals of fatherhood, but she was determined to focus on reality. And the reality was that her life, her family and her career were in California.

It wasn't likely that they were going to figure anything out—certainly not easily. She suspected it was more likely that there would be a lot of disagreement before any decisions were made, but it wasn't a battle she wanted to wage right now. Not while she was cradled in the warm strength of his arms, her body still sated from their lovemaking.

Within a few minutes, his breathing had evened out, and she knew he'd fallen asleep. As her own eyes started to drift shut, she found herself thinking about his impromptu offer of marriage. Not that she intended to accept—there were too many reasons to refuse, too many barriers to a relationship between them. But she couldn't deny that the prospect of sharing a bed with him for more than a few hours was undeniably tempting.

Chapter Four

When Jesse woke up, he was alone.

He could still smell Maggie's scent on his sheets, and there was an indent on the pillow where she'd slept, so he knew she couldn't have been gone long. He rose from his bed and moved to the window.

He didn't realize that his chest felt tight until he saw that her rental car was behind his truck in the driveway and the tension lessened. He'd been left with nothing more than a note on his kitchen table once before, and he didn't want to go through that again. He hadn't chased after Shaelyn—he'd had no interest in forcing her to stay in Rust Creek Falls when it was obvious she didn't want to be there.

But the situation with Maggie was different—she was carrying his baby, and that meant they had to figure out a way to work things out. If she had gone, he would have chased after her. He was glad he didn't have to.

He retrieved his jeans from the floor and tugged them on, then shoved his arms into the sleeves of his shirt and headed down the stairs. He found her standing at the stove, a spatula in her hand. The pressure in his chest eased a little more.

A glance at the numeric display on the stove revealed that it was after eight o'clock. "I guess we skipped dinner."

She looked up and offered a shy smile. "I hope you don't mind—I woke up hungry, and I thought you might be, too."

"I don't and I am," he told her. "French toast?"

"Is that okay?"

"Perfect."

She flipped the last piece of bread out of the frying pan and onto the plate, then carried the plate to the table, already set for two.

As she sat down across from him, he put a couple of slices on his plate, then liberally doused them with maple syrup. She took one slice, slowly ate it, cutting neat little squares that she dipped in a tiny puddle of syrup on her plate.

"I thought you said you were hungry."

"I was." She popped the last piece of toast into her mouth, then folded her napkin and set it on top of her plate. "And now I've eaten."

"You had one piece of French toast."

"I had two." One corner of her mouth tilted up in a half smile. "I ate the first one as soon as I flipped it out of the frying pan."

"Two whole slices?" He transferred another two to his own plate. "You must be stuffed."

"Don't make fun of me—I'm just happy to be able to keep down what I'm eating these days."

"I'm sorry," he said, sincerely contrite. "That must have been awful."

"It wasn't fun," she agreed.

"You should have called me."

She nodded. "I'm sorry I didn't."

He wanted to stay angry with her, but what was the point? Nothing could change what had happened since she left Rust Creek Falls in July, nothing could give them back the first four months of her pregnancy. But he couldn't help but think that, if she'd told him sooner, they might be in a different place right now.

Instead, he'd spent weeks dealing with the tangled emotions inside of him. He'd been hurt and angry and frustrated that he couldn't stop thinking about her. He'd tried to get over her—he'd even let his younger brother, Justin, set him up with a friend of the girl he was going out with. The date had been a complete bust, primarily because he couldn't stop thinking about Maggie. But recently he'd managed to convince himself that he was starting to forget about her—right up until the minute he saw her standing outside the paddock at Traub Stables.

"So," he began, thinking that a change of topic was in order, "things have been busy for you at work over the past couple of months?"

She nodded. "Busier than usual. Maybe too busy."

"Can you cut back on your hours?"

"Not if I want to keep my job."

"Do you?"

"Of course," she answered immediately, automatically. Then her brow furrowed as she picked up her glass of water and sipped.

"Tell me about your new job," she finally suggested. "When I was here in the summer, you were working here, at your family's ranch, and now you're training horses."

"I still help out here, but it's the horses that have always been my focus."

"I heard they call you the horse whisperer in town—what exactly does that mean?"

"It's not as mystical as it sounds," he told her. "It just means that I don't use restraints or force when I'm training."

"How did you end up working at Traub Stables? I thought there was some long-standing feud between the Crawfords and the Traubs."

"There is," he acknowledged. "Although no one really

seems sure about its origins, whether it was a business deal gone bad or a romantic rivalry. Whatever the cause, I think my sister's marriage to Dallas Traub in February has helped build some bridges between the two families."

"So your family doesn't mind that you're working for Sutter Traub?"

His lips curved in a wry smile. "I wouldn't go that far," he acknowledged. "My father saw it as a betrayal. My mother warned that I was being set up—for what, she had no idea, but she was certain it was some kind of disaster in the making."

"Did you take the job despite their objections—or because of them?"

"Despite," he said. "I've wanted some space from my family for a long time, but that doesn't mean I don't love and respect them."

"And you don't mind that your boss is a Traub?"

"Sutter's a good guy who values the animals in his care and appreciates what I bring to his stables."

"I read a series of books when I was a kid, about a girl who lived on a ranch and raised an orphaned foal," she told him. "She fed it and trained it and entered riding competitions with it. After reading those books, I was desperate to experience the feeling of racing across open fields on horseback. I begged my parents to put me in a riding camp for the summer.

"They were always encouraging us to try new experiences, so they found a local camp and signed me up. I was so excited...until the first day. I'd never seen a horse up close until then," she confided. "And when we got to the Northbrook Riding Academy and I saw real, live horses galloping in the distance, I was terrified."

"What happened?" he asked, both curious about and grateful for this voluntary glimpse into her childhood.

"I begged to go home as passionately as I'd begged for the camp, but they made me stay. My parents are very big on commitment and follow-through. I was the one who wanted the experience, and they weren't going to let me quit."

"Did you ride?"

She shook her head. "The instructors tried to help me overcome my fear of the horses, but whenever I got too close, I would actually start to hyperventilate. Of course, the other kids made fun of me, which made the whole experience that much worse.

"Then I met Dolly. She was a white Shetland pony who was too old and lame to do much of anything, but she had the softest, kindest eyes.

"I spent most of the week with her. I brushed her and fed her and led her around her paddock. At the end of the week, I still hadn't been on the back of a horse, but I'd fallen in love with Dolly. For the next six months, I went back to Northbrook once a week just to visit her."

He didn't need to ask what had happened after six months. Considering that the pony had been old and lame, he was certain he knew. Instead he said, "Did you ever get over your fear of horses?"

"I haven't been around them much since that summer."

He pushed away from the table. "Get your coat and boots on."

"What? Why?"

"I want to introduce you to someone."

She shook her head. "I got over my childhood fascination with horses—I'm good now."

"Not if you're still afraid," he told her.

"I wouldn't say *afraid*," she denied. "More…cautious."

He took her coat from the hook, brought it over to her.

"I need to clean up the kitchen."

"The dishes will wait."

"Has anyone ever told you that you're pushy?"

He took her hand and guided it into the sleeve of her coat. "Not pushy—persuasive."

"I'm not feeling persuaded," she told him, but she put her other arm in her other sleeve. "My boots are still, um, upstairs."

In his bedroom, where he'd taken them off her along with the rest of her clothing before he'd made love with her.

"I'll get them," he said.

When he came back down, she had her coat zipped up to her chin, a hat on her head and a scarf wrapped around her throat.

He held back a smile as he knelt at her feet and helped her on with the boots. To someone who had lived her whole life in Southern California, Montana in November—even the first of November—was undoubtedly cold, but he knew it would be a lot colder in December, January and February.

He hoped she would be there to experience it.

Maggie could tell that Jesse was amused by her efforts to bundle up against the climate. As she carefully tucked her hands into woolen mittens, he stuffed his feet into his boots and tugged on a jacket, not even bothering to button it.

She stepped outside and gasped as the cold slapped her in the face and stole the breath from her lungs.

"It was seventy-two degrees when I left Los Angeles," she told him.

He slid an arm across her shoulders, holding her close to share body heat—of which he seemed to have an abundance. "The weather takes some getting used to for a lot of people."

She couldn't imagine ever getting used to the cold—or wanting to. Thankfully, the barn was only a short distance from his house, and she was grateful to duck into its warm shelter.

The facility was brightly lit and immaculate. The alleyway was interlocking brick and the wooden walls fairly gleamed. Jesse pulled the door closed and stood beside her, giving her a minute.

"Are you okay?" he asked gently.

She nodded, because she wanted it to be true, but she wasn't entirely certain. She'd heard that the olfactory sense was one of the strongest for evoking memories, but she'd never experienced it herself until she stepped inside the barn and breathed in the scent of hay and horses. Suddenly her brain was flooded with memories of that long-ago summer camp, and with the memories came apprehension and anxiety.

"Just breathe," he said.

It was only then that she realized she'd been holding her breath. She let it out now, and drew fresh air into her lungs. But that fresh air carried the same scent, and made her heart pound hard and fast inside her chest. "I feel stupid."

"Why?"

"Because I'm scared," she admitted.

"I won't let anything bad happen to you," he promised.

"It's late," she said. "I should get back before Lissa starts worrying."

He took her hands, holding her in place. "Do you trust me?"

She nodded without hesitation.

"So let's just stand right here for a minute until you relax."

"I'm not going to relax in here."

"You just need to focus on something other than the horses," he said.

And then, before she could assure him there was absolutely nothing that would take her focus off the enormous beasts behind the flimsy wooden doors, his lips were on hers. And within half a second, her mind went completely, blissfully blank.

He released the hands he'd been holding to wrap his arms around her, pulling her closer. Then his hands slid up her back, and even through the thick layers of clothing, she could feel the warmth of his touch. Or maybe the heat was all in her veins, stoked by his caress. His tongue traced the curve of her bottom lip, teasing, coaxing. Her mouth parted on a sigh, not just allowing him to deepen the kiss, but demanding it, as her tongue danced in a slow and seductive rhythm with his.

Her blood was pumping and her head was spinning as she gave herself over to the pleasure of his kiss. She could still smell hay and horses, but mixed in with those scents was the essence of Jesse. His heat, his strength, his heart.

He eased his mouth from hers, but continued to hold her close as they each took a moment to catch their breath.

"What are you thinking about now?" he asked.

"That I won't ever be able to walk into a barn without thinking about you and remembering this moment."

He smiled. "Good."

"My heart's still racing."

"But not because you're afraid," he guessed.

"No." She blew out a breath and tipped back her head to meet his gaze. "Is that your usual method for helping people overcome their apprehensions?"

"It's not one I've ever used before," he told her.

Her brows lifted. "So I was a guinea pig?"

"No, you're the woman who makes me forget all thought and reason."

The words, and the sincerity in his tone, mollified her.

"But I haven't forgotten why we came out here," he said, looping his arm around her waist and gently guiding her along the alleyway.

They'd moved only about six feet when a huge head appeared over the top of the door of the closest stall. She let out a squeak and immediately jumped back.

Jesse's arms came around her, holding her steady. He didn't force her to move any closer, but he didn't let her back any farther away, either.

"This is Honey," he told her. "And she is as sweet as her name."

"She's...beautiful," Maggie realized. The animal had a sleek chestnut coat that gleamed in the light, a white blaze, glossy mane and tail and eyes the color of melted chocolate. "And...big."

The horse tossed her head, almost as if she was nodding, and Maggie couldn't help but smile.

Jesse chuckled softly, and she felt the warmth of his breath on the back of her neck.

"Do you see how her ears are turned forward?"

She nodded.

"That shows that she's relaxed and paying attention to you."

"Is she hungry?"

He chuckled again. "No, she's had her dinner," he promised, reaching around Maggie to tug her mittens off. Then he took her hand and guided it toward the horse's long muzzle.

She felt herself start to tremble and had to fight against the urge to snatch her hand away.

"Steady," he murmured.

The mare watched her, its huge, liquid eyes patient and trusting. With Jesse's guidance, she stroked the smooth hair of its blaze. Honey blew out a breath—an equine sigh of contentment—and Maggie fell in love.

"Now I really wish I'd learned to ride," she admitted.

"I could teach you," Jesse said. "Not now, obviously. But after."

After.

The word seemed to hang in the air for a long minute, teasing her with possibilities. Neither of them knew what would happen *after*—they didn't even know what the next five months would hold, but she couldn't deny that she liked the idea of *after*.

"I think I'd enjoy that," she finally said.

"What are the rest of your plans for the weekend?" Jesse asked Maggie, as they made their way back to the house.

"I didn't really have any other plans," she told him. "I came to Rust Creek Falls to tell you about the baby, and I've done that."

"Maybe we could spend some more time together," he suggested. "Get to know one another a little better before we bring a baby into the world."

"That baby's coming in another five months whether we know one another or not," she pointed out.

"Then we shouldn't waste any time."

"What did you have in mind?"

"Nothing too crazy," he assured her, opening the back door to lead her into the house. "Maybe a drive up to Owl Rock to see the falls or a walk through town. Dinner at my parents' house."

"I'm sorry—what was that last part?"

"Dinner at my parents' house," he said again.

"You want me to meet your parents?"

"And I want them to meet the mother of their grand-child."

She blew out a breath. "I didn't think about the fact that our baby will have a lot more family in Rust Creek Falls than a daddy."

"We don't have to tell the grandparents-to-be right away. I just thought it might be nice if they had a chance to meet you before I told them that I got you pregnant."

"I guess that's reasonable," she allowed.

"We don't even have to spend a lot of time with them," he promised. "In fact, I'd prefer if we didn't."

She smiled at that. "Are you trying to talk me into—or out of—this?"

"I'm not sure."

"Okay, we'll have dinner with your parents."

"What about *your* parents?"

"It's a long way for them to come for dinner."

He managed a wry smile. "Don't you think I should meet them?"

"Maybe not," she teased. "Because they already know I'm pregnant."

"Then they should also know that I want to marry you."

"I thought we'd agreed that wasn't a good idea."

"You said it wasn't a good idea, then we spent some time together in bed, proving that it is, in fact, a very good idea."

"That is definitely my cue to be going."

"Or you could stay."

She shook her head. "If I stay, we're both going to start thinking that this is something it's not."

"What do you think it isn't?" he challenged.

"A relationship."

He hung his coat on a hook. "We've had sex, we're hav-ing a baby, but we don't have a relationship?"

"We've spent the past four months in different states,"

she reminded him. "Does that sound like a relationship to you?"

"Obviously it's a relationship that needs some work."

Her lips curved, but the smile didn't reach her eyes. "I don't want to give anyone—including you—the wrong idea about us."

"I appreciate that," he said. "But this isn't LA, and I think people around here will have an easier time accepting the fact that you're having my baby if they believe we were involved in a real relationship—even if it didn't work out."

"Is that the story you want to go with?"

"I'd rather give the real relationship part a chance—to see if we can make it work."

"Jesse—"

"Don't say no, Maggie. Not yet."

She sighed. "I'll see you tomorrow."

"I'll pick you up around ten."

"Actually, I have an appointment with Lissa in the morning," she told him. "Can I meet you here again?"

"Sure." He brushed a quick kiss over her lips. "Drive safe."

"I was about to send out the sheriff," Lissa said, when Maggie walked into the house twenty minutes later.

The sheriff was currently lounging on the sofa in front of the television, so Maggie waved to him. "Hi, Gage."

He lifted his hand to return the greeting. "I told you she wasn't eaten by bears," he admonished his wife.

"As if that was all I was worried about," Lissa muttered.

"Well, you can see that I'm safe and all in one piece," Maggie said.

"Hmm." Her cousin's gaze narrowed, as if she wasn't entirely convinced. "How did it go?"

"Better and worse than I expected."

"What's the 'better'?"

"He's not disputing that the baby's his."

"I should think not," Lissa said indignantly.

Maggie shook her head. "I haven't seen him since July—he wouldn't be human if he didn't ask questions."

"And the 'worse'?" her cousin prompted.

"He thinks we should get married."

"Oh. My. God." Lissa jumped up and hugged her. "This is sooo great."

"Obviously you got kicked in the head by the same horse that he did."

Gage chuckled; Lissa scowled at him.

"You don't think it would be great if Maggie married Jesse and moved to Rust Creek Falls?" she said to her husband.

"I think your cousin has a life—and a job—in LA that need to be taken into consideration," he countered reasonably.

"Thank you," Maggie said to him.

"But you could get a job here," Lissa implored. "Unlike LA, Rust Creek Falls isn't plagued by an abundance of lawyers."

"Now you sound like Jesse," Maggie grumbled.

"Just think about it," her cousin suggested.

"I will." The problem was, she really couldn't think straight when she was around Jesse. When she was with him, she wanted to believe that they could defy both the odds and geography and somehow make a relationship work.

But that had been the plan when she'd gone back to SoCal after the night they spent together in July. They were going to keep in touch and see one another whenever possible. Except that complications—in the form of her job and then her pregnancy—hadn't allowed it to be possible, and Jesse had grown tired of her excuses and the distance and stopped communicating with her.

Of course, there was more incentive now to make it work. But their baby wasn't a magical glue that could bond them together, nor should they expect him or her to be.

And if she was ever going to say yes to a marriage proposal, she wanted to be in love with the man who was asking. She just wasn't ready to admit to anyone—even her cousin and best friend—that she already was.

Chapter Five

"There's been a little snag to our plans," Jesse said, when Maggie showed up at his house just after 10:00 a.m. Saturday morning.

"What kind of snag?" she asked curiously.

He stepped away from the door so she could enter. When she did, she saw a baby girl standing at the coffee table.

The child had wispy blond hair, big blue eyes and was dressed in a pair of pink overalls. And there was something about her—the shape of her eyes, the tilt of her chin—that launched her stomach into her throat.

She swallowed, and managed to find her voice. "You already have a baby?"

"What? No." The shock in his voice was real. "This is Noelle—my niece."

"Oh." She exhaled an audible sigh of relief.

Jesse scrubbed a hand over his face as he let out a nervous laugh. "Don't you think I would have told you something like that?"

She would have thought so, but she really didn't know him that well. If she had, she might have known that he had a niece. "I just saw the baby and my mind started spinning," she admitted.

"I would have warned you—if I'd had any warning myself," he told her. "Dallas took the boys to Kalispell to see a movie and Nina had to fill in at the store at the last minute. Usually she would take the baby with her, but Noelle's teething and cranky and Nina was afraid she'd scare off the customers."

"She doesn't look cranky to me."

"Give her a few minutes," Jesse said drily, hanging Maggie's coat on a hook.

"Do you babysit very often?"

"No. Nina can usually handle everything on her own, and when she does need help, there's a lineup of volunteers, including her husband, stepsons, grandparents on both sides and numerous aunts and uncles. But no one else was available today, so Noelle was dumped in my lap."

Maggie sat on the storage bench by the door and untied her boots. "So this wasn't part of your plan? Because I have to admit—this kind of feels like a test."

"A test?"

"To see how badly I'm going to screw up as a mother."

"It's not a test," he assured her. "And you're not going to screw up."

On the table in front of the sofa was a small plastic bowl containing a few cereal O's, with more scattered on the table and the carpet. When Maggie sat down, the little girl shuffled sideways toward her, holding on to the table as she went. Then she looked up at Maggie with a wide, droolly smile that revealed four tiny white teeth.

"She's adorable."

"She is pretty cute," he agreed. "But don't tell my sister I said so."

"Why not?"

"Because Noelle looks just like Nina when she was a baby." He sat on the floor and began to stack up the wooden blocks that were scattered around.

Noelle put her hand on Maggie's thigh and uncurled

her fist to reveal a crumbly cereal O. She left it on Maggie's pants, like a present, before she plopped down on the floor and crawled over to see what her uncle was doing.

Jesse was on the fourth level of blocks when his niece reached out with both hands and pushed them over.

"Oopsie," he said, and the little girl clapped her hands and laughed gleefully.

Maggie watched them play the same game for several minutes, amused by the easy interaction between them. "You're so natural with her."

"She makes it easy," Jesse told her. "She's a good baby."

"I don't have a lot of experience with kids," she admitted.

"That will change fast," he told her.

Noelle moved from the blocks to a ball that lit up and played music when it was rolled. When she gave up on the toys and went back to her cereal, Jesse decided it was time to make lunch, and he left Maggie supervising the baby.

She decided that she could stack blocks, too, and she sat down on the floor to do so. But Noelle wasn't overly interested in the structure Maggie was building. Instead, she was scouring the carpet for lost pieces of cereal. Only when she'd found them all did she crawl over to investigate Maggie's construction efforts. Of course, the house tumbled down and Noelle laughed and clapped. Then she picked up one of the blocks and shoved one corner of it into her droolly mouth.

"I don't know if you're supposed to be eating that," Maggie said dubiously.

The little girl continued to gnaw on the corner of the wood.

"I know you're probably hungry, but Uncle Jesse's getting your lunch ready so you might want to save your appetite."

Noelle kept her gaze fixed on Maggie, as if fascinated by what she was saying. Her lips curved in recognition of *Uncle Jesse*, but she continued to chew on the block.

"Why don't you give me that?" Maggie suggested, reaching for the square of wood. "Then we can use it to build a castle for—"

That was as far as she got, because when she managed to gently pry the block from the little girl's hand, Noelle started to scream like a banshee.

Panicked, Maggie immediately gave the piece of wood back to her. The little girl snatched the cube from her hand and threw it—bouncing it off Maggie's cheekbone and bringing tears to *her* eyes.

"What the heck—?" Jesse asked, appearing from the other side of the couch.

"I took her block away," Maggie admitted.

"Why?"

"I've read stuff…about lead paint and chemicals in children's toys, and I didn't think she should be chewing on the blocks."

"There's no paint on those blocks," Jesse pointed out. "They were handmade by my grandfather for Nina when she was a baby." Then he seemed to notice the red welt on Maggie's cheek and winced. "She's got a good arm, doesn't she?"

Maggie just nodded.

"I'll be right back," he said.

Noelle, having recovered her favorite wooden cube, was gnawing happily again, her explosive outburst apparently forgotten.

Jesse returned a minute later with a baggie filled with frozen peas and laid it gently against Maggie's cheekbone. "How's that feel?"

"Cold."

He smiled. "How do you feel?"

"Ridiculous," she admitted.

"Hungry?" he prompted.

"Sure."

Lunch was remarkably uneventful. Jesse had made grilled cheese sandwiches and French fries for everyone. He cut the little girl's sandwich into bite-size pieces, gave her a few fries and added a spoonful of corn niblets to her plate.

"Because her mother doesn't consider potatoes in fried form to be a real vegetable," he explained to Maggie.

Before the meal was done, Noelle was yawning and rubbing her eyes with a fist.

"Someone looks ready for her bottle," Jesse noted.

"Ba-ba," his niece confirmed.

"Why don't you give Noelle her bottle and I'll clean up the kitchen?" Maggie suggested.

"KP being the lesser of two evils?" Jesse teased.

She felt her cheeks flush. "It just seems fair, since you cooked, that I do the cleanup."

"In that case, I'll take you up on your offer," he said, scooping up the baby with his free arm. "But I think diaper change before bottle, because this little princess looks ready for a nap."

While Jesse tackled the diaper change—no way was Maggie ready for *that* challenge—she filled the sink with soapy water.

As she washed up and then dried the dishes, she could hear Jesse talking to the baby while she drank her bottle, his tone quiet and soothing. But as she put the dishes away, she realized he'd been silent for a while now, and she suspected that the little girl had probably fallen asleep.

She folded the towel over the handle of the oven and wandered into the living room.

She was right—the baby was asleep. So was Jesse.

And something about the image of the big strong man with the beautiful baby girl in his arms made her heart completely melt. There was absolutely no doubt that he loved his sister's child—or that he was going to be a fabulous father to their baby. She only wished she could be half as confident about her own parenting abilities.

Maggie touched a hand to her belly and thought of the tiny life growing inside her womb, suddenly assailed with doubts about her ability to meet all of her baby's needs, to be the mother her child deserved.

Noelle's mother worked full-time, but she was able to take her baby to work with her and she had family who were willing and able to help out with the baby as needed. Those same options weren't available to Maggie. Even if there was room in her shared office for a playpen—and there wasn't—she couldn't imagine the partners would ever approve that arrangement.

As for her family, she knew her parents would help in any way that they could, but they both had demanding careers of their own. And because she was at the start of hers, Maggie worked an average of ten hours a day, six days a week. Who would take care of her baby for all of that time?

Despite the size of the firm, there was no on-site day care at Alliston & Blake. Of course, most of the female lawyers on staff were primarily focused on their careers. She knew a few of them had children: Deirdre McNichol had three kids, but she also had a husband who was a playwright and able to work at home with their children; Lynda Simmons had invited her mother to move in so that she could look after her grandchild while Lynda was working; and Candace Hartman had a nanny—of course, she was a partner, so she could afford to pay someone to come into her house to take care of her child. Obviously none of those options was viable for Maggie, so she'd have to figure out something that was.

But first, she had to face dinner with Jesse's parents.

Dinner at the Crawfords' was always an experience—and probably not one that Jesse should have subjected Maggie to just yet. And definitely not while he was still hoping to convince her to marry him.

No one had ever accused his parents of being subtle, and as soon as Maggie sat down across from Jesse at the dinner table, the interrogation began. From "Where do you live in California?" and "What brings you to Rust Creek Falls this weekend?" to "How did you meet Jesse?" and everything in between.

No subject was off-limits, as his father proved when he asked, "What do you think about a woman planning to have a baby out of wedlock?"

Not surprisingly, the question made Maggie choke on her water.

"Really, Todd," his wife chided. "That's hardly appropriate dinner conversation." Which suggested that she at least had some boundaries, although Jesse didn't really believe it.

In an effort to divert the focus away from Maggie, he chimed in. "There are a lot of women who pursue nontraditional options to satisfy their desire for a family," he said, in a direct quote of the explanation his sister had once given to him.

"Nontraditional options," his father sputtered. "Nina got knocked up by some stranger through a turkey baster."

"Now she has a beautiful baby girl," his wife said soothingly. "*And* a husband."

"And three more kids she didn't plan on having," Todd noted.

"Three wonderful boys, who are now our grandchildren, too," Laura agreed. "And if we're lucky, Nate and Callie won't wait too much longer to give us even more."

"Give them time," her husband urged. "They're not even married yet."

"But they're so perfectly suited," Laura said. Then she turned to Maggie and said, in a confidential tone, "I had some concerns at first. There was a whole group of women who came here after the big flood last year, each one of them looking to hook up with a cowboy, and when Callie set her sights on Nate—as she did from the get-go—I was afraid she was just like them. Some of those women don't understand the life of a rancher—it isn't nearly as romantic as it looks in books and movies."

"Nothing ever is," Maggie agreed.

"But the important thing is that Callie and Nate are happy together." Laura paused to glance at her son. "We just hope Jesse will find someone who suits him so perfectly someday."

The implication being, of course, that Maggie couldn't be that someone. And though she kept a polite smile on her face, Jesse knew that his mother's remark had not been lost on her.

But still his mother had to hammer the point home, as she did when she asked, "So when are you going back to California?"

"Tomorrow," Maggie admitted.

"Well, I hope you'll stop by again the next time you're in town. Whenever that might be."

It was a dismissal—and not even a polite one. But he should have realized that Maggie wasn't the type of woman to let herself be dismissed, and while he was trying to figure out what he could say to clarify the situation, she responded.

"I'm sure it will be soon," Maggie said, matching his mother's cool tone. "We've got a lot to figure out before the baby comes."

Laura's fake smile froze on her face.

Todd turned to Maggie, his thick brows drawn together in a thunderous scowl. "You're pregnant?"

She nodded. "But don't worry—there were no turkey basters involved. I got knocked up the old-fashioned way."

Jesse hadn't intended to share the news of his impending parenthood with his own parents just yet, because he knew what they would expect him to do—it was the same thing he expected of himself: to marry the mother-to-be and give their child a family. And while he knew he wouldn't be able to keep Maggie's pregnancy a secret for much longer, he hadn't been anxious to go another round with his parents.

Their relationship had hit a serious snag when he'd told his mom and dad that he'd been offered a job at Traub Stables and they'd forbidden him to accept it. Forbidden him—as if he was a teenager rather than a twenty-nine-year-old man.

So while he hadn't planned to tell them about the baby, he couldn't regret that Maggie had done so—especially when her announcement had actually struck his mother mute for a whole three minutes.

"I can't believe I said that. To your parents." She dropped her face into her hands as they drove away from The Shooting Star. "I'm a horrible person."

"You were magnificent," he told her.

She shook her head. "Your mother pushed all of my buttons."

"She has a knack for that."

"I shouldn't have let her push my buttons. I should have just smiled and kept my mouth shut."

"I'm glad you didn't."

"Now they hate me."

"They don't hate you."

"They hate me," she said again. "And yet, they still expect you to marry me. How screwed up is that?"

He shrugged. "My family's big on taking responsibility."

"I thought they were big on finding someone who would suit you 'so perfectly.'"

"Apparently a baby trumps everything else."

"At least I understand a little better now why you felt compelled to propose."

He turned into the Christensens' driveway. "I do agree that a baby should have two parents."

"We've been through this once already tonight," she reminded him.

"But you still haven't agreed to marry me."

"Because I'm a big-city liberal who isn't morally opposed to nontraditional families."

"I'm not, either," he said. "Except when it comes to my child."

"Our lives aren't just in different cities but different states," she reminded him.

A fact of which he was painfully aware. And he didn't know what he could say or do to convince her to give them a chance to build a life together; he didn't have any new arguments to make. So he reiterated the most important one: "Our baby needs both of us."

He parked the truck in front of the sheriff's house, and although she was reaching for the handle before he'd turned off the engine, he scooted out of the vehicle and around the passenger side to help her out.

"There's no doubt your parents raised you to be a gentleman."

He lifted a finger to tip back the brim of his hat. "Yes, ma'am," he said, and made her smile.

But her smile quickly faded. "I wish I could say yes."

His heart bumped against his ribs. "It's a simple word—just three little letters."

"Those three little letters can't miraculously span twelve hundred miles." She started toward the house, and he fell into step beside her.

"We can figure it out," he said, desperately hoping it was true.

"I'm going back tomorrow," she reminded him. "I've got an early flight."

He sighed. "Will you let me drive you to the airport?"

She shook her head. "I've got to return my rental car, anyway."

"Can I call you?"

"Of course."

He caught her hand as she reached the door. "I know you have a lot to think about, but let me add just one more thing to the list," he said.

And then he kissed her.

Maggie didn't like to leave her car in the airport parking lot if she didn't have to, and she usually managed to cajole her brother Ryan into playing taxi driver. But when she got off the plane Sunday afternoon, she discovered that he'd somehow talked their mother into doing the pickup.

And when she saw Christa, Maggie felt her throat tighten and her eyes fill with tears. It both baffled and frustrated her that she could keep her chin up in the face of almost any kind of adversity, but as soon as she saw her mother, all of her defenses toppled and she felt like a little girl in need of her comforting embrace.

Christa, sensing that need, instinctively opened her arms and drew Maggie into them.

"What story did Ryan concoct to get out of airport duty this time?"

"There was no story," Christa said. "I volunteered."

"You hate driving around the airport."

Her mother shrugged. "I thought you might want to talk."

"I do," she agreed. "I just don't have the first clue where to begin."

Christa didn't press her. In fact, she didn't say anything else until they were in the car and driving away from the airport—except to ask for directions.

Once they were on the highway, Maggie finally vocalized the question that had been hovering at the back of her mind. "How did you manage to juggle a legal career and three kids?"

"I'd be lying if I said it was easy," Christa told her. "And I'm not sure I could have done it when you were babies."

"You weren't working then?"

Her mother shook her head. "I took a leave of absence when we adopted Shane and didn't go back to work full-time until you were in kindergarten."

"You took twelve years off?" She guessed at the number, since it was the age difference between herself and her oldest brother.

"It was actually closer to sixteen, although I did work a few hours a week at Legal Aid, to keep my hand in," her mother explained. "But your dad and I both agreed that if we were going to have children, our children needed to be a priority. I didn't want to work to pay someone else to raise you.

"That's not a choice every woman can make," she acknowledged, "but I was lucky to have your dad's support in that decision."

"I don't want to give up my career," Maggie said. "But I don't want to be so wrapped up in my career that I miss out on being a mother to my child."

"You don't have to choose one or the other," her mother pointed out.

"I'm not sure Brian Nash would say the same thing."

"Then maybe you need a new boss."

"I've dedicated almost half a decade to Alliston & Blake."

"Yes, you have," Christa agreed.

And Maggie heard what she didn't say—that maybe the time she'd already given them was enough. But leaving Alliston & Blake, trying something new and different, was a scary prospect. A little bit exciting but mostly scary, especially now that she had more than her career to think about—she had a baby on the way.

"I don't know what's the right thing to do," she admitted. "I know how to research precedent and draft motions and argue cases—I don't know how to be a mother."

"Being a parent is the toughest job you'll ever have, and the most important."

"What if I screw up?"

"You will," her mother said easily. "Every mother does once in a while. Every father, too."

"That was subtle, Mom."

Christa smiled. "I wasn't trying to be subtle."

"If you have questions about the baby's father, why don't you just ask them?"

"I don't have any specific questions—I just want you to tell me something about him. There was a time when you used to tell me everything about the boys you liked, but you've been awfully closemouthed since your trip to Montana in the summer."

Maggie wondered if it was possible to sum up Jesse in a handful of words, if there was any way to describe the way she felt when she was with him, any way to explain the conflicting emotions that she didn't understand.

"His name is Jesse Crawford," she said, deciding to start with the simple facts. "His family owns the general store in Rust Creek Falls and The Shooting Star ranch, but Jesse trains horses."

"So he's a cowboy," Christa mused.

Maggie nodded. "He's strong and smart, a little bit shy but incredibly sexy. There's an intensity about him, a single-minded focus. And he has a real gift for working with animals. They respond to him—his hands and his voice."

"I'm thinking he has the same gift with women," her mother noted drily.

Maggie felt her cheeks flush. "Maybe. But Lissa assured me he doesn't have that kind of reputation. In fact, since she's been living in Rust Creek Falls, she hasn't heard of him dating anyone at all."

"So what brought the two of you together?"

"Happenstance? Luck? Fate?"

Her mother's immaculately arched brows lifted. "Fate?"

"Something just clicked between us when we met," she said. "It was almost like…magic. I know that sounds corny, but I can't explain it any better than that."

"You're in love with him," Christa realized.

"I think…maybe…I am," she agreed hesitantly. "But is that even possible? I only met him a few months ago, I haven't spent that much time with him and I don't know him that well. But there's this almost magnetic draw that I can't seem to resist—that I don't want to resist when I'm with him."

"Have you told him how you feel?"

She shook her head.

"Why not?"

"Because I don't know how he feels."

"Love shouldn't be given with strings—it's a gift from the heart."

"Even if I told him, even if he—by some miracle—felt the same way, it doesn't really change anything."

"Honey, love changes everything."

"Maybe that's what makes me uneasy," Maggie finally admitted. "I like my life the way it is—and I get that having a baby will require some changes. But since I told Jesse, he's suddenly gone all Neanderthal, insisting that we should get married."

"You don't sound very happy about that."

"I'd be happy if I thought he wanted to spend the rest of his life with me," she admitted, startled to realize it was true.

"Isn't that usually the motivating factor behind a proposal?"

"The motivating factor for Jesse is our baby."

"Are you sure about that?" her mother asked gently.

"I told him I was pregnant and he said 'we should get married.'"

"And what did you say?"

"I said no."

"Did he accept that?"

"No," she admitted.

Christa smiled. "When do we get to meet him?"

Chapter Six

Since Jesse couldn't leave his animals unattended for a weekend, he called his brother Brad and asked him to take care of them. Of course, his brother showed up Friday just as Jesse was getting ready to head out.

"So where are you going this weekend?" he asked curiously.

"Los Angeles."

"California?"

"No, Los Angeles, Montana."

"Okay, it was a stupid question," Brad allowed. "But why are you going to California?"

"To see Maggie."

His brother narrowed his gaze. "That lawyer you were all ga-ga over in the summer?"

"No one over the age of twelve uses the expression *ga-ga*," Jesse chided. "But yes, Maggie is an attorney."

"I didn't even know you were dating her."

No one knew they were dating—because they weren't. But they were having a baby together and although his parents were now aware of that fact, they'd been surprisingly closemouthed about the situation. Probably because they were waiting for him to announce a wedding date, which he didn't think was going to happen anytime soon.

While he knew that Maggie's pregnancy couldn't remain a secret forever—and probably not very much longer—he wasn't ready to share the news with Brad. So he decided to go with the same explanation that Maggie had given to Jared Winfree. "We wanted to keep our relationship under the radar, to avoid small-town gossip."

"You definitely did that," Brad allowed. "I guess it's pretty serious, though, if you're going to LA to see her."

"I want to marry her," Jesse admitted.

His brother shook his head. "Why would you want to tie yourself to one woman when there are so many of them out there? And if you insist on settling down, why wouldn't you choose a local girl? Why would you hook up with another big-city gal who's only going to break your heart?"

"Thanks for the vote of confidence," Jesse said drily.

"You were devastated when Shaelyn left," Brad reminded him. "I don't want you to go through something like that again."

Actually, he'd been more relieved than devastated, having realized even before Shaelyn did that their engagement had been a mistake. But he didn't argue the point with his brother because Brad was right about one thing—Maggie was a big-city gal and it was entirely possible that he was making a big mistake.

Again.

Busy. Crowded. Frantic.

Those were Jesse's first impressions of Los Angeles, and that was before he left the airport terminal.

Thankfully everything he'd needed had fit into a carry-on, so he didn't have to battle the mass of people at baggage claim. He weaved through the crowd, feeling like a salmon swimming upstream. Or maybe the more appropriate analogy would be like a fish out of water.

Except that when he finally spotted Maggie, everything and everyone else seemed to fade away.

She offered him a quick smile and a kiss on the cheek. "Is that everything?" she asked, indicating the duffel bag slung over his shoulder.

"That's everything," he confirmed.

She nodded and led him toward the exit. "I got caught up in a meeting and didn't have a chance to pick up a file that I need this weekend. Do you mind if I make a quick stop at the office now?"

"Of course not," he said. In fact, he was curious to see where she worked—the big-city lawyer in her natural milieu.

But that was before she pulled out of the airport parking lot and onto the highway and he realized that Los Angeles traffic was insane. He'd never experienced anything like it and was beyond grateful that he didn't have to drive in it. And when Maggie began to zip from lane to lane, he just closed his eyes and held on.

They arrived at the offices of Alliston & Blake twenty minutes later. Maggie pulled into an underground parking garage and led him from there to a bank of elevators. She punched the call button for the one designated Floors 10–21, and once inside, they began the ascent toward the eighteenth floor.

"Are you okay?" she asked. "You look a little pale."

"I think so," he said. "I'd heard about California traffic, but I didn't anticipate anything quite like that."

"That was nothing compared to rush hour," she told him.

"I'll happily skip that experience, if it's an option."

She smiled. "I'll try to get in and out as quickly as possible."

He followed her into a small office with two desks and the same number of filing cabinets and bookcases. She went to the closer desk, the one with a neatly engraved nameplate that said Maggie Roarke. A similar nameplate on the other desk said Samantha Radke.

Maggie must have noted the direction of his gaze, because she said, "Sammi's working out of the San Francisco office this week."

While she sifted through a neat stack of folders, he moved farther into the room, checking out the diplomas on the wall and noting the summa cum laude designation on Maggie's certificate from Stanford Law.

"Got it," she said, just as a brisk knock sounded on the open door, immediately followed by a man's voice, "Good—you're back."

Maggie's smile froze on her face. "And on my way out again, Brian."

The man—Brian—didn't seem pleased by her response. And that was before he spotted Jesse standing beside her desk.

"Who's the cowboy?" he asked, speaking to Maggie as if Jesse wasn't even in the room.

"Jesse is...a friend of mine," she said. "Jesse Crawford. Brian Nash."

His hands were soft, his grip weak. The suit was obviously a pencil pusher who wouldn't be able to wrestle a fifty-pound sack of grain never mind a two-thousand-pound bull. Which didn't surprise Jesse or concern him—but he didn't like the way the other man put his hand on Maggie's shoulder, then let it linger there.

"I'm glad I caught you," Brian was saying to her now. "I have a meeting with Perry Edler tonight that I thought you might want to attend."

Perry Edler—the Chief Operating Officer of Edler Industries, one of Alliston & Blake's biggest clients. The invitation—and the possibilities that it implied—made Maggie's pulse quicken. Then she glanced from Brian to

Jesse, and her pulse quickened again, but for an entirely different reason.

"Tonight?" She shook her head with sincere regret. "I can't."

Brian frowned. "What do you mean—you can't?"

She couldn't blame him for sounding confused. In the almost five years that she'd worked at Alliston & Blake, she had probably never before uttered those same words. Her job had always been her number one priority and she'd happily juggled every other part of her life to accommodate it.

"I'm sorry," she apologized automatically. "But I already have plans for tonight."

"Plans?" Her boss's frown deepened as his gaze skipped to Jesse again. "Plans can't compare to opportunities, and this is an incredible opportunity for you, Maggie. Mr. Edler specifically asked that you be assigned to his team for this new project."

She looked at Jesse, her conviction wavering. His expression was guarded, giving her no hint of what he was thinking or feeling. He was leaving the choice entirely up to her, and she knew that if she told him this meeting was more important than their dinner plans because it had the potential to make her career, he'd probably wish her luck.

But was it?

Was one meeting with Perry Edler more important than the conversation she needed to have with her baby's father—a conversation for which he'd traveled more than twelve hundred miles?

Maybe the answer to that question should have been immediately obvious to her, but it wasn't. Because her job wasn't just important—it was vital. If she didn't have her job at Alliston & Blake, she'd have no income to provide the essentials of life—food, clothing, shelter—for her baby.

And okay, working as an attorney she'd have to add day care to that list, and day care was expensive, which meant that she'd have to increase her billable hours, which meant working more hours. The cycle was endless, and it made her head ache just to think about it.

If she let this one client meeting take precedence, where would it end? When would her job stop being more important than her life? When would the needs of her child finally matter more than the demands of her boss?

Brian took her silence as acquiescence. "We have an eight o'clock reservation at Patina—I'll see you there."

She looked at Jesse. "Can you give us a minute, please?"

"Sure," he agreed easily, already moving toward the door with the long, loose stride that was somehow both easy and sexy.

She waited until he'd closed the door before she turned back to her boss. "I'm sorry," she said again, but more firmly this time. "I can't make it."

His brows lifted. "This is a major career opportunity, Maggie."

She knew that it was—but she didn't much care for the strings that were obviously attached. "For the past five years, I've done everything you've asked of me—and more. I've come in early and stayed late. I've worked weekends and holidays that no one else wanted to work."

"And that's why you've earned this opportunity," he confirmed. "But if you're unavailable tonight, I'm sure Patricia will be pleased to join Mr. Edler's group."

Patricia was another junior associate who had made no secret of her ambitions—or her willingness to step on other people as she climbed her way to the top at Alliston & Blake.

"I thought Mr. Edler specifically asked for me."

"He asked for a young up-and-comer with lots of energy and enthusiasm." Brian amended his earlier claim. "I thought that was you."

"And now it's Patricia," she realized dully.

"You're good, but you're not indispensable," her boss said.

"I see."

"Do you?"

She was afraid that she did. And she was angry and frustrated because she knew there was nothing she could do—notwithstanding everything that she'd already done—to sway his opinion. If she couldn't be available to the firm every minute of every day, he would find someone who could.

She glanced from her boss to the door through which Jesse had exited. She could see him through the glass, leaning on a horizontal filing cabinet and chatting to one of the secretaries. Brian was a company man, from his neatly styled salon-trimmed hair to his immaculately polished Italian leather shoes. Jesse was every inch a cowboy—with a capital *C*. He was rugged and rough, charming and sweet, and he'd crossed state lines to be with her this weekend.

She'd never known anyone like him and it was immediately evident to her why—because he didn't, and wouldn't ever, fit in her corporate world.

Brian, obviously having followed the direction of her gaze, lifted his brows. "Do you really want to throw away this opportunity for some cowboy that you're having a fling with?"

"We're not having a fling," she told him. "We're having a baby."

He frowned. "You're joking."

"Actually, I'm not."

"You're really pregnant?"

She nodded. "Due in April."

"Well, that puts a different spin on the situation."

"Why is that?"

"As you already noted, I need someone who is available to come in early and stay late, someone who can work weekends and holidays. Are you still going to be able to do that when you have a baby at home?"

"I don't know," she admitted.

"That's not an answer that's going to get you very far in this firm," he warned.

"Are you firing me?"

"No," he said quickly. "Of course not. You're a valued associate and an important member of the Alliston & Blake team."

Which only meant that he knew he couldn't fire her without risk of being sued for unlawful termination.

"And I won't ever be anything more than an associate here, will I?"

"You know that's not my decision to make."

"You're a partner, Brian—one of the most senior, aside from Mr. Alliston and Mr. Blake. When you make a recommendation, the rest of the partners listen."

"If you're asking if I would recommend you for the partner track, I would have to say that, right now, I would not."

Though it was the answer she'd anticipated, it was still a shock to hear him say the words aloud. "That's not fair."

He shrugged. "It's a fact of life, Maggie. A partner is expected to put the needs of the firm first. Always."

"I can, and I would," she said, although without much conviction.

"Tell me," Brian said, "what you would do if you were on your way to court for closing arguments in a trial and the day care called because your child was feverish and vomiting?"

She didn't say anything, because she knew the answer

she would give him wasn't the answer he wanted to hear. And he knew it, too.

"Being a mother is a noble undertaking, but not one that's compatible with a partnership at Alliston & Blake."

Maggie dropped the file she'd come into the office to retrieve back on top of her desk.

"I'll see you on Monday."

Maggie didn't say anything to Jesse about her conversation with Brian. She didn't want him to feel sorry for her; she didn't want to give him any ammunition to manipulate her emotions to his own purposes; but mostly she didn't want his empathy, because she was afraid that would be her undoing.

"Do you like sushi?" she asked, when they exited the building.

He made a face. "No, and you shouldn't eat it, either, while you're pregnant."

"Suddenly you're an expert on pregnancy?"

"I've been reading up, learning a few things."

"Can I have steak?"

He nodded, either oblivious to or ignoring the sarcasm in her tone. "Red meat has lots of protein and iron, but it should be thoroughly cooked to ensure there is no residual bacteria."

"You really have been reading up," she noted, feeling duly chastised.

"I'm interested," he said simply.

She was, too, and she'd gone out to buy all of the best-reviewed books when her doctor had confirmed that she was going to have a baby. But they were still in a neat pile on her bedside table because she was usually too tired when she got home at the end of the day to want to crack the cover of a pregnancy guide or child-care manual.

"I'm hungry," she said, and led him through a set of frosted glass doors and into Lou's Chophouse.

The atmosphere was upscale casual, the decor consisting of glossy wood tables and leather-padded benches, with frosted glass dividers separating the booths and pendant-style lights hanging over the tables. When they were seated, the hostess handed them menus in leather folders, ran through the daily specials and promised that their server would be over momentarily to take their drink order.

Maggie ordered the peppercorn sirloin with basmati rice and steamed broccoli. He opted for the twelve-ounce strip loin with a fully loaded baked potato and seasonal vegetables.

But when her meal was delivered, she found she had no appetite. Mindful of the tiny life in her belly, though, she forced herself to cut into the steak and eat a few bites.

She didn't fool Jesse. He was halfway through his own steak when he said, "You're picking at your food."

"I guess I'm not as hungry as I thought I was."

"Is that all it is?"

She stabbed at her broccoli. "No," she admitted. "But I don't want to talk about it."

"Have you changed your mind?"

"About what?"

"Keeping the baby."

"No," she answered without hesitation. "I'm not sure about a lot of things, but I'm sure about that."

He exhaled an audible sigh of relief. "You probably know there aren't a lot of lawyers in Rust Creek Falls. In fact, Ben Dalton is it, but word around town is that he's interested in bringing in an associate."

"I have a job," she reminded him.

"I'm just presenting you with another option."

"Except that it's not an option, because I'm not licensed to practice in Montana."

"You'd have to pass the State Bar," he acknowledged.

"Have you been reading up on that, too?"

"A little."

"Then you should know that writing a Bar exam is a little more complicated than going to the store to pick up a quart of milk."

"Do you think the Montana exam is more difficult than the one you wrote here?"

"No," she admitted. "But I wrote the California Bar five years ago."

"And you've forgotten how to study since then?"

One side of her mouth tipped up in response to his teasing. "I don't think so."

"Then it's something you could at least consider?"

"Yes, it's something I could consider," she agreed. "But if I did get a job in Rust Creek Falls, what would I do about day care?"

"We have day care in Montana. In fact, the Country Kids Day Care is just a few blocks from Ben Dalton's office."

"Why are you okay with me putting our baby in day care in Rust Creek Falls but not in LA?"

"Because you wouldn't need day care for twelve hours a day," he pointed out logically. "Because even if you had to work late, I'd be there to help out, so our child would have more time with both parents."

"You make it sound so logical."

"It *is* logical."

She sighed. "I used to have a plan for my life and confidence that I knew exactly what I was doing. Now...I don't have a clue."

"So we'll figure it out together," he said.

"And what if we don't?"

"When you walk into a courtroom, do you worry that you can't handle the case?"

"I never walk into a courtroom unprepared."

"Exactly."

"I'm not sure the same rules apply to pregnancy and parenthood."

"I'm not sure there are any rules for parenthood—more like guidelines."

"Thanks, Captain Barbossa."

He grinned, pleased that she'd recognized the movie reference.

Maggie just sighed. "I used to be able to think things through—now my emotions seem to be all over the map, and I don't know if that's just the pregnancy hormones or…"

"Or?" he prompted.

"Or maybe this baby is giving me the excuse I need to make the changes to my life that I've wanted to make for a while."

"I have an idea for a change," he said. "You could marry me."

She shook her head.

"Why not?"

"Because I'm trying to be rational," she reminded him.

"You're pregnant with my baby, we have good chemistry—which might explain the baby," he acknowledged, earning a small smile from her. "You like to cook, I like to eat."

"Wow, your argument is…underwhelming."

"I'll be faithful, Maggie. I can promise you that." He knew it wasn't a declaration likely to make a woman swoon, but it was honest.

"I'm not sure that should be enough for either of us," she said softly.

"I'm not looking to fall in love."

"Why not?"

"Can we focus on what's relevant here?"

"What do you consider relevant?" she asked.

"The fact that I want to be a husband to you and a father to our baby." He reached across the table and covered her hand with his. "And maybe give that baby a brother or a sister someday."

"How do you know you want to be a husband to me?" she challenged. "You don't even know me."

"I know that you're beautiful and smart and warm and compassionate. I know that your family is important to you. You're close to your parents and your brothers and our baby is a real, biological connection to me and will bind us together forever.

"I know you enjoy your work, and I don't think you'd be happy to give up your career. But I also don't think you'll be happy, long-term, in a career that takes everything from you and gives nothing back—as it seems your job at Alliston & Blake is doing.

"The fact that you want to have and keep this baby proves you want to be a mother, and since you don't do anything in half measures, you want to be a good mother. Which means that you need to find a way to balance work outside the home with responsibilities to the child that we're bringing into the world."

She didn't know if anyone had seen into her heart so clearly, and the realization that he'd done so was a little worrisome. If he could read her thoughts and feelings that easily, it wouldn't take him long to figure out that she had strong feelings for him, and she was afraid he would manipulate those feelings to get what he wanted.

"You missed one thing," she told him.

"What's that?"

"I was raised by two parents who love one another as much as they love their children, and I always promised myself that if and when I did get married, it would be because I'd found someone that I loved the same way."

"I'd say the baby you're carrying trumps that idealistic dream."

Idealistic dream.

The dismissal in those two words cut to the quick. Just when she'd almost been ready to let him persuade her that they could make a marriage work, those two words told her so much more than he'd likely intended.

"She must have really done a number on you," Maggie mused.

"Who?"

"The woman who made you afraid to risk your heart."

Chapter Seven

Jesse didn't want to talk about the past but the future—his future with Maggie and their baby.

Except that her insight, as uncomfortable as it made him, was valid. And it forced him to ask himself some hard questions: Why *was* he pushing for marriage? Why was he trying to convince Maggie to move to Rust Creek Falls? How long did he really think an LA transplant would last in a small Montana town? Didn't he learn anything from his painful experience with his ex?

He'd met Shaelyn Everton when he was a student at Montana State University. She didn't really have a major—she was just taking some courses that interested her while she tried to figure out what she wanted to do with her life. Their paths had crossed at a pub on campus—his friend had been hitting on her friend, leaving the two of them to make conversation with one another.

She'd been pretty and sweet and he'd fallen fast and hard. Some of his friends had warned that she didn't want an education just an "MRS" degree, but he didn't care. All that mattered was that they were going to be together.

He'd proposed to her the day of his graduation, and she'd happily accepted. She'd promised that she was excited to go to Rust Creek Falls with him, to spend time with his family and start to plan their wedding.

She'd visited his hometown with him at Christmastime,

a few months earlier, but they'd been so busy with family and holiday events, she didn't have much time to experience the town. She admitted to him, after only a few days, that she was feeling a little bit of culture shock.

He didn't understand what she meant—having been born and raised in Rust Creek Falls, he was certain the town had all the amenities anyone could need. And anything that wasn't readily available in town—specialty shops and fancy restaurants—was close enough in Kalispell.

Her frustration had come to a head one night when she decided to make Salisbury steak for dinner. Unfortunately, she'd forgotten to buy mushrooms when she'd gone into Kalispell to get groceries. She went to Crawford's, but they only had canned, and she had a complete meltdown. Jesse tried to reassure her, suggesting that she could make the recipe without the mushrooms—he wasn't a huge fan, anyway. But she'd refused, insisting that it wouldn't be the same.

It hadn't seemed like a big deal to him, but it had been the beginning of the end for Shaelyn. She didn't know what to do with herself in Rust Creek Falls. She hated that his work at the ranch kept him busy for so many hours of each day. She wanted to spend time with him, to linger in bed late in the morning and enjoy long, leisurely lunches. Then she expected him to come in early and spend the evening hours entertaining her. After a few weeks, he talked his sister into giving Shaelyn a job at the store, but his fiancée had studied art history at university and was appalled by the idea of working in retail—especially in a small-town general store that sold cookies, canned goods and fishing gear, all under one roof.

He'd tried to make her happy. Though it got to the point where he almost dreaded coming home at the end of the day, he reminded himself that there had been a reason he'd fallen in love and planned to spend his life with her. So he would come in after working all day, shower off the dirt and sweat and take her into Kalispell to dinner or to see a movie. He wanted her to be happy, but trying to keep her happy was exhausting him. In retrospect, he was relieved it had only taken her three weeks to realize she couldn't stay in Rust Creek Falls.

She'd claimed to love him but, in the end, she hadn't loved him enough to really try to make their relationship work. He'd come in from checking fences one day to find her engagement ring on the table with a note.

Jesse,
I can't do this anymore. I really thought we would be together forever, but I can't stay in this town one more day. If you ever decide you want more than what you've got here, you know where to find me.
Love,
Shaelyn

Three weeks was all she'd lasted before deciding that Rust Creek Falls was too small-town for her. And she'd been from Billings. Billings had a population of 165,000 people—a booming metropolis in comparison to Rust Creek Falls, but an insignificant speck on the map in contrast to the more than three million that lived in Los Angeles.

If Shaelyn had been unhappy in Rust Creek Falls, what made him think that Maggie would feel any differently? Why was he pushing for marriage to another woman who would be completely out of her element in the small Montana town?

Maggie was a successful attorney comfortable with

the fast pace and bright lights of the city. She'd spent a few days in Rust Creek Falls—a few days that were an interlude from her ordinary life. In California she could have any kind of cuisine delivered to her door; food options in Rust Creek Falls were limited to the Ace in the Hole, Wings To Go and Daisy's Donuts. LA had concerts, comedy clubs, live theater and multiplexes; the only place to see a movie in Rust Creek Falls was the high school gymnasium, and only there on Friday or Saturday nights.

Of course, people were already talking about how the opening of Maverick Manor—his brother Nate's new resort—could change the atmosphere in Rust Creek Falls. Not everyone was in favor of those changes, but in Thunder Canyon, the opening of their resort a few years ago had brought about big changes and seriously boosted the local economy. It was hoped that Maverick Manor might do the same thing. There would be new shops and eateries, obviously targeting visitors but also benefitting local residents with the expanded availability of goods and services and the creation of new jobs. But those changes wouldn't happen overnight, and even when they did, would they be enough for Maggie? Could a big-city attorney ever be happy in a small town?

Because no matter how many more shops and restaurants moved into the area, Rust Creek Falls was always going to be a small town, and Jesse suspected that asking Maggie to stay would only be setting himself up for another heartache.

Unless he was careful to ensure that his heart didn't get involved.

Maggie had hoped to postpone the inevitable meeting between her parents and the father of her baby, but as soon as Gavin and Christa learned Jesse was coming to town, they were eager for the introductions. So after dinner, she drove to her parents' Hollywood Hills home, where Christa met them at the door.

After kissing her daughter on the cheek, she offered her hand to their guest. "You must be Jesse."

"Yes, ma'am," he confirmed.

And her mother, who rubbed elbows with judges and politicians and movie stars, almost swooned in response to his boyish country charm.

"Please," she said, "call me Christa."

"It's a pleasure to meet you," he said.

"We're eager to get to know you," she told him.

"Too eager to wait until tomorrow," Maggie noted.

Her mother just smiled. "It's a lovely night, so we're having drinks out on the patio, by the pool."

Jesse followed Maggie through the wide-open French doors that led to the enormous stone deck that spread out to encircle the hot tub and kidney-shaped swimming pool. Flames crackled in the outdoor fireplace, adding warmth and light to the seating area.

Her father had been relaxing on one of the dark wicker sofas with a glass of his favorite scotch in his hand, but he set the glass down and rose to his feet when they stepped out onto the patio.

"Maggie's brought her young man to meet us," Christa said to her husband.

Maggie winced at the *her* more than the *young man*, as the possessive pronoun suggested a relationship that didn't really exist.

"Jesse Crawford," he said, offering his hand to her father.

Gavin accepted, probably squeezing Jesse's hand with more force than was necessary—or even polite. She was confident that Jesse could handle anything her father dished out—she was more worried that her baby's father and her own father might find common ground in their belief that an expectant mother should have a husband.

"Can I get you something to drink?" Gavin asked Jesse. "Whiskey? Wine? Beer?"

"I'll have whatever you're having," Jesse said.

"Maggie?"

"I'll just have a glass of water."

Her father dispensed the drinks, then resumed his seat beside his wife. He asked Jesse about his education and his employment, his family and friends, and life in Rust Creek Falls. The questioning wasn't dissimilar to what she'd been put through by Jesse's parents, although she liked to think hers were a little more subtle.

Jesse answered the questions with more patience than Maggie had. When her father paused to sip his drink, she finally asked, "Is the interrogation part of the evening finished yet?"

"I'm just making conversation," Gavin told her.

"Really? Because you've served me steaks that haven't been so thoroughly grilled."

"Maggie," Christa chastised.

But her husband chuckled.

"She's always been quick to defend," he told Jesse. "But if the baby she's carrying turns out to be a girl, she'll undoubtedly be asking the same questions someday."

"Or I will," Jesse said.

Gavin nodded. "Or you will."

"Don't forget you've got a seven-fifteen tee time with the governor's son-in-law in the morning," Christa said to her husband when he got up to refill his drink.

"*If* it doesn't rain," he clarified.

"There's no rain in the forecast," his wife assured him.

"But every time I think there's no rain in the forecast, we get rained out."

"What are you two up to tomorrow?" Christa asked, turning back to her daughter.

"I'm going to show Jesse some of the local sights," Maggie responded. "And since we plan to get an early start, we should head out."

"I know you don't have a spare bedroom in your condo, but you've got a pullout sofa," her father said pointedly.

"Gavin," his wife chided.

He ignored her gentle admonishment. "She might be twenty-eight years old and on her way to becoming a mother herself, but she's still my baby girl," he said.

"Maybe I should move to Montana," Maggie muttered under her breath.

"If only you really meant that," Jesse said, not under his breath at all.

There was a lot to see and do in Los Angeles, and Maggie was happy to play tour guide for Jesse. She took him to Venice Beach, where they skated along the bike path, browsed the shops along the boardwalk, admired the public art walls, detoured around a filming crew and had lunch at a vegetarian café—but only after he made her promise she would never tell any of his friends or family in Montana. He seemed to enjoy spending the time with her, just talking and laughing and getting to know one another. And when they finally got back to her condo at the end of the day, she was sorry to realize the weekend was more than half over.

Less than twenty-four hours after that, she took him back to the airport again. She was glad that he'd come to Los Angeles, that he'd made the effort to see her. Except that she knew it had been an effort, that maintaining a relationship—or trying to establish one—over such a long distance wasn't easy.

And despite the time they'd spent together during the days—and their lovemaking in the nights—they hadn't resolved anything with respect to the baby or their future, and she was afraid they wouldn't anytime soon.

"We're not going to be able to do this every weekend, are we?" he asked when she walked him through the airport to the security checkpoint.

His question confirmed that his thoughts had been following the same path as her own. "Probably not," she admitted.

"When do you think you'll be able to get back to Rust Creek Falls?"

"I don't know. I've got a lot of stuff going on at work this week—" and she hadn't told him the half of it "—but I'll figure something out."

"I wish I had more to offer you."

"What do you mean?"

"My life in Montana is a lot more modest than everything you've got here."

She lifted a shoulder. "Believe me, the shine of Tinseltown wears off after a while."

And as much as she'd enjoyed this weekend in the city with Jesse, she couldn't deny there was a part of her that wished she was going back to Montana with him.

She was still feeling restless and unsettled when she went into work Monday morning. She'd always loved being part of the well-oiled machine that was Alliston & Blake and had thrived in the busy environment. But after her conversation with Brian Nash on Friday, she realized that it really was a machine—and she was just one of hundreds of gears—interchangeable and replaceable.

By early afternoon, she'd reviewed a restructuring proposal, drafted a motion for an injunction and written her letter of resignation—although she hadn't yet decided what, if anything, she was going to do with it.

Needing to stretch her legs, she went into the staff room to get a drink of water.

On her way, she crossed paths with Perry Edler as he was leaving Brian Nash's office.

"Mr. Edler," she said, offering her hand to the man she'd worked with on numerous occasions in the past.

He shook it automatically.

"I'm sorry I wasn't available to meet with you Friday night."

His expression was polite but blank, as if he wasn't entirely sure who she was or why he might have been meeting with her.

"I trust that Amanda was able to respond to any concerns you might have had about your new venture." She was well aware that it was Patricia and not Amanda who had attended the meeting, but she wondered if the COO of Edler Industries was aware.

"Yes," the older man assured her. "Amanda was most helpful."

Which confirmed Maggie's suspicion that he had never asked for her by name, that the associates at Alliston & Blake were all one and the same to the clients. So long as the work was done, they didn't care who did it. And that was okay—the head of an international company was obviously more concerned with the answers to his questions than the identity of the person answering them.

"But maybe you'll be at the next meeting," he said solicitously, because the head of an international company understood that it was easier to stay on top when you had people below to keep you there.

"Maybe I will," she said, but she didn't think it was likely.

She knew that her work mattered, but she was only beginning to realize that she wanted more than that—she wanted to matter. And she would never be anything more than one of those interchangeable gears if she stayed at Alliston & Blake.

She went back to her office and printed her resignation letter.

Chapter Eight

Maggie wasn't usually an impulsive person, but less than twenty-four hours after her brief conversation with Perry Edler, she was back in Rust Creek Falls to meet with Ben Dalton.

"We do a little bit of everything here," the attorney said, in response to her question about his areas of practice. "Although most of it is wills, real estate transactions, the occasional divorce, traffic offenses, minor criminal stuff. What did you do in LA?"

"Mostly corporate law for the past few years, with a focus on mergers and acquisitions," she admitted. "I've already looked into taking the Montana Bar, and I know it's only offered twice a year—in Helena in February or Missoula in July. I was hoping to write in February, but I missed the registration deadline."

"If you think you can be ready to write in February, I might be able to get your name on the list."

"I think I'd do better writing it in February," she admitted. "Because I'm expecting a baby in April."

"Are you planning to get married before then?"

The unexpected question made her pause, because she couldn't imagine any interviewer in LA ever daring to ask any such thing.

"It's a possibility," she told him.

"Because folks around here are pretty conservative,"

Ben warned. "And likely to be suspicious enough of a big-city attorney setting up practice in their backyard. But if you were married to a local boy—assuming the baby's father is a local boy—that would go a long way with the people in this town."

And she knew that if he did offer her a position, she'd have to remember that things were done a little bit differently here. With that thought in mind, she nodded. "One of the reasons I wanted to move to Rust Creek Falls was to be closer to the baby's father, so that we can share the parenting."

"A smart decision," Ben told her. "My wife chose to be a stay-at-home mother, and I'm grateful our six kids had the benefit of having her around full-time, but she'll be the first to admit that every aspect of parenting is made easier by sharing it with someone."

He talked about his wife with an easy affection that spoke of their thirty-seven years and the experience of raising half a dozen kids together. He had a copy of their wedding picture in a gold frame on his desk and told Maggie it was a lucky man who could, after almost four decades, honestly say he loved his wife even more now than the day he married her.

Rust Creek Falls might have been a small town, but there were still a lot of people that Maggie had yet to meet and a lot of familial connections she hadn't begun to make. For example, it wasn't until Ben pulled out his cell phone to show off the latest snapshots of his brand-new grandson that she learned his daughter Paige was married to Sutter Traub, the owner of Traub Stables—Jesse's boss. They'd recently had a baby boy—Carter Benjamin Traub—and the proud grandpa had more than a hundred photos of the little guy on his cell phone.

The baby was adorable, and just looking at the pictures

made Maggie long for the day when her baby would finally be in her arms. Except when she remembered her first interaction with Jesse's ten-month-old-niece—then her anticipation was tempered by a healthy dose of apprehension.

"He offered me a job," Maggie told Lissa, when she got back to her cousin's house after the interview.

"Of course he did," Lissa said smugly. "He's never going to find a more qualified candidate than you to add to his practice."

"I'm not qualified yet," she reminded her cousin. "I still have to pass the Montana Bar."

Lissa waved a hand dismissively. "I'm more interested in the details about your wedding, such as what your matron of honor will be wearing."

Maggie shook her head. "The only thing I accepted today was a job, not a marriage proposal."

"But you *are* going to marry Jesse, aren't you?"

"I don't know," she admitted.

"So let me see if I'm following this," Lissa said. "You felt an instant connection to Jesse and fell into bed together. It was the best sex of your life and you hoped it was the start of a real relationship, then you found out you were having his baby and he proposed, but you don't know if you should marry him?"

Maggie nodded. "That about sums it up."

"I need a little help with the 'why' part," her cousin admitted.

"Why what?"

"Why you don't want to marry him."

"Because I love him."

Lissa took her hands. "Sweetie, you're not just my cousin but one of my best friends in the world, but I have to admit that right now, I have serious concerns about your sanity."

Maggie managed a smile even as her eyes filled with tears. "I want him to love me, too."

"You don't think he does?"

"I know he doesn't." And she told Lissa what Jesse had said about common goals being more important to the success of a marriage than love.

"Clearly Jesse Crawford is an idiot. But," Lissa continued, when Maggie opened her mouth to protest, "since he's the idiot you love, we're going to have to come up with a plan."

"A plan?"

"To make sure he falls in love with you, too."

"I don't think that's something you can plan," Maggie said.

Her cousin smiled. "A smart woman has a plan for everything."

Gage and Lissa decided to go into Kalispell for dinner. They invited Maggie to go with them, but she declined. She needed some time to think about her future—and she needed to call Jesse. Before she had a chance to do so, there was a knock on the door, and when she opened it, he was there.

"Jesse—hi." Her instinctive pleasure at seeing him was mixed with guilt as she realized that she hadn't told him about her plans to come to Rust Creek Falls this week. "I guess news travels fast in a small town."

He nodded. "Of course, I didn't believe it when Nina told me she overheard Lani Dalton tell Melba Strickland that her father was interviewing 'that city lawyer.' But then Will Baker told me that he saw you and Ben having lunch at the Ace in the Hole."

"Who needs Twitter when you've got the Rust Creek Falls grapevine?"

"Why are you here?" Jesse asked. "I thought you had some big project to work on with your boss at Alliston & Blake."

She stepped away from the door so that he could enter. "Why don't you come in so we can talk about it?"

He followed her into the kitchen, hanging his jacket over the back of a chair before settling into it.

"Do you want anything to drink?"

He shook his head. "No, I'm fine, thanks."

She turned on the kettle to make herself a cup of peppermint tea, more because she wanted something to do than because she wanted the tea.

"I handed in my resignation at Alliston & Blake yesterday."

He opened his mouth, closed it again, as if he wasn't quite sure what to say, how to respond to her news. "Okay—I'll admit I didn't see that one coming."

She shrugged. "It was time. Maybe past time. Technically, I'm supposed to give two weeks' notice, but since I haven't used all of my vacation this year—actually, I haven't used all of it in any of the past few years—I'm officially on vacation right now."

"And your lunch with Ben today?" he prompted.

"He offered me a job." She didn't tell him that she'd accepted, because she didn't want him to immediately rush to the same conclusion that Lissa had done.

"You're thinking about moving to Rust Creek Falls?"

She nodded. "I'm not sure of any of the other details yet, but I'm sure that I want you to be part of our baby's life." She poured the boiling water over the tea bag inside her cup, then carried it to the table and sat down across from him. "You went away to school, right?"

"Montana State University in Bozeman."

"When you graduated, did you ever think about exploring options anywhere else?"

He shook his head. "Nowhere else is home."

She couldn't help but smile at his conviction. "It must be nice, to know without a doubt that you are exactly where you belong."

"You don't feel like that in LA?"

"I wouldn't be making this move if I did," she told him.

"Are you going to marry me?"

She hesitated. "I still think marriage is a little extreme."

"And yet people have been doing it for thousands of years."

She smiled. "Yes, and since it's the twenty-first century, our child is unlikely to be ostracized by society if his or her parents aren't married."

"Archaic attitudes are still pervasive in society," he said, in an echo of Ben's comments earlier that day.

"And more so in Montana than California," she acknowledged.

"Undoubtedly," he agreed.

"Despite that, there are aspects of this town that really appeal to me, too."

"Such as?"

"The teacher-to-student ratio in the schools. It's widely theorized that students in smaller classes learn better. The public high school I went to had two thousand students. The secondary school here has a population that isn't even one-tenth of that."

"And only one teacher."

She laughed, because she was almost 100 percent certain he was joking. "And I like the sense of community," she said. "Everywhere you go, you cross paths with someone you know."

"I don't always consider that a plus," he admitted.

"It is," she insisted. "You might not always agree with your friends and neighbors, but you know you can count on them.

"Lissa told me what it was like, after the floods last year. How the residents rallied to help one another. Even the Crawfords and the Traubs worked together."

"That's true."

"You don't see a lot of that in LA. I'm not saying that neighbors don't ever help neighbors, but it's not the usual mindset. It's a town built on glitz and glamour and climbing over other people to get to the top."

"Why would you ever want to leave such a place?"

She smiled at his dry tone. "I also like the idea of a job with more regular hours, so that I'd have more time to spend with my baby."

"And your husband."

She shook her head. "You're like a wave crashing against a rock, determined to erode my resistance."

"Is it working?"

"It might be," she acknowledged. "And if I did decide to marry you, then what would you do?"

"Call the preacher to book a date for the wedding before you changed your mind," he replied without hesitation.

"The wedding is the easy part—it's the marriage I'm worried about."

"I'm not going to tell you that you shouldn't worry," he said. "Because I think you're right—if we want our marriage to succeed, we're both going to have to work at it. But the fact that you're having my baby means that we both have a vested interest in its success, and I'm willing to do whatever it takes to give our child the happy and stable family that he—or she—deserves."

"Then I guess, since it seems we both want the same thing, you should call the preacher."

"Really?"

She nodded.

He whooped and lifted her off her feet, spinning her around. And the sheer joy of being in his arms and sharing his joy convinced Maggie that she'd made the right decision.

She still had some concerns—aside from agreeing to marry a man who didn't love her, there was the uncertainty about whether or not she would be able to make the transition to life in the country. But if Lissa could do it—if her cousin could make the change from Manhattan to Montana—then Maggie was confident she could adjust, too.

But Lissa had worked her butt off to prove herself to the people of Rust Creek Falls after the flood the previous year. On behalf of Bootstraps, a New York–based charitable organization, she'd rallied volunteers, coordinated their schedules and duties, and essentially gone door-to-door assisting families in need and helping repair damage. Along the way she'd fallen in love with the highly respected sheriff, which had helped the townspeople fall in love with her. Even so, Gage's mother had expressed concern when her son had got involved with Lissa. Apparently the local residents had some pretty strong opinions about "city people" and not necessarily good ones.

And then Maggie had swept into town from Los Angeles, and what had she done? She'd helped get Arthur Swinton out of jail—and while his illegal activities had targeted the residents of Thunder Canyon, the people of Rust Creek Falls weren't unaware of what he'd done. As if representing the convict wasn't bad enough, she'd seduced Jesse Crawford and got pregnant in order to trap him into marriage.

Of course, that wasn't at all how things had really happened, but she didn't doubt that at least some of the locals would view the situation in exactly that way.

"At the risk of you changing your mind before I've even put a ring on your finger, I have to ask—do you think you'll miss the hustle and bustle of LA?"

"It's not as if I'm never going back there," she pointed out. "I do still have family in California."

"How are they going to feel about you moving so far away?"

"My parents have always encouraged me to follow my own path."

"Even if that path leads you to a small town in the middle of nowhere?"

"Are you trying to convince me to stay or go?"

"I just want to be sure you know what you're getting into," he told her. "I couldn't imagine living anywhere else, but I know the open space and isolation aren't for everyone. Winters, in particular, can be harsh, especially for someone who is accustomed to having all the amenities of the big city within walking distance."

"So who was she?"

"Who was who?"

"The girlfriend from the big city who did a number on you," she clarified.

He didn't say anything.

"Don't make me go into town searching for tidbits of gossip," she teased.

It wasn't a sincere threat, of course, but Jesse finally answered.

"Her name was Shaelyn," he said. "And for all of three weeks, she was my fiancée."

"Oh." And how silly was it that Maggie was disappointed to realize she wasn't the first woman he'd ever proposed to. "How many times have you been engaged?"

"Just two."

"Was she pregnant?"

He shook his head.

"So you proposed to her because you loved her," she realized.

"I thought I did," he admitted.

But Maggie knew it had been more than a thought to have scarred him so deeply.

He'd told her he didn't want to fall in love—but that was only because he'd already been there, done that. And while her heart was filled to overflowing with feelings for him, his heart was still in pieces, broken by another woman.

Not exactly the auspicious start she'd envisioned for their life together.

True to his word, Jesse called the preacher that same night, and their wedding was scheduled for Saturday afternoon—only four days away.

Christa, Gavin and Ryan all had to do some serious rearranging of their schedules, but they managed to fly into Montana on Friday. Shane and his wife, Gianna, drove up from Thunder Canyon on the same day, and the Roarkes had an impromptu family reunion at Strickland's Boarding House, where they were all staying.

On Wednesday, Lissa had taken Maggie into Kalispell to go shopping. Maggie didn't want to buy her wedding dress without her mother's approval, so every dress that she tried on, Lissa took a picture and emailed it to Christa, who would email back her thoughts and suggestions.

After the fourth picture, Lissa's cell phone rang. Christa was crying happy tears on the other end of the line because she knew that dress was "the one," and she gave her credit card information to the clerk over the phone to ensure that Maggie walked out of the store with it in hand.

And on the day of the wedding, as she helped her daughter into the gown, Christa's eyes misted over again. "Look at you," she said softly, almost reverently.

Maggie did so, smiling as she took in her reflection in the full-length mirror. "I look like a bride," she said, turning to show off the dress from all sides.

It was a strapless design with a sweetheart neckline, a bodice covered in sparkly beads that hugged her breasts, and a full skirt that skimmed the floor.

"The most beautiful bride I've ever seen," her mother said, brushing moisture from her cheeks.

"I'm sure Dad would have something to say about that," Maggie countered. Then she lifted up the hem of her skirt to show her the cowboy boots on her feet. "What do you think? Lissa says she's going to make a cowgirl out of me yet."

"I think, if Lissa says so, I wouldn't bet against it."

Maggie smiled again. "I can't believe it's my wedding day already."

"It seems like only yesterday that you called to tell us you'd accepted Jesse's proposal," her mother said.

"You mean instead of actually being four days ago?"

Christa fussed with the headpiece. "I've never heard of anyone putting together a wedding in four days."

"That's because no one else had Lissa taking care of all the details."

"Probably true," her mother agreed.

Maggie turned to take her hands. "Are you disappointed that we wanted to get married here?"

"It's *your* wedding," her mother said. "And I can understand why you'd want to take your vows where you're going to start your life with your new husband. If I'm disappointed about anything, it's only that we didn't have enough time to plan a proper wedding."

"So you think this is going to be an improper wedding?"

The gentle teasing made Christa smile, even through her tears. "You always did know how to twist words to make your point. It's one of the reasons you're such a good attorney."

"I learned from the best," she said.

"Hopefully I also taught you that there's more to life than the law."

"That's why I left my job at Alliston & Blake."

"I only wished you'd left there sooner," her mother admitted. "They demanded far too much of you and gave you very little in return. If you'd come to work at Roarke & Associates—"

"I would have always wondered if I earned my position or got it on the basis of my name."

Christa sighed. "As much as it frustrates me to know that you believed it, I can understand."

"You'll get to meet my new boss and his wife at the wedding."

"I'm looking forward to it," her mother said.

"Knock, knock," Lissa said, pushing open the door. "Mabel sent me up to let you know that the photographer's here."

"Then I'll go get the father of the bride and meet you both downstairs in ten minutes."

Since Jesse had to pick up his tux in Kalispell the day of the wedding, he decided to take it directly to the church and get ready there.

So much had happened since the day Maggie told him she was pregnant, it was hard to believe that only two weeks had passed. He'd known right away that he wanted to marry her and be a father to their child, and his conviction had not wavered. But as the clock ticked closer and closer to four o'clock and their scheduled wedding, he found himself worrying more and more that Maggie might be having second thoughts.

He suspected Shaelyn's most recent phone call was responsible for some of his concern. Although he hadn't spoken to his former fiancée, there had been a message on his machine when he got home the night that Maggie had finally agreed to marry him. Shaelyn had asked him to call her back, but of course he hadn't. She was his past and he was determined to focus on his future with Maggie.

He should feel jubilant—Maggie was going to make her life with him and their child in Rust Creek Falls. He was getting everything he wanted. But what was she getting? She was moving away from her family, her friends, giving up a career. Yes, she was planning to write the State Bar exam in the new year, and he had no doubt that she would soon be licensed to practice in Montana, but he also knew that she wouldn't have the same kind of career here that she could have if she stayed in LA.

Which was one of the reasons she'd agreed to do this— to give her life balance, so that she could be a mother *and* an attorney. But it seemed to him that she was giving up more than she was getting in return, and he couldn't help but wonder if she might come to resent him because of the changes she'd felt compelled to make to her life.

But if there was another—a better—way to work things out, he couldn't see it. He didn't want to live more than twelve hundred miles away from his child. And he didn't want his child raised by someone else while Maggie worked sixty hours a week to pay for that care.

Chapter Nine

"Shaelyn."

Jesse stared at her for a long moment, not knowing what else to say. He couldn't believe she was here, and he couldn't begin to fathom why.

"Hello, Jesse." She smiled at him—the same slow, seductive smile that used to be the prelude to all kinds of things.

She looked good—but then, Shaelyn always did. She had the fragile beauty of a china doll: silky hair, porcelain skin, delicate features. She was the type of woman that a man instinctively wanted to cherish and protect, as he'd once vowed to do.

But looking at her now, he felt nothing more than surprise—and maybe some apprehension. He hadn't seen her in seven years and couldn't understand why she'd shown up after so long—and on his wedding day, no less. "What are you doing here?"

"I saw your mother and your sisters in Missoula," his former fiancée explained. "Natalie told me that they were shopping for dresses for your wedding."

"Why were you in Missoula?"

"I've been working at the university for the past four years—at the Museum of Art & Culture."

"I thought you were in Helena. Isn't your husband some kind of advisor to the governor?"

A knock on the door jolted him out of his reverie. Assuming it was Nate, his best man, he invited him to come in.

But when the door opened, it wasn't his oldest brother who walked through it—it was his former fiancée.

"Ex-husband," she said with a small smile. "I moved to Missoula after the divorce, almost three years ago."

"Oh." He wasn't quite sure what else he was supposed to say. "I'm sorry it didn't work out?"

She offered a weak smile. "I should have realized our marriage was doomed from the start—because I never stopped loving you."

She waited a beat, but Jesse remained silent.

"I was hoping you would say that you feel the same way."

"I don't," he said bluntly.

"I know it's been a long time—"

"Speaking of time, I really don't have time for this right now."

"If we don't do this now, it's going to be too late."

"It's already too late."

She shook her head. "You told me that you loved me."

"Because I did," he confirmed. *"Seven years ago."*

"And now?"

"Now I'm marrying someone else."

She lifted her chin, her gaze challenging. "Do you love her?"

"Why else would I be marrying her?"

"That's what I'm trying to figure out," she said.

"We've been apart longer than we were together," he pointed out. "And I promise—I'm *not* still in love with you."

As he said those words, he realized—without a doubt—that they were true. He was completely over Shaelyn. Yes, he'd loved her once, but that was in the past. He'd been young and infatuated, wanting to be with the woman who claimed she wanted to be with him. When she'd gone, he'd realized that he hadn't missed Shaelyn so much as he'd missed being with someone.

"But you still haven't said that you're in love with her."

"I'm in love with Maggie," he said, because it seemed that speaking the words was the only way to get his former fiancée out of the way so he could marry the mother of his child.

"Okay, then—" she took a step back "—I guess I should offer my congratulations."

"Thank you, Shaelyn."

But, of course, she couldn't leave it at that. "I hope she loves you, too, Jesse. Enough to trade in the glitz and glamour of Hollywood for the tedium and simplicity of Big Sky Country."

And with those words, she tossed her hair over her shoulder and stalked out, passing the groom's best man on the way.

"What the hell was *she* doing here?" Nate wanted to know.

"I'm not entirely sure," Jesse admitted.

His family had never taken to Shaelyn, despite the fact that he'd planned to marry her. Nate, specifically, had expressed disapproval of her apparent lack of ambition to do anything other than get married.

"What did she say to put that look on your face?"

Jesse just shook his head.

"Don't let her mess with your mind," Nate warned.

"She didn't say anything that I haven't already heard a thousand times."

Except for the fact that she was still in love with him, and he wasn't going to get into that with his brother. Because, as he'd said to Maggie when he first proposed to her, he wasn't looking for love.

So why was he bothered by Shaelyn's suggestion that Maggie might not love him enough?

* * *

As his wife fussed with his tie, determined to get it just right before he walked their daughter down the aisle, Gavin stared stonily ahead, trying *not* to think about the reason he was in this tux.

"You're the father of the bride—try to look happy."

"Even if I'm not?"

Christa sighed. "You should be happy for your daughter—this is what she wants."

"She's only twenty-eight years old and she's been so busy building a career, she's barely dated. How can she know what she wants?" he demanded.

"No one knows her mind like our Maggie," his wife assured him. "A fact that you've been lamenting since she was a toddler."

He smiled, because it was true, but the smile quickly faded. "You don't think he coerced her into this marriage because she's pregnant?"

"I think she wouldn't let herself be coerced if she didn't want to be."

He continued to scowl. "She's our baby girl."

"Our baby girl's going to have a baby of her own in a few months," Christa reminded him gently.

"And she's going to have that baby more than a thousand miles away from us."

"I know you think Montana is the middle of nowhere, but we managed to get here today, didn't we?"

"You think I'm being ridiculous," he realized.

"I think you're being a father." She tugged on his tie, bringing his mouth down to hers for a quick kiss. "And a very handsome father of the bride you are."

"The mother of the bride looks pretty good, too."

She arched a brow. "Pretty good?"

He grinned and slipped his arm around her waist. "I love you, Christa."

"I love you, too."

"I just hope that, forty years from now, Maggie and Jesse will be as happy as we are."

"No one can know what the future holds," she told her husband, "but I have no doubt that when you walk our daughter down the aisle today, she will be marrying the man she loves."

The groom's parents, already seated in the church, weren't any more enthusiastic about the forthcoming nuptials than the bride's father.

"I hope he isn't making a mistake," Todd Crawford said, drumming his fingers on his knee.

His wife clasped her hands together in her lap. "What else could he do, under the circumstances?"

"Nothing," her husband admitted. "A man needs to take responsibility for his actions, and a child needs a father."

"Then why are you griping?"

"I just wish, if he had to knock up someone, he'd chosen a local girl who might actually stay put in this town."

"Except that one or more of his brothers has dated most of the single women in Rust Creek Falls," she pointed out drily.

"There are plenty of women in Kalispell or even other parts of Montana."

"Like Billings?"

He winced at the mention of the hometown of the groom's former fiancée. "Okay, so that didn't work out so well for him. But I'm not sure this is going to be any better. She's from Los Angeles for Christ's sake."

"Don't swear," his wife admonished.

"She's not going to be happy here."

"You don't know that—look at her cousin, Lissa. She came from New York and yet she settled in with the sheriff with no difficulty."

As was usual when Todd couldn't refute an argument, he said nothing. But his jaw remained stubbornly set.

"This all started when he went to work at Traub Stables," he said, after another minute had passed.

Laura frowned. "What?"

"It's those damn Traubs—they lured Jesse away from home, from his roots."

His wife sighed. "You know Jesse's heart has always been with the horses."

Todd shook his head. "As if it wasn't bad enough that everyone in town knows that our son is working for a Traub, now he's marrying a California girl."

"Could you try to focus on something else—at least for today?"

"Like what?"

"Like the fact that we're going to be grandparents again."

"That's if she sticks around long enough for us to meet the baby," her husband grumbled.

Maggie had lived her whole life in Los Angeles, where there was no shortage of handsome men. She worked in a law firm where men lived in suits. But she was certain she'd never seen anyone as handsome as Jesse Crawford. And she knew none of those other men had ever affected her the way he did. Never had any one of those men made her breath catch in her throat or her heart pound so hard and fast against her ribs she was certain everyone must be able to hear it.

But when she took her first steps down the aisle and saw Jesse standing at the altar, that's exactly what happened.

She didn't even remember the exchange of vows; the words were somehow lost in the excitement of the realization that she was going to be Mrs. Jesse Crawford. She did remember the kiss. Although it was chaste in comparison to other kisses they'd shared, there was heat in the brief touch of his mouth to hers, enough to heighten her awareness and anticipation.

Now she was in his arms again, sharing their first dance as husband and wife.

As she turned around the floor, she caught a glimpse of her parents—Christa dabbing her eyes with Gavin's handkerchief—and Jesse's parents—Laura's smile obviously forced, Todd's attention on the drink in his hand.

"I think your mother disapproves of the fact that I'm wearing a white dress," Maggie said.

Jesse looked down at his bride—the most beautiful woman he'd ever known, looking even more beautiful than ever. "You don't need to worry about my mother's—or anyone else's—approval."

At nineteen weeks, Maggie wasn't obviously pregnant. It was only because he'd been intimate with her slender body that Jesse was aware of the subtle bump that was proof of their baby growing inside of her.

"I'm not really. But I know people are already speculating about the reasons for our getting married so quickly."

"People are always going to talk about something."

"I know," she admitted. "Although it's a little unnerving to realize that the Hollywood paparazzi has nothing on the Rust Creek Falls grapevine."

"You're a celebrity here," he told her.

"The city slicker who shamelessly seduced the quiet cowboy and trapped him into marriage?"

He tipped her chin up, forcing her to meet his gaze.

"I don't feel trapped," he promised her. "I feel incredibly lucky."

Then he brushed his lips against hers.

And the way she kissed him back gave him hope that, before the night was out, he'd get even luckier.

After the cake-cutting ceremony, Maggie slipped away to use the ladies' room. Lissa had been taking her duties as matron of honor seriously and had barely left the bride's side, but she was dancing with her husband now and Maggie didn't want to interrupt.

It was a bit tricky to maneuver her skirts in the narrow stall, but she managed and was just about to flush when she heard the *click-clack* of heels on tile. Several pairs, by the sound of it, accompanied by talking and laughter.

The words she heard made her pause with her fingers on the handle.

"Guess who stopped by to see the groom before the wedding," an unfamiliar female voice said.

"Who?" a second woman wanted to know.

"Shaelyn Everton."

"Who?" the second speaker asked again.

"Jesse's ex," yet another voice responded, sounding impatient. "The one he was engaged to for all of three weeks."

Inside her bathroom stall, Maggie sucked in a breath. Thankfully, the other women were too focused on their conversation to hear her.

"How do you know this?"

"Brad told me that Nate caught them together in the anteroom before the ceremony."

"Caught them doing what?" There was more glee than curiosity in the tone, suggesting that the second woman enjoyed a juicy scandal.

Maggie pressed a hand to her stomach, desperate to still its sudden churning.

Her friend laughed. "Nothing like that," she chided. "They were just talking."

"Oh." Woman Number Two didn't hide her disappointment while the bride exhaled a long, slow breath. "What was she doing here?"

"Trying to make a final play for Jesse would be my guess."

"Because breaking his heart once wasn't enough?"

"She messed him up, that's for sure," the first woman commented. "I remember hearing his mom tell my mom that she didn't think he'd ever get over her."

"That was a long time ago," someone else said. "And he seems happy with Maggie."

"For now," the first speaker allowed.

"Give her a chance," the third woman suggested.

"Kristin's just mad that Maggie got him into bed and she never did."

"I've always liked the strong, silent type," the first speaker, now identified as Kristin, admitted. "But Brad is every bit as cute as his brother—maybe even more."

"But why was Shaelyn here?" The second woman finally circled back to the original topic of conversation. "I thought she married some other guy."

"She did, but they're divorced now. And while she might have been the one to leave Jesse, the rumor is that she never got over him."

The women had apparently finished their primping and started toward the exit, as evidenced by the *click-clack* on the tiles and their fading voices. "I don't think he..."

Maggie stayed in the bathroom stall until she was sure they were gone, and then for a few minutes more to compose herself.

She didn't know what to make of that entire exchange. What she did know was that, even if Shaelyn still wanted Jesse, she wasn't going to get him.

Because the shy, sexy cowboy was Maggie's husband now.

Jesse warily eyed the beer that Maggie's oldest brother offered to him. "Is it poisoned?"

Shane Roarke grinned. "You haven't given me any reason to want to make my sister a widow...yet."

"Then I'll make sure I don't," he said, accepting the bottle.

"I wish I could be sure that Maggie will be happy here."

"You don't think she will be?"

"Let's just say I have my doubts." Shane sipped his own beer.

"Wasn't it just a couple of years ago that you decided to make your home in Montana?"

"Yeah, but I moved around a lot before then," his new brother-in-law pointed out. "Maggie, on the other hand, has been working her tail off for the past five years to establish herself at Alliston & Blake."

"From my perspective, she worked too long and too hard for too little."

"I don't disagree—but it was her choice."

"So was this," Jesse assured him.

"That's what I have to wonder about," Shane said. "Because this whole situation—quitting her job, moving twelve hundred miles away, having a whirlwind wedding—isn't Maggie. She doesn't rush into anything."

She hadn't dragged her feet at all the day they met, but that was hardly something that would gain him points with her brother.

"She walked down that aisle of her own free will."

"It looked that way," Shane agreed. "But one of the women I work with just had a baby, and I have to tell you—pregnant women have all those hormones to deal with that mess with their heads and their hearts.

"I'm not sure Maggie knows what she wants right now, but you managed to convince her that you should be together for the sake of your baby. She's smart, but she's probably scared, too. The prospect of having a baby on her own had to be a little daunting, especially when her pregnancy ended any hopes of ever getting a partnership at Alliston & Blake."

He must have noticed Jesse's scowl, because he swore softly. "I guess she didn't tell you about that."

"No, she didn't."

"I think she was planning to leave, anyway," Shane said now. "But when her boss found out she was pregnant, it expedited the process."

"So you think she married me because she was in danger of losing her job?"

"No. She wouldn't have had any trouble getting another job in LA—and not just at our parents' firm. But I think marrying you gave her the excuse she needed to make a big change.

"I'm just not sure, because everything happened so fast, that she's not going to regret it in a month or two and realize she isn't cut out for life in Small Town, Montana."

Jesse thought about what Shane had said for a long time after the other man had gone.

There was no doubt he'd pushed Maggie to the altar because it was what he wanted for their baby. She'd voiced some objections, and he'd disregarded each and every one. Even her concerns about her clients in LA had been discounted, because they hadn't been as important to him

as giving their baby a family. But they'd been important
to her…

Damn.

He didn't know if what Shane had said about pregnancy
hormones was true—but in case it was, he was going to
give her time and space to decide if this was truly what
she wanted.

As was usual for a bride, Maggie spent a lot of time
dancing with various guests. After the first dance with her
new husband, she took a turn around the floor with her
father, then Jesse's father, then Ben Dalton. She danced
and chatted with each of her new brothers-in-law and several other residents whose names she wasn't even sure she
would remember. When her brother Ryan snagged her for
a spin, she was grateful that she didn't have to keep up any
pretenses—at least for the next three minutes.

"When you decide to make some changes in your life,
you do it in a big way," he mused.

"It was time," she said lightly.

"Maybe," he acknowledged. "But this is the twenty-first
century—you don't have to get married to have a baby."

"I know," she said, and she loved her brother for his
ability to support nontraditional choices.

"You should also know that I'm having a really hard
time not kicking that cowboy's ass for doing the things he
did with you that resulted in you getting pregnant."

She held back a smile. "You could *try* to kick his ass."

Her brother's eyes narrowed. "You don't think I could
take him?"

"I'm a big girl, you know. It's not like I was an innocent
virgin seduced by a big bad cowboy. I wanted him every
bit as much as he wanted me."

Ryan winced. "I don't need to know things like that."

"Apparently you do."

"I just want you to be happy, and I'm not convinced you will be with him. He's not at all like any of the other guys you've dated."

"No, he's not," she agreed. "And I think it says something that I never fell in love with any of those other guys."

He looked at her carefully. "You really are in love with him?"

"This is the twenty-first century," she said, echoing his words back to him. "I wouldn't be marrying him for any other reason."

"So I can't kick his ass?"

"You can't even try."

"Okay," he relented. "But if he ever makes you unhappy, you let me know."

"I'll let you know," she promised.

"Maybe I should kick Shane's ass," Ryan suggested.

"Why?"

"Because if he hadn't enlisted our help to get Arthur Swinton out of jail, there wouldn't be any Grace Traub Community Center, and you would never have come to Rust Creek Falls and met Jesse Crawford."

"I would have come anyway for Lissa and Gage's wedding," she pointed out to him.

"I guess you would have," he allowed.

"Look on the bright side—now you have twice as many reasons to visit Montana. And maybe you'll find the woman of your dreams in Big Sky Country, too."

"There's only one woman for me—Lady Justice."

"Does she keep you warm at night?"

"No, but there are other women who satisfy those needs."

"I don't need details," Maggie said.

"You weren't going to get any," he assured her.

The song ended, and he stepped back but continued to hold her hands. "I'm going to miss you."

"You're going to miss stealing the Yorkshire pudding from my plate at Sunday-night dinner."

He grinned. "That, too."

Jesse caught up to his bride as she was kissing her younger brother's cheek. Since he'd already done the verbal sparring routine with her older brother, he merely nodded to Ryan and spoke to Maggie.

"Apparently the guests want the bride and groom to share one last dance."

"It's barely ten o'clock," she protested.

"Most of the people here are ranchers who will be up before the sun rises in the morning," he reminded her.

"Then I guess we should have that dance."

He took her hand and led her back to the middle of the floor. His youngest sister, acting as DJ, announced their final dance, and Maggie lifted a brow when she recognized the opening bars of the song.

"Did you request this?" she asked, as they moved in time to the Rolling Stones' "Wild Horses."

He shook his head. "It was Natalie's choice."

But Maggie just smiled, appreciating his sister's off-beat sense of humor. Or maybe she just appreciated that it wasn't a traditional sappy ballad.

"How are you holding up?" he asked her now.

"I'm doing okay."

"It's been a long day."

"It's been a crazy week," she clarified. "I can't believe we managed to put together a wedding in only three days."

"With a little help from our friends and families."

"A *lot* of help."

He nodded his agreement. Shane Roarke, head chef at

the Gallatin Room, the four-star restaurant at the Thunder
Canyon Resort, was their connection to the resort's pas-
try chef, who had agreed to make the wedding cake; Nina
had a friend who did the flowers; Lissa, Maggie's matron
of honor and the undisputed queen of organization, had
supervised the decorating, ensuring that the utilitarian
community room was transformed into a winter wonderland, including potted Christmas trees with white lights
and silver bows, silver and white streamers, bouquets of
helium-filled balloons and white poinsettias in silver pots
on the tables.

It was beautiful and festive, but what made the day perfect for Maggie was the identity of her groom.

And she was looking forward to their perfect night that
would follow their perfect day.

Chapter Ten

Someone had brought Jesse's truck to the front door of the community hall to expedite the bride and groom's exit from the reception.

Maggie smiled when she saw that the vehicle had been decorated with paper flowers and an enormous heart proclaiming Just Married. Jesse offered his hand to help her into the cab, and when she took it, a definite frisson of electricity passed between them.

Neither of them said much on the drive back to his house. Maggie's mind and heart were so cluttered with emotion and anticipation, she could barely hold on to a thought. But when she looked down at the hands folded in her lap, and at the rings on her finger that confirmed that she was definitely and undeniably Jesse Crawford's wife, she knew—maybe for the first time in her life—that she was exactly where she wanted to be.

It wasn't until he shut off the engine that she realized they'd arrived at his house. Now her home, too. And it was their wedding night. Nerves and excitement tangled in her belly as she reached for the gift bag that Lissa had thrust into her hands as she was leaving the hall.

Jesse came around to her door again and helped her out of the truck. But she'd barely put her feet on the ground when he swept her off them and into his arms.

"What are you doing?"

"It's traditional for the groom to carry his bride over the threshold," he told her.

She knew that, of course. And the fact that he'd insisted they marry before the birth of their child proved he was a traditional guy. But both of those facts were lost in the giddy excitement and sheer pleasure of being carried in strong arms.

He turned the handle and pushed open the door. "Welcome home, Mrs. Crawford."

She smiled at him. "Thank you, Mr. Crawford."

He gently set her onto her feet, only then seeming to notice the silver bag in her hand with the pale pink tissue sticking out of the top. "What's that?"

"A gift. From Lissa."

"I thought Justin loaded all of the presents into his truck to bring over tomorrow."

"All except this one," she confirmed.

Thankfully, he didn't ask any more questions about it. Instead he said, "I'll go get your suitcases."

"Okay."

He disappeared outside again, returning a few minutes later with the two bags of what she'd deemed to be essential clothing items and toiletries. The rest of her belongings were still in LA, but packed up and ready to be shipped. He set them down inside the door to remove his coat and boots, then carried the suitcases up the stairs.

Maggie hovered inside the door, not quite certain what to do. Reminding herself that she wasn't a guest here—although she still felt like one—she sat down on the bench beside the door and removed her wrap and boots.

She'd loved the sleeveless-style dress when she'd tried it on in the bridal shop in Kalispell, but she wished now that someone had warned her that a November bride in Montana should have sleeves. Long sleeves. And a high collar. But then she remembered the way Jesse had looked at her when he first saw her in the dress, how the heat in his eyes had warmed every inch of her body from her head to her toes.

She moved toward the stone fireplace and imagined flames crackling and flickering as they'd been the first day she'd been here—was it really only two weeks earlier? So much had happened since the day that she'd told Jesse about their baby, it was hard to believe such a short span of time had passed.

She wondered if Jesse would build a fire tonight. She had a fantasy—perhaps born of reading too many romance novels—of making love by a fire, and the thick sheepskin in front of the hearth only fueled that fantasy.

She curled her toes into the fluffy rug as the scene played out in great detail in her mind. He would move slowly toward her, his eyes—filled with unbridled heat and wicked promises—locked on hers. Then he would take her hands in his, drawing her down to the carpet, so they were kneeling and facing one another. Then he would slowly peel away her clothes as he kissed her, his lips moving from her mouth to her throat to her breasts—

"Maggie?"

She gasped, as his voice jolted her out of her fantasy. "I didn't hear you come back down the stairs," she admitted.

"Are you okay?"

"Fine," she said quickly. "I was just thinking a fire might help take the chill of the air."

"It's kind of late," he told her. "If I started one now, I wouldn't be able to go to bed until it was completely out."

"I didn't think about that," she admitted, trying not to feel disappointed that his response had been more practical than romantic. Besides, he'd carried her over the threshold, which was an undeniably romantic gesture. Not quite as romantic as carrying her directly upstairs and to his bed, but romantic nonetheless.

"Did you want anything?" Jesse asked. "A cup of tea or a glass of water?"

She shook her head. "I think I'll just go get ready for bed."

"Okay."

"Can I just get your help with something?" She turned around, showing him her back. "There's a little hook at the top of the zipper that I can't reach."

"Oh. Um. Sure."

She felt the brush of his knuckles against her bare skin as he wrestled with the tiny closure, and goose bumps danced up her spine. The catch released and he lifted his hands away.

"And the zipper," she prompted. "If you could just lower it a couple of inches."

The soft rasp of the pull tracking along the twin rows of tiny teeth—the only sound in the quiet room—was tantalizingly seductive. As the zipper inched downward, the fabric of her bodice parted, exposing a V of skin between her shoulder blades. The air was cool, but she felt hot all over. Hot and achy and needy.

"How's that?" His voice was low, husky, and she knew he was as aroused as she was.

Maybe he didn't love her, but he wanted her, and that would be enough for now.

"That's great—thanks."

She picked up the gift bag again and carried it upstairs to the bathroom.

She didn't know what was going on with Jesse—why, after campaigning relentlessly for her to marry him, he'd been keeping her at arm's length since she'd agreed to do so. Maybe it was another one of those traditions—abstaining from lovemaking until the night of the wedding. Again the horse-and-barn-door analogy came to mind, but she could pretend to be understanding. Because tonight, finally, was their wedding night.

She unzipped her dress the rest of the way and slid it down her body, then hung it on a hook on the back of the door. The snug bodice had eliminated the need for a bra, so she was left in only a pair of lacy bikini panties and thigh-high stockings. She debated for a minute and then removed them, too, before reaching into the bag for the peignoir set her cousin had bought for her.

The sleeveless gown had a soft, stretch lace bodice that dipped low between her breasts, and an empire waist from which fell a long flowing skirt of semi-sheer chiffon. It was feminine and romantic and sexy, and Maggie loved the feel of the soft fabric against her skin. The long-sleeved chiffon wrap had wide lace cuffs and delicate pearl buttons with satin loop closures at the bodice. She slipped her arms into the sleeves but decided to leave the wrap unfastened, then eyed herself critically in the mirror.

Would he see the truth of her feelings for him when he looked at her? Did it matter if he did? She knew he didn't feel the same way, but she couldn't help hoping that maybe, someday, he would.

She was under no illusions about why he wanted to marry her: *it's about giving our baby the family he or she deserves.* He wasn't looking for love, and now—thanks to the conversation she'd overhead in the ladies' room—she knew why. It was because Shaelyn had broken his heart so badly even his mother had worried that he'd never get over her.

She pushed the conversation between those unknown women to the back of her mind. Maybe Jesse's former fiancée had come back to Rust Creek Falls hoping to lasso her cowboy once again, but he'd sent her away and married Maggie. Even if he didn't love her, she knew he cared about her and he loved their baby. That was a pretty good starting point, and she wasn't going to let anything or anyone ruin her wedding night.

They'd shared a connection in the bedroom, and she was confident they would reconnect tonight. She craved not just the physical joining but the emotional intimacy they'd shared; she wanted to make love with him, to show him the true depth of her feelings with her lips and her hands and her body. But she would hold on to the words until he was ready not just to hear them but to believe them.

With her heart pounding against her ribs, she opened the door and stepped out of the bathroom.

"Jesse?"

She tapped her knuckles on the partially closed bedroom door. There was no response. She pushed it open and found the room was empty. His tuxedo was draped over the back of the chair in his bedroom, but her husband was nowhere to be found.

She made her way down the stairs, past his dark office, through the quiet kitchen to the empty living room.

"Jesse?" she said again.

It was then that she noticed his boots and coat were missing from the hook by the back door.

He was gone.

Her husband had left her alone on their wedding night.

Or maybe she was being melodramatic. He'd probably expected it would take her longer to get ready for bed, and he'd decided to go out to the barn to check on the horses while he was waiting. Her spirits buoyed by this thought, she went back upstairs. It was then that she noticed a light spilling out of the doorway of one of the spare bedrooms farther down the hall.

She pushed open the door and found her suitcases neatly aligned at the foot of the bed, undeniable evidence that her husband didn't plan on sharing a bed with her tonight—or anytime in the near future.

She felt the sting of tears behind her eyes as hurt and confusion battled inside of her.

Had she been so blinded by her own feelings that she'd misinterpreted what she'd believed was evidence of his desire for her? How were they supposed to make their marriage work if they were sleeping in separate rooms? And why had he insisted on marrying her if he didn't want to be with her?

Of course she didn't have the answers to any of these questions. All she had was an aching emptiness in her heart, and all she could do was slip between the cold sheets of a bed that wouldn't be shared with her husband and cry herself to sleep.

The next morning, Maggie's first as Jesse's wife, she woke up as she'd fallen asleep: alone.

She climbed out of bed and headed for the bathroom. After she'd washed her face and brushed her teeth, she stepped into the hallway. The scent of fresh coffee wafted up the stairs, luring her to the kitchen. Jesse wasn't there, but the empty cereal bowl and mug in the sink confirmed that he was up—and probably already out in the barn. Rumor around town was that Jesse Crawford liked animals more than he liked people, but Maggie hadn't believed it was true. At least not until he'd left her alone on their wedding night.

She opened three different cupboards before she found the mugs. Although she'd severely cut back on her caffeine consumption as soon as she knew she was pregnant, she still needed half a cup of coffee at the start of the day to feel human in the morning.

She looked out the window over the sink, slowly sipping her coffee and wondering if she might catch a glimpse of her husband. She didn't see him, but she heard the back door open and then close, indicating that he'd returned to the house.

As his footsteps came toward the kitchen, her heart started to pound a little bit faster. But she kept her eyes focused on the window, not wanting to appear overly eager to see him.

"Good mor—" The greeting halted as abruptly as the footsteps.

Her curiosity piqued, Maggie slowly turned to face him, and caught his gaze—hungry and heated—skimming over her.

"What—" He swallowed. "What are you wearing?"

She'd forgotten about the ensemble she'd donned in anticipation of her husband taking it off for her on their wedding night. Had she been thinking about anything but how much she wanted her daily half cup of coffee, she might have covered up. But the blatant masculine appreciation in his eyes warmed every inch of her—from the top of her head to the bare toes on the ceramic tile floor—and made her glad that she hadn't.

"It's called a peignoir set," she told him. "Lissa bought it for me."

He continued to stare at her, as if he couldn't tear his eyes away, but when he spoke, his tone was gruff. "Your cousin should know by now that the winter nights are cold in this part of the country. You'd be better off with something a little less see-through and a little more flannel."

Flannel—as if separate bedrooms wasn't a big enough hint that he didn't want her.

Except that he hadn't looked at her as if he didn't want her. Even now, even though he was staying on the far side of the kitchen, there was something in his gaze—and it wasn't disinterest.

But she only nodded in answer to his statement. "I guess I'm going to have to do some shopping."

He moved to the fridge and yanked on the door handle. "I can't ignore my responsibilities to take you around the shops today."

She blinked, sincerely baffled by his response. "I didn't ask you to take me anywhere."

He dropped a package of bacon on the counter. "No," he finally acknowledged. "I guess you didn't."

That did it. Maggie put her mug on the counter with a thud. "What's going on, Jesse?"

"What do you mean?" He set a frying pan on the stove, turned on the flame beneath it.

"We've barely been married—" she glanced at the clock "—fifteen hours, and you're acting like you're sorry you ever proposed."

"I'm not," he said quickly. "You know this is what I wanted."

"I *thought* it was what you wanted," she acknowledged. "But clearly I'm having trouble reading your signals, because when you asked me to marry you, I didn't think you intended for us to sleep in separate bedrooms."

He opened the bacon, peeled off several strips and placed them in the pan. "When you accepted my proposal, you didn't say you wanted to share a bed," he countered.

"I'm carrying your baby," she reminded him. "And there was nothing immaculate about the conception."

"We've done some things out of order in our relationship," he said, keeping his gaze focused on his task as he moved the slices of bacon around with a fork. "I just thought we should take some time now to get to know one another."

She tried to think about what he was saying objectively. The words sounded reasonable—considerate, even. But she couldn't help but wonder when exactly he'd decided they should take this time: Before or after he'd seen Shaelyn?

Maybe seeing the woman he'd once loved had made him realize he'd made a mistake in proposing to Maggie. But if that was true—why hadn't he called off the wedding?

"If it's so important to you that we take time to get to know one another, why didn't you want to take that time *before* we got married?"

He shrugged. "I wanted to make sure our baby would be born to parents who were legally married."

She nodded. From the moment he'd learned that she was pregnant, he'd been clear that the baby was his primary concern. Maybe his only concern.

What I want—what you want—isn't as important as what our baby needs.

She'd accepted his proposal because she'd been certain that there was more between them than their baby. She'd believed that their relationship was founded on mutual attraction and growing affection.

Now she knew the truth. Jesse didn't want her—he only wanted their baby.

If her silence wasn't evidence enough that he'd said something wrong, the white-knuckle grip in which Maggie held her cup further substantiated the fact.

He'd never been good with words—or relationships, but he'd never had so much at stake before. He decided a shift in topic toward something less personal was warranted.

"Did you have breakfast?" he asked.

She shook her head. "No. I'm not hungry."

"You have to eat," he admonished. "Skipping meals isn't good for the baby."

Apparently he'd said the wrong thing again, because when he glanced up, he saw that her eyes shone with telltale moisture.

Damn. His brain scrambled for something, *anything*, to divert the ensuing flood of tears and recriminations, but he came up empty.

To his surprise—and relief—Maggie lifted her chin. "You're right." She took a banana from the bowl of fruit on the counter. "I'm going to check my email."

And then she was gone, and he didn't know whether he was relieved or disappointed.

The only thing that was certain was that he'd lost his mind—most likely sometime between the minister proclaiming he and Maggie to be husband and wife and his return to the house to make breakfast this morning. It was the only possible reason that might explain why he'd suggested his wife should sleep in something less see-through and more flannel.

Not that what she'd been wearing was exactly seethrough, but the morning light coming through the window had backlit her so that her silhouette was clearly visible. And those delicious curves had tempted him to touch, to trace her feminine contours and revel in the satiny softness of her skin. He'd had to curl his fingers into his palms to prevent himself from reaching out for her. And then she'd turned to face him, and the outline of her peaked nipples pressed against the gauzy fabric had actually made his mouth water.

The first time he saw her, he wanted her. In the five months that had passed since their initial meeting, he hadn't stopped wanting her. And being with Maggie had escalated rather than satiated his desire.

She was right—he hadn't planned on separate bedrooms when he'd asked her to marry him. He couldn't think of anything he wanted as much as he wanted Maggie in his bed again—just imagining her naked body wrapped around his was enough to make him ache. He'd been eager for their wedding day to conclude so that their wedding night could begin. And then he'd been cornered by her brother at the reception.

His conversation with Shane Roarke had made him realize that he'd pushed Maggie into this marriage because it was what *he* wanted. He hadn't asked what she wanted. In fact, he'd ignored her efforts to tell him.

On more than a few occasions, he'd been accused of being stubborn and single-minded, because he rarely gave up until he got what he wanted. And usually the end justified the means—except that, in this situation, he wasn't entirely sure what "end" he wanted. Why had he insisted on this marriage? To ensure he would have a place in his child's life? Or to hold on to Maggie?

Because he didn't know the answers to those questions, and because he wasn't comfortable acknowledging the possibility that he might have pushed her into a marriage she wasn't ready for, he'd forced himself to take a step back.

The fact that she'd slept in that—what had she called it?—peignoir set, suggested that she hadn't planned on sleeping alone.

But the weight of her brother's words continued to echo in the back of his mind.

He'd never even taken Maggie out on a date. They'd gone from introductions to intercourse in a matter of hours. They'd both been on the same page, had both wanted the same thing, but their compatibility in the bedroom aside, what did he really know about her?

After she'd gone back to LA, they'd had several long

telephone conversations, they'd exchanged emails, they'd planned to get together again. But it hadn't happened.

Weeks and then months had passed, and he'd been certain their relationship was over. If what they'd shared could even be categorized as a relationship. After a few more weeks, he'd even managed to convince himself that he didn't care. Yeah, and that conviction had lasted right up until he'd looked up and saw her standing outside the paddock where he was working with Rocky.

He'd been genuinely happy to see her—and mad at himself for being so happy. She'd unceremoniously dumped him, and then reappeared out of nowhere, and his heart had practically leaped out of his chest.

Now, only two weeks later, they were married.

He didn't doubt that they'd done the right thing for their child. Whether it was right for him and Maggie remained to be seen.

Chapter Eleven

Over the next few days, Maggie and Jesse started to become accustomed to living together—albeit as roommates rather than husband and wife. They shared conversation and ate their meals together, but it was all superficial.

They talked mostly about the weather, which Jesse described as alternately chilly/nippy/frosty/blustery or simply cold, and which Maggie interpreted as unbelievably mind-numbingly and bone-chillingly frigid, and the local news: old Mr. Effingham slipped outside of the post office and broke his hip; six-foot-five-inch local basketball star Wendell Holmes was caught with his girlfriend in a compromising position in the backseat of a Chevy Spark at the high school; three ranch hands spent a night in lockup after the most recent brawl at the Ace in the Hole; and Tom Riddell's yellow lab had given birth to a litter of puppies that confirmed the doggy daddy was Liza Weichelt's German shepherd, despite her repeated assertions that Rex never showed any interest in Taffy. The discussion of which might have been more interesting if Maggie knew any of the people involved.

Maggie did most of the cooking, because she enjoyed it, and Jesse did the cleanup. And as they went about their respective duties, he didn't touch her—either by accident or design. It was as if every movement he made was deliberately intended to ensure there was no contact between them. If she asked him to pass the salt, he put the shaker in front of her plate rather than in her hand. If she needed help reaching something on the top shelf of the pantry, he'd wait until she moved aside rather than reach over her.

On Wednesday morning, just four days after her wedding, Maggie was scheduled to start working for Ben Dalton. She woke up early—both nervous and excited about her first day.

Although she'd learned a lot in her tenure with Alliston & Blake, she'd also had almost limitless resources at her disposal. At Ben's office, there weren't a dozen other junior associates to ask for help, there was no senior associate assigned to review her work. There was only Ben, his secretary, Jessica Evanson, and his paralegal, Mallory Franklin. Which meant that if she didn't know how to do something, she would have to ask her boss.

She hoped she didn't have to ask her boss, because she really wanted to make a good impression.

She knew that the people of Rust Creek Falls were reserving judgment—that they were wary of outsiders and didn't trust her not to run out on Jesse the way his former fiancée had done. Only time would convince them of that. She was more concerned with proving that she was smart and capable and independent of the man she'd married.

Ben had confided that he was usually in the office before eight-thirty, but he told her that she could start at nine. Since she was accustomed to early hours and Jesse was up as well, she decided she might as well head into town. She pulled into the small parking lot beside the building at eight-twenty-two and found Ben's Suburban was already there.

She picked up her briefcase and drew in a deep breath, trying to calm the butterflies that were swooping around in her tummy. Apparently it was early for most of the townsfolk, as the streets were quiet. Quite a different scenario from the nearby ranches, where the men would have been up at the crack of dawn, feeding stock and mucking out stalls and whatever else ranch hands did at the start of the day.

Jesse always began his morning at The Shooting Star. After he'd taken care of the animals there, he'd drive over to Traub Stables, where he'd put in several hours training other people's horses. She didn't know what exactly it was that he did, but she knew that when people spoke his name, they did so with respect. Aside from the fact that he had an undeniable gift when it came to animals, he was also universally regarded as a good man.

Maggie didn't disagree, but she would add *enigmatic*, *confusing* and *frustrating* to his list of attributes. And apparently, since their marriage, *celibate*—which contributed in no small part to the *frustrating*.

As she made her way around the building, she was startled to find Homer Gilmore sitting on the bottom step that led to the front door of the law office. She'd seen him around town before, but she didn't know much about him. She didn't put much stock in gossip or rumor, although the consensus was that he was a crazy old coot. She thought *lost* was a more apt description, as if he wasn't quite sure where he was or how he got there, but he seemed harmless. Certainly she'd never had reason to fear him, so she greeted him pleasantly now.

"Good morning, Mr. Gilmore."

He scrambled up from the step and moved out of her way. "The past is the present."

She wasn't sure if the mumbled words were intended as some kind of cryptic response to her greeting or if he was talking to himself.

"It's a little chilly this morning," she said, making her

way up the steps. Actually, it was more than chilly by LA standards, but she knew that saying so would only highlight her status as an outsider.

"The past is the present."

"O-kay."

"The past is the present." He muttered the same statement again, so quickly now the words almost ran together.

"Well," she kept her tone cheerful, "I should get in to work."

"Thepastisthepresent."

She opened the door and stepped into the outer office, concerned that the rumors about his sanity might be true.

Maggie spent the first hour and a half in her new office reviewing the client files her boss had put on her desk for later discussion. Jessica arrived just before nine and settled at her desk; Mallory came in a few minutes later, after she'd taken her niece Lily to school.

Everyone seemed to have their own routines and enough work to keep occupied—except for Maggie.

Just before ten o'clock, Ben Dalton knocked on her open door. "I've got a settlement conference in Kalispell," he said. "If you want to come with me, I can introduce you to the court staff and some of the local Bar members."

"I'd like that," she agreed readily.

On the way, he gave her some background information about the issues to be discussed, his client—an employer trying to negotiate an agreement with a former employee— the opposing counsel and the judge who was scheduled to preside over the conference.

Afterward, they went for lunch and while they were waiting for their food to be delivered, they discussed the files Ben had asked her to review. One was an application for a variation of a custody agreement, another was a landlord-tenant dispute and the third was a breach of contract case. Maggie had not just familiarized herself with the details of the cases but made notes of relevant statutes and precedents for each.

Ben seemed pleased with her initiative and insights, and confided that he'd been thinking about expanding his practice for a few years. Hiring Mallory Franklin as a paralegal had been the first step, and because she now did a lot of the paperwork that he used to do, he was able to keep more regular hours than he had in years. He hadn't given up on his plan to bring in a second lawyer, but there hadn't been any qualified candidates in Rust Creek Falls—until Maggie.

"With your background and experience, we can expand the services offered to our clients," he told her.

"I'm looking forward to being able to help," she said.

Ben nodded. "And maybe we can even work out some kind of partnership agreement after you pass the Montana Bar, so that you can work with me instead of for me."

Maggie stared across the table at him, too stunned to reply.

"What do you think—should it be Dalton & Roarke or Dalton & Crawford?"

She hadn't thought about whether she would take Jesse's name professionally. As for a partnership, she hadn't thought about that at all.

"Or maybe that's more responsibility than you're looking for?" he asked, when she didn't respond.

"No," she said quickly. "That's *exactly* the kind of responsibility I'm looking for.

"I guess I'm just…surprised," she admitted. "I worked more than sixty hours a week for years at Alliston & Blake before there was any mention of a promotion, and I haven't even worked here for six hours and you're offering me the possibility of a partnership."

"You think a small-town Montana lawyer doesn't have sense to know what he's doing?"

"On the contrary, I think you're a lot smarter than any of my bosses in Los Angeles."

He chuckled. "And I like to think you'd be right. I did my research," he assured her. "Beyond the work experience that was outlined on your résumé, I know that you graduated in the top five percent of your class from Stanford Law and passed the California Bar on your first try. In addition to the sixty-plus hours a week that you worked at your firm, you somehow found time to be an active member of the Women Lawyer's Association of Los Angeles and volunteer at a local women's shelter."

"That's pretty thorough research," she noted.

"I assure you, Maggie, I didn't hire you on a whim because your husband works for my son-in-law or because your cousin is married to the sheriff. I hired you because I want to expand the range of legal services available to the people of Rust Creek Falls and because I want to know this firm will be in capable hands when I decide to retire."

"Then I guess we should talk about the specific areas of expansion," she said, already looking forward to it.

Jesse spent the majority of his time at Traub Stables with the horses, but he always ended his day in front of the computer. He made detailed notes of his interactions with every animal and meticulously documented those notes in individual folders on Sutter's computer so they could be easily referenced by the owner.

He was at the computer on Thursday when Sutter strolled into the office with a baby carrier in hand.

Jesse looked over and couldn't help but smile at the wide-eyed infant.

"Good-looking kid," he said. "Must take after his mama."

Sutter chuckled, unoffended. "That he does. But his mama had a meeting at the school today, so the men are hanging out together."

"Drinking beer and smoking cigars?"

"Maybe in a few more years."

"Good call," Jesse told him.

"I hear you're going to have a baby of your own in a few months."

"News travels," he said, not at all surprised by the fact.

"Are you excited or terrified?"

"Both," Jesse admitted.

"I was, too," Sutter said. "Truthfully, I still am. But I wouldn't give him back for anything in the world."

As he spoke, he set the baby carrier on the desk to pull his cell phone out of his pocket and glance at the display.

"Brooks is here," Sutter said, naming the local vet. "Do you mind if I leave Carter with you while I go talk to him?"

"No problem," Jesse assured him.

"I won't be more than ten minutes," his boss promised.

It was the longest ten minutes of his life.

While Carter had seemed perfectly happy to gurgle and coo while his daddy was in his line of sight, as soon as Sutter walked out of the room, the baby began to squirm and fuss. Jesse tried rocking the carrier, to no avail. The fussing escalated to crying. He unbuckled the straps and lifted Carter out.

The little guy looked at him, his big blue eyes filled with tears, his lower lip trembling.

"Daddy's going to be right back," Jesse promised.

Carter drew in a long, shuddery breath, as if considering whether or not to believe him. But when "right back" was not immediate, the crying started anew.

Jesse tucked him close to his body, the baby squirmed; he cradled him in the crook of his arm—a favorite position of his niece Noelle's when she was younger—the wails grew louder; he propped him up on his shoulder and patted his back. The baby let out a belch surprisingly disproportionate to his size—and the crying began to quiet and, finally, stopped.

"That feels better now, doesn't it, buddy?"

Of course, the baby didn't respond. He let out a long, shuddery sigh, rubbed his cheek against Jesse's shoulder, and his eyes drifted shut.

Jesse couldn't help but smile.

His sister's little girl was the epitome of sugar and spice. She was soft and feminine and heartbreakingly beautiful. Sutter's son, although only four months old, was already snakes and snails. He was solid and sturdy and 100 percent boy.

Jesse hadn't given much thought to the gender of his own baby. When he'd learned that Maggie was pregnant, his primary concern had been marrying her to ensure his place in their baby's life. Now, however—

That thought was severed by the sudden realization that the back of his shirt was wet.

Carter hadn't just released an air bubble—he'd spewed the contents of his stomach all over Jesse.

"Why is there a sticky note on the fridge that says 'burp cloths'?" Maggie asked when Jesse came in for dinner later that night.

"I thought we should start making a list of things we'll need to get before the baby comes," he said.

She eyed him skeptically. "And the first thing that came

to mind wasn't a car seat or crib or even diapers—it was burp cloths?"

"I spent some time with Sutter and Paige's little guy today."

"His proud grandpa has shown me about a hundred pictures," she said.

"He puked all down my back."

She laughed. Then pressed a hand to her lips in a belated attempt to hide the fact that she was laughing.

His gaze narrowed.

"I'm sorry," she apologized, not sounding sorry at all. "I'm sure it was disgusting."

"I know that babies puke and poop and cry," he acknowledged. "But it's one thing to read about it in a book and another to experience firsthand."

"Noelle never puked on you?"

He shook his head. "She's spit up a little, but nothing more than that."

Maggie put a plate of chicken parm on the table in front of him.

"How was your day?" he asked her.

"Well, I didn't have to deal with any puking babies." She sat down across from him with her own plate. "In fact, I didn't have to do much of anything.

"Ben took me to Kalispell for an arbitration today. We chatted on the drive, lingered over coffee when we got there, he presented his case to the arbitrator, then we had lunch and returned to Rust Creek Falls around three o'clock, at which point he decided we'd done enough for the day."

"Most people would be happy to finish their day at three o'clock," he pointed out to her.

"I know. I just felt kind of...useless," she admitted. "Ben

promised he'd make me earn my salary, but I'm not sure that will happen until I pass the Bar."

"Maybe you need to remind yourself that you're not in LA anymore and relax a little bit," he suggested.

"That's what Ben said," she admitted.

"Imagine... I gave the same advice as an attorney without charging two hundred dollars an hour for it."

"Which is less than half the rate of most lawyers in California. Of course, the cost of office space is a lot higher there, too."

"Do you miss it?"

She shook her head. "Having time on my hands is a new experience but I think, once I get used to it, I'll enjoy the slower pace and lessened pressure. And I really like Ben and Mallory and Jessica—I'm not sure I could say that about any of the people I worked with at Alliston & Blake. I'm sure they were all great people, but I was so busy focusing on my clients and cases that I never really got to know any of them very well."

"I didn't have the chance to get to know your boss very well, but I'm sure I didn't like him," Jesse told her.

"Brian was always fond of saying he was in the business of business, not making friends."

"That's probably one of the reasons I prefer to work with animals than people." He pushed away from the table and carried his empty plate to the sink.

She appreciated that Jesse always insisted on doing the dishes if she did the cooking, but she wished he didn't shoo her out of the kitchen so that he could do the cleaning up. She just wanted to be with him, to do the things that most married couples did together. And since—for reasons she still didn't understand—that didn't include sex at the present, she was so pathetically eager to spend time with him she would settle for sharing chores.

She began to clear away the rest of the table. When she picked up a towel to dry the dishes he'd already washed, Jesse said, "I'll do that."

But this time, she didn't let him ban her from the room. "I don't mind," she told him.

Short of wrestling the towel from her, there was nothing he could do, so he shrugged and focused his attention on the washing again. He didn't say anything while he completed the chore, but she didn't mind the silence.

She put the last pot back in the cupboard then turned to hang the towel on the oven handle. She hadn't realized he was right behind her, and when she turned, her breasts brushed against his chest. The shock of the contact might have jolted her backward, except that the counter was at her back and Jesse was at her front, so she had nowhere to go.

She lifted her gaze to his and saw both heat and hunger reflected in his eyes. Her heart pounded harder and faster and her mouth went dry. The atmosphere crackled with heat and tension. She instinctively moistened her lips, and his eyes darkened as they followed the movement of her tongue. His gaze shifted from her mouth to her breasts, zeroing in on nipples that were already peaked, begging for his attention.

Jesse drew in a slow, deep breath. Then he took a deliberate step back, away from her.

"I have to go out...to check on Lancelot."

She swallowed, torn between frustration and disappointment. "Now?"

"Nate asked me to take a look at him—said he was favoring his right foreleg."

She nodded, because she could hardly dispute the importance of checking on an injured animal.

But as she watched him grab his coat and walk out the

back door, she wondered if she'd have to grow a tail and a mane to make him take a look at her.

And so it went for the next several days—except that Maggie banned herself from the kitchen after dinner. She didn't mind playing with fire, but she hated being the only one who felt the burn.

She tried to talk to her cousin, in the hope that Lissa might have some insights into Jesse's behavior. But although Lissa was puzzled by the distance he was deliberately keeping from his bride, she had no words of wisdom except to say that no man could resist a woman intent on seduction—especially if that woman was his wife.

The problem was that Maggie didn't know the first thing about seduction. She could count the number of lovers she'd had on one hand, with two fingers left over.

The first had been the editor of the law review. She'd fallen in love with his mind and decided that she liked the rest of him well enough to take their relationship to the next level. But the actual event, when it finally happened, was less than spectacular. Still, they'd stayed together for another four months before the relationship eventually fizzled away.

The second had been a former client at Alliston & Blake. She'd never actually worked with him, but she'd been in the elevator when he'd left a meeting with David Connors, one of the senior IP attorneys. He'd asked her to have dinner with him; she'd declined, telling him that it was against company policy for attorneys to fraternize with clients. He'd responded by calling David Connors on his cell phone, right then and there, and firing him. They'd dated for almost a year, and while the physical aspect of their relationship had been pleasant enough, he hadn't exactly rocked her world.

No one had—until Jesse.

She didn't know if the sex had been so great because she felt a deep, emotional connection that she'd never experienced with anyone else, or if she felt a deep, emotional connection to him because the sex had been so great.

Or maybe it hadn't been as great as she remembered... Or maybe it had been great for her but not for him... Or maybe she should stop driving herself crazy speculating about things and figure out what was keeping her husband so busy he was out of the house more than in it.

Because it seemed that every night he had one excuse or another to escape from the house right after dinner. If she'd still been working at Alliston & Blake, she wouldn't have minded being married to a man who was absent for frequent and extended periods—she probably wouldn't even have noticed.

A glance at her watch revealed that it was just past eight o'clock. Jesse's truck was parked out front, so she knew that he hadn't gone far.

She put on her boots and bundled into her coat, wrapping her scarf around her throat, tugging a hat onto her head and slipping thick mittens over her hands. She didn't know if she'd ever get used to Montana temperatures, but she was learning to cope with them.

It helped if she didn't check the daily forecast for LA, as she'd done that morning, only to discover that it was sixty-four degrees in SoCal—forty degrees warmer than in Rust Creek Falls. No wonder she hadn't owned a winter coat until she'd gone shopping in Kalispell with Lissa before the wedding. Unlike the peignoir set her cousin had purchased for her, she actually used the coat.

Her breath puffed out in little clouds, and the snow crunched under her feet as she made her way toward the stables. It wasn't a long trek from the house, but her cheeks and nose were numb by the time she reached the door. The light inside gave her hope that she would find her husband there.

The scent of hay and horses no longer filled her with panic. Instead, it reminded her of Jesse's kiss—the comfort of his arms around her, the warmth of his mouth against hers—and renewed her determination to track down her errant husband.

Honey poked her head over the gate when Maggie ventured near. She was tempted to go closer, to rub the animal's long nose the way Jesse had taught her, but she wasn't nearly as brave without him beside her. She just kept walking, toward what he'd explained was the birthing stall at the back of the barn and from which the light emanated.

She didn't know what she expected to find him doing—but whatever possibilities had crossed her mind, finding him rubbing sandpaper over a carved piece of wood was not one of them.

She didn't know if she made some kind of sound or if he sensed her standing in the open doorway, but his movements suddenly stilled and he looked up at her.

She stepped into the stall, her curious gaze taking in the assortment of pieces spread out over a large worktable—along with the plans for a baby's cradle.

"Oh." Her heart, already his, went splat at his feet. "Is this why you didn't put *crib* on one of your sticky notes?"

He smiled. "We'll need one eventually, but I wanted to do this."

"I thought horses were your thing."

"They are—but sometimes I like to putter."

She looked at the pieces of wood, meticulously carved and sanded. "You're a very talented putterer."

"Is that even a word?"

"I don't think so," she admitted, running her hand over

what she guessed—based on the picture—was the top of a side rail. But referring to him as a putterer was safer than saying that he was good with his hands. Because he undoubtedly was, but that kind of comment would bring to mind all kinds of things that he could do with his hands, things he had done with his hands, things she wished he would do with his hands again. Pushing those tantalizingly torturous thoughts aside, she asked, "Where did you learn to do this?"

"My grandfather was a carpenter as well as a rancher. He taught me a lot of tricks to working with wood."

"The one who made Noelle's blocks?" she guessed.

He nodded.

"Did he make the blanket chest at the foot of my bed?"

"No. I made that."

She'd thought it was a family heirloom, and knew that someday it would be. Just as this cradle would be enjoyed by their child, and maybe, eventually, their child's child.

"There's something else on your mind," he guessed. "You didn't come out here to talk about puttering."

She managed a smile. "No, because I didn't know about the puttering until I got out here."

"Something you want to talk about?"

"I'm not sure," she admitted.

He picked up a soft cloth and began to wipe down the sanded pieces in preparation for staining. "When you decide, you can let me know."

It would be easier, she decided, to ask the question when he wasn't looking at her. When he couldn't see the doubts and insecurities she feared might be reflected in her eyes.

So with his attention focused on his task, she blurted out, "Why didn't you tell me your ex-fiancée was in town?"

Chapter Twelve

Jesse looked up, sincerely startled by the question. "I didn't know that she was."

"I don't mean today," Maggie amended. "I meant the day we got married."

"Oh."

"Why didn't you tell me?" she asked again.

"Because I didn't think it was important."

"The woman you were once planning to marry shows up in town on the day of our wedding and you don't think it's important?"

He sighed. "I don't know how much you know about that engagement—"

"As much as you've told me, which is nothing."

"Because there isn't much to tell. We were engaged for a few weeks—not even long enough to plan a wedding."

"That's longer than we were engaged," she pointed out.

"What do you want me to say, Maggie?"

"I don't know," she admitted. "But I guess I've been wondering… Are you still in love with her?"

"No." His response was immediate and unequivocal.

She didn't look convinced.

"The truth is, I hadn't seen her in almost seven years," he told her. "And I never knew if seeing her again might stir up any old feelings. But it didn't. Any feelings I once had for her are long gone."

"Well, I guess that's good," she said. "Considering that you're now married to me."

"And I'm happy to be married to you."

She opened her mouth, then closed it again without saying a word.

"If there's something you want to say, just say it," Jesse suggested. "I'm not a mind reader."

"One of the first things a lawyer learns is to never ask a question that she doesn't already know the answer to."

"Was it a legal question you were wondering about?"

"No," she admitted. "But in this situation, I think the same rule applies."

He decided to ask a question of his own. "How did you find out about Shaelyn's visit?"

"I overheard some women talking about it at our reception."

"Why didn't you ask me about it then?"

"Because I was hoping you would tell me about it," she admitted.

"I didn't tell you because I forgot about her the minute she walked out the door."

She had no reason not to believe what he was telling her, but his casual dismissal of his former fiancée made her wonder if, during the four months that he and Maggie had been apart, he'd forgotten about her just as easily.

If she hadn't been pregnant, she might not have seen him again. She wouldn't have had any reason to seek him out, and he hadn't shown any inclination to track her down. They were only together now because of their baby—and while she was exactly where she wanted to be, she wasn't convinced the same was true for Jesse.

"I'm sorry I interrupted your work," she said.

"I didn't mind the interruption," he told her. "But you kind of ruined the surprise."

"I'll be surprised when it's all put together," she promised him, heading toward the door.

"Maggie—"

She paused with her fingers wrapped around the handle and turned back.

"I don't want to be with anyone but you," he told her.

She managed a smile. "Same goes."

As she headed back to the house, she told herself that she should be satisfied. He wanted to be with her, and that should be enough.

But it wasn't—she wanted him to love her as much as she loved him.

At Alliston & Blake, there was an office manager in charge of ensuring supplies were documented and maintained. At Ben's office, Jessica usually went into Kalispell once a month to replenish supplies as required. If anything was needed in the interim, it could usually be obtained from the General Store.

Which was why Maggie was at Crawford's to pick up a package of printer paper on Friday afternoon. Natalie directed her to the stationery section at the back of the store, where she found Nina pacing with Noelle in her arms.

"Someone doesn't look too happy today," she said, noting the runny nose and teary eyes of the little girl in her mother's arms.

"That's why my sister's working the register and I'm hiding out back here," Nina admitted.

"Is she sick?" Maggie asked.

"Teething," her sister-in-law clarified. "She's been teething for six months—but every new tooth seems to make her grumpier than the previous one."

Maggie stroked the back of a finger over the child's red cheek. Noelle looked at her and let out a shuddery sigh.

"I was just about to take her upstairs to see if she'll nap," Nina said. "Do you have time for a cup of tea?"

Maggie glanced at her watch, although, aside from printing the memorandum she'd drafted and which didn't need to be submitted until Monday, she had absolutely nothing pressing at the office. "I do if you do," she told her sister-in-law.

Nina led the way through the store to the staircase behind women's sleepwear.

"I lived up here before I moved in with Dallas. Because I manage the store, it was convenient. I decided to keep the apartment, at least for now, so that Noelle can be close by when I'm working. It makes it easy for me to slip away to nurse her—or take a nap with her."

"You're nursing even while she's teething?"

"For now," Nina agreed. "We've been supplementing with formula for a few months, because it gives me a little more freedom, but they say that breast milk is best for the first year, so even when I'm not nursing, I'm pumping."

The door opened into a big living room that was separated from the kitchen and dining area by an island counter. It was bright and spacious but as warm and inviting as the woman who had decorated it.

"This is nice," Maggie said sincerely.

"I like it," Nina said. "It was where I originally planned on living with Noelle—until I fell in love with Dallas. Now he's going to add on to his house—our house—so that we'll have a master suite on the main level and then the current master bedroom can be divided into two rooms and each of the kids will have their own."

"Are you planning to add to your family?" Maggie asked.

"I think four is a good number." Nina passed the baby to her sister-in-law so that she could make tea. "But I have to admit, I've been thinking that it would be nice to have a baby with Dallas."

"What does he say about that?"

"It took some getting used to for him with Noelle. Robbie is seven now, so dealing with midnight feedings and dirty diapers was a big adjustment for him, so I haven't even mentioned the idea yet. I was thinking I'd give him a little more time before I bring up the subject—and to make sure it isn't just a whim on my part."

Watching Nina's ease with and obvious love for her baby, Maggie didn't think it was a whim. Jesse's sister was clearly one of those women who was meant to be a mother, and she knew that her husband was lucky to have found a woman who loved the children from his first marriage as much as she loved her own.

"Speaking of homes," Nina said. "Did you know that Jesse built his? Well, not by himself," she clarified. "My dad and my brothers helped."

"He didn't tell me." But the information reminded her that she'd wondered about something else. "How long has he lived there?"

"Four years, I think." And then, demonstrating a startling insight into her sister-in-law's mind, she said, "It was definitely post-Shaelyn."

Maggie nodded, grateful for the information. "Did he design it, too?"

"Inside and out," Nina confirmed.

"He's got a good eye—and great hands."

"Please," Nina said. "There are some details a sister doesn't need to know."

Maggie felt as if her cheeks were as red as Noelle's. "I meant that he's good with tools."

Her sister-in-law raised a brow.

She blew out a breath. "I saw the cradle he's making for the baby."

"He's making a cradle?" Nina's eyes misted. "That's so sweet—and so Jesse."

"Is it?"

"He's over the moon about this baby."

Maggie looked down at the little girl now sleeping in her arms. "I'm pretty excited, too. I can't wait to hold my own baby just like this."

"He—or she—will be here before you know it, and then what you'll want more than anything in the world is a few hours of uninterrupted sleep."

"I'm sure that's true," Maggie agreed. "But I still can't wait. Of course, I'm as terrified as I am excited, but since there's no turning back now, I'm trying to focus on the positive."

Nina was silent for a minute, seemingly content to just watch Maggie cuddle with Noelle. But when she spoke again, the sincere concern in her tone even more than the question warned Maggie that the other woman suspected all was not wedded bliss for her brother and sister-in-law.

"Is everything okay?" she asked gently.

Maggie managed a smile, in an effort to convince Nina as well as herself. "Everything's great."

"The day that you and Jesse got married, you were absolutely glowing," Nina said. "You're not glowing anymore."

Since Maggie couldn't dispute that, she said nothing.

"Are you unhappy here?" her sister-in-law prompted.

"No. I'm really coming to love Rust Creek Falls."

"Are you missing your family?"

"Sure," she admitted. "But I'm building a new family here, with Jesse." When Nina's only response was patient silence, Maggie sighed. "I guess I just hoped that we'd have more time together. He's so busy, between his work at Traub Stables and chores at The Shooting Star, that I hardly ever see him."

Nina's brow furrowed. "I would expect a new husband to make more time for his bride."

"You know why we got married," Maggie reminded her.

"I know why you got married as quickly as you did," her sister-in-law allowed. "I also know that Jesse started to fall for you the first time he saw you—long before there was a baby in the picture."

Maggie was surprised by the statement. What Nina apparently "knew" was news to her.

Yes, Jesse had been attracted to her from the start—which was why there was a baby on the way—but she didn't know if she'd go so far as to say that he'd fallen for her. Even if she'd fallen head over heels for him a long time ago.

"Did he tell you about Shaelyn?" Nina asked.

"Only that he was engaged to her, briefly."

"That's true, but not even close to being the whole truth." She picked up her tea, sipped. "It's not really my place to tell you the story—or at least what I know of it—but I think you should know the basics, so that you won't lose all patience with my idiot brother."

"I'm not sure how to respond to that," Maggie admitted, making Nina laugh.

"You don't have to—as much as I love him, I'm not blind to his faults."

She sipped her tea again while she considered what—or maybe how much—to say. Maggie set aside her own cup, unable to drink her tea while her stomach was twisting itself into knots.

"He loved her," Nina finally said, and with those words, the knots tightened painfully. "In that innocent first love kind of way. You have to understand what it was like for

Jesse growing up in our family. He's always been the quiet one, the more introspective one. And he's sensitive, which is probably why he's so good with animals, and why he doesn't like to play with anyone's emotions.

"All of the local girls chased after Nate and Justin and Brad. Jesse was every bit as good-looking, smart and charming, but he was overlooked because he let himself be.

"When he went away to college, he was no longer competing with our brothers for attention, and the girls started to notice him for who he was. Shaelyn set her sights on him from day one. He didn't have a lot of experience deciphering subtle signals, but there was nothing subtle about Shaelyn."

"You didn't like her," Maggie realized.

"I wanted to—for Jesse's sake. But Shaelyn didn't have many redeeming qualities, aside from the fact that she loved my brother."

"And he loved her."

"He was infatuated," Nina allowed. "I'm not sure it was anything more than that, although he certainly thought it was, at least at the time.

"And his experience with Shaelyn did make him wary. So I'm going to ask you to try to be patient with him. To give him the time he needs to accept how he feels about you."

"What if you're wrong about his feelings?"

"I'm not," her sister-in-law promised.

Maggie wished she could be half as certain, but her conversation with Nina had at least given her hope.

Jesse's excited anticipation about the impending birth of his child was tempered by his fear that the baby's mother would wake up one day and realize she hated life in Rust Creek Falls. Because if that happened and Maggie decided to go back to Los Angeles, he'd lose everything that mattered most to him.

It was this fear that kept him from admitting—to her and himself—the true depth of his feelings. It was easy to keep busy around the ranch: mending broken fences, mucking out stalls and working with the horses. But that hadn't taken up all of his time, so he'd decided to build a cradle. It was something he wanted to do, and it gave him an excuse to stay out in the barn, away from Maggie. Because he couldn't be around Maggie without wanting Maggie, and giving in to that want would inevitably tangle up his heart, and he wasn't ready to go down that road again.

Except that he was almost finished the cradle, and he didn't know what project to tackle next. Maybe he would see if he could find a good plan for a crib.

He was assembling the stand when Honey nickered a happy greeting. Curious, he left the worktable and rounded the corner to discover Nina rubbing an affectionate hand down the horse's muzzle.

"What brings you out here?" he asked his sister.

"Maybe I just wanted to see my big brother."

"More likely you want something from your big brother," he guessed. "Like a babysitter?"

She smiled, unoffended by the assumption. "I really just wanted to see how you were doing—how you're settling into married life."

"Fine."

She lifted her brows in response to his single-word answer. "I don't know if I can express how incredibly reassured I am."

"I don't know why you'd need reassurance," he said. "But I'm glad I could help."

"Maggie told me you were making a cradle for the baby."

"When did you see Maggie?"

"She came to the store yesterday?"

"Yesterday?" he echoed incredulously. "And you waited a whole twenty-four hours to track me down to no doubt tell me that my marriage is doomed?"

"I don't think your marriage is doomed," she denied. "Although it's interesting that you would project that forecast onto me."

"I'm not projecting anything."

"Can I see the cradle?"

Happy to turn her attention to something other than his marriage, he led her to the workbench.

"Oh," she said, when he removed the protective cloth he'd draped over it. "Wow. Jesse, this is—" she ran a hand over the smoothly curved footboard "—gorgeous."

"I think it turned out pretty good," he agreed.

"This was obviously a labor of love."

"I wanted the baby to have—"

"This isn't for the baby," she interjected softly. "It's for Maggie."

"I'm pretty sure Maggie won't fit in it."

"You know what I mean," she chided. "This is your way of showing Maggie—because God forbid you should actually use words—how you feel about her."

His only response was to pull the blanket back over the cradle.

Nina sighed. "What are you afraid of?"

"I'm not afraid of anything."

"Good—because she married you, Jesse. She let you put a ring on her finger and she put one on yours and she promised to stay with you 'so long as you both shall live.'"

"Your point?" he prompted.

"You've got to stop waiting for her to leave," she said gently.

He scowled. "I'm not."

"Maybe not consciously, but I know you, and I see the way you look at her—and the way you don't let her see you look at her."

He frowned. "I'm not sure what you just said even makes any sense."

"Okay, I'll put it in simple terms that even you can understand—Maggie isn't Shaelyn. Don't make her pay for what Shaelyn did to you."

"I know she's not Shaelyn."

"Do you?" his sister challenged. "Do you realize that she looks at you as if you're everything she wants and needs? Or do you look at her and think—she's going to hate it here? That after having lived her whole life in Los Angeles, she's never going to adjust to life in Rust Creek Falls?"

"I can't deny that the possibility has crossed my mind, but I'm not waiting for it to happen."

"Here's another question—when you asked her to marry you, did you tell her how you feel about her or did you make it all about the baby?"

"I'm really glad that you're in love and happily married—even if you did choose to marry a Traub—but I don't want or need your marital advice."

She shook her head. "You haven't told her how you feel, have you?"

"Maggie and I both know why we got married."

"I don't think either of you has a clue about the other's reasons."

He scowled at that.

"She's not going to break your heart," Nina told him. "But if you're not careful—or maybe I should say if you don't stop being careful—you might break hers."

"I've got things to do, so if that's all…"

"There is one more thing."

"What is it?" he asked, not bothering to disguise his impatience.

"The holiday pageant at the elementary school is on Monday night. Ryder's part of the stage crew, and Jake and Robbie both have parts. I'd like you and Maggie to come."

"I don't think—"

"Most of Dallas's family has already said that they'll be there," she interjected to cut off what she no doubt knew was going to be a refusal.

He tried again. "I'm not sure a school play is Maggie's kind of thing."

"You might be surprised—by a lot of things."

He scowled. "What's that supposed to mean?"

"It means, ask her," his sister said, heading toward the door. "The show starts at seven."

So Jesse asked her.

When he got back to the house, Maggie was on her computer, looking on Pinterest for decorating ideas for the nursery. Her study manuals for the Bar exam were closed on the table beside her.

"My brain needed a break," she said.

He took a bottle of beer from the fridge, twisted off the cap. "I'm not surprised," he said. "You've been working nonstop since you got here."

"I used to take work home from the office all the time. Now I'm lucky if I have enough work to keep me in the office until five o'clock."

"Are you bored?"

"No, I enjoy what I'm doing. I'm just not accustomed to having so much time on my hands."

He felt another twinge of guilt as he realized it was true. Not only did her job demand fewer hours, but she didn't have the number of friends and acquaintances that she'd had in California. Yes, her cousin, Lissa, was here—but Lissa and Gage were head over heels in love and rarely more than ten feet away from one another.

"Do you have some time Monday night?"

"For what?" she asked, just a little warily.

"There's a Christmas pageant at the elementary school," he explained.

"Actually, it's a holiday pageant."

"Huh?"

"They're billing it as a holiday pageant this year because of the earlier date. There's going to be a short Thanksgiving play, holiday songs performed by the school choir and then the Christmas production."

"How do you know all of this?"

"Ben's daughter Paige teaches at the elementary school. Well, she's not teaching right now because she just had the baby, but she was talking about it when she came into the office last week. The earlier date—apparently a result of Winona Cobbs forecasting some big snowstorm—left the teachers scrambling to get everything ready on time."

He chuckled. "She's forecasting a big snowstorm?"

"You think she's wrong?" she asked hopefully.

"I think winter snowstorms in Montana are inevitable."

She sighed. "Obviously I'm going to need more than one pair of long johns."

She was making a joke—at least, he thought she was joking—but just the mention of her needing more long johns started him thinking about her nonthermal underwear. He'd had the pleasure of undressing her a few times now and he remembered—in scorching detail—that she liked to match her panties and her bras. But even more tempting were the feminine treasures he'd discovered hidden within the delicate scraps of lace.

"About the pageant," he prompted, in a desperate attempt to get his own thoughts back on track. "Do you want to go?"

"Sure," she agreed. "But why do you sound less than enthusiastic?"

"It's not exactly my idea of fun."

"Then why did you ask me to go?"

"Because misery loves company, and Nina guilted me into going."

"How did she do that?"

"She said that all of the Traubs were going to be there."

"So?"

"You know about the rivalry between the Crawfords and the Traubs," he reminded her.

"I thought Nina and Dallas getting married had put an end to all of that."

"Their wedding might have started to bridge the divide," Jesse allowed. "But the tension between the two families is still there, beneath the surface, with this ongoing one-upmanship. If Dallas's family is all going to be there, then Nina's family all needs to be there to show that we're just as supportive as they are."

"Sounds...exhausting," Maggie decided.

"Yeah," he agreed. "And mostly I don't care, but since Nina asked..."

"You feel obligated."

He nodded. "But if you don't want to—"

"I'm not going to be your excuse for begging off," she told him.

"I wasn't going to use you as an excuse, but only because I didn't think of it," he admitted. "I was just going to say that you aren't under the same obligation, so if you don't want to go, you don't have to."

"And give your parents another reason not to like me?" She shook her head. "I don't think so."

He frowned. "My parents don't dislike you."

"They think I trapped you into marrying me."

"No, they don't," he denied, uncomfortable to realize that she believed such a thing, and that he'd done nothing to reassure her. "They do have some concerns about the fact that we got married quickly and don't know each other very well, but they'll come around."

"Before or after our child graduates from college?"

He smiled at her wry tone. "Hopefully before."

"Well, in the meantime, I would like to go to the holiday pageant with you."

"You would?"

"Sure," she agreed. "What time does it start?"

"Seven o'clock. But we should probably be there by six-thirty if we want to get a seat in the auditorium."

"Are you expecting the show to sell out?"

"There's not a lot of entertainment in Rust Creek Falls," he reminded her.

Chapter Thirteen

It hadn't taken Maggie long to realize the trick to tolerating the frigid Montana weather was layers. Lots of layers. So she started with long johns under her dark jeans and a long-sleeved knit top beneath a bulky cable-knit sweater in pale pink. Then she added some dangly earrings, just for fun.

She didn't miss the cocktail parties and dinner meetings that were so much a part of her life in LA, but she did miss dressing up and feeling pretty. In need of a little extra boost, she added mascara to her lashes and a darker than usual shade of gloss to her lips.

Jesse was ready and waiting for her when she came downstairs. He'd showered and changed into a clean pair of jeans with a dark blue V-neck sweater over a lighter blue crewneck T-shirt. He hadn't bothered to shave, and the dark shadow on his cheeks and jaw made him look even more rugged and sexy—and made her heart slam against her ribs.

It was the closest thing they'd ever had to a date. She wondered if he would hold her hand, and chided herself for the flutters of anticipation that danced in her tummy.

She'd had sex with him—more than once even, but not at all since their wedding—and now she was desperate for any sign of interest or affection.

Sometimes when he looked at her, she thought she saw

a flicker of heat, a glimpse of desire, but then he'd look away, leaving her to wonder if she'd only imagined it. She didn't understand why he'd pushed so hard for her to marry him, and then completely withdrawn once his ring was on her finger.

He looked at her, his gaze skimming from the boots on her feet to the top of her head, lingering at certain spots in a way that made her breasts ache and her thighs tingle. But when he spoke, it was only to say, "You're going to want a hat. It's cold outside."

"It's November in Montana—of course it's cold outside," she noted drily. But she found the new pink hat and matching gloves she'd bought on a recent trip into Kalispell and put them on.

"How many hats do you own?"

"Hopefully enough."

"You do know that you can only wear one at a time?" he teased, flicking the pom-pom on top of her head.

"I like to accessorize."

"You look good in pink," he told her.

She was surprised—and pleased—by the compliment.

"And in skirts," he said. "Although I haven't seen you in one since we got married."

"And you probably won't until spring," she warned. "There's no way I'm baring my legs in this weather."

"That's too bad—because yours are spectacular. Especially when you wear those heels that make them look a mile long."

The comment seemed to surprise him as much as it surprised her. But she kept her tone light when she said, "So you're a leg man, are you?"

"I like *your* legs," he admitted, his gaze skimming down her body, then slowly up again. "Actually, I like every part of you."

"Really?"

"You're a beautiful woman, Maggie," he said.

She blew out an unsteady breath. "And you're a confusing man."

He held her gaze for a long minute, as if there was something more he wanted to say. But in the end, he only asked, "Are you ready to go?"

As soon as they got to the doors of the auditorium, Maggie realized that Jesse had not exaggerated the popularity of the event. Although there was still more than half an hour before the pageant was scheduled to start, almost all of the seats were taken.

"This is quite the gathering," Maggie noted.

Jesse shrugged. "Folks around here will take their entertainment any way they can get it."

"Or maybe they appreciate the time and effort that the teachers and students put into the productions."

"Maybe," he allowed, guiding her closer to the front, where his sister and the rest of the family were sitting.

Looking around as they made their way down the center aisle between the rows of seats, Maggie was surprised by how many familiar faces were in the crowd.

Caleb Dalton was there with his fiancée, Mallory Franklin, whose niece Lily was singing in the choir and one of the angels in the pageant. In addition, Maggie recognized several members of the Rust Creek Falls Newcomers Club, including Vanessa Brent—recently engaged to Jonah Traub—Jordyn Leigh Cates and Julie Smith. She knew some of their stories—Lily Franklin had played a big role in bringing her aunt and the boss's son together; Vanessa had met Jonah while they were both working onsite at the soon-to-be-completed Maverick Manor—and that some of the others were still looking to lasso the cowboy of their dreams.

She also knew that several of the single newcomers probably envied her the attention of the handsome cowboy she'd married. But while she might have Jesse's ring on her finger, she didn't have the one thing she really wanted: his heart.

Although she was undoubtedly a newcomer, too, she'd married Jesse so quickly after moving to Rust Creek Falls that a lot of people viewed her as his wife first, forgetting that she was also a transplant. Which was funny, because Jesse never did. In fact, she didn't think a single day had gone by since they'd married that he hadn't made at least one passing reference to the life she'd left behind in LA.

He wants you to stay, but he's afraid you won't.

Nina's words echoed in the back of her mind as Maggie took a seat beside her husband. In the row immediately in front of them was Jesse's sister with her husband. On the other side of Nina were her parents, and on the other side of Dallas were his. The Hatfields and the McCoys of Rust Creek Falls playing nice—or at least pretending to—for the sake of their children and grandchildren. Seeing them here together gave Maggie hope that the baby she was carrying might also succeed in bringing her and Jesse closer together.

As far as school plays went, Jesse decided it was entertaining. But not quite entertaining enough to keep his attention on the stage while he was seated beside his bride. He wasn't usually so easily distracted, but being close to Maggie made it impossible for him to focus on anything else.

With every breath he took, he breathed in the scent of her skin—something light and spicy. The scent was too subtle to be perfume, so he guessed it was probably some kind of lotion she rubbed on her body. A conclusion that tantalized his mind with the mental image of her delicate hands smoothing fragrant lotion over the bare, silky skin of her shoulders, her arms, her breasts…

The sound of applause jolted him back to the present. He automatically put his hands together as the kids on stage took a bow.

"There will now be a fifteen-minute intermission," the eighth-grade emcee announced. "Please help yourself to the cookies and hot drinks available outside."

The auditorium was suddenly filled with the sound of chair legs scraping against the floor as parents and grandparents and other guests hurried for the snacks.

"Do you want anything?" he asked Maggie.

She shook her head as she rose to her feet. "Just to stretch my legs."

He noticed that several older kids, not in costume, were on the stage now, pushing aside the long table that had been the setting of the Thanksgiving feast to set up a makeshift stable for the upcoming nativity scene.

"It's hard to believe that we're going to have a son or a daughter up on that stage someday," he said.

"Not for several years yet," Maggie pointed out to him.

"I know, but it started me thinking… Do you know if our baby is a boy or a girl?"

She shook her head. "Do you want to know?"

"I'm not sure," he admitted. "In some ways, I think it would make planning easier."

"We'd know whether to buy pink or blue burp cloths."

He smiled in response to her teasing. "There is that."

"I have an appointment for an ultrasound tomorrow. We should be able to find out the baby's gender, depending on his or her position." She hesitated a second, then said, "I know it's short notice, but you could come with me, if you want."

"I'd like that," he immediately replied.

"I should have asked you before, but you've been so busy..." Her explanation trailed off.

Yes, he'd been busy making himself busy, and he suspected that she knew it. But he still couldn't admit it to her now, because that would also require admitting that he didn't know how to be the husband she wanted—the husband he wanted to be to her.

Before he could manufacture an appropriate reply, Tara Jones—the third-grade teacher—stopped beside them.

"Mr. and Mrs. Crawford—how wonderful to see you here tonight."

Although her greeting encompassed both of them, she seemed to be speaking to Maggie, making Jesse suspect that she was a client. Her next words dispelled that theory.

"I know I said it before—but I have to thank you again for all of your help with the costumes and props."

"I really didn't do very much," Maggie said.

"We would never have had everything ready on time without you," Tara insisted. Then she turned to Jesse. "In case your wife didn't tell you, she made thirty pilgrim hats and an equal number of native headbands, painted the starry sky for the nativity scene and designed the wings and halos for the angels."

"You might want to save your thanks until after the pageant, in case the sky falls down."

Tara chuckled. "It's not going to fall down. And even if it did, it wouldn't matter. What matters is that you gave us the extra hands we desperately needed to get everything done in time for tonight."

Maggie smiled. "And that the kids all seem to be having a good time."

"They definitely are," the teacher agreed. "And now I'm going backstage to make sure their costumes are on before we continue the show."

Jesse waited until she was out of earshot before he turned to his wife. "I didn't know you'd helped out with this."

"I put in a few hours when I had nothing to do at the office," Maggie admitted, settling into her chair again as the other audience members began to return to their seats.

"It sounds like you put in more than a few hours."

She shrugged. "I had time on my hands."

He impulsively reached for one of those hands—it was small and soft in comparison to his, but for all of its delicacy, it was also strong. Not unlike Maggie herself.

She was a California girl experiencing a Montana winter, and he wondered if it was only her first or also her last. If she made it through the season, would she stay through the spring and the summer? How long would she last so far away from the bright lights of the big city? And how long did she need to stay before he stopped anticipating that she'd pack her bags and hightail it back to LA?

Right now, she seemed happy enough, and he hadn't been doing anything to make her happy. He'd been leaving her to her own devices, certain she would get bored and be gone. Maybe he was pushing her away, or at least testing her steadfastness. And yeah, it had only been a couple of weeks, but so far, she'd stuck. Which got him to thinking… What if he actually let her know that he wanted her to stay? What if he made an effort to make her want to stay?

There was a connection between them—he'd felt it from the first. It was real and strong. She made him want to open up to her in a way that he hadn't opened up to a woman in a long time, to share not just his home but his life and his heart, and that was more than a little scary.

Watching her watch the kids onstage, he let himself consider the possibilities. Maybe she could grow to love Montana—and him—enough to want to stay. Maybe they really could raise this child—and other children—together.

But there was still a part of him that was afraid to let himself believe, certain that as soon as he started to plan for their future together, she'd knock him down and stomp on his heart.

Don't make Maggie pay for what Shaelyn did to you.

Nina's words echoed in the back of his mind.

He knew that most of his family had had concerns when he'd told them that he and Maggie were getting married—and why. And although only ten days had passed since the wedding, Nina had become her new sister-in-law's biggest cheerleader.

But not her only supporter. Ben Dalton had nothing but praise for the young attorney he'd taken on. And even Sutter had mentioned how appreciative Paige was of Maggie's work at the law office, because it freed her father up to spend more time with his family.

Obviously their faith was well-placed. She was willing to tackle whatever legal issues were assigned to her, she was studying for her exams, and even outside her area of expertise she'd stepped in to help where help was needed. She was making an effort to fit in, to be accepted by the community, and the residents of Rust Creek Falls were starting to give her a chance—which, he realized, was more than he'd done.

Even while she'd been reciting her vows, he'd been holding his breath, waiting for her to announce that she'd changed her mind.

But despite his best efforts, he'd got used to having her around. He looked forward to seeing her at the breakfast table in the morning and having dinner with her every night. He enjoyed talking to her about his day and hers, and he enjoyed the silence when they didn't feel like talking. He felt comfortable around her—except when being in close proximity to her was decidedly *un*comfortable because she tempted him to want more, to believe they could have more.

They were connected by their baby and their marriage. But he'd meant it when he'd told her he wasn't looking for love, and he knew that he needed to maintain some kind of boundaries between them if he was going to protect his heart. He was already sharing his name, his house and almost every part of his life. If he shared his bed, there would be no more boundaries between them, nothing to prevent him from falling the rest of the way in love with her.

It was that certainty that prevented him from giving in to the ever-growing desire he felt for her.

At least for now.

Maggie had been referred to Dr. Gaynor in Kalispell by her ob-gyn in Los Angeles, and the first time she met her, she was impressed by the doctor's warmth, compassion and efficiency. Dr. Gaynor didn't believe in overbooking her patients, which meant that while emergencies did occasionally arise, it was unusual for there to be more than one or two women in the waiting room.

So it didn't surprise her that she was taken into an exam room at 10:59 a.m. for her eleven o'clock appointment, or that the doctor entered the room only three minutes later.

It did surprise her when the doctor said to Jesse, "You must be the husband."

He nodded and offered his hand. "Jesse Crawford."

"Susan Gaynor." She must have noticed Maggie's surprise, because she smiled. "The last time I saw you, you said that you might be getting married," the doctor reminded Maggie. "This time, you came with a man and a ring on your finger."

"We got married on the fifteenth," Maggie confirmed.

"Congratulations," Dr. Gaynor said to both of them. "And thank you—" her gaze shifted to Jesse "—for taking the time to come here today. It's always nice to see a husband supporting his wife through her pregnancy."

"I'm happy to be here," he said sincerely. "And to do anything I can to help Maggie over the next five months."

"The next five months are the easy part," the doctor teased. "The real challenges—and joys—come with the baby."

Jesse reached for her hand, linked their fingers together. "We're looking forward to both."

"Good answer," Dr. Gaynor said. "And I'm happy to report that everything looks great with both your wife and the baby. In fact—" she turned to Maggie now "—you've gained two pounds since I last saw you."

"I knew I shouldn't have eaten those Christmas cookies that Nina sent home with us last night," the mom-to-be grumbled.

The doctor chuckled. "A special treat every once in a while isn't going to hurt you or your baby so long as you're also eating lots of fruits, vegetables, whole grains and proteins."

"I'm eating lots of everything," Maggie confirmed.

"Good. That first trimester weight loss could have been problematic, but it's apparent that you've been taking good care of yourself and your baby.

"Have you felt any movement?"

"I don't think so," Maggie said, her grip on his hand instinctively tightening.

"It's nothing to be concerned about," the doctor assured her. "A lot of first-time moms don't recognize the little flutters as fetal movement. If you haven't noticed anything yet, you will soon enough."

Dr. Gaynor's glance shifted from Maggie to Jesse and back again. "Do either of you have any questions at this stage?"

He looked at Maggie, who shook her head.

The doctor followed the silent exchange, then directed her next comment to him. "A lot of first-time fathers worry about sex."

"Nope," he said quickly, vehemently. "No worries there."

"Good." The doctor nodded, but she didn't leave it at that. "But just in case you were wondering, there are absolutely no restrictions on intercourse right up to the day of delivery, so long as Maggie's comfortable and there aren't any complications in her pregnancy."

"Okay...um...yep. That's great."

Maggie didn't know if Jesse was looking at her, because she didn't dare look at him. Obviously they'd had sex—she wouldn't be here otherwise. But the doctor couldn't know, thankfully, that they hadn't been intimate for some time. In fact, for reasons she didn't understand and that her husband hadn't bothered to share with her, they hadn't even consummated their marriage.

Not that she was going to discuss that with him in the doctor's office—or anywhere else, apparently. Because although it was a question that continued to keep her awake at night, she wasn't entirely sure she wanted to know his answer. She didn't want to hear him confirm that he didn't want her—he only wanted their baby.

But she couldn't help wondering when and why he'd stopped wanting her. When they'd made love the first time after she'd told him that she was pregnant, he'd seemed captivated by the subtle changes in her body, awed by the realization that there was a tiny life growing inside of her.

Of course, with each day that passed, that tiny life was getting a little bit bigger. And although she'd only gained two pounds since that day, she was barely able to fasten the button on her pants now, which meant that she was going to have to start wearing maternity clothes soon. And if Jesse found her barely noticeable baby bump unappealing, how was he going to feel in a few more months?

"Are you ready to have a look at that baby of yours now?" Dr. Gaynor's question interrupted her musing.

It was only when Jesse squeezed her hand that Maggie realized he was still holding it—had been holding it almost from the minute they walked into the doctor's office. She nodded in response to the doctor's inquiry.

"I'll send the technician in."

The technician, who introduced herself as Carla, wheeled in a cart with the ultrasound machine on it. It only took her a minute to set up, then she asked the mom-to-be to lift her shirt.

Maggie's pregnancy wasn't yet obvious—at least not to Jesse and not in the clothes she usually wore. In fact, she did such a good job of hiding any evidence of her pregnancy that he sometimes almost forgot she was pregnant—except he knew that she would never have chosen to move to Rust Creek Falls and marry him if not for their baby. He suspected the loose-fitting tops were a deliberate choice, to postpone the inevitable gossip and speculation that would run rampant when her condition became public knowledge. While he understood her reasons, he wanted to shout the news of her pregnancy from the rooftops for all of the world to hear. But because she'd done such a good job disguising her baby bump, he was surprised when she lifted the hem of her tunic-style top and he saw that there was an undeniable roundness to her belly.

The technician squirted gel onto the exposed skin and pressed a probe to her belly. A rhythmic whooshing sound filled the silence and the fuzzy display on the monitor screen began to take shape.

"Oh. Wow."

Jesse felt stunned—and humbled—as he registered the shape of their baby: the outline of the head and the body, even the skinny little legs and arms, and—most awesome and overwhelming—the rapid beating of the heart inside the chest.

He had some experience with ultrasounds—mostly with respect to equine fetuses. But this was completely outside his realm of experience. This was an actual human baby—his and Maggie's baby. He knew that he'd done very little to help grow this miracle inside of her. Yes, he'd contributed half of the baby's DNA, but since then, he'd done nothing. She was the one who was giving their baby everything he or she needed, the only one who could.

He wanted to say something to express the awe and gratitude that filled his heart, but his throat was suddenly tight, so he settled for squeezing Maggie's hand.

"Your baby is almost eight inches long and weighs about fourteen ounces," Carla told them. "Completely within normal range for twenty-one weeks."

"I've gained eight pounds and less than one of that is the baby?"

"Which is completely normal," the technician said patiently. "Now that I'm finished with all the measurements, do you want to know your baby's gender?"

Maggie looked at Jesse. They'd talked about the possibility but hadn't made a final decision, and he was grateful that she was asking for his input now. He considered, wavered, then nodded.

"Can you tell?" Maggie asked.

"I can tell," Carla said. "But I never do unless the parents want to know."

"We want to know," she decided.

The technician smiled. "It's a girl."

A girl.

Maggie honestly hadn't thought she had any preference, but she would have guessed that Jesse wanted a boy. But when she looked at him now, trying to gauge his reaction to the news, he didn't look disappointed. In fact, he was smiling like the proud father he would be in another few months.

"Were you hoping for a boy?" she asked softly.

He immediately shook his head. "My only hope is that both you and the baby are healthy."

The sincerity in his tone assured Maggie that he meant it. And the way he was looking at her—with warmth and affection—gave her hope that sharing the experience of "seeing" their baby for the first time together might bring them closer.

The technician gave her a paper towel to wipe the gel off her belly, and the moment was broken.

"Do you feel up to making another stop before we head back home?" Jesse asked when they left the doctor's office.

"Does that stop include lunch?"

He chuckled. "That stop can definitely include lunch," he promised. "What do you want to eat?"

"A burger," she answered without hesitation.

"Then we'll get you a burger."

Chapter Fourteen

They found a diner around the corner from the medical center. It was an old-fashioned-style eatery with Formica tabletops and red vinyl benches and stools lined up at the counter. The menu was quite extensive, offering more than a dozen different types of burgers with countless toppings, French fries, sweet potato fries, onion rings, coleslaw or green salad, and milk shakes and ice-cream floats.

Maggie ordered a bacon cheeseburger and a side salad, then picked at the fries on Jesse's plate. Not that he minded—it was all he could do to finish the spicy barbecue chicken sandwich on sourdough bread that he'd ordered—but he was curious.

"If you wanted fries, why didn't you just order fries?" he finally asked.

"Because the salad is healthier."

"But you're eating fries, anyway."

"Only a few," she said defensively. "And only after I ate my veggies."

He nudged his plate closer to her. "I don't mind sharing," he assured her. "I was just wondering about your rationale."

"I never even used to like French fries all that much," she said. "But lately, I can't seem to get enough."

"Any other unusual food cravings?"

"Red meat," she said.

"I noticed we've been eating a lot of beef."

Her gaze tracked the slice of apple pie that a waitress carried past their table to deliver to another customer.

"And apple pie?" he prompted.

She turned her attention back to him. "Sorry?"

He smiled. "Do you want dessert?"

"I probably shouldn't."

"Which doesn't actually answer the question," he said.

"I'm not sure if I want dessert or if that pie just looked really good."

"Should I get a slice of pie and ask for two forks?"

"Only if you want pie," she said. "With ice cream."

So he ordered the apple pie with ice cream and two forks.

After it was delivered, he watched her fork slide through the flaky crust and layers of sweet, sticky apple slices. Her lips closed around the tines of the fork, her eyes drifted shut and she let out a sigh of pure pleasure that stirred an appetite inside him that had nothing to do with dessert.

She chewed slowly, savoring the flavor, and finally swallowed.

"You have to try this," she told him.

"I ordered it for you."

She shook her head. "I'd feel way too guilty if I ate the whole thing myself."

So he picked up the second fork and took a bite.

There was something intimate about sharing a dessert. Maybe it went back to the communal consumption of ancient times, when a hunter shared his catch with his mate and their children, proof of their relationship to one another. Or maybe it was that watching Maggie eat was an incredibly erotic experience.

The pie was good, but he much preferred letting Maggie savor it.

Her tongue swept over her bottom lip, licking away the smear of ice cream. He knew that her lips were even sweeter than ice cream, and he had an almost insatiable desire to lean across the table and sample her flavor. It seemed as if it had been years since he'd kissed her, rather than the ten days that had passed since their wedding. But it wasn't easy holding his want of her in check, and he knew that if he gave in to the urge to kiss her, he wouldn't be able to stop with one kiss.

"I'm glad you're enjoying your dessert," he said.

"It's always a treat to eat something that someone else has prepared."

"And I haven't taken you out to eat anywhere since we got married," he realized. Equally startling was the realization that he hadn't taken her out at all *before* they were married. They had gone out for dinner in LA, and although he'd insisted on paying the bill, she'd chosen the restaurant, so he didn't figure he should get credit for that.

"We're going to your parents' house for Thanksgiving."

"That hardly counts."

She shrugged. "I don't need to be taken out or entertained."

And maybe it was because she didn't that he found himself wanting to make the effort. "I haven't been a very attentive husband," he acknowledged. "My only excuse is that I don't have a lot of experience with this kind of thing."

"It's my first marriage, too," she said lightly.

"I meant…dating and other courtship rituals."

"I'm your wife, Jesse. You don't have to court me."

"I should have courted you properly before we were married."

"I guess we did things a little out of order," she agreed. "But I'm not sorry, because they got us to where we are now."

"You don't miss LA?"

"Only my family," she told him. Then she gave him a half smile. "And the weather."

"The weather can be a challenge, even for those who were born and bred in Montana," he admitted.

"I asked Lissa how she survived her first winter in Rust Creek Falls—she said she wouldn't have survived at all if she hadn't had Gage to snuggle up to every night."

"I don't think I like the idea of you snuggling up to your cousin's husband," he teased.

"I don't think Lissa would, either," she admitted.

And although she smiled, her gaze shifted away, as if she was disappointed by his response. Which made him wonder—had she been suggesting that she wanted to snuggle up to him?

Before he could decide whether or not to pursue the possibility, the waitress brought the bill to their table.

When Jesse asked if they could make a stop before heading back to Rust Creek Falls, she'd assumed it was to pick up something that he needed for the horses. So she was more than a little surprised when he pulled into the parking lot of a strip mall—and parked in front of a toy store.

He strode purposefully through the front doors, as if he'd been there before and knew exactly where he was going. Considering the way he doted on his eleven-month-old niece, she would bet he'd been there several times before. He guided her down the main aisle to a section titled Cuddly Critters that was lined with big cubes stacked floor to ceiling and filled with stuffed animals of various breeds, sizes and colors.

Jesse zeroed in on the pink teddy bears, rifled through the selection, then pulled one out and handed it to Maggie.

Her fingers sank into fur that was unbelievably soft and plush. The bear was the color of cotton candy, with skinny arms and legs ending in oversized paws. The head was big, too, with a slightly paler muzzle, a brown nose, and eyes and a half smile stitched onto the fabric. It was, without a doubt, the cutest baby teddy bear she'd ever seen, and when he put it in her arms, her heart just melted.

She looked up at him. "For our baby?"

He shook his head. "For you. To remember the day that we found out about our baby girl."

"I have a very old pink teddy bear that sits on my bedside table at home," she said wistfully.

"I saw it when I was there," he admitted.

"My parents gave it to me the day I was adopted."

"I guess teddy bears are a pretty common theme."

But there was nothing commonplace about his gesture, and tears filled her eyes as she impulsively hugged him, squishing the bear between them. "Thank you."

"I should be thanking you," he said gruffly. "You're giving me the greatest gift of all in our baby, and I don't know how to tell you how grateful I am. Looking at our daughter on the ultrasound monitor, I realized how different things might have been…if you'd chosen not to tell me…or if you'd decided to give her away."

"I wouldn't have," she promised him. "It might have taken me a while to share the news, but I would never have kept it from you."

He brushed a strand of hair off her cheek, tucked it behind her ear. His deep blue eyes reflected so much of what he was feeling: affection, warmth—want?

Her breath caught in her throat as she thought, for one brief moment, that he was actually going to kiss her. She didn't care if they were standing in the middle of a toy store, she wanted to feel his lips on hers. It had been so long since he'd kissed her, too long.

But instead of lowering his head toward her, he took a step back, away from temptation. Or maybe she was the only one who was tempted.

She'd seen the surprise on his face when she lifted her shirt and he realized the tiny curve of her belly was bigger and rounder since the last time he'd seen her naked. And although she was still on the small side for twenty-one weeks, there was no longer any denying that she was pregnant. The body that he'd so thoroughly explored with his hands and his lips back in the summer was growing and changing—her subtle curves weren't nearly as subtle anymore, and his desire for her wasn't nearly as palpable.

She sat with the teddy bear in her lap throughout the drive home and consoled herself with the knowledge that at least now she'd have something to cuddle up with at night.

It wasn't what—or rather who—she wanted to be with, but the company of a plush bear was better than nothing…

Maggie went into the office for a couple of hours after she and Jesse returned from Kalispell. He, predictably, went to Traub Stables and warned her that he wouldn't be home until late. When the phone rang around nine o'clock that night, she thought it might be him calling to tell her that he was on his way home. She was only a little disappointed when she heard her mother's voice on the other end of the line.

"I just called to see how you're doing," Christa said when her daughter answered. "You had a doctor's appointment today, didn't you?"

Maggie had to smile. "You're twelve hundred miles away, in the middle of discoveries for a multimillion-dollar class action lawsuit, and you remembered the date of my doctor's appointment?"

"Of course," her mother said simply.

"Everything's fine," Maggie told her. "The baby is healthy and growing."

"And the baby's mom?"

"She's fine, too. In fact, I've gained back almost all of the weight I lost in the first trimester."

"That's good."

"I think I'm going to wear that Isabella Oliver wrap maternity dress that you sent to me for Thanksgiving." She didn't tell her mother that she'd also be wearing faux fur–lined knee-high boots and a down coat, because she did not want to hear about the balmy weather in SoCal.

"Maybe you could make a quick weekend trip this way sometime soon for us to do some more shopping," Christa suggested. "For you and for the baby."

"I'd like that," Maggie agreed.

"I wish you could be here for Thanksgiving," Christa said. "Both you and Jesse, I mean."

She was glad for the distance that separated them, so her mother couldn't see the tears that stung her eyes. "We'll make the trip for Christmas," she promised.

"Christmas still seems so far away."

"It will be here before we know it."

"So what are your plans for this holiday?"

"We're having a big meal with Jesse's family—all fifteen of them."

Christa laughed. "That should be an experience."

"No doubt."

"How's the new job?"

"Good," Maggie said. "Different, but good. I'm doing a little bit of everything, but not a lot of anything."

"I'm sure you don't miss working sixty hours a week for Brian Nash."

"No," she agreed. "I feel a little bit like I'm at loose ends right now, but I know I'll be glad for the slower pace when the baby comes."

They chatted a little more, about the class action suit, a new movie star client—unnamed to protect the solicitor-client privilege—who had hired Gavin to fight a paternity claim, and the new woman—a Laker girl—that Ryan was dating.

"Are you sure everything is okay?" Christa asked when their conversation had finally wound down. "Because LA might seem like a long way from Rust Creek Falls, but if you need anything at all, you just say the word and I'll be there."

Maggie was glad that her mother couldn't see the tears that filled her eyes. "Thanks, Mom. But everything's fine."

"You don't sound fine."

"I guess I'm just missing you and Dad. I've never not been home for Thanksgiving."

"You don't feel like Rust Creek Falls is your home now?" her mother asked gently.

"No, I do," Maggie hastened to assure her, again grateful that her mother couldn't see her face because Christa always could tell when any of her kids was being less than honest. "Like I said—I'm just missing you and Dad. Even Ryan."

That made her mother chuckle. "Happy Thanksgiving, Maggie."

"You, too, Mom."

Maggie was putting her boots on when Jesse came in from his final check on the animals Wednesday night.

"Going somewhere?" he asked.

"To the grocery store."

Because she'd specified *grocery*, he knew she didn't mean Crawford's. "We were just in Kalispell yesterday for your doctor's appointment," he reminded her.

"I know," she admitted. "But I wasn't thinking about Thanksgiving then."

"And you're thinking about Thanksgiving now?"

"Because it's tomorrow," she reminded him. "And I can't show up at your parents' house empty-handed."

"My mom's been doing Thanksgiving dinner for more years than I've been alive," Jesse pointed out. "I assure you, everything is covered."

"I want to make something," she insisted.

He sighed. "It's late and it's already been a long day."

"I don't expect you to go with me—I just thought you might want to know where I was going."

"Is Lissa going with you?"

"No."

He frowned. "You're going by yourself?"

"I know the way," she assured him.

"But it's late," he said again.

"It's not quite seven-thirty and the store's open until nine."

She made the statement matter-of-factly, as if she was perfectly capable of driving twenty minutes to an out-of-town grocery store to pick up a few items. And, of course, she was—he was just taken aback by her independence.

He'd lost count of the number of times he'd suggested to Shaelyn that she should go into Kalispell to go shopping or to a movie or even just to get one of those fancy over-priced iced coffee drinks that she liked and that couldn't be found in Rust Creek Falls.

But she never wanted to go anywhere without him. And she had a knack for making him feel guilty for even suggesting she should be on her own for half an hour when he'd been away from her for most of the day. And what if something happened when she was driving *all the way* to and from Kalispell?

As if he needed any further proof that Maggie was nothing like Shaelyn, she already had her boots and coat on and her keys in hand.

"Wait."

She paused at the door. "Did you want something from the store?"

"I want to go with you," he decided.

"That's really not necessary."

And he knew it was true. She didn't need him to go to the grocery store with her. In fact, she didn't seem to need him for much of anything. There wasn't anything she couldn't do on her own—including having and raising a child.

Which supported what Nina had said—that Maggie wasn't with him because she needed him but because she wanted to be with him.

And he realized that he didn't like the idea of her driving to Kalispell on her own. Not because he was worried about anything that might happen, just because he wanted to be with her.

"I know," he finally said. "But I'd like to come, anyway."

She looked at him for a moment, then turned back to the door. "Then let's go."

Maggie was undeniably apprehensive about spending Thanksgiving with Jesse's family. Partly because the last time she'd been invited to Todd and Laura's house, she'd abruptly—and rudely—dropped the bombshell about her pregnancy on them, and partly because this was the first time since the wedding that she'd be in the same room with all of Jesse's siblings—and the first time she'd see most of them since her husband had shared the news about their baby.

"What have you got there?" Laura asked, gesturing to the covered bowls in each of Jesse's and Maggie's hands.

"This one's coleslaw," she said, holding it up. "And Jesse's got the mac and cheese carbonara."

"Mac and cheese *what*?" Todd asked.

"It's got bacon in it," Jesse said, knowing that was his father's weakness.

"Well, I'll have to try that," he decided.

"You didn't have to bring anything," her mother-in-law protested.

"It's a lot of work to make a meal for so many people," Maggie acknowledged. "I wanted to at least make a small contribution."

"Well, that was real thoughtful," Laura said, basking a little in her new daughter-in-law's compliment. Then she gestured for them to join the rest of the family in the living room. "Come in, come in. We'll be putting dinner on the table shortly."

"Can I give you a hand with anything?" Maggie offered.

Her mother-in-law shook her head. "We've got everything covered. Oh—except that we do need one more place set at the table."

"I'm doing it now," Callie said from the dining room.

"One more?" Jesse queried.

Laura nodded to her husband. "Ask your father."

His father shrugged. "When I stopped by the store to pick up a pint of ice cream, I saw Homer Gilmore wandering the street. Since I knew we'd have more than enough food to feed the army reserves, I asked him to join us for the meal."

"That was…generous," Jesse noted.

And, Maggie could tell by his tone, unexpected.

"Everybody sit," Laura directed, as Nina and Natalie began to set bowls and platters of food around the table. "Justin—you can pour the wine. Brad—get Noelle's high chair from the kitchen. Jesse—you make sure everyone finds a seat. Nate—you come get the turkey."

Justin made his way around the table, pouring the wine. "Oops—forgot about the bun in the oven," he said, lifting the bottle away from Maggie's glass.

"Gramma took the buns out of the oven," seven-year-old Robbie said, pointing to the basket on the table.

"Yes, I did," Laura confirmed, sending a narrow-eyed look in her son's direction.

"What would you like to drink?" Natalie asked Maggie.

"Water's fine," she replied, because glasses of that were already set around the table along with a pitcher for refills.

When everyone was settled, Todd said grace, expressing thanks for the bountiful feast on the table and the gathering of family and friends. Then the bowls and platters were passed around, and people chatted easily as they filled their plates.

Laura Crawford had indeed prepared enough food to feed an army—or at least the army reserves—confirming Jesse's assertion that Maggie's contribution was unnecessary. But she was pleased to note that Dallas's three sons all wanted to try her mac and cheese.

"What's that?" Brad asked, warily eyeing the bowl that Jesse offered to him.

"It's coleslaw."

Brad scowled as he looked more closely at the salad. "But it's got raisins…and nuts."

"And it's delicious," Natalie said.

"Did you make this?" Brad asked his youngest sister.

"Maggie did."

"Oh." He glanced apologetically at his new sister-in-law. "I usually eat my fruit after dinner, inside a pie crust."

"He says as he spoons cranberry sauce onto his plate," Nina noted drily.

He scowled at that. "Cranberry sauce isn't fruit—it's a condiment."

"It's fruit," his mother informed him.

"Well, my plate's kind of full right now," Brad said, passing the bowl of coleslaw to Nate's fiancée, Callie, on his other side. "I'll try some on the next go-round."

"Can I have some more mac 'n' cheese?" Robbie asked, lifting his plate up.

"Eat some of your veggies and meat first," his father admonished.

"But I like the mac 'n' cheese best," the little boy said.

Which reassured Maggie that she'd at least made one good choice.

"What kind of cheese is in that sauce?" Laura asked.

"There are four different kinds," Maggie said. "Cheddar, Asiago, Fontina and Parmigiano Reggiano."

"Do we carry those in the store?" Laura asked her oldest daughter.

"Cheddar and Parmigiano," Nina said. "But even I go shopping in Kalispell to pick up items that we don't stock on a regular basis."

And all three of Dallas's boys were devouring the mac and cheese carbonara as if they'd never tasted anything so good.

Jesse slid an arm across her shoulders. "Better than the stuff that comes out of a box, that's for sure."

"You haven't tried the coleslaw."

"Fruit and nuts are for dessert," he echoed his brother.

"And I can say that because I don't eat cranberry sauce, either."

Across the table, Justin was drowning his mashed potatoes in gravy as he spoke to Nate. "How is construction of the resort coming along?"

Other conversations quieted as everyone wanted to hear the details. Maggie had been surprised to learn that, only a few months earlier, Nate had been thinking about leaving Rust Creek Falls. Instead, he'd decided to buy a piece of local property to open a resort, similar to what was in Thunder Canyon. Work had progressed steadily, and Maverick Manor was scheduled for a Christmas Eve grand opening.

"Is there going to be a honeymoon suite?" Nina asked.

"You've already had a honeymoon," her oldest brother reminded her.

"But Jesse and Maggie haven't," she pointed out.

"There is a honeymoon suite," Callie confirmed. "On the top floor, of course, with a gas fireplace in the lounge area and a jetted tub big enough for two in the bath."

"It sounds impressive," Maggie said, because Callie seemed to expect her to say something.

"Let us know when you've got a couple of days free and I'll reserve it for you," Nate promised.

Jesse looked at his wife. "What do you think?"

She was tempted to ask Nate if the room had two beds, because she didn't think Jesse would be willing to go if they actually had to sleep under the same covers.

"That's a generous offer," she said instead. "But we're going to be in Los Angeles for Christmas this year."

Which would present them with the same dilemma under a different roof. As close as Maggie was to her parents, she didn't want to explain to them that she wasn't sharing a bed with her husband. So they were going to have to share a bed—or one of them would have to sleep on the floor, and it wasn't going to be her.

But they had several weeks before they had to worry about that. Right now, she was focused on getting through this holiday with Jesse's family.

She was grateful that his siblings seemed to have accepted her. His parents were still lukewarm, and she didn't really blame them. They didn't know her well enough to know that she hadn't set out to trap their son.

On the other hand, her parents didn't know Jesse very well, either, but they didn't blame him for the situation. Maybe because they at least knew her well enough to know that she wouldn't be here now if she didn't want to be. Baby or no baby, she wouldn't have married him if she didn't love him. She wondered if Jesse was ever going to figure out the same thing.

"How about New Year's Eve?" Nate suggested now. "We've taken a few reservations for December 31 already, but the honeymoon suite is still available."

"I promise you'll love it," Callie said to Maggie. "The painting's done and the window coverings are going to be installed this week. Then it's just the finishing touches—bedding, towels, decorations, et cetera. If you get a chance, you should stop by for an informal tour."

Maggie appreciated the overture. "I'd like that—thanks."

"I'll pencil you in for New Year's Eve, then," Nate decided.

To which Homer responded, "We must rescue the child."

Maggie looked at Jesse, not sure if the old man was referring to their unborn child or Noelle or one of Dallas's sons. The old man didn't appear to be looking at anyone in particular but was staring at his plate and shaking his head. "We must save the child."

"Why's he saying that?" Robbie asked Nina.

"I have no idea," she admitted to her youngest stepson.

"He's creepy," Ryder muttered.

Thankfully the boy was far enough away from Homer that the old man couldn't hear him. And, truthfully, Maggie couldn't help but agree, at least with respect to his behavior today.

"Who wants pie?" Laura asked brightly.

"I think we're going to skip dessert and get the kids home," Nina told her mother.

The family matriarch looked as if she wanted to protest, then she glanced at Homer again and finally nodded. "I'll get you some pie to take with you."

Nina and Dallas ushered the kids away from the table, and Homer turned his attention to Maggie.

"We must rescue the child," he told her, his tone imploring.

While his eyes were on her, his gaze was unfocused, and she realized he wasn't looking at her so much as past her.

Were his strange prognostications merely the ramblings of a crazy old man—or were his words intended as some kind of warning to her? Was it possible that the child he was referring to was her own? And if so, why did he think her child needed to be saved?

Chapter Fifteen

"**I** think we should invite Homer Gilmore to the table every time we have dinner with your parents," Maggie said to Jesse when they got home that evening.

"Why is that?" her husband asked, sounding amused.

"Because his sporadic outbursts meant that people were staring at him instead of me every once in a while."

"Was it that bad?"

She shrugged.

"Well, you survived your first Crawford family Thanksgiving relatively unscathed."

"Pun intended?"

He just grinned.

"Since it's a day to count our blessings, I'll say that your mother is a fabulous cook."

"And she always makes sure there's enough so that everyone has some leftovers to take home."

"She even packed a turkey sandwich for Homer Gilmore before your dad took him back to town."

"Did he freak you out?"

"Homer or your dad?"

Her husband chuckled. "Homer."

She shrugged again. "Not really. Although sometimes, the way he looked at me when he talked about saving the baby, I wondered if he was talking about our baby."

"I don't think even he knew what he was talking about," Jesse said. "He's just a crazy old man."

"Maybe," she allowed. "But he seemed sincerely worried. Does he have any children?"

"I have no idea. He's not originally from around here. And while it's hard to imagine him in a relationship with anyone, I suppose it's possible."

"I just wish there was something I could do to help him."

"Maybe you should keep your distance from him."

"He's not dangerous."

"Probably not," Jesse agreed. "But I'd rather you didn't take any chances."

"I wouldn't do anything to risk our baby," she assured him.

"I'm not just worried about the baby."

She looked up at him, obviously surprised by his statement.

"Don't you realize how much I care about you, too?"

Care. There it was—a four-letter word that described his feelings for her. Unfortunately, it wasn't the four-letter word she'd been hoping to hear.

"Well, I'm not going to let anything happen to me or our baby," she said lightly.

He nodded. "Good. Now, how about a turkey sandwich?"

She shook her head. "I can't believe you're hungry again already."

"Turkey sandwiches are a Thanksgiving evening tradition."

"Not for me," she told him. "I couldn't eat another bite."

"How about pie?"

She started to shake her head again, paused. "Pumpkin?"

He chuckled. "We've got apple and pumpkin."

"Maybe just a sliver," she allowed, and followed him to the kitchen.

"Sit," he said, pointing to the breakfast bar. "I'll get it for you."

She sat. He cut a slice of the pie his mother had sent home, slid it onto a plate, added a fork and set it on the counter in front of her.

"I said a sliver," she reminded him.

"You're eating for two."

Actually, her doctor had warned her that was a fallacy, but considering the fact that her weight wasn't an issue—not yet, anyway—she picked up the fork and dug into the pie without further comment.

"I wish we had some of that mac and cheese left over," he said. "I barely got to sample it."

"It was a hit with the kids," she agreed.

"Not just the kids—even Brad had two helpings."

"But he wouldn't try the coleslaw."

Jesse just shrugged and washed down his sandwich with a tall glass of milk.

She expected him to push away from the table and escape to the barn with the excuse of one chore or another. Sure enough, he slid back his chair and stood up to clear away both of their plates, but then he surprised her by asking, "Do you want to watch some of the football game with me?"

She shook her head. "It's been a long day and I'm ready for bed."

"Are you feeling okay? You didn't overdo it, did you?"

"I'm fine," she assured him. "Just…tired."

And she was—not just physically, but emotionally. She was tired of wanting what she knew she couldn't have, tired of pretending that their marriage was something it wasn't, tired of hoping that he might one day love her the same way that she loved him.

It was her own fault. He'd told her from the beginning that he didn't want to fall in love—he just wanted their baby to have two parents.

It had seemed like a reasonable request at the time, but after almost two weeks of living together, so close and yet with so much distance between them, she realized this was going to be more difficult than she'd anticipated. Not just difficult, but painful, and she wasn't sure that she could continue like this for much longer.

They'd been married for twelve days and living like roommates. She thought they'd made some progress today. They'd spent several hours together, shared some quiet moments and comfortable silences. And he'd admitted that he cared about her. True, it was a long way from caring to loving, but she had to believe it was a step in the right direction.

Maybe she should stay up with him, at least for a little while. But being near Jesse wreaked havoc on her mind and her heart. What she really needed was distance— some time away from him to figure out what she really wanted and needed.

"I talked to my mom yesterday," she told him. "She invited me to LA for a shopping trip. Well, the invitation was to both of us, but I don't imagine that would be your idea of fun."

"It's not," he agreed. "And it seems a long way to go to do some shopping."

"Aside from the fact that I'd also get to spend some time with my parents, there are some fabulous baby stores in SoCal."

"Rust Creek Falls might not be a shopping mecca," he acknowledged, "but it has other advantages."

"I wasn't making a comparison."

But obviously he thought that she was, because he said, "I just wanted to remind you that this is a great place to raise a child.

"That's why I'm here," she reminded him. "So that we can raise our child in Rust Creek Falls, together."

"You're sure this is where you want to be?"

"This is exactly where I want to be," she said, wanting to reassure him. But then she realized that while it was true, it wasn't the whole truth. "Or *almost* where I want to be."

He frowned at the clarification. "Almost?"

She hesitated, doubts creeping in. Did she really want to go down this path without knowing where it might lead? But she decided that she did, because it beat the alternative of continuing to live the way they'd been living for almost two weeks. She hadn't married Jesse so they could live separate lives under the same roof.

She'd married him because she loved him and she wanted to be his wife in every sense of the word. But she didn't think he was quite ready for that heartfelt declaration just yet, so she only said, "I'd rather be in the bed across the hall from where I've been sleeping."

Across the hall was…his bed.

Jesse's gaze locked with hers, silently seeking—begging for—confirmation.

She didn't falter, didn't blink, and in the depths of her eyes he saw a reflection of the same desire that hummed in his veins. She wanted him—and he wanted her. He would be a fool to turn down what she was offering, and he never liked to be a fool.

But he realized now that he had been. Living in close proximity to Maggie since the wedding had been a delicious torture. She'd been close enough to touch, but he hadn't been certain she wanted his touch. He'd let himself be swayed by her brother's concern that she didn't know what she wanted instead of asking her what she wanted.

"I put your stuff in the other room because I didn't want to assume we'd share a bed just because we were married."

"I kind of hoped we'd share a bed because we wanted to," she told him. "If that is what you wanted."

"It's what I wanted—what I want," he confirmed. "I haven't stopped wanting you since the first day I saw you, and believe me, I've tried."

"Why?"

"Because I pushed you into marriage, and then it bothered me to think that you only married me because I pushed."

"If you knew me better, you'd know that nobody pushes me to do something I don't want to do."

"You wanted to marry me?"

She nodded. "I've never felt about anyone else the way I feel about you. And I've never experienced anything like the pleasure I've known in your arms."

In response to that, he lifted her into his arms and carried her to his bedroom.

He set her back on her feet beside the bed and lowered his mouth to hers. Her eyes drifted shut as her lips parted, welcoming a deeper kiss. Her tongue danced with his, a sensual rhythm that had his blood pounding in his veins, hot and demanding.

It took him a minute to figure out the wrap-style dress she was wearing. He thoroughly enjoyed running his hands over her torso, tracing her feminine curves in an effort to find the hidden zipper, but he really wanted to feel her bare skin beneath his palms. When he finally discovered the tie at her side—when she finally guided his searching hands to it—he nearly chuckled with giddy relief. With one quick tug, the knot loosened and the fabric parted. Then he was touching *her*, and the silky softness of her skin was even more tantalizing than he remembered.

He pushed the dress off her shoulders and let it fall to the floor, then he took a step back to look at her. She was wearing a pale pink bra, matching bikini panties and those thigh-high stockings that he'd always suspected were designed to drive a man to his knees. Literally.

He dropped to the floor in front of her, splayed his palms on her belly then slid them around to her back, pulling her closer to kiss her belly. Then his mouth moved lower to nuzzle the sweet heat between her thighs. Maggie sucked in a breath. He stroked her with his tongue, through the thin barrier of lace, and felt her thigh muscles quiver. He wanted her to tremble for him, but he didn't want her to sink to the floor.

He rose to his feet again and peeled away her bra, her panties, one stocking and the other. Then he eased her back onto the mattress and started to lower himself over her.

She lifted her hands, holding him away. "I want you naked, too," she told him.

He quickly stripped away his own clothes, then glanced at her with his brows raised. She answered his silent question with a smile and lifted her arms to embrace him.

He kissed her again, softly, sweetly. "You are so beautiful," he told her.

When Jesse looked at her the way he was looking at her right now, with warmth and affection in his gaze, Maggie felt beautiful. When he touched her the way he was touching her now, gently and reverently, she knew he saw her that way.

But if she was beautiful, he was breathtaking.

Maybe the life of a rancher wasn't as romantic as it was

depicted in the movies, but there wasn't any big-screen star who could hold a candle to Jesse Crawford. She let her hands roam over him, absorbing the smooth texture of bronzed skin stretched taut over all those glorious muscles, sculpted not in some Hollywood gym to look like a cowboy but through years of hard work actually *being* a cowboy.

She'd never known anyone like him, had never felt the way she felt with him, and the memory of what he had done—could do—to her body left her breathless and aching for him.

"Jesse...please."

"I will please you," he promised.

And he did. He made his way down her body, kissing and caressing every inch of her. Loving her with his mouth and his hands until everything inside of her twisted and tightened—and released.

He held her close—he was her anchor in the storm as endless waves of sensation washed over her. When those waves gradually subsided to ripples, he finally parted her thighs and buried himself in the wet heat between them, and the storm started all over again.

As they moved together in the thrillingly familiar rhythm of lovemaking, she felt connected to him in a way that was so much more than physical. And the way he looked at her, their gazes linked as tangibly as their bodies, she was sure that he must feel it, too.

Afterward, he held her tight against him, as if he couldn't bear to let her go. And she fell asleep listening to his heart beating, steady and strong, beneath her cheek and knew she was exactly where she wanted to be.

Maggie wasn't sure why she'd awakened—a quick glance at the clock on the bedside table confirmed that it was still early. Not surprisingly, Jesse was already up—and getting ready to walk out the door.

"Where are you going?"

"You're awake."

"After last night, I didn't expect to wake up alone." She sat up, tugging the sheet to cover her breasts.

"I got a message from Sutter."

"It's the day after Thanksgiving—a holiday for almost everyone in this country who doesn't work in retail."

"One of his friends has a yearling with some behavioral issues and he asked me to take a look at him," he said, as if that explained everything.

"And you have to go right now?"

"I told him I would."

And because Jesse was nothing if not a man of his word, she nodded. "When do you think you'll be back?"

"I don't really know."

It wasn't just the noncommittal response, it was the way his gaze kept shifting away, as if he couldn't bear to look at her, as if he was already out the door.

No—she wasn't going to jump to conclusions. They'd had a fabulous night together. She wasn't going to assume anything was wrong and sabotage the closeness they'd shared.

"Will you be home for lunch?"

"Probably."

But he didn't say that he'd keep her posted, and he didn't kiss her goodbye. He just said, "I'll see you later," and then he walked out the door.

She sat there for another minute, naked in his bed, staring at the empty doorway through which he'd disappeared and trying to make sense of what had just happened. But she couldn't, and tears welled up along with her frustration. She didn't understand what was going on with him.

The night before, she'd felt so connected to him, not just physically but emotionally. She'd been certain that they'd turned a corner, that they were finally going to start living as husband and wife, building a life and preparing for the birth of their child together.

She'd expected to wake up in his arms; she'd even hoped they might make love again. She knew he had things to do around the ranch, that even on the day after Thanksgiving, stalls needed to be mucked out and animals fed, so she didn't expect he'd stay in bed with her all day. But she'd hoped he'd at least show *some* reluctance to leave her side.

Instead, he'd already been up and dressed and on his way out the door when she'd awakened. She wasn't just hurt by his disappearing act, she was baffled. Why was he so anxious to put distance between them? Did he really not have any feelings for her?

No, she didn't believe that. There was no way he could have kissed her and touched her and loved her the way he had unless he felt something. But she was tired of guessing the breadth and depth of those feelings. She couldn't keep doing this—she couldn't keep putting herself out there only to have him pull back every time they started to get close. She couldn't continue to live under the same roof with the man she loved if he didn't feel the same way.

She dried her tears and picked up the phone.

When the call connected at the other end, she took a deep breath and said, "Nina—I need to ask you a huge favor."

Jesse was more than halfway to Traub Stables before he finally acknowledged the question that had been hammering at his mind since he'd responded to Sutter's text: *What was he doing?*

Why had he walked away from the beautiful—and

naked—woman who was still in his bed? What was he afraid of?

Maggie wasn't Shaelyn. The woman he'd married wasn't anything like the girl he'd been engaged to for a short time so many years before. Maggie was smart and beautiful, warm and compassionate, sexy and fun. She was also making a real effort to meet people and make friends, to fit in—and she was succeeding. He'd heard nothing but positive comments from everyone who had got to know her, his brothers and sisters all liked her, and even his parents were starting to come around.

And most significant to Jesse, she'd left her job and her family in LA and moved to Rust Creek Falls so that they could raise their baby together. He'd been so grateful for that decision he hadn't really asked why. He hadn't dared let himself hope that she'd made the choices she had because she loved him—as he loved her.

And with sudden clarity, he realized that was exactly what he'd been afraid of.

They'd both agreed to this legal union in order to give their baby a family. He'd made it clear that he didn't want to fall in love. But apparently his heart hadn't got that memo, because that was exactly what had happened.

He should have known, from day one, that he was fighting a losing battle. Because he'd started falling the first day he met her—no, even before then. The first time he saw her.

Had he really thought he could share a life with her—his home, his bed—and keep his emotions out of it? If so, he was obviously a bigger fool than he thought.

He might not have wanted to fall in love, but that's what had happened. And now he wanted more. He wanted everything.

So why was he pulled over on the side of the road near

Traub Stables instead of with Maggie, telling her how he felt?

His tires kicked up gravel as he made a quick U-turn and headed toward home.

As he took the stairs two at a time, he could hear Maggie moving around in the spare bedroom. He paused in the doorway to catch his breath and saw she was removing her clothes from the dresser. At first, he actually thought she might be moving her things across the hall to his room.

Then he saw the suitcases open on the bed.

For just a moment, his heart actually stopped beating.

"What are you doing?"

She looked up, and he saw the wet streaks on her cheeks, evidence of the tears she'd recently shed. His heart, beating once again but in a slow, painful rhythm now, twisted inside his chest, because he knew that he was responsible. He'd hurt her and made her cry, and he'd never wanted to do that.

"This is your house," she said to him. "Instead of you always making excuses to run off, I figured it made more sense for me to go."

"Go," he echoed numbly, not wanting to believe it. He'd rushed home to tell her that he loved her—and she was leaving him? He felt as if she'd reached inside his chest and ripped his heart out.

And yet, there was a part of him that wasn't really surprised, that understood he'd been on tenterhooks since their wedding in anticipation of this exact moment. But expecting it didn't mean that he was prepared for it—especially not now. Not when he'd finally accepted how much she meant to him.

"Don't do this," he said. "Please, don't go."

She folded a sweater and placed it in the suitcase. "I can't live like this."

"I know we have some things to figure out, but we can't do that if you're not here."

"I'm not the one who rushed out of here this morning," she pointed out to him.

"I told you where I was going."

"I know," she admitted. "And the fact that you'd rather spend time with a horse than me says everything that needs to be said."

"That's not true," he denied.

"Isn't it?"

"No," he insisted.

But she continued to pack.

"If you won't stay for me, please stay for our baby."

"I'm not going to keep you from our baby," she assured him.

"You don't have to—the twelve hundred miles between here and Los Angeles will do it for you."

"I'm not going back to LA."

"You're not?"

"My job and my life are here now. I have no intention of leaving town. I'm just going to Nina's apartment over the store until I can find something else."

He was torn between relief and confusion. "Why would you stay in Rust Creek Falls if you're not staying with me?"

"I'm staying in Rust Creek Falls because I made a promise to Ben Dalton when he hired me, and I don't renege on my promises."

"Really?" he challenged. "What about the promise you made to me when we exchanged wedding vows?"

She zipped up the first suitcase, and when she looked up at him, the tears that shone in her eyes were like another dagger to his heart. "I would have been happy to love, honor and cherish you for the rest of my life," she said softly, "if I thought there was any chance you might someday feel the same way."

"Wait a minute." He pried her fingers off the handle of her suitcase, linked them with his. "Are you saying that you love me?"

"I would never have married you if I didn't." She kept her gaze riveted on the suitcase as she responded. "But I can't live with someone who doesn't feel the same way."

"But I do," he told her. "I was just too stubborn and stupid to admit—even to myself—how I felt." He nudged her down onto the edge of the mattress, then sat beside her. "I fell for you, hard and fast, even before we were officially introduced. I know it sounds crazy, but it's true. And when you shook my hand—it was like something inside of me just clicked."

She eyed him warily, as if she didn't trust what he was saying. "I thought it was just me."

"And I thought it was just me—until you kissed me."

That first kiss was tame compared to the intimacies they'd shared since then, but her cheeks colored at the memory.

"I think I fell in love with you that night," he told her. "The next morning, I was so happy, certain it was only the first night of many. Then I found out that you were going back to LA that same day.

"And yes, I wondered if our relationship would end the same way my relationship with Shaelyn did. But when you promised to come back, I believed you. I *wanted* to believe you."

"And then I kept making excuses as to why I couldn't," she realized.

He nodded. "And I thought you were brushing me off. I figured you'd gone back to LA and realized you couldn't consider giving up your glamorous life in the city to settle down with a quiet cowboy."

"You barely got a glimpse of my life in LA," she said. "Or you would have known that it wasn't very glamorous."

"But you had palm trees and temperatures that rarely ever dip below freezing."

She managed a small smile. "There is that."

"My point is that I was so worried that you wouldn't want to stay here, with me, that I acted like an idiot in an unsuccessful attempt to protect my heart."

"Are you done acting like an idiot?"

"Probably not completely," he warned. "But I'm done pretending that I don't love you with my whole heart, because I do. And if you can forgive me for being such an idiot, I promise that I will never give you reason to doubt my feelings for you ever again."

"I can forgive you."

He leaned forward and brushed his lips against hers. "I love you, Maggie."

"Show me," she said.

He shoved the suitcases aside, onto the floor, and complied with her request.

Afterward, while their bodies were still joined together and sated from lovemaking, he held her as if he would never let her go. Maggie, her head cushioned on his shoulder, exhaled a soft, contented sigh.

Jesse stroked a hand over her hair, down her back. "I'm sorry."

"For what?"

"Missing out on almost two weeks of mornings just like this because I was an idiot."

"I thought we moved past that part."

"I guess it's easier for you than for me."

She pulled back, just far enough to prop herself up on an elbow so she could see his face. "Well, stop beating up on the man I love."

He lifted a hand to cradle her cheek. "What did I ever do to deserve you?"

"You loved me," she said simply.

"I do," he told her. "You are everything to me—my wife, the mother of my children, my partner in life and the woman I love, for now and forever."

"And you are everything to me," she replied. "My husband, the father of—" Her breath caught as she felt a little flutter low in her belly. "Oh."

His brows lifted. "Oh?"

The flutter happened again, and she took his hand and placed it over the curve of her belly. "Can you feel that?"

"What?" And then he felt it, too. His eyes went wide, his lips curved. "Is that…our baby?"

She nodded. "I think she's happy that her mommy and daddy are finally, truly together."

"And always will be," Jesse promised.

Epilogue

"Thanks for helping me out with this," Nina said to Maggie and Jesse. "The Tree of Hope was a big success last year and I wanted to do it again, but decorating with a baby underfoot turned out to be more difficult than I imagined."

The newlyweds, who had stopped in at Crawford's just to pick up a few staples before Nina conscripted them into service, were happy to help.

"This time next year, we'll have a little one of our own to interfere with our decorating," Maggie said to her husband, already anticipating that day.

Jesse grinned. "An eight-month-old baby whose mother graduated summa cum laude from Stanford Law will probably be directing our every move."

"Unless she takes after her father," his sister teased.

Maggie hooked another ornament over a branch and turned to her sister-in-law. "She?"

"You've slipped up and used the feminine pronoun a few times," Nina told her. "But if the baby's gender is supposed to be a secret, I won't tell."

"I don't know that we'd planned to keep it a secret," Maggie admitted. "But I didn't realize I'd given it away so quickly."

"We only found out at Maggie's ultrasound appointment last week," Jesse told his sister.

Since then—and since his wife's move across the hall

Help! **She was still tingling and zapping from having him take off her coat.**

This was such a dangerous moment. She only had to give the slightest hint of acceptance and Zac Corrigan would be kissing her. And she couldn't pretend that she didn't want to be kissed. His lips were so close, so scrumptious, so wonderfully tempting.

The air between them was crackling and sizzling. At any moment he was going to lean in…

Now she was struggling to remember why this was wrong. "Zac, we can't—"

"Shh." He touched her arm, sending dizzying warmth washing over her skin. "Forget about the office for one night."

"How can I? How can *you*?"

"Chloe, you're an incredibly sexy woman, and I'm absolutely smitten by you."

A VERY SPECIAL HOLIDAY GIFT

BY
BARBARA HANNAY

MILLS & BOON

Published in Great Britain 2014
by Mills & Boon, an imprint of Harlequin (UK) Limited,
Eton House, 18-24 Paradise Road, Richmond, Surrey, TW9 1SR

© 2014 Barbara Hannay

ISBN: 978-0-263-91331-6

23-1114

Harlequin (UK) Limited's policy is to use papers that are natural, renewable and recyclable products and made from wood grown in sustainable forests. The logging and manufacturing processes conform to the legal environmental regulations of the country of origin.

Printed and bound in Spain
by CPI, Barcelona

Reading and writing have always been a big part of **Barbara Hannay**'s life. She wrote her first short story at the age of eight for the Brownies' writer's badge. It was about a girl who was devastated when her family had to move from the city to the Australian Outback.

Since then, a love of both city and country lifestyles has been a continuing theme in Barbara's books and in her life. Although she has mostly lived in cities, now that her family has grown up and she's a full-time writer she's enjoying a country lifestyle.

Barbara and her husband live on a misty hillside in Far North Queensland's Atherton Tableland. When she's not lost in the world of her stories she's enjoying farmers' markets, gardening clubs and writing groups, or preparing for visits from family and friends.

Barbara records her country life in her blog, *Barbwired*, and her website is: www.barbarahannay.com.

For Elliot, with huge, *huge* thanks
for your unfailing faith in my writing…
It would never have happened without you.

CHAPTER ONE

THE PHONE CALL that changed Chloe Meadows's life came when she was poised on tiptoe, on a chair that she had placed on top of a desk in a valiant attempt to tape a loop of Christmas lights to the office ceiling.

It was late on a Wednesday evening, edging towards nine p.m., and the sudden shrill bell in the silent, empty office was so unexpected Chloe almost fell from her precarious perch. Even so, she slipped as she scrambled down awkwardly in her straight grey business skirt and stocking feet.

She was slightly out of breath as she finally grabbed the phone just as it was due to ring out.

'Hello? ZedCee Management Consultants.' She wondered who would call the office at this late hour. On a Wednesday night.

There was a longish beat before she heard a man's distinctly English voice. 'Hello? I'm calling from London. Could I please speak to Mr Zachary Corrigan?' The voice was officious, like the command of a bossy teacher.

'I'm sorry. Mr Corrigan isn't in the office.' Chloe politely bit back the urge to remind the caller that it was well after office hours in Australia and that her employer was almost certainly at a social function.

On any given week night, Zac Corrigan was likely to be socialising, but that possibility had become a certainty *this* week, the week before Christmas, when almost everyone was at some kind of party. Everyone, that was, except Chloe, whose social calendar was *quiet* even at this busy time of the year.

Sadly, the red letter date in Chloe's festive season was the office Christmas party. This was the third year in a row that she'd put up her hand to be the party's organiser. She'd ordered the champagne, the wines and beer, as well as a selection of delicious canapés and finger food from François's. And she'd been happy to stay back late this evening to decorate the office with festive strings of lights, shiny balloons and bright garlands of tinsel and holly.

Secretly, she loved this task. When she'd first landed her job at ZedCee she'd also moved back home to care for her elderly parents, who weren't overly fond of 'gaudy' decorations, so this was her chance to have a little Christmas fun.

'To whom am I speaking?' the fellow from London barked into the phone.

'I'm Mr Corrigan's PA.' Chloe was used to dealing with bossy types, matching their overbearing manner with her own quiet calm. 'My name's Chloe Meadows.'

'Ms Meadows, this is Sergeant Davies from The Metropolitan Police and I'm ringing from The Royal London Hospital. I'm afraid the matter is urgent. I need to speak to Mr Corrigan.'

'Of course.' Instantly alarmed, Chloe forgave the policeman his bossiness and reached for a pen and paper.

She was appalled to think that this urgent matter was in any way connected to her boss. 'I'll call Mr Corrigan immediately and tell him to ring you.'

Sergeant Davies dictated his number, Chloe thanked him and her stomach clenched nervously as she connected straight to Zac Corrigan's mobile.

The zip in the young woman's black silk dress slid smoothly downwards and the fabric parted to reveal her delightfully pale back. Zac Corrigan smiled. She was lovely. Tipsy after too many champagne cocktails and without very much to eat, but at least they'd escaped the party early, and she was quite irresistibly lovely.

With a practised touch, he caressed the creamy curve of her shoulder and she giggled. Damn. Why did champagne make girls giggle?

Still. Her skin was soft and warm and her figure was exquisite and, for a repeat of the night they'd shared last weekend, Zac could forgive her giggling.

With a firm hand cradling her bared shoulders, he leaned closer to press a kiss to the back of her neck. His lips brushed her skin. She giggled again, but she smelled delicious and Zac's anticipation was acute as he trailed a seductive line of kisses over her shoulder.

The sweet moment was spoiled by the sudden buzz of his mobile phone and Zac swore beneath his breath as he sent a frustrated glare in the direction of the armchair where he'd dumped the phone along with his jacket and tie.

'I'll get it!' the girl squealed.

'No, don't bother. Leave it.'

Too late. She'd already wriggled free and was diving for the chair, laughing excitedly, as if answering his phone was the greatest game.

Chloe suppressed a groan when she heard the slightly slurred female's voice on the line.

'Hi, there!' a girl chirped. 'Kung Fu's Chinese Take-away. How can I help you?'

'Hi, Jasmine.' Chloe was unfortunately familiar with most of her boss's female 'friends'. They were usually blessed with beauty rather than brains, which meant they were always ringing him at work, and Chloe spent far too much time holding them at bay, taking their messages, placating them with promises that Mr Corrigan would return their calls as soon as he was free, and generally acting as a go-between. 'Hold the jokes,' she said now. 'And just put Zac on.'

'Jasmine?' The voice on the end of the line was slightly sloshed and distinctly peeved. 'Who's Jasmine?' Her voice rose several decibels. 'Zac, who's Jasmine?'

Oops. Under other circumstances, Chloe might have apologised or tried to reassure the silly girl, but tonight she simply spoke loudly and very clearly. 'This is Mr Corrigan's PA and the matter is urgent. I need to speak to him straight away.'

'All right, all right.' The girl was sulky now. 'Keep your hair on.' There was a shuffling, possibly stumbling sound. 'Mr Corr-i-gan,' she said next, sounding out the syllables in a mocking sing-song. 'Your PA wants you and she says you'd better hurry up.' This was followed by a burst of ridiculous giggling.

'Give that here!' Zac sounded impatient and a moment later he was on the line. 'Chloe, what's up? What the hell's the matter?'

'An urgent phone call has come through for you from London,' she said. 'From the police. At a hospital.'

'In *London*?' There was no missing the shock in his voice.

'Yes. I'm afraid it's urgent, Zac. The policeman wants you to call him immediately.'

There was a shuddering gasp, then another sound that might have been—

No. It couldn't have been a sob. Chloe knew her ears were deceiving her. During three years in this job she'd never detected a single crack in Zac Corrigan's habitual toughness.

'Right.' His voice was still *different*, almost broken and very un-Zac-like. 'Can you give me the number?'

Chloe told him and listened as he repeated it. He still sounded shaken and she felt a bit sick. Normally, she refused to allow herself any sympathy for her boss's personal life, which was as messy as a dog's breakfast, as far as she was concerned. But this situation was different. Frightening. She couldn't recall any connection between her boss and London and she thought she knew almost everything about him.

'I'll let you know if I need you,' he said.

Zac was as tense as a man facing a firing squad as he dialled the London number. This emergency *had* to involve Liv. He was sure of it. He'd been trying to convince himself that his little sister was an adult now and quite capable of running her own life, especially after she'd ignored his protests and left for England with her no-hoper boyfriend... But...

Liv.

His baby sister...

All that was left of his family…

His responsibility…

'Hello,' said a businesslike English voice. 'Sergeant Davies speaking.'

'This is Zac Corrigan.' His voice cracked and he swallowed. 'I believe you're trying to contact me.'

'Ah, yes, Mr Corrigan.' The policeman's tone was instantly gentler, a fact that did nothing to allay Zac's fears. 'Can I please confirm that you are Zachary James Corrigan?'

'Yes.' What had Liv done? Not another drug overdose, surely? When he'd rung her two weeks ago, she'd promised him she was still off the drugs, *all* drugs. She'd been clean for over a year.

'And you're the brother of Olivia Rose Corrigan?'

'Yes, I am. I was told you're calling from a hospital. What's this about?'

'I'm sorry, Mr Corrigan,' the policeman said. 'Your sister died a short while ago as the result of a road accident.'

Oh, God.

It wasn't possible.

Shock exploded through Zac, flashing agonising heat, threatening to topple him. Liv couldn't be dead. It simply was *not* possible.

'I'm sorry,' Sergeant Davies said again.

'I—I see,' Zac managed. A stupid thing to say, but his mind was numb. With terror. With pain.

'Do you have any relatives living in the UK?' the policeman asked.

'No.' Sweat was pouring off Zac now. Vaguely, he was aware of the girl, Daisy, with the black dress dangling off her shoulders. She was hovering close, frowning at him, her heavily made-up eyes brimming with vacuous curiosity. He turned his back on her.

'Then I take it you'll be prepared to be our contact for any arrangements?'

'Yes,' Zac said stiffly. 'But tell me what happened.'

'I'll pass you onto someone from the hospital, sir. The doctor will be able to answer all your questions.'

Dizzy and sick, Zac waited desperately as the phone went through several clicks and then a female voice spoke.

'Mr Corrigan?'

'Yes,' he said dully.

'This is Dr Jameson from the maternity ward.'

Maternity? She was joking, surely?

'I'm very sorry, Mr Corrigan. Your sister was brought to our hospital after a vehicle accident. There were extensive head and chest injuries.'

Zac winced. Head and chest. The worst.

'Olivia was rushed to theatre and we did our very best, but the injuries were too extensive.' A slight pause. 'I'm afraid we couldn't save her.'

Zac went cold all over. So there it was. Two people had confirmed the impossible. His greatest fear was a reality. After all these years when he'd tried and failed with Liv, he'd now failed her abysmally...

And it was too late to try again.

He couldn't breathe, couldn't think. Horror lashed at him as he fought off images of Liv's accident. Instead he clung to a memory of his beautiful, rebellious young sister from years ago when she was no more than sixteen... He saw her on the beach, during a holiday on Stradbroke Island, her slim tanned arms outstretched, her dark gypsy hair flying in the sea wind, her teeth flashing white as she laughed and twirled with child-like joy.

He remembered it all so clearly. With her brightly co-loured sarong over a skimpy yellow bikini, she'd looked so tanned and beautiful. Innocent, too—or so Zac had thought—and, always, *always*, so full of fun.

That was how he'd thought of Liv back then—full of fun and life.

Now…he couldn't believe that her life had been ex-tinguished.

'But we were able to save the baby,' the English doc-tor said.

Baby? Now Zac sank in weak-kneed horror onto the edge of the bed. What baby? How could there be a baby?

'Are you there, Mr Corrigan?'

He swallowed. 'Yes.'

'You're listed as your sister's next of kin, so I'm as-suming you knew that Olivia was pregnant?'

'Yes,' he lied when in truth he'd had no idea. When he'd phoned Liv only two weeks ago, she hadn't said a thing about being pregnant. Right now, he felt as if the world had gone quite mad.

'Your sister was already in labour,' the woman said. 'We believe she was on her way to hospital when the accident occurred.'

'Right.' Zac sagged forward, elbows on knees. 'So—' he began and then he had to stop and take a shuddering breath, which wasn't much help. He forced himself to try again. 'So—this baby. Is it OK?'

'Yes, a beautiful baby girl, perfectly unharmed and born by Caesarean section only a couple of weeks be-fore her due date.'

Zac pressed a shaking hand to his throbbing forehead. His stomach churned. He was sweating again. This woman was trying to tell him that some crazy twist of fate had snatched his beautiful sister's life and left a baby in her place. How bizarre was that?

He wanted to drop the phone, to be finished with this absurd conversation. No way did he want to deal with the gut-wrenching news that had just been so calmly delivered.

But, of course, he knew he had no choice.

With a supreme effort, he shut off the hurt and pain and, like the cool-headed businessman he usually was, he forced his mind to confront practicalities.

'I presume you've contacted the baby's father?' he said tightly, recalling the man who'd convinced Liv to run away with him. A guy from a band—a band no one had heard of—an older man with dreadlocks streaked with grey and restless eyes that could never quite meet Zac's gaze.

'Your sister wasn't able to tell us the name of the baby's father. There was a man in the car with her, but he assured us he was only a neighbour and not the father, and our blood tests have confirmed this.'

'But he could tell you—'

'I'm afraid he doesn't know anything about the father's identity.'

'Right.' Zac drew a deep, shuddering breath and squared his jaw. 'So this baby is, for all intents and purposes, my responsibility?' Even as he said this, he knew it hadn't come out right. He'd sounded uncaring and hard. But it was too late to try to retract his words. He could only press on. 'I'll…er…make arrangements to come over to London straight away.'

* * *

Chloe had just finished pinning the last decoration in place when her boss rang back.

'Chloe, I know it's late, but I need you to book me a flight to London.' His voice was crisp and business-like, but tight, too, the way people spoke when they were fighting to keep their emotions in check. 'You'd better make it the soonest flight possible. First thing tomorrow morning, if you can.'

'Of course, and would you like a hotel reservation as well?' Chloe hoped she didn't sound too surprised, or worried... If there was a crisis, the last thing Zac needed was an anxious, fussing PA.

'Yes, book a hotel room, please. Somewhere central.'

'No problem.' Already she was firing up her computer.

'And I'll need you to sort out those accounts with Garlands.'

Chloe smiled to herself. 'All done.'

'Already?' He sounded surprised. 'That's great. Well done.'

'Anything else?'

'Could you ring Foster's and tell them that Jim Keogh will represent me at tomorrow's meeting.'

'No problem.' Chloe paused, in case there were any more instructions. 'That's all then?'

'Actually, Chloe...'

'Yes?'

'You'd better book two flights to London. Just two one-way seats at this stage. I'm not sure how long I'll need to be over there.'

Ridiculously, Chloe's heart sank. An annoying reaction. Why should she care if her boss wanted to take the giggling girl who'd answered the phone with him on an all-expenses-paid trip to London? Of course, she couldn't help wondering how much use the girl be would if Zac had been called away to something urgent.

'What name for the second ticket?' she asked smoothly as the company's preferred airline's website came up on her computer screen.

'Ah…good question. Actually…'

Another pause. Chloe began to fill the boxes on the flights search. Point of departure… *Brisbane, Australia*. Destination… *London, UK*. Date of flight…

'How busy are you, Chloe?'

'Excuse me?'

'Could you spare a few days?'

'To fly to London?'

'Yes. This is an emergency. I need someone…capable.'

Chloe was so surprised she almost dropped the phone. Was Zac really asking her to go to—to London? *At Christmas?*

'I know it's short notice and it's almost Christmas and everything.'

Her head spun, first with shock and a fizz of excitement, and then with dismay as she thought about her elderly parents at home, waiting for her, depending on her to look after the shopping and to cook Christmas dinner and to drive them to church. They would never cope without her.

'I'm sorry, Zac. I don't really think I could get away at such short notice.'

As she said this, there was the sound of a door opening behind her and she jumped. Turning, she saw her boss striding into the office. Of course, he'd had his phone in the hands-free cradle while he was driving.

As always, Chloe's heart gave a pitiful little skip when she saw him, but at least she was used to that nuisance reaction now. She knew it wasn't significant—pretty much the automatic reaction shared by most women who encountered Zac Corrigan's special brand of tall, dark and handsome.

This evening he looked paler than usual and his grey eyes betrayed a shock he hadn't been able to shake off.

'If you can come with me, I'll pay you a hefty Christmas bonus,' he said as he strode across the office to Chloe's desk.

But he'd already paid her a generous Christmas bonus. 'Can you explain what this is about?' she asked. 'What's happened?'

What's happened?

Zac lifted his hand and rubbed at his brow, where a headache had been hovering ever since he took the call from the hospital and now throbbed with renewed and vicious vengeance.

'Are you all right, Zac? You look…'

Abruptly, Chloe pulled a swivel chair from the nearest desk and pushed it towards him. 'Here, sit down.'

He held up a hand. 'It's OK, thanks. I'm fine.'

'I'm sorry, but I don't think you are.'

To Zac's surprise, his PA took a firm grasp of his elbow, gripping him through his coat sleeve. 'I think you should sit down now before you fall down.'

Zac sat.

'Can I get you a cup of tea?'

If he wasn't feeling so strung out, he might have

smiled at this old-fashioned response from his conservative and over-conscientious PA. She was dressed in one
of her customary businesslike suits. Her white blouse
was neatly buttoned and tucked in, and there wasn't a
strand of her light brown hair out of place. Good old,
reliable Chloe.

He was so relieved to see her tonight. He'd been
desperate to get away from the giggling Daisy and, by
contrast, cool, collected Chloe was a reassuring and
comforting sight.

'I don't need tea,' he said. 'I'd just like to get these
flights sorted, and I could really do with your assistance in London.'

'I assume this is all because of the phone call…from
the hospital.'

'Yes.' Zac swallowed, trying to clear the sharp, per-
sistent pain that seemed to have lodged in his throat. 'I'm
afraid it wasn't good news,' he said with quiet resignation. 'It was bad. Really bad. The worst.'

'Oh, no… I'm so sorry.'

Sorry… Zac was sorrier than he'd ever thought possible. He looked away from the sympathy in Chloe's soft
brown eyes. Then, staring bleakly at a spot on the grey
office carpet, he told her the rest of his news…

When he finished, Chloe took ages to respond. 'I…I
don't know what to say,' she said at last. 'That's so terrible. I…I never realised you had a sister.'

'Yeah…well…' He couldn't bring himself to admit his
estrangement from Liv, or that he hadn't known about
the baby, that Liv had never even told him she was pregnant, that she almost hadn't told him about going to England.

How could he admit to this prim and conscientious

cliché of a secretary that his reckless sister's pregnancy was just another of the many secrets she'd hidden from him?

'I guess you'll need help...with the baby girl...if they can't find her father,' Chloe suggested awkwardly.

'Yes. I'll be it's...I mean...*her* guardian.' He knew this, because the one thing he'd insisted on after Liv's overdose was that she made a will. He'd hoped that a measure of reality would shake some sense into her. 'I couldn't possibly manage on my own.'

Babies had never registered on Zac's radar. He'd always supposed they were a dim possibility in his far distant future...when he eventually settled down and chose a wife and all that went with a wife... But, even though he was a godfather twice over, he'd never actually held a baby. There had always been plenty of women with willing arms and he'd been more than happy to buy expensive gifts and the best champagne to wet the baby's head and then stay well in the background...

'I'm sure we can find someone.' Chloe was busy at her computer screen, scrolling through some kind of spreadsheet.

'Find someone?' Zac asked, frowning. 'How do you mean? What kind of someone?' He didn't need to *find* someone. He had Chloe.

She turned back to him with a smile that was almost sympathetic. 'This is a list of your personal female contacts.'

'You have them on a spreadsheet?'

'Well, yes. How else do you think I manage to—?'

'All right, all right.' He gave an impatient wave of his hand. He knew Chloe was a marvel at managing his female friends—sending them the appropriate invi-

tations or flowers, birthday or Christmas presents, get
well cards, even, at times, offering excuses on his behalf…but he'd never given any thought to how she kept
track of them.

'What about Marissa Johnson?' Chloe said now. 'She
always struck me as sensible.'

'No,' Zac said curtly, remembering the awkward way
he and Marissa Johnson had broken up. He jumped to
his feet, seized by a fit of restless impatience. 'Look,
there's no point in looking at that list. I don't want any
of *them*. I want you, Chloe. We've worked together for
three years now and I know you'd be perfect.'

To his surprise her cheeks went a deep shade of
pink—a becoming shade of pink that unsettled him.

'I don't know very much about babies,' she said.

'Really?' Zac frowned at her. She was female, after
all. 'But you know enough, don't you? You know how
to put on a nappy. And when it comes to bottles and that
sort of thing, you can follow instructions. It's just for
a few days, Chloe. There's a remote possibility that I
might have to bring this child home. I'll need help, just
till I have everything sorted.'

Not that he had any idea how this problem could be
sorted. At the moment he was still too shocked. Too
sad. He didn't want to think about a little new life when
Liv was—

'I'm sorry,' Chloe said quickly. 'I'd like to help, but
I'm not really free to rush overseas at the drop of a hat.
Not at this time of year. I have my parents to consider…'

'Your parents?' Zac frowned again. Why would a
woman approaching thirty be so concerned about her
parents? Then again, he knew he was out of touch with
the whole family thing. His own parents had died when

he was eighteen and he'd been managing without them for almost seventeen years.

But now there was a baby...a niece...another little girl who was his responsibility. A slug of pain caught him mid-chest. History was repeating itself in the most macabre way.

'It's Christmas,' Chloe said next, as if that explained everything. She looked up at the surprisingly attractive decorations she'd arranged about the office. 'Would you like me to look into hiring a nanny?'

Zac let out a weary sigh. 'The last thing I need now is to start interviewing nannies.'

'I don't mind doing the interviews.'

'No,' he snapped. 'We don't have time.'

Besides, for this delicate operation, he needed someone he already knew, a woman who was loyal and trustworthy, and sensible and efficient—and a woman who wouldn't distract him with sex.

Chloe Meadows ticked every box.

CHAPTER TWO

CHLOE COULDN'T QUITE believe it was actually happening. Here she was in the executive lounge of Brisbane International Airport, enjoying coffee and croissants with her boss, with a boarding pass for a flight to London in her handbag, a grey winter jacket and rosy pink scarf folded on the seat beside her, and a neatly packed carry-on bag at her feet.

She still wasn't quite sure how Zac had convinced her to do this, but from the moment he'd learned she had an up-to-date passport the pressure had begun. He'd argued that the company was winding down for the Christmas break anyway and, thanks to her superb organisational skills, the office Christmas party could run brilliantly without her.

He'd brushed aside her concerns that she knew very little about babies. After all, the child's father might yet be found.

To Chloe's amazement, even her very valid concerns about her parents had been duly considered by her boss and then swiftly and satisfactorily smoothed away.

She'd been stunned when he'd asked last night if he could visit her parents. She'd tried to protest. 'Sorry, no. Mum and Dad will be in bed already.'

'Why don't you ring them to check?' he'd said confidently.

To Chloe's surprise, her mother and father were still up, watching *Carols in the Cathedral* on TV, and, even more surprisingly, they said they'd be happy for her boss to call in, if he didn't mind finding them in their dressing gowns and slippers.

Zac said he didn't mind in the least.

'Chloe, there's sherry in the pantry and we can break open that box of shortbread you bought last week,' her mother suggested, sounding almost excited.

Zac had poured on the charm, of course, and, when it came to being charming, her boss was a genius. Even so, when he offered to put her parents up in the River-slea Hotel, all expenses paid, with all their meals, most especially Christmas lunch, included, Chloe was sure they would refuse. It would be all too flash! They didn't like flashiness.

But, before her parents could object, Zac had thrown in a car with a driver to take them to church on Christmas Day, or to the doctor, or anywhere else they needed to go, and he'd offered to hire a nurse to check daily that they were keeping well and taking their correct medication.

Chloe's mother had looked a bit doubtful about this, until she'd received an elbow in the ribs from her dad.

'It would be like a holiday, love,' he'd said.

Still, Chloe had expected her parents to have second thoughts and say no. But then Zac also told them with commendable sincerity how extremely important, no, *invaluable*, their daughter was to him and how much he needed her for this very important mission in the UK.

Somehow he'd struck just the right note, which was

clever. If he'd praised Chloe to the skies, her parents would have been suspicious and he would have blown it.

Instead, by the time he'd finished, they were practically squirming with delight, like puppies getting their tummies rubbed just the way they liked it.

And now…this morning, her parents, with their out of date, simple clothes and humble, shabby luggage, including her dad's walking frame, had looked a trifle out of place in the luxurious hotel suite with thick white carpet, floor-length cream linen curtains, golden taps in the bathroom, not to mention panoramic views up and down the Brisbane River…but the grins on their faces had said it all.

'Chloe, you go and look after your nice Mr Corrigan,' they'd said, practically pushing her out of the door. 'Don't you worry about us.'

Chloe had closed her gaping mouth.

Remembering her parents' delight, she could almost imagine them exploring their hotel room like excited children, checking the little bottles of shampoo and bubble bath, flushing the loo and bouncing on the king-sized mattress. Zac Corrigan had achieved a minor miracle.

And Chloe was going to London!

Right. Deep breath. She only hoped she wasn't making a very serious mistake. After all, she knew why her boss had been so keen to avoid asking any of his female 'friends' to accompany him on this very personal journey. He liked to keep his relationships casual and this sojourn to London would be anything but casual.

Chloe also knew why her boss regarded her as a suitable choice. She was capable, conscientious and uncomplicated, and he trusted her to remain that way. Which suited her just fine. It did. Really.

Yes, there was a danger that those annoying long-ings she sometimes felt for Zac would surface, but she'd had plenty of practice at keeping them in check and she was sure she could survive his close proximity for a few short days.

So perhaps it was OK now to admit to herself that she was a tiny bit excited, or at least she would be if she wasn't concerned for Zac and the sad ordeal that still awaited him when they landed.

Eventually, they boarded and took off, making the long flight across Australia, and now they were, according to the map on the screen, flying high above the Indian Ocean…

The cabin lights were dimmed, Zac and Chloe had eaten an exquisite meal and had drunk some truly de-licious wine, and their business class seats had been turned into beds.

Beside Chloe, her boss appeared to be asleep al-ready, stretched out in jeans and a black T-shirt, with his shoes off and his belt removed and his feet encased in black and purple diamond-patterned socks. He had also plugged in earphones and was listening to music and he had slipped on the navy silk eyeshade the air-line provided.

He was used to flying and she supposed he would sleep now, possibly for hours. He'd probably had very little rest during the previous night and she was sure he needed to sleep. Actually, Chloe's night had been sleep-less as well, so she knew it would be sensible to try to follow his example. Otherwise, she'd end up in Lon-don, useless with jet lag, with a boss who was ready and raring to go.

Unfortunately, however, Chloe was too *wired* to sleep. The past twenty-four hours had been such a whirlwind and the thought of London was simply too exciting. She'd acquired her passport in happier times, when she'd thought she knew exactly where her life was heading…

But she'd never used it. So she'd never been on an international flight before, had never flown business class, and had certainly never been to England. It was hard to believe she would soon be seeing the famous Tower Bridge and Big Ben and Buckingham Palace.

Needing to calm down, she fished in her bag for the magazines she'd bought from the airport newsagent while Zac was busy with a phone call. The mags were all about mothers and babies and parenting and Chloe hoped to find an article or two about caring for newborns. Just in case…

Luckily, there were plenty of stories and columns covering all kinds of newborn issues. Chloe soon discovered what to do if a baby had colic, jaundice, an umbilical hernia…and masses of information about bath time, skin care, crying, feeding, burping…

She read the information conscientiously, trying to take it all in, wondering if she would actually be called on to apply any of this in practice and hoping she'd remember the important details. Her real-life experience of babies was limited to admiring her friends' offspring, and she'd found them cute to cuddle or play with and then she'd been happy enough to hand them back to their mothers.

After her life turned upside down several years ago, she'd given up her own dreams of motherhood, so she'd never given much thought to the finer details of green nappies or colic or projectile vomiting.

Even now, she blocked those images. Not every baby had those problems, surely?

Instead, Chloe allowed herself to picture a tiny, warm, sweet-smelling bundle in her arms, a dear little baby girl, with soft pink skin and perhaps dark hair like Zac's. A darling rosebud mouth.

'Aren't you sleepy?' murmured a deep voice beside her.

Startled, she turned to see that Zac had lifted his eyeshade and removed an earplug, and was watching her with marked curiosity.

Chloe's insides began to buzz—an annoying reaction to having him so close. 'I…er…thought it might help if I read for a bit first,' she said.

Zac leaned closer, frowning. 'What on earth are you reading?'

The magazine in her lap was unfortunately open at a full-page picture of a tiny baby attached to an enormous breast.

Chloe felt her cheeks heat. 'I…um…just thought…in case…you know, the baby…it would be handy to have a few clues.'

'It would indeed.' Zac spoke smoothly enough, but his eyes once again held the bleak shadows that had arrived with the terrible news about his sister. 'Good thinking, Ms Meadows.'

Chloe swallowed. It was more than a little unnerving to find herself lying so close to her boss's disconcerting, sad grey eyes. She could see his individual thick, dark eyelashes and the grainy texture of the skin on his jaw. She hadn't been this close to a man since—

'I'm sure I'll be sleepy soon,' she said quickly, before her thoughts could be hijacked by haunting memories.

'Tell me something you've learned,' Zac said, keeping his voice low so he didn't disturb the other passengers, many of whom were sleeping. 'I'm intrigued.'

'Something about babies?' Chloe whispered back.

He cast another glance at the photo in her lap. 'Or breasts, if you prefer.' He gave her a teasing smile.

Despite the rising heat in her cheeks, Chloe sent him a drop-dead look and closed the magazine.

'Babies then,' Zac amended, his lips still twitching in a smile. 'Tell me what you've learned about babies.'

In truth, she'd learned an awful lot that she hadn't really wanted to know—about a newly delivered mother's hormonal fluctuations, the stitches she might have in awkward places, her leaking or sore and swollen breasts.

'OK,' she said as she remembered a snippet of practical information that was safe to share with him. 'Did you know that you should wash the baby's bodysuits and nightgowns in hypoallergenic dye- and scent-free detergent?'

'Fascinating.' Zac yawned, clearly already bored.

Good, he might leave her in peace.

Chloe waited for him to replace his eye mask. Instead, he pointed to one of the magazines in her lap. 'Do you mind?'

This time, she didn't try to hide her surprise. 'You want to read one of these? A mother and baby magazine?'

Her corporate executive playboy boss could not be serious. The Zac Corrigan she knew wouldn't be caught dead with such an incriminating piece of reading material in his hands, not even in the relative anonymity of an international flight.

'Yes, please,' he said, holding out his hand and smiling blandly. 'I'd like to be educated.'

Lips compressed to stop herself from making a smart retort, Chloe handed him a magazine that focused on a baby's first six months. She supposed he was probably teasing her, but he might be trying to distract himself from thinking too much about his sister.

It was even possible that he genuinely wanted to learn. After all, if a father for Liv's baby couldn't be traced, Zac might soon find himself in complete charge of a newborn.

For a while they both read in peaceful silence, the small glow of their reading lights making golden cones in the otherwise darkened cabin. But Chloe couldn't relax. For one thing, she was too curious about how Zac might be reacting to the contents of his magazine.

But it wasn't long before he leaned close, speaking softly. 'Did you know that babies can stare at you while they sleep?'

'Excuse me?'

He smiled. 'It says here that they can sleep with their eyes half open. It looks pretty spooky, apparently.'

Although his smile, up close, was dangerous for Chloe's heart health, she couldn't help smiling back at him. 'Well, the article I'm reading warns that babies sometimes don't sleep at all.'

'No.' Zac feigned complete shock. 'That can't be right.'

'Well, I guess they sleep eventually, but some stay awake for much longer than they're supposed to.'

'A bit like us,' he said, looking around the business class cabin at all the other passengers, who appeared to be contentedly sleeping.

Chloe sighed. 'I guess we really should turn our lights out and try to sleep.'

'Yes, we should.' He closed the magazine and handed it back to her. 'Thanks for that. Most enlightening.'

By the time she'd stowed the magazines away, Zac had turned off his reading light, pulled down his eye-shade and folded his arms over his wide chest. 'Good-night, Ms Meadows.'

He usually only addressed her this way when he was in a playful mood, which wasn't very often, mostly when he'd pulled off some extraordinarily tricky business coup. Chloe wondered if the playboy was coming out in him now, simply because he was lying beside a young woman who was close enough to touch and kiss.

That thought had no sooner arrived than her body re-acted, growing warm and tingly and tight.

Oh, for heaven's sake.

Where had such a ridiculous reaction sprung from? Chloe gave herself a mental slap and glared at Zac.

'Goodnight, sir,' she said icily.

'And try to sleep.' He spoke without lifting his shade and he sounded now like a weary parent. 'We've a long way to go.'

Chloe didn't answer and she was relieved that she would not have to speak to her boss again until morning. She pulled on her own eye mask and tried to settle comfortably, hoping that the steady vibration of the plane and the hum of its engines would soothe her.

Her hopes were not realised.

She couldn't relax. She was too upset by her mental slip about kissing and touching her boss. Too busy deliv-ering a good, stern lecture to herself. After all, she knew very well that Zac had asked her to accompany him on this trip precisely because he needed a female companion to whom he was *not* sexually attracted.

Her momentary lapse had no doubt been brought on by her over-tiredness. She knew nothing like *that* would happen. Zac had spent a good section of almost every working day in the past three years in her company without once trying to flirt.

Besides, she didn't want it to happen. She was far too sensible to ever fall for her boss's superficial good looks and charming wiles. Apart from the fact that she'd had her heart broken once and never wanted to experience that pain again, there was no way on this earth that she would allow her name to end up on the spreadsheet of his *Foolish Females*.

Unfortunately, her attempt to sleep only lasted about ten or fifteen minutes before she had to wriggle and fidget and try for a more comfortable position. Beside her, she heard a weary sigh. 'Sorry,' she whispered.

Zac lifted the eye mask again and pinched the bridge of his nose.

'Sorry,' Chloe said again. 'I disturbed you, didn't I?'

He shook his head. 'Not really.' He yawned. 'I'm dog-tired, but I have a feeling I'm not going to sleep tonight.'

'Do you normally sleep on long haul flights?'

'Eventually.'

She wondered if he couldn't stop thinking about his sister. Was he simply too upset to sleep? She wished she could help.

'I don't have any brothers or sisters,' she said tentatively.

Zac frowned.

'Sorry,' she said quickly, wincing at her third apology

in as many minutes. 'I just thought you might want to talk, but I shouldn't have—'

'No, no, it's OK.' He sighed again, and lay staring into space, apparently thinking...

Chloe waited, not sure what else to say.

'Liv was eight years younger than me,' he said quietly. 'When our parents died, she was only ten, so I felt more like her father at times.' His mouth was a grim downward curve. 'She was my responsibility.'

Chloe stared at him now as she tried to take this in. Was the poor man blaming himself for his sister's accident? Did he feel completely responsible? 'But you must have been very young, too,' she said.

'I was eighteen. An adult.'

Only just, by the skin of your teeth. 'How awful for you to lose both your parents so young.'

'Yeah,' he agreed with another sigh.

Chloe didn't like to ask, but her imagination was running wild. 'How did it happen, Zac? Was there an accident?'

He shrugged. 'We'll never know for sure. My parents were sailing somewhere in Indonesia when their boat just disappeared. My father was a geologist, you see, and my mother was a marine biologist and they were mad keen on science and exploration, always on the lookout for a new discovery. I suppose you'd call them nutty professors. Eccentrics.'

So they'd just disappeared...? Poor Zac. How terrible to have his parents simply vanish, to never know if they'd been taken by pirates, or capsized in a tropical storm, or drowned when their boat struck a coral reef...

'They—they couldn't be still alive, living on some jungle-clad island, could they?'

Zac's mouth tilted in a wryly crooked smile. 'I've played with that fantasy, too. But it's been seventeen years...'

Chloe couldn't imagine how awful it must have been for him—a mere eighteen years old and forced to carry on living without answers, just with terrible possibilities.

'Right from the start I was worried about Liv,' he said next. 'I couldn't bear to see her disappear into a foster home, so I applied to be her guardian. I dropped out of uni and got myself a job, so we could live together and I could look after her.'

'Goodness,' Chloe said softly, hoping she didn't sound as surprised as she felt.

Zac's lips curled unhappily. 'It was possibly the stupidest decision I ever made.'

'Don't say that. I think it was incredibly brave of you.'

She was stunned to realise that Zac had sacrificed his own goals to try to keep what was left of his family intact. All she'd ever known about his private life was the revolving door of lookalike leggy blonde girlfriends. He'd never seemed to really care about any of them beyond their sex appeal and she'd assumed the 'care factor' gene was missing from his DNA.

But it was clear to her now that he'd cared very deeply about Liv.

'I couldn't keep her on track,' Zac said, so softly Chloe almost missed it. 'Liv never really looked on me as a parent. She wouldn't accept me in a fathering role, so I had very little influence, I'm afraid. I think she was mad at our parents for disappearing the way they did and she saw me as an inadequate substitute. Before she was out of her teens she was into drinking and trying drugs. And then she was like a nomad, never wanting to settle. She didn't want to study and she would never stay in one job for long enough to get any real skills. She was like a butterfly, always searching for a brighter flower.'

'Might she have inherited that urge from your parents?'

'Quite possibly, I guess.'

He stared unhappily up at the cabin's ceiling and Chloe wished she could offer him wise words of consolation.

She did her best. 'Honestly, I don't think you should blame yourself for this accident, Zac.'

But he simply shook his head and closed his eyes.

It was ages before Chloe drifted off to sleep and when she woke a soft grey light filled the cabin and flight attendants were bringing around hot towels to freshen their hands and faces, as well as glasses of orange juice.

'Morning, sleepyhead.'

Zac's seat was already back in the upright position and he looked as if he'd been to the bathroom and washed and shaved.

Chloe yawned and hoped her hair wasn't too messy. In a minute she would follow his example and freshen up. 'What time is it?'

'Seven forty-five. That's Greenwich Mean Time, of course. If we were still at home it would be five forty-five in the evening.'

So...her parents had almost completed their first day in the hotel. Chloe hoped they were still enjoying themselves.

If she'd been in Brisbane, she would be putting the final touches to the office's decorations and making last minute checks about the drinks and ice.

'I hope you're not worrying about your parents.'

'No, I'm not.' She knew they were in good hands and she'd left the hotel desk, the hired nurse and the chauffeur with all the phone numbers and information they could possibly need. 'I was thinking about the office Christmas party tonight, actually.'

'Really, Chloe?' Zac was frowning at her now, although his eyes glinted with puzzled amusement.

'I was looking forward to the party,' she admitted, no longer caring if this revealed her inadequate social life.

'You were looking forward to watching half the office staff get plastered and then staying behind to clean up their mess?'

She opened her mouth to protest.

Zac's smile was gently teasing. 'You're going to see London at Christmas. I promise you that's a thousand times better than the office do.'

'I suppose it would be. When should we get our first glimpse of England?'

'Oh, in about an hour.'

CHAPTER THREE

IT WAS RAINING when they touched down at Heathrow, but somehow that couldn't dim Chloe's excitement. As business class passengers with only carry-on baggage, she and Zac didn't have to hang around in long queues and soon they were outside, suddenly very grateful for their warm overcoats and scarves.

While they waited for a taxi she made a quick phone call to her parents.

'We're about to go down to the dining room,' her mum told her excitedly. 'We've already checked out the menu and we're having lamb cutlets and then rhubarb crumble. Give our love to Zac.'

They were having the time of their lives and, within moments, Chloe was climbing into a proper shiny black London taxi and her excitement mounted as they whizzed along busy rain-slick streets filled with other taxis and cars and bright red double-decker London buses. Ahead, on a pedestrian crossing, people huddled beneath umbrellas glistening with rain.

Zac asked the taxi driver to stop at their hotel to leave their luggage and Chloe caught a brief impression of huge glass doors, massive urns filled with greenery and enormous gold-framed mirrors in a white marbled foyer.

'Now, we'd better head straight to the Metropolitan Police,' Zac said when he returned.

'Yes.' Chloe dug out her phone and checked the arrangements she'd made for Zac to meet with Sergeant Davies. She gave their driver the address and then they were off again.

Three blocks later, they had stopped at traffic lights when she saw the trio of soldiers. The tall, broad-shouldered men were simply standing and chatting as they waited to cross a road, but all it took was the sight of their camouflage uniforms and berets to bring back memories of Sam.

It could still happen like that, even though she'd had three and a half years to recover. The smallest trigger could bring the threat of desperate black grief.

Not now...I can't think about him now...

But now, on the far side of the world with her handsome boss, this painful memory was a timely reminder of the heartache that came with falling in love. Chloe knew she had to be super-careful...and she was grateful she'd trained herself to think of Zac as nothing but her boss...glad that she'd become an expert at keeping a tight lid on any deeper feelings...

At the police station, Sergeant Davies was very solicitous as he ushered them into his office. He told them that Liv's death had been clearly accidental and there was no reason to refer it to the coroner.

'The young man who was driving your sister to the hospital is definitely in the clear,' he added. 'He's a Good Samaritan neighbour. He was injured, but he's going to be OK. A badly broken leg, I believe.'

Zac sat stiffly, his face as grim as granite, as he received this news.

'We'll be laying serious charges against the driver of the other car,' the sergeant then told them.

'Driving under the influence?' Zac asked.

This was answered by a circumspect nod of assent. Zac sighed and closed his eyes.

Outside, Chloe wanted to suggest that they found somewhere for a coffee. She was sure Zac could do with caffeine fortification, but perhaps she shouldn't have been surprised that he was determined to push on with his unhappy mission. At work he always preferred to confront the unpleasant tasks first. It was one of the things she'd always admired about him.

Within moments of hitting the pavement, he hailed another taxi and they were heading for the cold reality of the Royal London Hospital.

Once there, Zac insisted on seeing his sister, but as Chloe watched him disappear down a corridor, accompanied by a dour-looking doctor in a lab coat, she was worried that it might be a mistake. Her fears were more or less confirmed when Zac returned, white-faced and gaunt, looking about ten years older.

She had no idea what to say. There was no coffee machine in sight, so she got him a drink of water in a paper cup, which he took without thanking her and drank in sips, staring at the floor, his eyes betraying his shock.

Eventually, Chloe couldn't bear it. She put an arm around his shoulders and gave him a hug.

He sent her a sideways glance so full of emotion she felt her sympathetic heart swell to bursting. He offered her a nod, as if to say thanks, but he didn't speak. She was quite sure he *couldn't* speak.

For some time they sat together, with their overcoats

bundled on the bench beside them, before one of the hospital staff approached them, a youngish woman with bright red hair. 'Mr Corrigan?'

Zac lifted his gaze slowly. 'Yes?'

The woman's eyes lit up with the predictable enthusiasm of just about any female who met Zac. 'I'm Ruby Jones,' she said, holding onto her bright smile despite his grimness. 'I'm the social worker looking after your case.'

'Right. I see.' Zac was on his feet now. 'I guess you want to speak to me about the…the child?'

'Yes, certainly.' Ruby Jones offered him another sparkling smile, which Chloe thought was totally inappropriate. 'Am I right in imagining that you'd like to meet your niece?'

'Meet her?' Zac looked startled.

'Yes, she's just on the next floor in the maternity ward.'

'Oh, yes, of course.' He turned to Chloe. 'You'll come, too, won't you?'

'Yes, if you like.'

Ruby, the social worker, looked apologetic. 'I'm afraid—in these situations, we usually only allow close family members into—'

'Chloe is family,' Zac intervened, sounding more like his usual authoritarian self.

Chloe stared at the floor, praying that she didn't blush, but it was a shock to hear Zac describe her as family. She knew it was an expedient lie, but for a crazy moment her imagination went a little wild.

'I'm sorry.' Ruby sounded as flustered as Chloe felt. 'I thought you mentioned a PA.'

Zac gave an impatient flick of his head. 'Anyway, you couldn't count this child's close family on two fingers.' He placed a commanding hand at Chloe's elbow. 'Come on.'

Chloe avoided making eye contact with Zac as the social worker led them to the lift, which they rode in silence to the next floor.

'This way,' Ruby said as they stepped out and she led them down a hallway smelling of antiseptic, past doorways that revealed glimpses of young women and bassinets. From all around were sounds of new babies crying and, somewhere in the distance, a floor polisher whined.

Zac looked gloomy, as if he was hating every minute.

'Have you ever been in a maternity ward before?' Chloe asked him out of the side of her mouth.

'No, of course not. Have you?'

'Once. Just to visit a friend,' she added when she saw his startled glance.

Ahead of them, the social worker had stopped at a glass door and was talking to a nurse. She turned to them. 'If you wait here at this door, we'll wheel the baby over.'

Zac nodded unhappily.

Chloe said, 'Thank you.'

As the two women disappeared, Zac let out a heavy sigh. His jaw jutted with dismal determination as he sank his hands deep into his trouser pockets. Chloe was tempted to reach out, to touch him again, to give his elbow an encouraging squeeze, but almost immediately the door opened and a little trolley was wheeled through.

She could see the bump of a tiny baby beneath a pink blanket, and a hint of dark hair. Beside her, she heard her boss gasp.

'Oh, my God,' he whispered.

The trolley was wheeled closer.

'So here she is.' The nurse was middle-aged and hearty and she gave Zac an encouraging smile. 'She's a proper little cutie, this one.'

Chloe couldn't help taking a step closer. The nurse was right. The baby was incredibly cute. She was sound asleep and lying on her back, giving them a good view of her perfectly round little face and soft skin and her tiny nose—and, yes, her perfectly darling rosebud mouth—just as Chloe had imagined.

The baby gave a little stretch and one tiny hand came out from beneath the blanket, almost waving at them. There was a hospital bracelet around her wrinkled wrist. Chloe saw the name Corrigan written on it and a painful lump filled her throat.

Zac was staring at the baby with a kind of awestruck terror.

'So what do you think of your niece, Mr Corrigan?' asked Ruby, the social worker.

He gave a dazed shake of his head. 'She's tiny.'

'Her birth weight was fine,' the nurse said, sounding defensive, as if Zac had directly criticised her hospital. 'At least seven pounds.'

The social worker chimed in again. 'Would you like to hold her?'

Now Zac looked truly horrified. 'But she's asleep,' he protested, keeping his hands rammed in his pockets and rocking back on his heels as if he wished he could escape. For Chloe, by contrast, the urge to pick the baby up and cuddle her was almost overwhelming, as the maternal yearnings that she'd learned to suppress came suddenly rushing back.

She saw a frowning look exchanged between the nurse and the social worker and she worried that this was some kind of test that Zac had to pass before they could consider handing the baby into his care.

'Go on,' Chloe urged him softly. 'You should hold her for a moment. You won't upset her. She probably won't even wake up.'

Zac felt as if the air had been sucked from his lungs. He couldn't remember when he'd ever felt so out of his depth. The nurse was peeling back the pink blanket to reveal a tiny baby wrapped tightly in another thinner blanket. This was going to happen. They were going to hand her to him and he couldn't back out of it.

'Our little newborns feel safer when they're swaddled firmly like this. It also makes them easier to hold,' the nurse said as she lifted the sleeping bundle.

Reluctantly, Zac drew his hands from his pockets and hoped they weren't shaking.

'Just relax,' the nurse said as she placed the baby in his arms.

Relax? She had to be joking. It was all right for her. She did this every day. He was still getting over the agony of seeing Liv. And now he was so scared he might drop her baby…

She was in his arms.

He could feel the warmth of Liv's baby reaching him through the thin wrap. Could feel her limbs wriggling. Oh, dear God, she was so real. Alive and breathing. He forced himself to look down into her little pink face, so different from the deathly white one he'd so recently witnessed…

And yet…the similarity was there…

He found it so easily in the baby's soft dark hair, in

the delicate curve of her fine dark eyebrows, and in the tiniest suggestion of a cleft in her dainty chin.

'Oh, Liv.'

His sister's name broke from him on a desolate sob. His vision blurred as his throat was choked by tears.

Chloe's heart almost broke when she saw the silver glitter in Zac's eyes.

Even now, under these most difficult circumstances, it was a shock to see her boss cry. Zac was always so in control. In the day-to-day running of his business, it didn't matter how worried or upset or even angry he was, he never lost his cool. Never.

He usually viewed any kind of trouble as a challenge. In fact, there were days when he seemed to thrive on trouble and conflict. Twice, to her knowledge, he'd taken his company to the very brink of economic peril, but he'd never lost his nerve and had emerged triumphant.

Of course, there was a huge gulf between the challenges of the business world and a personal heartbreaking tragedy.

Now Zac Corrigan, her fearless boss, was caught in the worst kind of heartbreak and he was shaking helplessly as tears streamed down his face.

'Here,' he said, thrusting the baby towards Chloe. 'Please, take her.'

Her own emotions were unravelling as she hastily dumped their coats to accept the warm bundle he pressed into her arms. The poor man had been through so much—*too* much—in such a short time and, on top of everything else, he was dealing with jet lag. But, even though he had every reason to weep, Chloe knew he would be mortified to break down like this in public.

She wasn't at all surprised when Zac turned from them and strode back down the corridor, his head high and his shoulders squared as he drew deep breaths and fought for composure.

Watching him, she held the baby close, inhaling the clean and milky smell of her. She thought how perfectly she fitted in her arms.

Beside her, Ruby, the social worker, said, 'It's such a very sad situation.'

Indeed, Chloe agreed silently.

The baby squirmed now and beneath the blanket she gave a little kick against Chloe's ribs. Chloe wondered if this was how it had felt for Liv when she'd been pregnant. *Such a short time ago.*

Oh, help. If she allowed herself to think about that, she'd start weeping, too.

Perhaps it was just as well that she was distracted by Zac's return. He seemed sufficiently composed—although still unnaturally pale.

'I'm so sorry for your loss,' the nurse said.

Zac held up a hand and gave a brief nod of acknowledgement. 'Thank you.' His manner was curt but not impolite. Then he said, in his most businesslike tone, 'I guess you need to bring me up to speed.' He shifted his now steady gaze to the social worker. 'What's the current situation? Has anyone been able to locate the father?'

Ruby shook her head. 'I'm afraid we've had no luck at all.'

'You've definitely ruled out the fellow who was in the car with Liv?'

'Yes.'

At this news, Zac looked bleaker than ever.

'We've also interviewed the people who lived in the

share house with your sister,' Ruby said next. 'But they haven't been able to help us. They said Olivia wouldn't tell anyone the father's name. She simply told them that he wouldn't be interested in a child and she didn't want anything more to do with him.'

Zac stared at her for a long moment, his grey eyes reflecting a stormy mix of emotions. Eventually he nodded. 'That sounds like my sister, I'm afraid. But there was a boyfriend. I'm pretty sure Liv was still with him last Christmas. An Australian. A singer in a band.'

'Bo Stanley?'

Zac nodded grimly. 'Yes, I'm pretty sure that's his name.'

Again, she shook her head. 'A housemate did mention him and he's still in the UK, so we made contact and had him tested. It was easy to disqualify him. He's completely the wrong blood type.'

This time, Zac stared at her as if he was sure she had to be mistaken, but eventually he gave an unhappy shake of his head and shrugged. 'I guess he's off the hook, then.'

In Chloe's arms, the baby gave a little snuffling snort. When Chloe looked down she saw that her eyes had opened. The baby blinked and stared up at Chloe, straight into her eyes.

How much could those newborn dark grey eyes see? The baby's expression was definitely curious. Trusting, too. Her intense, seemingly focused gaze pierced Chloe's heart and she was enveloped by a rush of warmth, a fierce longing to protect this tiny, sweet girl. *It would be so easy to love her.*

She realised that Zac was watching her.

His gaze lingered on her as she stood there with the

baby in her arms. Surprise flared in his eyes and then a softer emotion. Chloe held her breath and for a winded moment her mind played again with hopelessly ridiculous possibilities…

Fortunately, Zac quickly recovered. 'OK,' he said, looking quickly away and becoming businesslike again. 'I guess my next question is about the baby.'

'What would you like to know?' the nurse asked guardedly.

'Is she healthy?'

'Perfectly.' She sniffed as if his question had offended her. 'You would have been informed before now if there was a problem.' Then, more gently, she asked, 'Do you have a particular concern?'

Zac grimaced uncomfortably. 'My sister had a drug habit, or at least she used to.' He shot a quick glance to Chloe and then looked away, as if he was embarrassed to have his employee hear this admission. 'It was some time back,' he added quickly. 'And Liv assured me she's been clean ever since, but I assume you've run the necessary tests?'

'Yes, Mr Corrigan. I can reassure you there were no signs that the baby has been adversely affected by alcohol or drugs.'

'Well, that's good news at least.' He swallowed. 'So…' Looking from the nurse to the social worker, he summoned a small smile, a glimmer of his customary effortless charm. 'What's next?'

Ruby, the social worker, was clearly surprised. 'Well…as you're next of kin and you've been named as guardian—'

'Yes, I've brought a copy of my sister's will if you need to see it.'

'And you've come all the way from Australia,' Ruby continued. 'I—I mean *we* were assuming that you planned to care for the baby.'

Zac nodded and his throat worked as he swallowed again.

Chloe knew he felt overwhelmed. He'd fielded successive shocks in the past twenty-four hours and she felt compelled to speak up. 'We've only just arrived from Heathrow and Mr Corrigan hasn't had any time to adjust, or to buy any of the things the baby will need.'

The nurse nodded. 'Of course. I understand.'

Shooting Chloe a grateful look, Zac added, 'If the baby could remain in your care for a little longer, I'd be happy to pay for any additional costs.'

This could be arranged, they were told, and Zac was also given a list of funeral parlours, as well as the name and address of Liv's share house, so that he could collect Liv's belongings. On that sobering note, they departed.

Outside the hospital a brisk December wind whipped at them, lifting their hair and catching at the ends of their scarves. Standing on the footpath on Whitechapel Road, Zac almost welcomed the wind's buffeting force and the sting to his cheeks. He dragged in an extra deep lungful of chilled air, as if it might somehow clear the raw pain and misery that roiled inside him. But there was no way he could avoid the two images that kept swimming before his vision. The pale, bruised, lifeless face of his beautiful sister and the small, red, but very much alive face of her tiny newborn daughter.

His niece.

His new responsibility.

The frigid air seemed to seep into Zac's very blood

along with this chilling reality. This baby, this brand new human being had no other family. He was *it*. She would be completely dependent on him.

He shot a glance to Chloe, whose cheeks had already turned quite pink from the cold. The high colour made her look unexpectedly pretty and he thought how fabulous she'd been this morning. In fact, his decision to bring his PA with him to London had been a stroke of pure genius. On the long flight, at the police station and again at the hospital, Chloe's no-fuss efficiency and quiet sympathy had been exactly the kind of support he'd needed.

'I vote we go back to the hotel now,' he said. 'We can check in and get a few things sorted.'

Chloe nodded. 'I'll check out those funeral parlours, if you like. It might be hard to find a—a place—with Christmas and everything.'

Zac was about to agree, but then he remembered the heartbreaking decisions he might be required to make. 'I'd better talk to them, Chloe. Anyway, you're probably exhausted.'

'I feel fine, actually.' She smiled. 'Being outside and grabbing a breath of fresh air makes all the difference.'

You're a breath of fresh air, he almost told her, and then thought better of it. Even minor breaches of their boss-PA boundaries seemed to make Chloe uncomfortable and now that she'd given up her Christmas and had come all this way, he didn't want to upset her. Instead he said, 'And I'll also make contact with the share house people.'

'Yes, it might be worth finding out what Liv's already bought before you start shopping.'

Zac frowned. Suddenly, his mega-sensible PA wasn't making any sense at all. 'Shopping?'

'For the baby.'

'Oh.' He gulped nervously. 'Yes, of course.'

A vision of a mountain of nappies and prams and tins of formula mushroomed in Zac's imagination. He felt overwhelmed again as he raised a hand to hail their taxi.

In a matter of moments, they were heading back into the city centre. Chloe leaned back in the seat and closed her eyes. She was probably worn out, even though she'd denied it. Zac had never seen her like this—with her eyes closed, her dark lashes lying softly against her flushed cheeks, her lips relaxed and slightly open.

She looked vulnerable and he found his attention riveted…

This wasn't the first time he'd entertained the idea of kissing Chloe, of making love to her, but, just as he had on the other occasions, he quickly cut off the thought.

From the start, when he'd first employed Chloe, he'd quickly recognised her value as his PA and he'd set himself clear rules. No office affairs. Ever.

Of course, there'd been times when he'd wished to hell that wasn't so principled where Chloe was concerned. More than once they'd been deep in a business discussion when he'd been completely distracted by her quiet beauty, but it was almost certainly for the best that his common sense had always prevailed.

And now, once again, Zac dismissed ideas of tasting her softly parted lips and he wrenched his thoughts back to his new responsibilities.

A tiny baby…such an alarming prospect for a commitment-shy bachelor. If he took Liv's little daughter into his care, she would rely on him for everything—for food, for shelter, clothes...love. As she grew older she would look up to him for wise guidance, for entertainment, for security. She would require vast amounts of his time and patience.

No doubt she would view him as her father.

Her daddy...

The thought brought shivers fingering down Zac's spine. He couldn't deny he'd been hoping that the baby's biological father would emerge and make a claim, but he'd also been worried by the prospect. Knowing Liv, the guy was bound to be a no-hoper. Now, the possibility of a father galloping up on a white charger to save the day was fast disappearing and this left Zac with a different, but equally worrying set of problems...centring on his own, very real inadequacies...

He was very aware that his personal life was at best... haphazard...but there was a good reason for that—in more recent years he'd been making up for lost time.

Liv had been so young when their parents died, and for many years Zac had made her his first priority. He'd juggled several part-time jobs so that he could be at home for as much of Liv's out-of-school time as possible.

It was only *after* Liv had turned eighteen and struck out on her own, that he'd decided he might as well have some fun, so when it came to dating women he'd been a late starter. By then he'd also discovered he had a head for business as well as a talent for attracting gorgeous girls. He'd enjoyed the combination of work and play so much that he hadn't felt a need to settle down.

Now...as he stared out at the busy London traffic, at the towering modern buildings and the occasional ancient stone church hunkering within the skyscraper forest, he wondered if adoption might be the best option for Liv's baby.

It wasn't the first time Zac had toyed with the idea. Ever since the first shocking phone call from London , the possibility of adoption had been there, nagging at the back of his thoughts.

A huge part of him was actually quite willing to hand the baby over, and not because he was keen to shirk his responsibility, but because he was so totally scared of failure. With Liv, he'd tried his damnedest and he'd failed spectacularly, so how could he hope to be any more successful with her baby?

And yet…

Zac dragged an agonised hand over his face as guilt squirmed unpleasantly inside him. Could he really bring himself to hand that tiny bundle, that little 'mini-Liv', over to strangers?

After all, his sister had named him as guardian of her children in her will, and surely she wouldn't have made that weighty decision if she'd wanted her baby to be adopted.

Problem was…if the child was *not* adopted, there were very few alternatives. He certainly couldn't care for a baby on his own and he shuddered at the idea of a procession of housekeepers and babysitters and nannies.

He had to find a better solution. Fate had handed him a second chance to care for a member of his family and he simply *had* to get it right this time.

Liv's child needed security and continuity and she needed someone else besides him, someone who would balance his strengths and weaknesses. But a baby also needed someone who would really care about her and love her and, most importantly, stay with her…

What the poor kid needed was a mother...

With a heavy sigh, Zac closed his eyes, recalling a long ago image of Liv as a baby. He could picture their house in Ashgrove in a street lined with Bunya pines. Their mother was bathing Liv in a special little baby bath on the kitchen table, holding her carefully in the crook of her arm as she squeezed water from a facecloth over her fat little tummy.

Their mum had made a game of it and every time the water touched Liv's tummy, the baby would laugh and splash. Zac remembered the happiness of that squealing baby laughter, remembered the shining joy and impossible-to-miss love in his mother's face.

At the time he'd been a bit jealous and oh, so aware of the vital importance of a mother's love.

Oh, Liv, Liv...you should have been a mother, too.

Watching from the seat in the taxi beside Zac, Chloe saw his face twist with pain. He was looking away, out of the window, and he had no idea he was being observed. His mouth was trembling and then he grimaced and bit down hard on his lip as if to hold back a sob, and she could see tears again, could see the raw, agonising pain in his face. She longed to reach out, but she knew he would hate to be caught on the brink of breaking down yet again.

Still staring bleakly through the window, Zac's weary mind threw up a picture of Chloe at the hospital this morning. He remembered how perfectly the baby had fitted into the cradle of her arms, remembered the warm glow in Chloe's chocolate eyes as she looked down at her. He remembered the equally warm, melting sensation that he'd felt as he'd watched the two of them.

So natural and right…

Yes, there could be no question. What the baby needed most definitely, *absolutely*, was a mother.

And suddenly, arriving with the lightning jolt swiftness of every great idea, Zac discovered the perfect solution.

'You know what this means, don't you?' he announced in sudden triumph.

Beside him Chloe jumped and blinked as if she'd been woken from sleep. 'What?' She was frowning. 'Excuse me?'

'This baby,' Zac said impatiently. 'Liv's baby. There's only one way to take proper care of her.'

Despite Chloe's puzzled frown, her eyes widened with curiosity. 'What is it?'

'I'll have to take the plunge.'

'What plunge?'

'Into wedded bliss.' He tried to sound more excited. 'I'll have to get married.'

CHAPTER FOUR

MARRIED?

Zac Corrigan married?

Chloe stared at her boss, too stunned to speak. There was every chance she wasn't breathing and she had huge doubts about her hearing.

Surely she must have dreamt that Zac, the serial dater, truly wanted to get married?

He was watching her with a smile that didn't quite reach his worried eyes. 'Don't look so shocked,' he said.

She gave a dazed shake of her head, as if to clear it, and sat up straighter. 'Sorry. I think I must have nodded off and didn't hear you properly. What did you just say?'

'I've found the perfect solution to the baby problem.'

'Which is…?' she prompted cautiously.

Zac lifted his hands in a gesture of triumph, as if he was announcing the latest boost in company profits to a group of delighted shareholders. 'It's obvious that I need to get married.'

Good grief. She had heard him correctly.

For no more than a millisecond the word 'marriage' uttered by Zac Corrigan sent a strange thrill zinging through Chloe, skittering across her skin and lifting fine hairs. But, almost immediately, she came to her senses.

He was pulling her leg, of course. If she hadn't been so tired she would have seen the joke immediately.

'Marriage?' She laughed. 'Yeah, right.'

'I'm serious, Chloe.'

'Yes, of course you are.'

'I mean it.' He said this forcefully, as if he was growing impatient with her. 'It's the perfect solution.'

For some men, possibly, but not for you, Zac.

Clearly, jet lag had caught up with her devilishly handsome playboy boss. Jet lag plus too many personal shocks in a short space of time.

Unless...

Chloe supposed it was possible that Zac had fallen deeply in love very recently, without her knowing. 'I should have asked,' she said quickly. 'Do you already have a lucky lady in mind?'

Please, don't let it be that giggling girl who answered his phone the other evening.

Perhaps it was just as well that their taxi pulled up outside their hotel at that precise moment. Zac didn't answer Chloe's questions and the crazy conversation was dropped. Instead, he turned his attention to signing for the fare, making sure it included a generous tip.

Then a young man, resplendent in a uniform with tassels, opened the taxi door for Chloe. She had an almost film star moment as she went up the short flight of stone stairs with Zac to enormous glass doors, opened for them by another man in livery.

Once inside the glamorous high-ceilinged foyer with an exquisitely decorated soaring Christmas tree, they were greeted by more smiling staff who attended to the business of collecting their luggage and checking in.

It all went super-smoothly, with a level of service

that exceeded Chloe's experiences on previous business trips. She'd certainly never stayed anywhere this glamorous before.

Zac had interrupted her last Wednesday evening, when she'd been about to make the hotel booking.

'Hang on,' he'd said, as he hunted in his desk and produced a business card. 'Try this place. I stayed there once. It's central and rather good.'

It was much pricier than his usual budget, but Chloe hadn't liked to argue and now, here they were, in a lift with an intricately tiled floor and mirrored walls, taking them silently swishing upwards…

Seconds later, they were standing in the carpeted hallway outside their adjoining rooms. 'Take your time settling in,' Zac said. 'Perhaps you'd like to rest up for a bit?'

Chloe was tempted, but she knew it wouldn't be wise. 'If I fall asleep now, I'll probably find myself wide awake and prowling around at midnight.'

To her surprise, he responded with a sparkling-eyed, slightly crooked smile.

She frowned. 'Did I say something funny?'

'No, as always you were eminently sensible, Chloe, but I have a very curious imagination. I couldn't help playing with the idea of my Ms Meadows on a midnight prowl.'

To her dismay, her mind flashed an image of the two of them meeting out here in the corridor when she was wearing nothing but a nightie and heat flared as if Zac had struck a match inside her. 'Don't be ridiculous,' she snapped.

He wiped the smile, but irritating amusement still lurked in his grey eyes. 'Seriously, it's probably best if you can manage to stay awake until this evening. How about we meet in half an hour for lunch?'

'Sounds fine. Would you like me to make you a cup of tea, sir?' She added this in her most deferential manner, to remind them both of the very clear lines drawn between his status and hers.

Zac's response was another unsettling smile and, for a moment, he looked as if he was going to make yet another inappropriately playful remark, but then he gave a slight shake of his head and the amused light in his eyes died. 'No, thanks. I'll manage.'

Chloe was annoyed that she still felt unsettled as she slid the key in her lock and went into her room.

But she was soon distracted by the room's jaw-dropping gorgeousness. It had an enormous bed, a thick, pale carpet and comfortably padded armchairs, as well as vases of roses. Everything was in tasteful shades of pink and cream, and the view was beautiful, too, through elaborately draped windows to green English parkland with enormous ancient trees spreading winter-bare branches above smooth velvet lawns.

She set her bag down and took off her coat and scarf and laid them carefully on the end of the bed. She slipped off her shoes, and when her stockinged feet sank into the deep pile carpet she gave a blissful little twirl and then a skip.

She thought of her parents back in Brisbane, enjoying their lovely hotel stay, which was also courtesy of Zac. It seemed wrong somehow that both she and her parents were enjoying a luxurious and other-worldly experience for such a very sad reason.

Sobered by this thought, she located the tea-making facilities hidden discreetly behind white-painted doors.

Soon she had the jug boiled and a bag of Lady Grey tea brewing in a delicate china cup and, with milk and a half-teaspoon of sugar added, she took the cup to an armchair. For the first time in days, she had a little time to herself, to relax and unwind. But she couldn't stop thinking about her boss and the difficult phone calls he was making right next door.

As an only child, she didn't know what it was like to lose a sibling, but she knew all too well what it was like to lose someone she loved…and, without warning, she was swamped by memories.

Once again she was feeling the crushing weight of the raw grief caused by Sam's death. It had sent her retreating home to her elderly parents and, once there, their increasing age and health issues had become her excuse to withdraw from the pain of her old life…

Now, curled in the armchair, clutching the lovely cup to her chest, Chloe wept for Sam, her fiancé…and for her lost dreams…and also, in a more complicated way, she found herself weeping, as well, for her boss.

'Are you sure you're OK, Chloe? You're looking a little peaky,' Zac commented when they met again thirty minutes later.

She looked surprised. 'I'm perfectly fine, thanks.'

He might have quizzed her further, but he knew he probably looked rather pale and drawn, too. He'd certainly felt flattened after his discussions with the funeral director.

'Liv's share house is in Islington,' he said, referring to one of the other phone calls he'd made. 'It's probably just as easy to take the Tube and we can go out there first thing in the morning.'

Chloe nodded.

'I was hoping you'd come, too.'

'Yes, of course.'

The enormity of his relief was out of all proportion but, with that small issue settled, they headed for Oxford Street, hunting for a place to eat. Or at least that was Zac's plan until Chloe was completely captivated by the extravagant Christmas displays in the shops' windows.

He was patient enough while she admired them— blinding white snow scenes complete with pine trees and clever mechanical toys, glittering tables laden with sumptuous feasts, fantastic fashions displayed against a stunning snowy backdrop.

He knew the shop windows were incredibly inventive and artistic, but he found it difficult to enjoy them. He was finding it impossible to shake off the burden of his new and weighty responsibilities.

He'd been slightly miffed that Chloe had laughingly dismissed his brilliant solution of marriage without giving it so much as a moment's thought. He was also surprised she'd been so forthright. Usually, if his PA disagreed with him, she kept her opinions to herself, unless he specifically asked for her input.

Of course, he'd never discussed his private life with Chloe until now, but everything had changed last Wednesday evening. And it had changed again this morning when he saw his sister's tiny baby. He was overwhelmed anew by the huge pressure of his *duty*, and now, as Chloe turned from a clever display of robots made from children's building blocks, he was gripped by a new kind of urgency.

'You know, I'm at a loss about this child,' he said. 'I can't possibly care for her on my own.'

Perhaps he spoke a little too loudly. A woman rushing past them, laden with shopping parcels, sent Chloe a distinctly disapproving glance.

Fortunately, Chloe ignored her and simply stepped closer to Zac, lowering her voice. 'You can have all kinds of help with a child, you know. There are nannies and—'

Zac cut her off in a burst of impatience. 'Nannies come and go. I want—' He sent another glare to the steady stream of Christmas shoppers flowing around them and gave an impatient shake of his head. They couldn't talk about this here, and the cafés in Selfridges were bound to be packed at this time of the year.

'Come on.' He tugged at her coat sleeve. 'I've remembered a pretty good pub just around the corner.'

As Zac charged off, Chloe almost had to run to keep up with him.

She soon forgave him, though, when he located the pub. It had a very appealing wonderfully 'old English' atmosphere created by small paned windows with white trims, a green door and a window box spilling red, white and purple petunias.

Inside, the dark, timber-panelled space was as warm and cosy as the outside had promised. Appetising aromas drifted from the kitchen, and there was a friendly buzz in the room as diners, who were taking a break from their Christmas shopping, chatted quietly at tables covered in white linen.

Chloe and Zac took off their coats and scarves and hung them near the door, which was quite a novel experience for Chloe after subtropical Brisbane, and a friendly young waiter showed them to a table in a corner.

Several of the female diners turned and unashamedly

followed Zac with their eyes. Chloe was used to this, of course, but Zac hardly seemed to notice them.

As they made themselves comfortable, Chloe was tempted to relax completely and soak up the centuries-old atmosphere, but she was too conscious of the tension coming off Zac in waves. She wondered if he was still stewing over his crazy marriage idea. Surely he would soon wake up to himself?

At least he didn't try to raise the delicate subject until after they'd ordered. Chloe chose a Stilton and potato soup with a glass of white wine, while Zac ordered a beef and Guinness pie and half a pint of beer.

With that settled, Chloe decided that she should at least humour her boss. 'So are we still discussing this marriage plan, Zac?'

His grey eyes narrowed. 'On the assumption that you're prepared to be reasonable.'

'Of course I'll be reasonable, but you never did tell me if you had a future wife in mind.'

'Well…no.' He smiled a little ruefully. 'I'll admit that's a problem.'

Chloe stomped on the ridiculous flush of relief that swept through her.

'But I'm still quite sure marriage is the perfect solution.'

'Because…?'

'The baby will need a mother,' Zac said simply.

Ah, yes…

In a heartbeat, Chloe was remembering the sweet little bundle in her arms, the warm weight of Liv's baby, and she was reliving that amazing moment when she'd looked deep into the baby's bright little eyes and had felt her heart turn over.

The memory made her throat ache and she had to swallow before she could answer. 'Finding a mother would be the ideal solution,' she said, hoping the emotion didn't show in her face. 'But plenty of babies have been brought up by nannies.'

Ridiculous tears threatened and she looked away quickly to the end of the dining room. What on earth was the matter with her? She had to be very careful that she didn't become too emotionally caught up in Zac's problems. There was no point in becoming maudlin just because she'd given up her own dreams of a family when she'd gone home to her parents.

She turned her attention to the far wall, where a huge mantelpiece lent the restaurant a gracious Victorian air. With her gaze centred on it, she said lightly, 'Wasn't the British Empire practically raised by nannies in its heyday?'

Zac's jaw stiffened, a clear sign that he was annoyed. 'Let's stick to the twenty-first century.'

She tried again, in placating tones. 'I believe the modern nannies are very well trained.'

'But no nanny these days is going to stick with a child until she's an adult.'

'That might be a stretch.' Across the table, Chloe eyed her boss boldly. 'Then again, modern marriages don't always last very long either.'

A stubborn light gleamed in Zac's eyes as he stared unblinkingly back at her. 'I still think marriage is the most sensible option. I want this child to have stability, parents who'll stick around, perhaps a little brother or sister—a life as close to normal as possible.'

Such an alluring picture…

Chloe took a deep breath. Zac wanted to give the

baby everything Liv had lost.He wanted this quite badly, and desperate times required desperate measures. 'You have to do what you think is right, Zac. It's none of my business, anyway.'

'Actually…that's not quite true…'

Her heart began a frantic hammering. What did he mean?

'I thought you might be able to help me,' Zac said.

'Really? How?'

'You have that spreadsheet. We could go through it together—take another look at the possibilities.'

The spreadsheet… It was so ridiculous to feel disappointed in him. Why on earth might she have thought…?

'Please tell me you're joking,' she said quickly.

'I'm not. I'm deadly serious.'

'But trawling for a wife through a database is so—' *So wrong on so many levels.* 'So unromantic.' Chloe had to look away again.

She was remembering the day Sam proposed. They'd been walking in the rain along a cliff top, with the sea crashing and foaming on the rocks below. Sam had produced a ring and he'd actually gone down on one knee. It was *so-o-o-o* romantic. He'd told her how madly he loved her and their kiss in the rain had been the most exciting moment imaginable…

'I mean,' Zac was saying. 'For all we know, these modern marriages might fail for the very reason that they're based on romantic notions instead of common sense and logic.'

'So what are you saying now, Zac? That you don't believe in romance?'

Before he could respond, the waiter approached with their drinks.

'Meals won't be long,' the young man said cheerfully.

Zac thanked him and, as the waiter left, he raised his glass and smiled. 'Anyway…here's to you, Chloe Meadows, best PA ever.'

It was such a sudden turnabout, she knew she looked flustered and was possibly blushing. Again.

'I'm extremely grateful to you for agreeing to come here at such short notice,' Zac went on. 'And at such a difficult time of the year.'

As they clinked glasses, his smile was so sincere that Chloe gave a little laugh to cover her reaction.

'How could I turn down an all-expenses-paid trip to London?' she said, but she was actually wondering how Zac could be so exasperating one moment and then so charming the next.

After a sip of wine, which was exceptionally fine, she veered back to their previous discussion. Now that Zac had raised the thorny subject of marrying someone with the aid of a computer spreadsheet, it was like a prickle buried in her skin that she had to dig out. 'So I take it you don't believe in romance?' she challenged him again.

He shrugged. 'I think romance is problematical. I don't see how people can make a decision that lasts a lifetime based purely on their feelings. It's highly possible that there would be more successful marriages if everyone took a more practical approach.'

'Like arranged marriages?'

'Why not? They seem to work quite well in many cultures.'

Chloe took a deeper sip of her wine as she considered this. She had to admit it was true that arranged marriages often worked. Her parents' neighbours from Afghanistan were prime examples. The Hashimis' marriage had been arranged by their parents when they were still in their teens and they'd been happily together for forty years. In fact, Mr Hashimi seemed more devoted to his wife than ever.

'You know, you're *almost* making sense,' she said. 'Except—'

'Yes?' Zac prompted eagerly, but then the waiter appeared again with their meals.

Chloe was grateful for the interruption. She'd been about to say that she couldn't imagine many Australian women falling for Zac's scheme, but then she'd remembered the names in the list of his *Foolish Females* and she knew that quite a few of those girls would probably leap at the chance to marry her boss. After all, Zac Corrigan was exceptionally eligible.

'So it sounds as if you'd like to approach this marriage like a business strategy?' she said instead as she sprinkled croutons over her soup.

Zac nodded as he cut into his crusty pie to reveal rich dark meat and gravy. 'As a starting point, at least.'

'And how would you make your choice? Draw up a list of the attributes you want in this wife? Then try to find the perfect match from the *Fool*—from the list of girls you've already dated?'

'Exactly,' he said with a grin. 'I knew you'd come on board.'

An hour later, they were still in the pub.

Having finished their meals and drinks, they were onto their second cups of coffee, hoping to keep jet lag at bay for a little longer, and Chloe, to her own amazement, was helping to draw up Zac's list of wifely qualities.

'OK, let's see what you have so far.' She read from the

notes she'd typed into her phone. 'We—I mean *you*—want someone who's sensible—' She'd been majorly surprised that this had headed his list. 'Smart, sympathetic, reliable, has a sense of humour, likes kids, is not too loud…'

Zac nodded. 'That sounds about right.'

What about size eight and blonde? This described most of the girls he liked to date, but somehow Chloe restrained herself from asking this and took a kinder approach. 'I don't think you really need a database, Zac. You must already know which of your girlfriends has these qualities.'

A deep frown furrowed his brow as he stared at his coffee cup. 'It's hard to find them all in one person, though, isn't it?'

When he looked up, he seemed genuinely perplexed. 'Angie Davis has a great sense of humour and she's probably good with kids, but I'm not sure she's all that reliable. And Sasha Franks would run a terrific household, but she's a bit…cold.'

'What about Marissa Johnson?' Of all Zac's girlfriends, Chloe had liked Marissa the best. She was a very friendly young woman who worked in a sports store on the Gold Coast, and she had short dark hair and a natural, make-up-free glow of the outdoors about her, which made her a little different from his usual choices.

Zac, however, was shaking his head. 'Why does Marissa's name keep cropping up? You told me to invite her here to London and I said no then.'

Chloe shrugged. 'I just think she's really nice, the sort of girl I could be good friends with.' She smiled sheepishly.' But I don't suppose that's helpful to you.'

'Actually, you're probably right about Marissa.' He

sighed heavily. 'But of all the girls I know, she's probably the least likely to be interested in marrying me.'

'Are you sure?'

He nodded. 'I'm afraid I stuffed things up with her. I...er...kind of forgot to mention that I was still seeing someone else.'

Chloe groaned. 'For heaven's sake, Zac.'

He shrugged. 'The other girl was in Melbourne and it was only ever occasional, but Marissa still gave me the boot.'

Good for her, Chloe thought, but she kept the thought to herself. Instead, she found herself saying, 'You never know, she might forgive you if you asked very nicely. Putting a ring on her finger could make a world of difference.'

She wished she felt happier about offering that last piece of unasked-for advice. It didn't help that Zac's response was a gorgeously brooding smile that made her wonder what he was thinking.

Was he actually in love with Marissa?

Why should I care? It's not as if I want him for myself. Chloe knew she was far too sensible to make such a foolish mistake.

'I've never actually asked about *your* credentials,' Zac said suddenly.

'Mine?' A zap, like an electric spark, shot through Chloe. 'Wh-what d-do you mean?'

'Well, here I am seeking your advice and I don't even know if you're qualified. I know nothing about your social life. You're such a private girl, Chloe. I've never heard you mention going on a date.' He was looking at her now as if she was a very amusing riddle. 'For example…is there a boyfriend I should have apologised to when I dragged you away at Christmas?'

Chloe gulped. 'No—there's…er…no one at the moment.'

'You're a lovely girl…so there must be an explanation.'

Stifling her delight at his use of the word 'lovely', she decided that she wouldn't tell him about Sam. How could a man who didn't believe in romance possibly understand her pain, or why she'd retreated so completely from the dating scene?

Zac was still smiling, but the expression in his grey eyes was piercing now. It seemed to skewer her. 'You're not going to share that explanation, are you?' he said.

'No, I'd rather not.'

He frowned and, for the longest time, he regarded her with a look that was unexpectedly sympathetic, but, to Chloe's intense relief, he dropped the subject.

They walked back to their hotel through the gathering gloom of a wintry London afternoon. Street lights had already come on and the window displays made eye-catching splashes of colour.

Zac was beginning to feel a little better after a warming meal and a reasonably profitable chat with Chloe, as if he'd been trapped in a nightmare but was gradually finding his way out. He would certainly give the Marissa option more careful thought.

'I suppose you might have to think of a name for the baby,' Chloe said suddenly when they were about a block from their hotel.

'A name?' With a soft groan, Zac threw back his head

and stared helplessly up at the dark lowering clouds. 'I wouldn't have a clue where to begin.'

'Oh, I'm sure you'll have fun once you get started, Zac. There are so many pretty girls' names.'

'I guess.' But when he tried to think, he could only think of past girlfriends' names and he didn't want any of them. Beyond these, however, his mind drew a blank. 'Do you have any suggestions?'

Chloe laughed. 'Where do I start? Mind you, I'm no expert, but I think all the old classic names are still very popular—names like Emma and Sophie or Rose. Or, let me see, there's Isabella or simply Bella.'

'Bella's cute,' Zac admitted, thinking of the tiny pink-cheeked baby he'd been handed at the hospital.

'I guess you'd also want to choose something that went well with Corrigan.'

'Would I? Yes, I guess…'

'For example, Chloe Corrigan would sound a bit off.'

Inexplicably, Zac's chest tightened. 'Would it?'

'Definitely,' Chloe said gruffly. 'Too many Cs and Os. Although Kate or Katy might work. Katy Corrigan sounds catchy. Or maybe something pretty starting with M like Megan or Molly or Mia—or, if you wanted to be modern, you could go for something like Mackenzie.' His PA was obviously warming to this task.

'Molly,' Zac said quickly. 'I don't mind that. I don't know why, but the baby sort of looks like a Molly, doesn't she?'

Chloe turned to him. She was smiling, but her brown eyes were so soft and warm with emotion that the band around his chest pulled tighter.

'Molly's very cute,' she said. 'Or if you wanted to tie in a Christmas link, you could always go for Holly.'

'No, I'm warming to Molly,' Zac said. He liked to arrive at firm decisions. 'Molly Corrigan sounds all right, doesn't it? Or are there too many Os?'

'Molly's great.'

'Or Lucy. What about Lucy Corrigan? That sounds better, doesn't it?'

'Yes, Lucy's lovely,' Chloe said softly.

'Lucy Francesca Corrigan,' Zac refined, proud of his sudden inspiration.

'Oh, Francesca's gorgeous. What made you think of it?'

'It was my mother's name, although most people just called her Fran or Frannie.'

'It would be very fitting to name the baby after her grandmother. Lucy Francesca's so pretty. I love it!'

'Excellent. We can sleep on it and see if we still like it in the morning.'

For a moment, Zac thought he saw a glistening dampness in his PA's eyes, but she turned quickly to study another shop window, so he couldn't be sure.

He wondered if he'd said something wrong.

CHAPTER FIVE

ZAC WASTED NO time in getting to the share house the next morning. Having finally succumbed to jet lag on the previous evening, he and Chloe had opted to skip dinner in favour of much needed sleep and, consequently, they'd both woken early. A hearty hotel breakfast and a Tube ride later, they stood outside the house Liv had shared for the past twelve months.

Zac had no idea what to expect, but he wasn't totally surprised when his knock was answered by a girl with purple hair and a silver ring through her nose.

'Good morning,' he said rather formally. 'I spoke to someone called Skye on the phone.'

'Yeah,' the girl said. 'That's me.'

Zac lifted the empty suitcase he'd brought to collect Liv's belongings. 'I'm Zac Corrigan.'

Skye's face broke into an unexpectedly warm smile. 'Lovely to meet you, Zac.' She offered her hand, complete with black nail polish. 'Liv told us so much about you.'

'Really?' He couldn't hold back his surprise.

'Yeah, of course she did. She was dead proud of you, you know.'

But as she said this, her eyes filled with tears and—dammit—Zac felt his own eyes begin to sting.

'Come on in,' Skye said in a choked voice, blinking hard as she opened the door wider and stepped back to make room for them. 'Pete and Shaz have both left already for work.'

'We're not holding you up, are we?'

She shook her head. 'I don't work Saturdays.'

In the narrow hallway a faint smell of incense lingered. Zac introduced Chloe.

'Pleased to meet you.' Skye smiled now and regarded Chloe with interest. 'Are you Zac's girlfriend?'

'PA,' Zac and Chloe said together.

The girl gave a slightly puzzled frown, then shrugged and headed down the hall, nodding for them to follow.

'We miss Liv so much,' she said over her shoulder. 'But you must know that, Zac. You know what she was like. Such a live wire and always so lovely and kind.'

'Yes,' Zac said faintly as they entered the lounge room, which wasn't nearly as dilapidated as he'd expected.

The furniture was almost certainly second-hand and the sofa was draped in a hand-knitted shawl of red and purple wool, while the walls were hung with huge amateurish paintings in equally bright and gaudy oils. But everything was clean and tidy and the overall effect was surprisingly appealing. Artistic and cosy.

'Before I show you Liv's room,' Skye said, 'I thought I should mention that Father Tom dropped by last night.' Her eyes widened with the importance of this news. 'He said he could squeeze in a funeral on Monday morning, even though it's Christmas Eve…' The girl looked from Zac to Chloe. 'That is, if you'd like a church funeral.'

Zac hoped he didn't look as surprised as he felt. Avoiding Chloe's gaze, he asked, 'Did—did Liv attend church?'

'Oh, yeah.' The look Skye gave him was almost pitying. 'Every Sunday morning and on Wednesday evenings as well. We all go together. It's lovely.'

'Um…what kind of church?' he dared to ask.

'Oh, you can check it out for yourself, Zac. It's the little chapel around the corner. Father Tom's marvellous. You should see the work he does in the streets around here.'

'I see.' Zac swallowed. 'I'm afraid I had no idea about this. I've…er…made arrangements with a funeral director for a cremation.'

'But wouldn't you want a church service with Liv's friends as well?'

He realised he'd given no thought to the friends Liv might have made. She'd only been in England a year and he'd somehow pictured her wandering around with the guy from the band, pretty much alone and drifting…

Somewhat dazed, he looked Chloe's way and she immediately smiled and sent him an encouraging nod.

'A church service would be…perfect,' he said.

'Wonderful. I'll give Father Tom a ring, shall I?'

'Thank you.'

'Right. It's this way to Liv's room.' Skye was pointing. 'Feel free to take any or all of her things. Anything left, we can sort out.' Her voice wobbled and suddenly there were tears in her eyes again and her nose was distinctly pink. 'And stay as long as you like.'

'Thank you. You're very kind.' Still feeling dazed, Zac went to the doorway and then came to an abrupt halt when he saw his sister's room.

As a teenager, Liv's bedroom had always been a dive, with the bed unmade and clothes left lying on the floor where she'd climbed out of them, the waste basket overflowing with scrunched balls of paper and drink cans. For Zac, the messy room had been a constant battleground, but in the end he'd hated carrying on like an Army sergeant major and he'd given up trying to get her to tidy it.

In this room, the bed was covered by a smooth, spotless white spread and there was an arrangement of bright flowers in a vase on the bedside table. On top of a chest of drawers sat a small yellow teddy bear and neatly folded piles of baby clothing. Beside that a collection of toiletries…talcum powder and baby lotion and a glass jar filled with snowy cotton wool balls.

Taking pride of place in the corner stood a white bassinet of woven cane made up with clean sheets and with a soft pink blanket folded over one side, ready and waiting for a tiny occupant.

Stunned, Zac sagged against the doorpost.

The room said it all. His little sister had grown up and changed beyond recognition. Liv had found a true home here in London and she'd obviously been looking forward to motherhood. All evidence pointed to the fact that she'd planned to be a perfect mother, until fate cruelly robbed her of that chance, that *right*.

Without warning, he was swamped by a fresh deluge of sorrow and his chest swelled to bursting point as he felt his heart break all over again. He had no hope of holding back his tears.

It was a while later when he heard Chloe whisper softly behind him, 'Zac.'

He felt her hand on his arm, rubbing him through

his coat sleeve, and he found her touch unexpectedly comforting.

Straightening, he scrubbed a hand over his face. 'Sorry. I'm afraid I lost it again.'

'Oh, don't worry,' she said, swiping at her eyes. 'I've been blubbing, too.'

'It was such a shock.' He waved a hand at the room. 'I wasn't expecting this. Everything's so damn...*neat*.' He managed a broken laugh.

'It's charming,' Chloe said. 'Picture perfect.'

'The little monkey. Liv would never tidy a thing for me.'

They both laughed shakily, and stood looking about them. Then, drawing a deep breath, Zac set down the empty suitcase on a mat at the end of the bed. 'If only I had a clue where to start.'

Chloe crossed the room to the chest of drawers. 'I guess you'll definitely need these baby things.' She picked up the top item of clothing and held it out to him.

It was the tiniest singlet he'd ever seen. 'Wow, it's so little.'

'It's minuscule,' Chloe whispered, sharing his awe.

'I can't imagine trying to dress a wriggling baby in that,' Zac added with mild alarm.

Chloe smiled, but made no comment and he thought how lovely she looked. Actually...what man wouldn't be entranced by those shapely legs, that shiny, touchable hair? And how could he ignore the lovely warmth of her dark brown eyes? Bizarrely, in the midst of these saddest of circumstances, Zac found himself wondering why he'd always been so black and white about the boundaries he maintained with his PA.

'I'll get started, shall I?' she said, turning to open

the top drawer. 'I'm assuming you'll only take the baby clothes?'

'I think so.'

'There are plenty here. It looks like Liv was well prepared.'

Zac nodded and pledged to concentrate on the task at hand. 'If we set Liv's clothes to one side, Skye will know what to do with them.'

'But you'll want to keep things like this, Zac.'

'Like what?'

Chloe was holding out a small blue album. 'Take a look,' she said, sending him a significant glance.

It was a photo album, he quickly realised as he turned to the first page. It showed a professional photograph of his family taken in a studio when he was around ten.

His mother had used this photo to make a personalised Christmas card, he remembered. And there his mother was…looking youthful and beautiful with short dark hair and lively grey-green eyes, and wearing her favourite dress of tailored green linen.

Beside her, his father was wearing a white business shirt and dark trousers with a maroon tie. His father's hair had already started to grey at the temples, but his face was tanned from all the time he spent outdoors in the bush, tracking down the plants and animals that were endangered by extensive mining.

His mum had dressed them all in Christmas colours, so Zac was wearing a dark red polo shirt with pale chinos, while Liv, aged two, was in a white dress with a green and red tartan sash. Zac smiled, remembering how hard it had been to get Liv to sit still for the photo.

Now…they were all gone.

He was the only one left…and, suddenly, looking

at the photo was unbearable. He shut the album with a snap. He'd had more than enough heartbreak for one day.

Without speaking, he walked over to the suitcase and dropped the album into it. Chloe glanced at it and then up at him, but she didn't say a word. Her eloquent dark eyes told him that she understood. For that, he almost hugged her.

It was as they were leaving and thanking Skye yet again that Zac remembered to ask, 'Do you know if Liv had any names chosen for the baby?'

Skye laughed. 'She had hundreds. You should have seen the lists. Liv knew she was having a girl, of course.'

'Did she have a favourite name?'

'Not as far as I could tell. The name seemed to change almost every day. The only thing Liv was certain about was that she wanted her mother's name, Francesca, for the middle name.'

'Ah…' Zac caught Chloe's eye and they shared a smile and he felt an unexpected glow inside. It was incredibly reassuring to know that his first important decision about the baby had been on the right track.

'Are you going to check out the church?' Chloe asked when they were once again outside.

'Yes, good idea. I wouldn't mind meeting this Father Ted, too, if he's around.'

'Tom,' Chloe corrected. 'Father Tom.'

Zac grinned. 'Thanks, Ms Meadows. I suppose the chances of finding him on a Saturday morning are slim.'

They saw the tiny stone church as soon as they rounded the corner. Surrounded by a narrow fringe of green lawn, it was like a relic from the past, smack bang next to a row of brightly painted modern shops.

The front door of the church was open, offering an enticing glimpse of a nativity scene, complete with a stable and straw and a plaster donkey. When Zac and Chloe detoured around it, they found two women in the church's darkened interior, arranging white gladioli and bunches of holly in tall copper urns.

'I was hoping to find Father Tom,' Zac told the nearest woman.

She nodded towards a small wooden arch-shaped door in the far wall. 'Over there in the vestry.'

'Thank you.'

'He's very busy with Christmas and everything, and there'll be a wedding here in an hour or so.'

'I won't take up much of his time.'

As he turned to head off, Chloe held out her hand for the suitcase. 'I'll look after that.'

'OK, thanks.' Leaving Chloe sitting in a pew, Zac realised how quickly he'd become used to having her right beside him. *Almost as if…*

He cut off that thought before it distracted him from the task at hand.

At the vestry he gave two short knocks and the door was opened by a young sandy-haired fellow in jeans and a black knitted sweater.

'Hi there,' he said. 'How can I help you?'

'I was hoping to speak to Father Tom.'

The young man grinned. 'And so you are.'

This was Father Tom? Zac swallowed his shock. He'd expected a grey-haired old fellow, possibly stooped and wearing spectacles. This Father Tom, with his designer stubble and flashing blue eyes and no hint of a dog collar, looked more like a rock star than a priest.

'How can I help you?' Father Tom asked.

'I'm Zac Corrigan. I—'

'Zac, of course, of course… Wonderful to meet you. Come on in.' The young priest opened the door wider and stepped back. 'Take a seat,' he added as he scooped a pile of hymn books from a chair.

Once the books were deposited on a crammed shelf, he held out his hand. 'Please accept my condolences.' His hand gripped Zac's firmly. 'Liv was an amazing girl, just wonderful. We're all devastated.'

'I'm very grateful that you've offered to fit in a funeral for her at such short notice.'

'Only too happy to help.' Father Tom sat behind his desk, pushed some paperwork aside and leaned forward, hands clasped. 'Is there anything else I can do for you while you're here?'

Zac deliberately tried to relax, with an ankle propped on a knee. 'I know you can't break confidence,' he said carefully. 'But I wondered if Liv ever spoke to you about the baby's father.'

'About his identity?'

'Yes.'

Father Tom shook his head. 'I had no luck there, I'm afraid. Of course, I did raise the question with Liv. I asked her if the father was going to be able to help her or at least support her. She was straight upfront and said that this was *her* baby and she would be the one to care for it. The father was completely out of the scene.'

Zac realised he'd been holding his breath and now he let it out slowly, surprised by an unexpected sense of relief. He wasn't sure how or when it had happened but, some time in the past twenty-four hours, he'd arrived at a point of acceptance and his feelings about the baby had changed. He would be disappointed now if a strange man stepped up to claim her.

'Of course I did talk to Liv about the challenges of being a single mother so far from home,' the priest said. 'I was concerned about her secrecy and I probed to make quite sure that she didn't want the father's help. She assured me that the baby's father hadn't abused her in any way. In fact, she impressed on me that he wasn't a bad guy, but she said she'd put a lot of thought into her future and she knew exactly what she was doing.'

He fixed Zac with a steady gaze. 'She liked to talk about her family and she told me all about you.'

'Her annoying big brother.'

Father Tom gave a smiling shrug.

'She never told me about her pregnancy.'

'Ah, yes, Liv admitted that. She seemed to think she'd given you enough worry over the years. She knew you would have felt compelled to rush over here and to—'

'Interfere,' supplied Zac, tight-lipped.

This brought another sympathetic smile. 'Micro-manage, perhaps.'

Zac nodded. He knew Liv was right. He would have been over here like a shot, bossing her around, trying to order her to come home.

'Liv certainly planned to tell you once the baby was born. She said—I want to show Zac that I can be a brilliant mum and I want him to be finally proud of me.'

Finally? Zac cringed and the back of his neck burned. 'I was already proud of her,' he said gruffly. 'I might have been bossy, but I—I loved her.'

Damn it, he was *not* going to break down again, and certainly not in front of this man.

'I know you loved her,' Father Tom said gently. 'And

I'm sure Liv knew it, too. She was looking forward to showing you her baby. She told me that she couldn't wait to meet you at Heathrow and she fantasised about the moment she handed you your little niece.'

Oh, God. Zac groaned with the effort of holding himself together. Somehow he managed to lurch to his feet and thank Father Tom for his time. They spoke briefly about the service on Monday.

'Thanks for calling in, Zac. I'll see you then.'

They said farewell and Zac was still shaking inside as he strode back through the church to Chloe.

'No leads on the baby's father,' he said tersely and he was infinitely grateful that Chloe didn't press him with further questions as they went outside, where the clouds had parted at last to reveal a glimmer of pale English sunshine.

Chloe knew Zac was tense after his discussion with the clergyman. As the Tube train rushed back into the city, she tried to talk about practical things.

'I don't think we need to buy many more clothes for the baby, unless we see something *really* cute. I've done a little research on the Net and, for now, I think we probably only need formula and bottles and a steriliser, although we should check with the airline to see what they provide for babies on long haul flights.'

'Yeah, and I suppose we'd better ring the hospital and arrange a time to collect Lucy.' Zac looked a little self-conscious as he said the baby's name and Chloe gave him an encouraging smile.

Unfortunately, the look in his eyes when he returned her smile made her stomach drop as if she'd plunged from a great height.

Which was a definite problem. She'd had a few too many of these moments recently. Spending so much time with Zac was taking its toll.

She told herself that it was only natural, that sharing his personal tragedy was bound to have an impact on her own emotions. But now she was beginning to worry about the future. After this time in London, it was going to be so hard to return to their former strictly boss-PA relationship.

It would be hard for her, at least. She would remember all the emotional moments when her feelings for Zac had felt so much deeper and sweeter. Quite possibly, Zac would have no difficulty, though. He was pretty much an expert at keeping his business and personal life in separate compartments.

For Chloe, however, it had become increasingly clear that the sooner she got back to Brisbane and normality, the better. She was thinking about this when she asked, 'Would you like to collect Lucy this afternoon?'

'I don't think so,' Zac answered slowly, as if he was giving the matter careful thought. 'I hope this doesn't sound selfish, but I feel as if I need a little more time to adjust.'

'How much time?' Chloe asked cautiously.

'A decade?'

She must have looked shocked and Zac laughed. 'A joke, Ms Meadows. Don't worry. I'll speak to the hospital about collecting her tomorrow. In the meantime...' His eyes suddenly gleamed with unexpected merriment. 'I think we've earned ourselves a night out, don't you?'

An unhelpful fizzing raced along her veins, as if they were filled with champagne. 'I...I'm not sure,' she said. A night out sounded risky.

Zac frowned at her. 'Surely you don't want to squander this perfect chance to enjoy a Saturday night in London town?'

Even to sensible Chloe it did seem like a wasted opportunity, and she found it especially difficult to voice her very reasonable concerns when her less sensible self was jumping up and down like an excited child.

'Of course you don't,' Zac answered for her. 'We'll have a fabulous night. It's my last night of freedom and it's your duty as my employee to help me enjoy it.'

Before she could summon an effective protest, the train pulled into Oxford Circus and Zac launched to his feet, so the subject was dropped until they'd battled their way out of the crowded Underground and found themselves once more on the footpath.

By then Zac had it all planned and he was quite exuberant. Even though it was at the last minute, he was sure he could wangle a table for two at a good restaurant.

'And what about theatre tickets?' he asked Chloe now, his eyes shining with expectation. 'What sort of show do you feel like seeing? I must admit I could do with a little comedy.'

'Definitely comedy.' Clearly, there was no point in trying to argue about going out with him for the evening. 'We've had enough of real life drama.'

'Great.' Zac was almost boyish in his excitement. 'We'll go shopping this afternoon to buy clothes—for ourselves, not for the baby. We don't have to worry about sticking to carry-on luggage for the journey home. We'll have the suitcase with Lucy's things, anyway, so why not lash out? I'll pay for your new outfit, of course.'

'No,' Chloe said swiftly and firmly.

Zac stopped abruptly and a pedestrian hurrying behind them almost bumped into him. 'Don't be silly, Chloe.' He reached for her hand, but she slipped it into her coat pocket.

'Now you're being stubborn. This night out is my idea.' Zac ignored the pedestrians streaming around them. His attention was solely on Chloe. 'Let me buy you a dress and hang the expense. Think of it as a thank you gift for everything you've—'

'No,' Chloe said again, even more firmly to make sure he got the message. 'Thank you very much, Zac. It's an extremely kind offer, but I can't let you buy me clothes.'

This was one line she knew she mustn't cross. It was the difference between being his PA and a member of his chorus line of girlfriends.

'It's just a dress, Chloe.' Zac's smile was charming now. Bone-meltingly charming.

Chloe could feel her skin warming and her limbs growing languorous. It would be so easy to give in, but she had to remember that this was the special smile Zac used to conquer his countless female victims.

'Chloe, come on, loosen up. You're in London, for heaven's sake. You can't be in London without buying at least one new dress.'

He was right about that, she conceded. She would regret it later if she arrived home without some kind of memento, and what better than a chic new dress from London's famous Oxford Street?

'I was planning to buy a dress anyway,' she said.

Without dropping the smile, Zac narrowed his eyes at her. 'No, you weren't.'

'Of course I was.' She lifted her chin for emphasis and kept her expression deadpan. 'It'll be my Christmas present to myself.'

CHAPTER SIX

BY THE TIME Chloe carried her shopping bags back to her hotel room she felt quite sick. She couldn't believe she'd spent so much money. On one dress.

The expense was almost obscene. She should never have tried the dress on, but as soon as she'd entered the store she'd been seduced, and she hadn't looked at the price tag until it was far too late.

The knee-length dress with cap sleeves had looked so simple and demure on its hanger. Admittedly, it was a bold red and Chloe had never worn such a bright colour before. She usually stuck to soft pinks or browns, but it was Christmas after all, and she was in a mood to be daring. And as soon as she'd stepped into the changing room and slipped the dress on, her senses had instantly fallen under its spell.

The silk lining whispered against her skin like a lover's kiss and when she closed the underarm zip, the dress settled around her like a second skin. Then she'd turned to the mirror and experienced a true *oh-my-God* surprise.

Was that really her?

How could one dress make such a transformation? The bright red seemed to give her complexion a fresh glow and the scooped neckline enhanced the line of her collarbone and décolletage so that she looked… amazing.

As for the fit of the dress, Chloe had no idea how the designer had done it, but he'd managed to give her an hourglass figure. In a blink she'd become positively vain. She couldn't help it. She twisted this way and that, looking at herself from every angle. She'd never dreamed she could look so good and she knew there was no question. She simply *had* to have this dress. She couldn't possibly walk out of the store without it.

It was only after she'd arrived at this decision that she reached for the label and tried to read the price with the help of the mirror. At first she thought she'd made a mistake—she'd read the price upside-down, or back to front or something—so she was still feeling reasonably calm as she took the dress off, once again delighting in the cool slide of the silken lining over her skin.

With the dress back on its hanger, she looked at the price tag again. And almost had a heart attack.

Just as well there was a seat in the changing room or she might have keeled over.

Huddling on the seat in her undies, Chloe wanted to cry. She'd fallen in love with the red dress. While she was wearing it, she'd been quite certain that the designer had dreamed it up just for *her*.

But, dear Lord, the price was horrendous. Normally, she could buy six dresses for that amount and, with the current exchange rate, it would be even worse in Aussie dollars.

A small voice whispered: *That's why this dress looks ten times better on you than any of your old ones.*

And then, in the next breath, Chloe pictured the expression in Zac's eyes when he saw her in this dress, and that was probably about the time her synapses fused and she stopped thinking clearly. She simply got back into her clothes, marched to the counter and handed over her credit card.

Now, as she hung her purchase in the hotel wardrobe, she tried to ignore the sick feeling in the pit of her stomach. She consoled herself that she'd got a bargain with the black platform heels she'd bought to complete the outfit. And she told herself she'd atoned for her sins by buying a beautiful expensive silk scarf for her mother and an equally costly cashmere pullover for her dad.

And now the only sensible thing was to make sure she enjoyed this evening. Surely that couldn't be too hard?

In fact, it was impossible not to enjoy herself. Zac had bought himself a new dark grey suit which he teamed with a fine grey turtleneck instead of a traditional white shirt, which meant that his already devastating good looks now took on an extra sexy European appeal. Chloe found herself staring. And staring some more.

Of course, Zac did quite a bit of staring, too, especially when they arrived at the romantic candlelit restaurant in Piccadilly and Chloe removed her coat.

After he recovered from his initial dropped-jaw shock, he stared at her with an almost bewildered smile, as if he couldn't quite get over the surprise of seeing her all dressed up.

Illogically, Chloe wanted to cry. The look in Zac's eyes was so out of character. So unguarded and intimate...and *unsettling*.

'Ms Meadows, you've outdone yourself,' he murmured and he didn't drag his shimmering gaze from her till the waiter cleared his throat.

'Sir? If you'll come this way, I'll show you to your table...'

'Yes, yes. Thank you.' Zac sent Chloe a wink, as if to cover any embarrassment, and he touched his hand to her elbow ever so lightly to indicate that she should go ahead of him.

To her dismay, his touch set off flashes and sparks and she almost tripped as they wound their way through the tables.

It was a relief to be finally seated but, throughout the meal, Zac's eyes revealed a range of emotions as his initial shock gave way to amused delight, and finally to a more serious smouldering heat that stole Chloe's breath and set her pulses drumming.

Later, she could barely remember the meal although, of course, everything was delicious. She was too absorbed in the experience of being with Zac in such a romantic setting. Everything was so different—their vast distance from Australia, her red dress, the romantic Christmas decorations—and for one night she stopped thinking of herself as his PA. She was a woman very much enjoying the company of an exceptionally handsome and charming man.

Zac was, not surprisingly, an excellent conversationalist, and once they'd been through the typical chat about favourite books and movies, Chloe encouraged him to talk about himself. He told her how, when Liv was three, his family had lived on an island on the Great Barrier Reef for two years while his mother studied, among other things, the nesting habit of sea turtles.

His father couldn't be with them all the time, apparently, because of his work in the central Queensland coalfields, so he used to fly in and out from the island in a seaplane, which also delivered the family's provisions.

To Chloe, who'd only ever lived in the same small house in a Brisbane suburb, this life sounded wonderfully adventurous and romantic. Zac had lived in a timber cottage perched on a hill overlooking the Coral Sea, and from his bedroom he could reach out of the window to pick coconuts. His mother had taught him how to skin dive, and at night she'd built campfires on the beach and, while Liv was curled asleep in her lap, she'd taught Zac all about the stars and planets.

'It's a wonder you didn't become a scientist, too,' Chloe said.

Zac shrugged. 'I started out studying marine science but, after my parents' boat disappeared, I—' A corner of his mouth tilted in a briefly awkward smile. 'I needed to try something completely different.'

'At which you're equally brilliant,' she told him warmly.

His eyes shimmered again as he smiled at her. 'Thank you, Ms Meadows,' he said with exaggerated modesty.

But Chloe was sure that talking about his family couldn't be easy and, as they dug their spoons into a shared dessert of sinfully divine chocolate mousse, she directed the conversation to Lucy. 'Would you like her to have an adventurous childhood like yours?'

'You know, I almost want her life to be boring,' Zac said.

Chloe couldn't help herself. 'That would be such a shame.'

'But boring's safe.'

'It might be safe,' she responded, perhaps a little too vehemently. 'But it's certainly not fun.'

Now Zac regarded her thoughtfully before he helped himself to another spoonful of mousse. 'Sounds to me like you're speaking from experience.'

'I'm afraid I am.'

Of course, he wanted her to explain about this, which was how she ended up telling him about her parents—how her dad had worked in a hardware store and her mum was a teacher's aide, how they'd married late and never expected to have a family, so when baby Chloe arrived at the last moment, she had been a complete and bewildering surprise for them.

'My parents were already very set in their ways, so it was a very quiet life,' she said. 'Mum gave up work to stay at home with me and we didn't have much money, so we didn't go out very much, or entertain, and we only went on holidays every second year. Then it was always to the same place, Maroochydore. I love the beach, of course, but I was too shy to make new friends, so I used to sit under a beach umbrella with my parents and watch the other kids having fun.'

She rolled her eyes. 'I know, I know…that makes me sound like such a loser.'

'A loner, perhaps,' Zac said kindly. 'But hardly a loser.'

'It's not what you'd want for Lucy, though.'

He smiled. 'I guess I'll have to aim for some kind of middle ground.'

A picture flashed into Chloe's thoughts of Zac and Lucy with Marissa Johnson, sharing a new 'middle ground' life together. She found the thought incredibly depressing, so it was probably just as well that they'd reached the bottom of the chocolate mousse and Zac checked his phone for the time.

'We'd better get cracking,' he said. 'Our show's starting soon.'

He took Chloe's hand as they left the restaurant. She knew it was only practical to hold hands as they hurried through the crowds in Piccadilly Circus but, as they passed beneath a dazzling wonderland of Christmas lights, she was excruciatingly conscious of his strong fingers interlinked with hers. She'd almost forgotten the heart-zapping intimacy of even the smallest amount of skin contact.

Then they were in the warmth of the theatre, taking off their coats and settling into comfy velvet-upholstered seats, with all the attendant excitement of the lights being dimmed and the curtain rising...

'My sides are aching from laughing so much,' Chloe said as they stood outside afterwards, waiting for a taxi.

'Mine, too,' said Zac. 'I can't remember the last time I laughed so hard.'

'I'm so glad you picked a comedy.'

'Yeah, laughter's certainly good medicine.'

They were freezing on the footpath, but the air was crystal-clear. Above them stretched a network of lights in the shapes of stars, snowflakes and angels that made the night even more enchanting.

Chloe was still feeling relaxed and happy when they reached their hotel, which was probably why she didn't object when Zac suggested a nightcap in the bar.

'Here, allow me,' he said, stilling her hands with his as she was unbuttoning her coat.

At his touch, she froze, and her heart began thumping as she looked up at him.

The world seemed to stand still and she was trapped by his smiling silver-grey eyes.

'I've been dying to do this all night,' he said softly.

She couldn't breathe as she dropped her gaze to his hands, as she watched his long fingers slowly undo each button, as he gently slipped the coat from her shoulders and let his gaze travel deliberately over her.

'You know this dress is…magnificent.'

Chloe could feel a blush rising from her neck to her cheeks.

'I'm so glad you wouldn't let me pay for it,' Zac said.

'Why is that?'

'You would have chosen something sensible and inexpensive and not nearly as attractive as this.'

Now she couldn't help smiling. Seemed her boss knew her only too well.

'Actually, I have a better idea,' Zac said next as he looked around him at the rather crowded bar. 'Let's not have a drink here. We should go upstairs and get room service.'

And, just like that, alarm bells began clamouring in Chloe's ears—loud and clear—a reality check as effective as the clock at midnight for Cinderella.

There was no way she could share late night drinks in her playboy boss's hotel room. But, before she could insist on staying at the bar, Zac took off for the lift, still carrying her coat. She hurried after him, planning to drag him back, but the lift doors were already opening and there were other guests inside. She didn't want to make a scene so she held her tongue until they reached their floor and were out in the corridor.

'Zac, I don't need a nightcap,' she told him quietly but decisively as they arrived at the door to her room.

He tipped his head to one side with the look a parent might give to a troublesome child. 'You're not going to be a spoilsport.'

Chloe sighed. She should have guessed that this would happen and she should have had a strategy already planned. 'Look, tonight's been wonderful. I've had a fabulous time, but we both need to remember this isn't a date.'

'But it so easily could be.'

This was true and in the confined space of the hallway Chloe could smell Zac's cologne, musky and expensive and very masculine. When she looked up, she saw that his jaw was now lined by an attractive five o'clock shadow.

Help! She was still tingling and zapping from having him take off her coat. Anything more intimate would probably cause her to self-combust.

This was such a dangerous moment. She only had to give the slightest hint of acceptance and Zac Corrigan would be kissing her. And she couldn't pretend that she didn't want to be kissed. It was such a long, long time since she'd been in a man's arms…and this wasn't just any man. It was *Zac!* His lips were so close, so scrumptious, so wonderfully tempting.

The air between them was crackling and sizzling. At any moment, he was going to lean in…

Now she was struggling to remember why this was wrong. *I'll only be another of his Foolish Females.*

'Zac, we can't—'

'Shh.' He touched her arm, sending dizzying warmth

washing over her skin. 'Forget about the office for one night.'

'How can I? How can *you*?'

'Easy,' he said as his thumb rode a sensuous track over her bare arm. 'Tonight you're not my PA and I'm not your boss.'

'But we—'

'Chloe, you're an incredibly sexy woman in a gloriously sexy red dress and I'm the poor, helpless guy who's absolutely smitten by you.'

His words sent shivery heat rushing over her skin. She longed to give in. She was only human after all and Zac was a ridiculously attractive man and she'd been half in love with him for the past three years.

And in the past few days she'd learned so much more to like about him. She'd seen past the handsome façade to the vulnerable boy who'd lost his family and still longed for the safety and security of belonging.

But the yearning that filled her now had little to do with respect or friendship. It was pure and simple lust and all Chloe wanted to do was say yes… She was sinking beneath an overwhelming temptation to close her eyes and lift her face to his.

Why shouldn't she? Just about any girl in her situation would.

What the heck? they'd say. *Why not have some fun for one night? What happens in London stays in London…*

Problem was…while Chloe had been half in love with Zac for all this time, she'd also felt smugly superior to the girls who'd fallen head over heels for him. She'd watched those girls from the sidelines and she knew all too well that one blissful night could so easily lead to weeks and months of regret.

There were so many ways that love could hurt and she'd taken ages to get over Sam's death. She was terrified of risking another version of that heartbreak and pain.

It was so hard to be sensible though. So hard when Zac was a heartbeat away from kissing her... When he was looking at her with a breath-robbing intensity.

'Chloe, has anyone ever told you, you have the most amazing—'

In panic, she pressed a hand to his lips, shutting off the rest of his sentence—which was a pity because she was actually desperate to hear why he thought she was amazing. But it was time to toughen up, time to summon every ounce of her willpower. She lifted her face. 'I have one word for you, Mr Corrigan.'

Zac smiled. 'Please, let it be yes.'

She eyed him sternly. 'Marissa.'

His smile vanished as if the name had landed in his chest like a smart bomb.

'Or, if not Marissa,' Chloe went on, needing to make her message clear, 'substitute the name of whichever girl you decide to marry. *That girl* is where your focus should be.'

She felt terrible though, especially when she heard the shudder of Zac's indrawn breath.

'Good shot, Ms Meadows,' he said softly, and then, with a heavy sigh, he took a step back. From a safer distance, he regarded her with a shakily rueful smile. 'I should have remembered that I can always rely on you to be sensible.'

'That's what you pay me for,' Chloe said crisply and then she turned quickly to open her door. 'As I said, I've had a fabulous evening, so thanks again, Zac, and...and goodnight.'

Without looking back, she stepped inside and closed the door swiftly before she weakened and did something very foolish.

Safely inside, she sagged against the closed door and saw her lovely lamplit room in front of her. *Don't think!*

On the other side of the door Zac was still holding her coat, but it was too bad. She would collect it in the morning. She couldn't see him again now. Not when stupid, stupid tears were streaming down her cheeks.

That was a very close shave.

Zac was scowling as he stared at Chloe's closed door. He'd almost lost his head and broken his own golden rule.

Tonight you're not my PA and I'm not your boss.

How could he have said that?

How could he have been so crass? With Chloe, of all people? His invaluable, irreplaceable Chloe.

He knew she already had zero tolerance when it came to his love life, and now he'd just proven to her that her low opinion was justified.

Damn it. How the hell had his plans to marry someone like Marissa slipped so easily out of his head?

Of course, everything might have followed its proper course tonight if Chloe had stuck to being Chloe. But she'd morphed into a goddess in the sexiest red dress on the planet.

Sure, Zac had always known that Chloe was an attractive young woman, but she'd always been safe as his conservative, efficient PA. Beautiful, yes, but a bit distant and shy. He'd never guessed she had the confidence to dress so glamorously, to reveal herself as a truly sensual, feminine woman.

Tonight's dress had been perfect on her. The rich red had given extra glowing warmth to her complexion, enhancing the lustre of her hair and the dark beauty of her eyes.

And as for the figure-hugging lines and the beguiling scooped neckline...

Zac had been stunned. Transfixed. It was the only explanation he could summon for why he'd stepped over the boss-PA line. For a moment there, he'd allowed himself to acknowledge his secret desire for Chloe. Truth be told, his feelings had felt way deeper than the mere desire he felt for his usual girlfriends.

But Chloe had promptly broken the strange hypnotic spell that gripped him and all it had taken was one word.

In a blink he was thudding back to earth, to his real life, to his new responsibilities, to the way the world would be for him from now on and for ever after.

He supposed he should be grateful to Chloe for reminding him, and for remaining so consistent and sensible. He *was* grateful, or at least he probably would be grateful...eventually...

Now, with a sigh of frustration, Zac unlocked the door to his room and went inside, tossing his and Chloe's coats into an armchair. He let out another sigh as he stood, hands on hips, staring down at the coats as they lay in a pool of lamplight—entangled—with a sleeve of Chloe's coat looped over the shoulder of his coat. Like an embrace.

Mocking him for his foolishness.

It was back to business at breakfast in the hotel dining room next morning. Last night's flirtatious smiles and warm camaraderie were safely relegated to the past.

Chloe was pleased that Zac was cool and serious again—at least she told herself she was pleased, just as she told herself she was relieved that he made no teasing or personal remarks as she started on her melon and yoghurt, while he tucked into his full English breakfast.

Apparently, Zac had even been up early and had already made phone calls to both the airlines and the hospital.

'I've decided that we don't need to buy a car seat while we're here,' he said, getting straight down to business. 'The requirements for fitting them into vehicles are slightly different from country to country. And apparently it's easy enough to get a taxi that's set up for a baby. As for the airlines, they provide bassinets and facilities for heating bottles or whatever.'

Chloe nodded. 'Let's hope Lucy doesn't cry too much during the flight.'

'Indeed,' he agreed gravely.

It was a daunting prospect, flying to the other side of the world with a brand new baby.

Zac frowned. 'Do you think three days will be enough time for us to get used to managing her here before we fly home?'

'Three days? Does that mean you're planning to fly home on Boxing Day?'

'As long as the passport comes through in time. Thank heavens you had the forethought to contact that brilliant agency before we left Brisbane. They've broken all records in fast-tracking Lucy's passport, because of our special circumstances. So do you think Boxing Day will work?'

'It should be fine, I guess.' Chloe was quite sure they shouldn't delay their London stay for a second longer than necessary. And she knew Zac must be eager to get home. He had a great deal to organise when he arrived in Australia—including the procurement of a suitable wife. 'As Lucy's so tiny, she might do a lot of sleeping,' she suggested hopefully.

'Yes, fingers crossed.' Zac handed her a sheet of note-paper. 'I asked the hospital about bottles and formula et cetera. Apparently, we should have collected a checklist, but I've jotted down the things we'll need.'

Chloe scanned the list as she sipped her coffee. Fortunately, she was used to reading Zac's scratchy handwriting. She nodded. 'I noticed there's a pharmacy nearby, so I'll get all these things straight after breakfast.'

'Great.' Zac lifted the coffee pot. 'Like a top-up?'

'Just half a cup, thanks.'

As he concentrated on pouring, he said, 'There is one other difficulty that we haven't discussed.'

'What's that?'

He kept his gaze focused on the coffee pot as he filled his own cup. 'We need to decide where Lucy should sleep.'

'Oh, yes.' This problem had occurred to Chloe, but she'd promptly dismissed it as far too awkward. Now it had to be faced.

Obviously, while they stayed in the hotel, Lucy would be installed in either her room or Zac's. But the big question was—which room was appropriate? Zac was Lucy's official guardian and uncle, but could a bachelor be expected to cope with a newborn baby on his own? Zac had been terrified of simply holding Lucy at the hospital.

'I understand small babies wake at all hours of the night,' he said. 'I read in one of those magazines of yours that newborns sometimes need feeding every two to three hours, even at night time.'

Chloe nodded carefully, certain she could see where this was heading. 'I wouldn't mind taking care of Lucy through the night.'

'No, no,' he said, surprising her. 'I wasn't angling for that. It's asking too much of you.'

'So you think you'll be OK looking after her?'

His mouth squared as he grimaced. 'Frankly, no. I imagine I'll be pretty hopeless.'

'Then, unless you hire a nanny, we don't really have an alternative.'

Zac watched her for a long moment and the smallest hint of a smile played in his eyes. 'Actually, we do have an alternative, Chloe, but I'm afraid you're not going to like it.'

In an instant she was sitting straighter. 'You're not going to suggest we share a room.'

'But it makes sense, doesn't it?' His smile had disappeared now and Chloe could almost believe that he wasn't teasing. 'Neither of us knows much about babies. We both need moral support.'

She groaned. Of course she was remembering last night's close call when Zac had almost kissed her, when she'd almost let him...when she'd so very nearly welcomed him into her arms...and of course the memory stirred all the yearnings that she'd spent an entire night trying to forget. 'Honestly, Zac, don't you ever give up?'

'Calm down. There's no need to get all stirred up and old-maidish.'

'*I am not an old maid,*' Chloe hissed in a rush of righteous fury. Actually, she might have yelled this fact if they weren't in a refined hotel dining room filled with dignified guests.

'I stand corrected.' Straight-faced, Zac pushed his empty plate aside and rested his arms on the table as he leaned towards her. 'I certainly wasn't going to suggest that we share the same bed,' he said, lowering his voice so that she also had to lean in to hear him. 'I've actually looked into hiring a suite with two bedrooms, but the hotel's fully booked with special Christmas deals, so there's nothing like that available. And we really don't want to have to start hunting for another place at this late stage.'

Chloe had to give him credit—there wasn't a trace of a smile or a smirk.

'So what do you have in mind?' She wished her voice didn't sound so shaky.

'Well, it's easy enough to break up a king-size bed into twin singles and then our problem's solved.'

'Solved?' *So we'd be sleeping side by side?* 'What kind of a solution is that?'

'I'm only trying to think of what's best for the baby.' He actually sounded genuine. 'I swear there'll be no funny business, Ms Meadows. I'll be on my best behaviour.'

'I'm sure you have good intentions, Mr Corrigan, but I'd much rather—'

Chloe stopped. She'd been about to say that she would much rather look after Lucy on her own, but then she realised how selfish that sounded, and she would be denying Zac an important chance to get to know his baby niece and possibly to bond with her.

Maybe she *was* being a trifle prudish. After all, if Zac had really wanted to seduce her, he wouldn't have given up so easily last night. And if he could resist her in last night's red dress, he wasn't likely to pounce on her as she walked the floor at midnight with a fretful baby in her arms.

'Look, all right,' she admitted reluctantly. 'I suppose your plan makes a crazy kind of sense. I'll…I'll give it a go.'

Her boss rewarded her with one of his spectacular smiles. 'I knew I could rely on you to be unfailingly sensible. I'll organise for the beds to be changed, and for a cot to be sent up to my room. And I certainly won't let your room go. You'll need it as a bolt-hole, at least to escape to for long hot baths.'

His grey eyes shimmered and she couldn't be sure if he was teasing her again.

CHAPTER SEVEN

'SHE'S AN ABSOLUTE angel, isn't she?'

Zac stood by the cot set in a corner of his hotel room, aware that he wore a sappy smile on his face as he stared down at the sleeping baby. As far as he could tell, Lucy Corrigan was perfect.

She'd been sound asleep when he and Chloe collected her from the hospital and she'd slept all the way during the taxi ride. She hadn't even stirred when they arrived back at the hotel, where he'd rather clumsily extracted her from the car seat before the excited hotel staff rushed to make a huge fuss of them.

Now the three of them were alone. Chloe was in an armchair by the window, reading yet another magazine about mothers and babies, and Zac was pacing the floor on tenterhooks, waiting for Lucy to stir and wake for her next feed.

Standing ready in the bar fridge were a row of bottles of formula that Chloe had made up and which she was going to heat with a special travelling contraption she'd found at the pharmacy.

Zac wasn't entirely happy about this. He'd planned to ask the kitchen staff to prepare the baby's formula and he'd been quite pleased with the idea of Lucy's bottles arriving via room service. He was rather amused by the prospect of signing for a baby's bottle delivered on a covered silver tray.

But Chloe, sensible as always, had wanted to be certain about the hygiene of the bottles and about getting the temperature of the milk exactly right, so now Zac's bathroom housed a sterilising unit as well as the heating gear and a collection of baby bath gels and lotions and wipes.

Still, he liked to think of himself as tolerant—and at least Lucy was very well behaved. Not a peep out of her so far. Then again, a quiet, sleeping baby was rather boring for a guy who wasn't used to sitting around...

'Isn't she due to wake up for a feed?' he asked Chloe as he checked the time yet again. By his reckoning, Lucy had slept twenty minutes past her mealtime.

Chloe looked up from her magazine. 'I suppose she'll wake when she's ready.'

'Isn't that a bit vague? I thought there was a schedule.' Schedules were usually his PA's forte. 'Isn't it important to get a baby into a routine?'

'Zac, give her time. She's only a few days old. She'll probably wake soon.'

Disgruntled, he picked up the TV remote and pressed the 'on' button. A loud blast of music erupted and Lucy gave a start, throwing one tiny arm in the air.

'Sorry,' he muttered as Chloe glared at him while he hastily searched for the 'mute' button.

Ridiculously, his heart was pounding now. No doubt he'd terrified the baby. He held his breath, waiting for her wails of terror. But, to his amazement, she was already asleep again, lying as still as a doll. Perhaps she'd never really woken.

Zac dropped into another armchair and began to flip restlessly through the channels with the sound turned down, but there was nothing he really wanted to watch and he found his mind meandering back over the previous night...

Rather than chastising himself yet again, he allowed himself to dwell on the pleasures of the evening. And there had been many. Chloe had been such good company—so relaxing and easy to talk to at the restaurant—and at the theatre she'd laughed uproariously, even at risqué jokes that he'd feared might upset her.

As for the red dress... Zac feared he was scarred for life by that dress.

He knew that from now on, every time Chloe walked into his office, he was going to remember the tormenting way the dress had hugged her delicious curves.

Why on earth had he paid such scant attention *to* those curves before now? He was beginning to regret that he'd been so disciplined from the day Chloe first joined his staff, never allowing himself to think of her as anything but his PA.

Of course, office romances were messy and bad for business—Zac had seen several of his mates fall by that particular wayside—but, last night, it was as if he'd had laser surgery and his vision had suddenly cleared. And today, even though Chloe had changed back into a sweater and jeans that he'd seen many times before, he was aware of her body in a whole new and entirely distracting way.

He couldn't help noticing the lush swell of her breasts and the dip to her waist, or the sweet tempting curve of her butt.

Which was hardly conducive to a good working re-

lationship, especially now that they were spending so
much time together, including sleeping side by side in
the same room. Clearly his brain had been out to lunch
when he'd come up with *that* bright idea. He'd presumed
the baby would keep them fully occupied…

With a heavy sigh, Zac switched off the TV, pushed
out of the armchair and began to prowl again. If Lucy
slept for too much longer he would have to take off—
go for a hike—hope that the freezing winter weather
outside might chill his inappropriately lustful thoughts.

'Are you quite sure we shouldn't wake her?' he demanded after yet another circuit of the room.

Chloe rose and came over to the cot. Her sweater had
a V-neck that exposed the soft pale skin of her neck and
a hint of the perfection of her collarbone.

'I'm not totally sure,' she said. 'Most of the information I've read is for breastfed babies.'

Zac wished she hadn't mentioned breasts. He was all
too aware of the way hers swayed gently beneath the soft
knit of the sweater when she walked.

He tried to concentrate on the tiny girl as they stood
together, looking down at her. Lucy was lying on her
side, giving them a view of her profile now—the newborn slope of her brow, her snub little nose and slightly
pouting red lips.

She was so still. So quiet. So *tiny*.

A tremor of fear rippled through Zac's innards. 'I
suppose she's still breathing?'

He saw his fear reflected in Chloe's dark eyes. 'Of
course. Well…I—I think so.'

Zac's fear spiked to panic. 'Should we check?'

'OK.'

One of Lucy's hands was peeking out of the blanket

and his heart hammered as he reached down and touched it with his finger. 'She feels a little cold.'

'Does she?' Chloe also sounded panicked now and she gave the baby a prod with two fingers.

Lucy squirmed and made a snuffling noise.

'Oh, thank God,' Zac breathed and he nearly hugged Chloe with relief.

Then they both laughed, shaking their heads at their foolishness, but, as their smiling gazes connected, Zac's heart thudded for a very different reason.

He felt a deep rush of gratitude for this woman. In the past few days he'd experienced some of the darkest moments of his life and Chloe's presence had been like a gently glowing candle, a shining light just when he needed it. Actually, he suspected that this feeling comprised something way deeper than gratitude.

Perhaps Chloe sensed this, too. Confusion flashed in her eyes and she hastily looked down. 'Hey,' she said suddenly. 'Zac, look.'

From the cot, two small bright eyes were staring up at them.

Zac grinned. 'Well, well…hello there, Lucy Francesca Corrigan. Aren't you the cutest little thing?'

'I guess we can pick her up now,' Chloe said. 'She probably needs changing. Do you want to do the honours?'

Zac swallowed. The nurse had handed the baby to Chloe when they left the hospital, which was fine by him. He'd planned to be an observer. Then again, he'd never been one to chicken out of a challenge.

'OK,' he said bravely, peeling back the top blanket. To reassure himself, he added, 'No worries.' But he held his breath as he carefully lifted the tiny bundle.

'You can change her on the bed,' Chloe said.

'Me?'

'Why not?' Her smiling dark eyes were daring him now. 'I've spread towels for you.'

'Right, sure.'

Anyone would think he was defusing a bomb, the way he gingerly set the baby down and began to unwrap her bunny rug. Beneath this, he found that she was wearing an all-in-one affair, like a spacesuit, so his task now was to undo countless clips.

Beside him, Chloe was on standby with baby wipes and a clean disposable nappy.

'Maybe you should take over,' he suggested. 'You're probably an expert. You've done this before.'

She shook her head. 'I haven't actually, but I've watched friends change babies, and I'd say you're doing a fine job.'

Soldiering on, Zac eventually managed to free Lucy from her nappy and it was a bit of a shock to encounter her naked lower half. Her hips were minuscule, her legs thin and red as she kicked at the air.

'She's like a little frog,' he said in awe.

'She's beautiful,' reproached Chloe.

'Well, yeah. A beautiful little frog.'

Chloe handed him a wipe. 'You can put on a new nappy and dress her again while I heat her bottle.'

'Right.' Zac felt a stab of alarm as Chloe disappeared, but then he took a deep breath and manfully got on with the job and, although it was tricky getting tiny limbs back into the right sections of the garment, he was absurdly pleased with himself when he had Lucy properly dressed again by the time Chloe came back with the bottle.

'She hasn't cried at all,' Chloe commented.

'No, she's frowned and looked cross-eyed at me once or twice,' Zac said. 'But not one wail.'

'Isn't she good?'

'Amazing.' In a burst of magnanimity, he said, 'You can feed her if you like. I'm happy to watch and learn.'

But Zac soon realised this wasn't such a great idea. The picture Chloe made as she settled in the armchair with Lucy made him choke up again. This was partly because he was suddenly thinking of Liv and the fact that she should be here with her baby. But also...even though he was missing Liv, he knew that Chloe looked so damn right in this setting.

Perhaps it was something about the tilt of her head, or the way the light from outside filtered through the hotel's gauzy curtain, making the scene look soft, like a watercolour painting.

Or perhaps it was the fondness in Chloe's face as she looked down at Lucy, and the way Lucy looked straight back at her, concentrating hard, so that she almost went cross-eyed again as she sucked on the teat.

He was damn sure those two were forming a bond.

'I should put the kettle on and make you a cuppa,' he said, wishing his voice didn't sound so gruff.

Chloe flashed him a brilliant smile. 'Thanks.'

As Zac went to fill the kettle he couldn't remember the last time he'd made a cup of tea for anyone else. He knew he should be dismayed by the sudden domestic turn that his life had taken, but the craziest thing was that he actually quite liked it.

Chloe was secretly amazed that the first day with Lucy went so smoothly. After the baby was fed and burped she went straight back to sleep again and she continued to sleep while Chloe and Zac watched an entire DVD.

Now, the short winter daylight had disappeared already and the dark streets outside once again flashed with traffic lights and neon signs and Christmas decorations.

'This baby-raising is a piece of cake,' Zac declared as he poured two glasses of the Italian wine he'd ordered from room service and handed a glass to Chloe. 'How much do they pay babysitters and nannies for sitting around like this?'

'I don't really know,' Chloe said. 'But I'm quite sure they earn it.'

'I can't see how.' Zac was grinning as he lifted the cover on the cheese platter he'd ordered to accompany the wine, and Chloe guessed he wasn't really serious. Then again, it was hard to argue that their new responsibility was onerous as they clinked glasses in a toast to the sleeping baby in the corner.

Their afternoon had been surprisingly pleasant. She and Zac had established clear ground rules and he'd been on his best behaviour…and this evening promised ongoing pleasantness.

They planned to have dinner here in Zac's room and perhaps watch another movie, having discovered an unexpected mutual liking for sci-fi. It was all very agreeable. Zac was so much more at ease about caring for Lucy now and Chloe was genuinely pleased for him. He'd been through so much turmoil over the past few days and he still had to face his sister's funeral in the morning, and heaven knew what challenges awaited him when he got back to Australia.

A quiet, relaxing evening was exactly what he needed

and so they'd planned for dinner at seven-thirty, allowing plenty of time for Lucy to wake and be changed and fed and settled back to sleep again.

Chloe always felt better when she had a clear plan...

'Is that someone knocking?' Zac shot a frowning glance to the door. He couldn't really hear anything with a baby screaming in his ear. 'What's the time?'

'Seven-thirty,' said Chloe, who'd been pacing anxiously beside him.

'That'll be our dinner.' Zac, who was fast becoming an expert, deftly shifted Lucy, plus a hand towel to catch spit-up milk, to his other shoulder. 'We should have rung through and told them to hold the meal till we got her down.'

Chloe winced, knowing that normally she would have thought of this. 'I guess I'd better answer the door.'

'Wait till I take Lucy through to the bathroom. We don't want to blast the poor guy's ears off.'

Chloe's stomach was churning as she watched Zac disappear with the red-faced, yelling babe. This had been going on for over an hour now and they weren't quite sure how or why Lucy was so upset.

She'd woken from her sleep and together they'd bathed her and changed her into clean clothes from head to toe. This had taken a little longer than it probably should have and by the time they'd finished Lucy was desperately hungry and letting them know. When Zac offered her the bottle—they'd decided it was his turn—she had sucked quite greedily and the milk had disappeared in no time.

'Piece of cake, this looking after babies,' he'd said again, smiling smugly as he laid Lucy back in the cot.

Thirty seconds later, the wailing had begun. Lucy kept pulling her little knee into her stomach as if she was in pain.

'She needs burping,' Chloe decided. 'There's a diagram of what you have to do in one of the magazines.' And, following the instructions carefully, she'd sat Lucy on her lap, holding her tummy firmly with one hand while she gently rubbed her back.

It hadn't worked—and neither had walking up and down with Lucy. The hoped-for burp never occurred and after more than an hour of valiant efforts to calm her, her cries still hadn't stopped.

Despite the closed bathroom door, the yells could be heard all too clearly now as their room service dinner was wheeled in...

Chloe gave the fellow a generous tip.

'Thanks.' His eyes were wide with curiosity and he sent more than one worried glance to the closed door.

'Colicky baby,' Chloe told him with the knowledgeable tone she imagined a nursing sister might use. 'She'll settle soon.'

The fellow nodded and hurried away and Chloe hoped they weren't going to be reported for creating a disturbance.

She opened the bathroom door for Zac and he emerged looking somewhat haggard, although Lucy's howls had finally begun to quieten to whimpers.

'Do you think she's settling?'

Zac's shoulders lifted in a shrug. 'I have no idea. From now on I'll admit to total ignorance and I take back everything that I said about nannies and babysitters. Whatever they're paid, it's not enough.'

Chloe couldn't help smiling and, although this wasn't

the right moment, she also couldn't help noticing how utterly enticing a strong hunky man could look with a tiny baby in his arms. Moments like this, she could almost imagine…

But no. She reined her thoughts back. Imaginations were dangerous.

'That dinner smells amazing,' Zac said, casting a longing glance to the trolley.

'I know. My tummy's rumbling.' Zac had ordered a Greek lamb dish for both of them and Chloe doubted any meal could smell more tempting. 'I wonder when we'll get to eat it.'

At that moment, Lucy's knee jerked upwards again and she let out another heart-rending yell.

'She's definitely in pain,' Zac said. 'Maybe we should ring someone. Do you think there's a helpline?'

'I'm pretty sure she just has colic.' Chloe said this more calmly than she felt. 'Early evening is supposed to be the worst time for it.'

'Perhaps it's my fault?' A totally uncharacteristic look of guilt appeared in Zac's eyes. 'Maybe I held the bottle the wrong way.'

'Of course you didn't. Here, let me take her for a bit. You eat your meal. It's getting cold.'

'No, no. You eat first.'

Chloe shook her head. She couldn't possibly eat while Lucy was still so upset. 'Perhaps we should try changing her again…'

In the end, they ate their cooling and congealing dinner in shifts, while taking it in turns to pace the floor with the baby. Several times her crying calmed down and she began to look sleepy and their hopes soared.

Twice she nodded off and they actually placed her back in the cot, holding their breath and hoping she would stay asleep as they backed silently away on tip-toe. Both times, just when they thought all was well, Lucy suddenly threw up her hand and began to cry more lustily than ever.

She kept crying on and off until it was her feed time again. This time, when they changed her, they encountered their first dirty nappy and Zac rose another notch in Chloe's estimation when he didn't flinch, but gamely went to work with the wipes.

He insisted that Chloe be the one to feed Lucy this time. She made sure that the baby didn't guzzle and she stopped the feed halfway through for a little burping session—this time with results—and, to their infinite relief, when they tiptoed away from the cot, Lucy remained sleeping.

As the silence continued, they let out relieved sighs. *Bliss.*

They shared tired smiles.

'I'm knackered,' Zac admitted with a sheepish smile. 'I was looking forward to kicking back with some more of that wine and cheese, but I'm not sure I have the strength.'

'Nor me,' agreed Chloe. 'Not if Lucy's going to wake again in three hours or so.'

She went back to her room to shower and to change into sleepwear and of course she chose the safety of a voluminous grey T-shirt and opaque black tights, but, when she came back, Zac was already in bed and he appeared to be sound asleep.

She smiled wearily. After making such an enormous fuss about the dangers of sleeping so close to Zac, the

reality was going to be a non-event. All either of the
wanted was the oblivion of deep sleep.

A small sound woke Chloe.

Drowsily, she rolled over without opening her eye
then nestled back under the covers. No sound now. A
was quiet again. Lovely. She didn't have to worry. T
sound wasn't Lucy.

Zap!

Lucy? Shocked into wakefulness, Chloe shot up, hea
thudding. The room was mostly in darkness, but the
was enough light from a lamp in the corner for her to s
that Zac was awake and sitting on the edge of his bed

'I thought I heard something,' she whispered. 'W
it Lucy?'

'It's OK,' he whispered in answer. 'Go back to sleep

'But there was a noise. How is she?'

'She's fine. I've just fed her.'

'*You've* fed her?' Chloe stared at him in amazeme
'You mean you've done it all—changed her and fed h
and burped her?'

'The whole deal.'

'So what's she doing now?'

'Sleeping again. Like a baby.'

Chloe gave a dazed shake of her head. 'Why did
you wake me?'

'Didn't want to bother you.' Zac yawned. 'You we
snoring your head off.' He yawned again. ''Night. S
you in the morning.' And then he lay down with his ba
to her and pulled the covers high.

Chloe was too surprised to fall straight back to slee
She was supposed to be moral support. She was slee
ing in this room because Zac needed her help. Exce

he clearly hadn't needed her at all…and she wasn't sure how she felt about that…

She'd grown accustomed to him needing her…

Although perhaps she shouldn't be so surprised. She knew that Zac threw his whole weight into any project he undertook.

As she lay staring into the darkness, she thought again about the fuss she'd made this morning over sharing this room with him. She'd expected him to try to seduce her again. She'd imagined having to fend off his advances, even though she didn't really want to…

If she was brutally honest, she'd probably hoped he might try…

But, as Zac had promised, this was an entirely practical arrangement. He hadn't shown the slightest glimmer of sexual interest in her and now she felt a bit foolish about the way she'd made such a hue and cry.

Of course, it probably helped that she'd chosen to wear these gym clothes to bed rather than slinky pyjamas, but tonight she'd gained the impression that Zac would probably have ignored her even if she'd been wearing a transparent negligee. His focus was entirely on Lucy. And Chloe was delighted about that. She was. Really.

But she wasn't sure if she would get back to sleep.

AFTERWARDS, ZAC'S MEMORIES of Liv's funeral were fragmentary at best. He could recall the harrowing hollowness he felt on entering the small church lit with candles and Christmas brightness, and filled with a surprising number of people. But he remembered very little of the short eulogy he gave, although he did his best to give his sister's new friends a few cheering pictures of Liv's happy family life in Australia, and of the deep love he'd always felt for her.

He thanked everyone gathered there for offering his sister the welcoming warmth of their friendship and for coming today to honour Liv's memory. He thanked Father Tom…having earlier handed him an envelope with a cheque that he hoped would convey his immense gratitude.

Moving outside again was the worst moment—bidding farewell to Liv's coffin before it was driven away. Zac felt as if he couldn't breathe. His throat burned as if he'd swallowed a hot ember and his hand was shaking as he reached into his coat pocket and drew out a piece of coral, one of two pieces he'd found on a shelf in Liv's room.

Bleached white and bony, like miniature antlers, Zac had recognised them immediately as coral their mother had collected when they'd lived on the island, pieces that Liv had always kept with her.

Today he placed one slender branching cluster on her coffin.

'Bye, Liv,' he whispered. Then, blinded by tears, he wrapped his fingers around the other piece still in his pocket.

When he felt an arm slip through his, he turned to see Chloe, who offered him a markedly wobbly smile.

'You were wonderful,' she told him, and her eyes were shiny with tears as she picked up the tail of his scarf and tucked it back inside his coat, before lifting her face to press a warm kiss to his cheek.

Zac closed his eyes, more touched by the simple gesture than was possibly appropriate. He suspected that, while other memories might fade, this particular moment would stay with him for ever.

Even though it was Christmas Eve, Skye and Liv's other housemates insisted on inviting everyone back to the house. In no time the place was crammed with a huge range of young people, including Father Tom.

As mugs of mulled wine and savoury platters were passed around, Chloe was introduced to a fascinating crowd with a wide range of British accents, as well as the more distinctive voices of people who were clearly new arrivals, just as Liv had been.

She met a Brazilian man, a kitchen hand who was not only stunningly handsome but extremely polite and charming. Next, she was introduced to two Polish plumbers with shaved heads who looked fierce but were actually super-friendly. A large West Indian girl showered everyone with her beaming smile.

Of course, all of Liv's friends wanted to make a fuss of Lucy and, to Chloe's surprise, they'd even brought presents for the baby—so many gifts, in fact, that Zac was going to need another suitcase.

Zac was extremely tolerant as the baby was passed around, and Chloe guessed that he was as touched as she was to discover how supportive Liv's community of friends had been. And, fortunately, Lucy seemed to enjoy all the attention.

'That went well,' Zac said quietly as a taxi took them back to the hotel. 'I had no idea what to expect, but it couldn't have been better, really.'

But he still looked sad...terribly sad...and Chloe's heart ached for him.

Almost as soon as they got back to the hotel, Zac made his excuses. 'There are one or two matters I need to see to,' he said enigmatically before disappearing.

Chloe knew he had to collect Lucy's passport, but she was also sure he needed a little time to himself. Actually, she was more than ready for some thinking space, too... There were one or two matters she needed to chew over...including the fact that the longer she was in close proximity to Zac Corrigan the more she liked him, the more she cared about him. Deeply. Maybe even *loved* him...

In the past few days her understanding of her boss had changed massively, especially since they'd begun caring for Lucy. There were times when Zac had looked at her with an emotion that went way deeper than teasing or desire. Moments when Chloe saw a kind of tenderness that made her heart tremble and hold its breath, as if…

Her more sensible self wanted to argue with this, of course, but Chloe was tired of her internal debates…or perhaps she was just plain tired. Lucy had been colicky again in the early hours…

Curled in the armchair, she must have nodded off, and she woke with a start when Zac returned.

'Sorry.' He sent her a smile as he tiptoed across the room to peek into the cot. 'I was trying not to wake you.'

'Doesn't matter. Is Lucy still asleep?'

'Out like a light.'

Chloe's limbs were stiff as she unfurled from her cramped position and sat straighter. She rubbed at her eyes and blinked. No, she hadn't imagined it. Zac was not merely smiling; he was looking particularly pleased with himself.

She'd assumed he'd been walking around London's streets, sunk in his grief, but his smile was definitely triumphant as he tossed his coat onto the end of his bed before he sank comfortably into the other armchair. 'I've collected Lucy's passport and I've sorted out our Christmas,' he said.

'Sorted it how?' Despite the beautiful decorations and lights and the frenzy of shopping all around them, Chloe had almost stopped thinking about Christmas. 'I thought we'd have turkey and plum pudding here in the room.'

'No, Chloe, you deserve better than that.'

'I do?' she asked, frowning.

'Yes, you do, Chloe Meadows.' Zac smiled gently and she wished he wouldn't. 'You've given up your own plans for Christmas without a word of complaint and you deserve some fun.'

An edgy uncertainty launched her to her feet. What was Zac planning? That she should go off and celebrate Christmas on her own while he stayed here with Lucy? She couldn't imagine she'd enjoy that very much.

'Zac, I don't need a fancy Christmas. I've said all along that I'm happy to help with Lucy.'

'Don't worry about Lucy. I've organised a sitter.'

She stared at him in surprise. 'But you don't believe in babysitters.'

Zac frowned. 'I don't think I ever said that exactly.' Now he rose from his chair to stand beside her. 'I'm not keen on nannies, particularly if they're used as a mother substitute. But this is different. It's not fair to you to be locked up in here on Christmas Day with someone else's baby.'

His eyes sparkled. 'After all, I did promise you a flash London Christmas to make up for missing our office party.'

'So you did.' Chloe found that she was smiling too as she remembered what a big deal the office Christmas party had been for her. Only a few days ago. So much had changed since then. And now...the very fact that Zac had obviously been thinking about her, making plans in an effort to please her made her feel unexpectedly happy and glowing...

'Actually, I've also been thinking ahead,' Zac said. 'I've been thinking about when I get home. I've realised that I can't expect *any* woman to be tied to the baby around the clock. She'll have to have help.'

Any woman... He was referring to his future wife, of course, and a shiver skittered down Chloe, as if he'd dropped a cold key down the back of her shirt. How silly she'd been to imagine...to think that he might possibly...

'So,' she said stiffly as she tried to ignore the chilling slap of ridiculous, unwarranted disappointment. 'What do you have planned for tomorrow?'

'Are you all right, Chloe?'

'Yes, of course.' She was working hard now to ignore the confusion and tumult that seemed to have taken up residence in her head and her heart.

Turning away from him to the window, she stared out at the park with its huge bare trees. She saw children in woolly hats chasing each other, saw businessmen with newspapers and furled umbrellas. An elderly couple were walking their dogs. And then her vision blurred.

She certainly wasn't all right. She was very afraid that, against her better judgement, she'd fallen in love with her boss.

She was as foolish as all his other females. More foolish actually, because she'd always known that falling for Zac was dangerous.

Somehow, over the past few days, she'd been seduced by their moments of deep connectedness. She'd been charmed by those times when he'd looked at her with a true appreciation that went way deeper than the mere respect of a boss for a trusted employee.

Saturday night had been different—Chloe had found it difficult but at least possible to resist Zac when he'd so clearly set out to seduce her. After all, she knew that Zac Corrigan would try to seduce any young woman he dated. But this morning, outside the church, Zac had needed her emotional support. And her heart had never felt so full…

'Chloe, what is it? What's the matter?' Zac was standing close behind her now and at any minute he was going to discover her tears.

'I—I was just thinking about…Christmas,' she said, grasping at any excuse.

'I suppose you must be missing your parents.'

'Yes.' Across the street a young woman was running through the park. The woman wore a red coat and her blonde hair was flying behind her like a banner.

'Chloe.' She felt Zac's hand on her shoulder and she tried to keep her head averted. The girl in the park was running to meet a young man. The young man was hurrying too and at any moment they would fall into each other's arms.

'You're crying,' Zac said and he made a soft sound of despair. 'Come here.' With sure hands, he pulled her around to face him. 'Let me see you.'

Chloe shook her head, made her eyes extra wide in a desperate attempt to hold back the tears. *I'm being an idiot.*

Zac had positioned her in front of him now, a hand on each of her shoulders as he searched her face, his grey eyes mirrors of her sadness. 'Chloe, what's the matter?'

How could she tell him? She shook her head and she might have held up her hand to ward him off but, before she could, his arms were around her, drawing her against him.

'Oh, Chloe.'

Now she was clinging to him, pressing her damp face into the comforting wall of his chest, and his arms were around her, warm and strong, holding her close. She could smell a faint trace of his aftershave, could hear his ragged breathing, could feel his heart thudding against hers. Now she could feel his lips brushing a soft kiss to her brow…and that tiny intimacy was all it took.

In the next breath she was coming undone, wanted nothing more than for Zac to kiss her properly. On the lips. And if he kissed her, she would kiss him back. She would kiss him deeply, passionately, throw caution to the wind.

With him suddenly so close, her emotions were a fiercely rushing tide. Desire churned deep inside her, and she knew she had no choice but to ride the flood... rising, rising... She was gripped by a kind of desperation. It was now or never... If Zac kissed her, she would surrender. She would give herself to him completely. Nothing else mattered.

Oh, how she longed for him to kiss her.

Fortunately, he was a mind reader.

With a hand beneath her chin, he lifted her face and touched his lips to hers and everything went wild. Their kiss flared from hello to explosive in a heartbeat and Chloe wound her arms around his neck, pressing close, turning to fire.

Neither of them spoke. It was as if they both feared that words might break the spell. This coming together was all about emotion and longing and heat...as their mouths hungered and their hands turned feverish...as clothing fell silently onto white carpet...as they stumbled in a lip-locked tango to the nearest bed.

For a fleeting second, as they landed together on the mattress, Chloe's more sensible self tried to slam on the brakes. But Zac was gazing down at her and he had that look in his eyes—a look that was a mix of heartbreak and surprise and unmistakable desire. A look that melted her.

And now his hand was gliding over her skin and

flames leapt to life wherever he touched. He lowered his lips to her breast and the longing inside Chloe bucked like a wild beast fighting to be free. All hope of resistance was lost...

Afterwards...the thrashing of their heartbeats gradually subsided as they lay side by side... And the silence continued...

Chloe couldn't find the right words. What did you say to your boss when you'd just shared blazing, uninhibited, mind-blowing sex with him? She had no idea, and it seemed Zac had been struck dumb as well.

Cautiously, she turned her face towards him. With equal caution, he turned to her and his eyes reflected the same shell-shock she felt.

They both knew this wasn't supposed to happen. They'd clarified on Saturday night that there were very valid reasons why this should never happen.

But now...their lovemaking had been so spontaneous, so flaming and passionate, it had taken them both by storm.

'Are—are you OK?' Zac asked gently, his words touching her skin and reaching into her heart, just as his kisses had, mere moments ago.

'Yes,' Chloe whispered.

He let out a huff of breath and a soft sound that might have been a sigh or the merest hint of a laugh. 'At least one of us is OK then.'

What did he mean? She knew she should ask, should at least say *something,* but she certainly wasn't willing to analyse the whys and wherefores of this, and she was still struggling to find the right words when Lucy woke with a lusty yell.

Grateful for the distraction, both Chloe and Zac rolled out of opposite sides of the bed and began to drag on clothes with the speed of commandos responding to an alarm.

'You can heat the formula,' Chloe said as she pulled her shirt over her head. Zac knew how to look after the formula now and he was quite expert at testing the temperature of the milk on the inside of his wrist. He was standing by with Lucy's bottle when Chloe had changed her nappy and re-dressed her.

'Why don't you feed her?' Chloe suggested, without quite meeting his gaze. 'I'll make a cup of tea.' OK, so perhaps it was another ploy to avoid talking to him about what had just happened, but the tea making had also become part of their surprisingly domesticated routine. 'Then you can tell me what you have planned for Christmas,' she added.

'Christmas?' Zac gave a soft, self-deprecating laugh. 'Went clear out of my mind.'

'And remember, don't let her guzzle,' Chloe warned, desperately needing to remain businesslike and matter-of-fact, but her thoughts were churning as she went to fill the kettle.

Zac found it hard to concentrate on feeding the baby. He had too much to think about. He'd always believed he was reasonably knowledgeable when it came to women and seduction. He'd also thought he knew his PA quite well. He'd been wrong on both counts and to say that he was stunned was putting it mildly.

He cringed now when he recalled accusing Chloe of being an old maid. Clearly, she was far more worldly than he'd ever dreamed. He didn't want to start mak-

ing comparisons, but something amazingly spontaneous and earth-shatteringly good had happened just now.
Something way, *way* beyond random meaningless sex...

No doubt he'd stuffed up the very fine working relationship he had with his PA, however, and that was damn
stupid. At this point, he had no idea where to take things
from here, but one thing was certain—he would have
to think this situation through very carefully before he
made another move.

Perhaps his Christmas plans would be a useful diver-
sion. He'd pulled off quite a coup, managing to wangle
tickets for the hotel's sumptuous Christmas banquet.
There was to be a six-course menu with every delicacy
imaginable.

He reckoned the best news was that he'd secured a
properly certified babysitter for the entire afternoon. Of
course, he'd had to pay an exorbitant sum for a sitter on
Christmas Day and at such late notice but, with the help
of the concierge, it was all settled.

He'd been really looking forward to sharing this news
with Chloe, but now...a Christmas feast paled into in-
significance after what they'd just shared.

As Chloe poured boiling water over tea bags, her mind
was spinning. Why hadn't she remembered that leaping
into bed with Zac was simply *not* an option? Clearly her
brain had snapped. She'd fallen into the oldest trap—
giving in to lust and confusing it with love.

Surely she knew better than that? She was opening
herself up to all kinds of pain.

Zac was never going to love her, so the outcome could
only be painful. After all, she'd experienced what it was
like to truly love someone and to be loved in return. And

she knew Zac's attitude to love was light years away from her own. He was focused on finding a wife from a database, rather than searching his heart.

Her problem was that she'd spent too much time in his company. She'd become too caught up in his personal life and, for a short time, she'd totally lost her perspective.

Her only choice now was to accept that she'd made a very silly mistake and then to forgive herself. Forgive and forget. That was what Zac would expect her to do and, with luck, she would survive the emotional fallout.

OK. She felt marginally better now that she'd thought this through. It meant she simply had to put her feelings for her boss on ice until she got back to Australia and then she should be safe. She would come to her senses. Surely that was a workable plan?

Their lunch of toasted ham, cheese and tomato sandwiches with coffee was a strained and quiet affair.

'I guess we should talk about…you know,' Zac said as he finished his second sandwich, but he still looked extremely uncomfortable.

Chloe drew a quick breath for courage. 'If you like… but I don't expect a post-mortem.'

'What about an apology?'

Shyly, she shook her head. They both knew this had been a two-sided affair.

'That's good,' Zac said. 'Because I wouldn't want to apologise for something so—'

He left the sentence unfinished, as if words were inadequate…or too revealing…

'Maybe it was inevitable,' Chloe said without looking at him. 'A guy and a girl in constant close proximity.'

When she looked up, she saw his puzzled smile. No doubt he'd expected tears and recrimination. That would have to wait till later when she was alone.

'Chloe, for the record, I'd like you to know that—' Zac hesitated again and his throat worked. 'It's so hard to express this properly, but you must know that kind of chemistry is pretty damn rare.'

Heat flooded her face. For her, their lovemaking had been astonishing, an outpouring of passion beyond anything she'd ever experienced—even with Sam—but she mustn't think about what that signified, or she'd end up with a broken heart. 'Maybe it's best if we don't say too much right now,' she said.

Zac nodded, a cautious smile still playing at the corner of his mouth as he picked up a final sandwich. 'A cooling-off period.'

'Yes.' She was too worried that she'd let her emotions show, that she'd burst into tears and make an awkward situation a thousand times worse.

'I'm sure that's probably wise,' Zac said, but he looked thoughtful, as if he was in the middle of a puzzle he hadn't quite solved. Then his expression lightened. 'Actually, to change the subject, I was wondering if we should brave the elements this afternoon and take Lucy for a walk.'

It was a brilliant idea. Chloe nodded enthusiastically. 'I think we're all in need of fresh air. If we put a little bonnet and mittens on her and bundle her in an extra warm blanket, she should be fine.'

Seemed they were both eager to hit the streets for a final Christmas shopping spree, and Chloe hoped fervently that the bustle of crowds and the dazzle of decorations would prove a very welcome distraction from her way too sexy employer.

'I'm keen to buy something for Lucy's first Christmas,' Zac said as they headed down Oxford Street. 'Any ideas?'

'I was thinking this morning, when Skye was madly taking photos, that it would be lovely to start an album for Lucy and to include shots of London.'

'Good thinking.' He didn't add *Ms Meadows* this time, but he was smiling again, almost back to the Zac of old. 'Lucy should have a record that begins right here with her very first Christmas.'

'I took photos of Skye and her friends with my phone. I'll email them to you, if you like.'

'Great. They should certainly be part of the record.' He definitely looked pleased. 'So an album's first on our list. What else? Liv already bought Lucy her first teddy bear.'

'Maybe you could buy her a gorgeous Christmas stocking while you're here, something that will become a tradition for her every year.'

'Yep, sounds good.' Zac trapped her with a private smile. 'Am I right in guessing you're a girl who likes traditions?'

'Possibly.'

For too long, they stood in the crowded and busy store, smiling goofily at each other until they realised they were blocking an aisle.

'And I think I'd like Lucy to have a little gold bracelet,' Zac said. 'I remember Liv used to wear one when she was a kid.'

'With a heart locket?' Chloe asked.

'Yes.'

She smiled. 'I had one of those too. I loved it, but I lost it once when my neighbours took me water-skiing.'

Zac's grey eyes shimmered and Chloe gulped. She was so susceptible to that look. 'What's the matter? Do I have a smut on my face?'

'I'm trying to picture you as a little girl.'

Her heart tumbled like a snowball on a very steep slope. 'Don't talk like that,' she said, almost begging him. 'Concentrate on the shopping.'

CHAPTER NINE

AT BREAKFAST ON Christmas morning, when Chloe announced that she would like to go to church, Zac surprised her by saying that he'd like to come too.

'Church two days in a row?' she queried.

'I've been reading about St Paul's Cathedral.' Apparently, Zac was fascinated by the cathedral's history. It was rebuilt after the Great Fire of London in 1666, and then later survived the Blitz in World War II when most of the surrounding buildings were flattened in bombing raids. 'It's become a symbol of resurrection and rebirth,' Zac said. 'And that seems rather fitting for Lucy's first Christmas.'

Considering the sad and miraculous circumstances of Lucy's birth such a few short days ago, Chloe had to agree.

'I don't think another outing will hurt her, do you?' he asked.

'She should be fine. She was actually better last night after all that shopping.'

While Zac checked the times of the services, Chloe rang her parents, who had almost finished their Christmas Day in Australia.

'It was wonderful,' they gushed. 'The loveliest Christmas, Chloe. The chauffeur took us to church and then brought us back here in time for lunch. And, my goodness, you should have seen the spread. We've never eaten so well. Please give our love to Zac.'

'My parents are probably your biggest fans,' she told Zac as she hung up, and she felt unexpectedly happy at the thought of going off with him and Lucy to celebrate Christmas in St Paul's.

OK, it might feel like the three of you are almost a proper family, but don't get ideas, girl.

'We've time for presents before we go,' Zac announced as they finished their simple breakfast of coffee and croissants, in lieu of the banquet to come. With a boyish grin, he crossed to the wardrobe and produced a small package.

'Hang on.' Chloe dived for the floor and rummaged under her bed. 'I have a little something for you, too.'

It was also a small gift, but the shop assistant had worked magic with a square of green and white striped paper and a bright red bow. Chloe set the gift on the table in front of Zac, rather than placing it in his hand. Probably an over-the-top precaution, but after yesterday's 'mistake', she was super-conscious of the dangers of any skin contact with this man.

Zac, however, had no qualms about kissing her cheek as he handed her his gift. 'Merry Christmas, Chloe,' he said warmly.

'Thank you.' She knew she couldn't refuse to return his kiss, but she did this so quickly she barely touched his cheek. 'And Merry Christmas to you.' She nodded towards the little green and white package.

'Thanks!' He looked so genuinely delighted that she

wondered how he normally spent his Christmases. It was possible that, without close family, he was often quite lonely. The thought stabbed at her soft heart.

'Aren't you going to open it?' Zac had already freed the red ribbon and had started ripping into the paper.

'Yes, of course.' Her parcel was wrapped in pink and silver tissue and topped by a posy of tiny silk roses. 'But it's almost too pretty to open.'

Zac grinned. 'Go on, get stuck into it. I dare you.'

Chloe laughed. She was actually far more excited than she should have been, but a hand-selected gift from Zac was quite a novelty. Back in Brisbane, it was her job to order his corporate gifts for employees and business associates, as well as sending flowers and perfume to his girlfriends.

His gift to her usually came in the form of a Christmas bonus and, generous and welcome as this was, she couldn't help being curious about what he might buy when he made the selection entirely on his own.

There was a box inside the wrapping and it looked like a jewellery box. Chloe's heart fluttered and she shot a quick glance to see if Zac had opened his gift.

He was watching her and smiling. 'You go first.'

'All right.' She knew her cheeks were pink as she lifted the lid to find, nestling inside in a bed of cream silk, a solid gold chain bracelet with a heart-shaped locket. 'Oh, Zac, it's beautiful. It's just like Lucy's.'

'Hopefully, a grown-up version.'

'Yes, a *very* grown-up version.' Unlike the delicacy of the baby's bracelet, this one was solid and shiny gold and Chloe knew it had probably cost a small fortune.

'I almost bought you a necklace,' Zac said, 'but I

knew you'd lost your bracelet when you were little.'
He gave a self-conscious little smile and shrugged. 'I
thought you might like a replacement.'

This was so much more than a replacement. It was a
gift that mirrored the one Zac had bought for his niece.
It wasn't only expensive, it was *personal*...

There was a good chance Chloe's blush deepened. 'I'll
love wearing this. Thank you.' On her wrist it looked
perfect. Toning beautifully with her skin, it made her
feel mega glamorous.

She looked pointedly at the box in Zac's hand. 'Your
turn.'

'Ah, yes...'

Chloe held her breath as he lifted the lid on the silver
cufflinks she'd bought him. She watched his face, saw
the flash in his grey eyes when he recognised the significance, and his face broke into a delighted grin. 'Sea
turtles!' His grin broadened. 'You remembered from
the other night.'

'I loved your story about living on the island and I
thought these were incredibly stylish but cute,' Chloe
said. 'But I also thought they might bring back happy
memories.'

'They do. They will. They're wonderful.' He looked
as if he might have hugged her, but perhaps he'd picked
up on her caution. Perhaps he was as afraid as she
was that they'd end up in bed again, ravishing each
other...

'Thank you, Chloe,' he said instead, but his eyes had
that look again, the one that told her he was remembering every detail of their passion, the look that made her
head spin and her insides tremble.

* * *

'I feel dangerously virtuous after all that carol singing.' Zac was in high spirits as they came back into the hotel room. 'I'm certainly ready to eat, drink and be merry.'

Chloe knew what he meant. She'd felt wonderfully uplifted by the beautiful music in the magnificent cathedral and it seemed somehow perfect to follow up with her first slap-up Christmas dinner in a posh hotel.

Just the same, Zac's flippant comment about dangerous virtue sent her thoughts off once again in inappropriate directions, which was probably why she made herself busy writing notes for the babysitter, double-checking with room service for the delivery of the sitter's special Christmas dinner, and ensuring that everything Lucy might need was already laid out for her.

'At least we'll only be a few floors away, so the sitter can call us if she has any worries.'

Zac pulled a face. 'I wouldn't encourage her to call.'

'But we have to leave her a phone number, Zac.'

'Oh, if you insist.' His smile was teasing again as he walked to the cot. 'You go and get ready, while I have a quiet talk to this child. It's time I delivered her first lecture. She needs to understand that we expect nothing from her but her very best behaviour.'

For Chloe, entering the hotel's special banquet room was like walking into the dining room of a royal palace. There was so much to take in—the high ornate ceiling and stunning red walls with huge mirrors that reflected back the splendour, a tall Christmas tree covered in fairy lights in the corner, candles everywhere in glass holders, chandeliers overhead.

Down the middle of the room stretched long tables covered in red tartan and set with sparkling glassware, shining silver, starched white napkins. The guests were beautifully dressed and Chloe was more pleased than ever that she'd lashed out on her expensive red number.

With a glass of Yuletide punch in her hand, Zac's lovely bracelet on her wrist and his tall, dark and exceptionally handsome presence at her side, she'd never felt more glamorous and confident.

She had such a good time. They met a lovely Canadian couple who'd come to England to track down their family history, two genial elderly Scottish brothers who apparently spent Christmas at this hotel every year, a group of New Zealanders...

There was even a famous American author called Gloria Hart, who was accompanied by a much younger man whom she openly introduced as her lover. Chloe had read a few of her books, so meeting her was quite a fan girl moment.

Gloria made a beeline for Zac and although she kept her arm firmly linked with her young man's, she made sheep's eyes at him, and then she turned to Chloe with a coy smile. 'I do like your young man,' she said. 'I'm almost jealous.'

'Ah, but I'm taken,' Zac said gallantly as he slipped his arm around Chloe's shoulders and dropped a proprietorial kiss on her cheek.

Chloe hoped her smile held. Zac probably had no idea that his simple gesture gave her lightning bolts of both pleasure and pain.

Champagne was opened as they all took their seats and settled in for a truly sensational meal. White-coated waiters brought the most amazing dishes—Colchester rock oysters, shellfish platters, roast middle white pork with winter jelly, roast goose with Brussels sprouts and all the trimmings. These were followed by mince pies, Christmas pudding, Ayrshire cream and cider and chestnut syllabub.

Fortunately, there was plenty of time between courses, plenty of laughter and storytelling. Zac, as always, drew more than his share of feminine interest, but he got on well with the men, too, and he was attentive to Chloe throughout the afternoon.

Like Gloria Hart, everyone assumed they were a couple. Chloe almost set them straight, but then she caught Zac's eye and saw an ever so subtle warning smile, as if he was urging her to leave things be. She could almost hear him say, *What's the harm in a little pretence?*

She just wished she could feel happier about it, wished she didn't mind that it was only a charade…

Of course, when she explained that the occasional texts she sent were to their sitter, it was also assumed that she and Zac were Lucy's parents.

'You've regained your figure so quickly,' one woman commented.

Chloe smiled her thanks and this time she avoided catching Zac's eye. But she couldn't help silly thoughts that began with the fireworks of yesterday's unforgettable passion and ended with the bleak sadness of *if only…*

Give up now, Chloe. You know it's never going to happen…and you're not in love with him. You can't be. She didn't want to fall in love again, couldn't bear to risk that kind of heartbreak. And falling for Zac could bring nothing but heartbreak. She knew him too well. *Just play the game. It's only for a few more hours and tomorrow you'll be on the plane, safely winging your way home.*

In the breaks between courses, people got up and moved about, mingling and chatting with other guests, going to the tall windows at the far end of the room to look out at the views across the park. Twice, Zac went back to the room to check on Lucy, which made Chloe smile.

The second time he left was just before their coffee arrived, and when he came back he hurried to Chloe and leaned close to her ear. 'Come with me,' he whispered.

Turning, she saw unmistakable excitement in his eyes and he nodded to the windows. 'I want to show you something.'

'What is it?'

His smile was the sort that made her ache inside. 'Come and see for yourself.'

Of course she was curious, so she excused herself from her neighbour and Zac grabbed her hand, hurrying her to the far end of the room.

'Look.'

Chloe looked and gasped.

Outside, it was dark, but the street lights and the lights of the buildings caught the dazzle of dancing, snowy white flakes. *Snow!* Real, no-doubt-about-it snow was falling silently, landing on tree branches, along railings and on the roofs of parked cars.

'Wow!' she exclaimed, gripping Zac's hand in her excitement. 'I've never seen snow before. Isn't it beautiful?'

'I thought you'd like it.'

'Oh, Zac, it's amazing. It's the perfect end to a perfect day.'

'I don't know how long it will last. I vote we skip coffee and go outside to dance about in it.'

'Yes, I'd love to. But we'll need to go back for our coats and gloves.'

'All sorted. I collected them while I was up checking on Lucy.'

Lucy. 'I forgot to ask. How is she?'

'She's fine, Chloe. The lecture I gave her paid off. She's a fast learner.' Zac slipped his arm through hers and gave a tug. 'Come on. Let's go.'

They made their farewells.

'It's snowing,' Chloe explained, which caused quite a stir. 'I'm afraid I've never seen snow before, so we're going outside. I want to catch the full experience.'

'Yes, off you go, lass,' one of the Scotsmen said. 'Although I should warn you that London doesn't have real snow.'

'Zac, make sure you keep Chloe warm,' called Gloria Hart.

They were laughing as they left amidst calls of 'Goodbye, lovely to meet you' and 'Merry Christmas'.

Chloe hadn't thought it was possible for her Christmas Day to get any better, but she was floating with happiness as Zac slipped his arm around her shoulders and they walked together along the paths in the park while the snow fell softly all around them.

'I'm going to wake up soon,' she said, holding out a red-gloved hand to catch a flurry of snowflakes. 'This is so magical. It's simply too good to be true.'

'It might not stay pretty, so I wanted you to enjoy it while it's fresh.'

She looked back to the hotel, where she could see the big window of the dining room, the twinkling lights of the Christmas tree and the chandeliers, and the silhouettes of people moving about inside.

'Thanks for dragging yourself away from the party

and bringing me out here,' she said. 'I would have hated to miss this.'

'So would I,' Zac said with a mysterious shy smile.

Even though it was dark now, the park was well lit and the space rang with the excited shouts and laughter of children and adults alike, making the most of the white Christmas. Chloe was zinging with excitement as she and Zac walked on, under bare-branched trees that now gathered white coats, and she loved the way he kept his arm securely around her...

They reached the far side of the park and were turning back when Zac said, 'Actually, while I'm in your good books, Chloe, I wonder if I could put a proposal to you.'

She frowned at this. Something about Zac's careful tone took the high gloss off her happiness. Thinking fast, she tried to guess what this proposal might be about. No doubt something to do with work, or with Lucy, or possibly with Marissa Johnson. She certainly hoped it wasn't Marissa. Not now. Not today.

'What kind of proposal?' she asked cautiously.

'Actually, I was thinking of a marriage proposal.'

Chloe's reaction was inevitable. Her silly heart toppled and crashed.

'Your proposal to Marissa?' She knew her shoulders drooped. She thought Zac had more tact than to bring this up now and spoil Christmas Day.

He gave a soft groan and came to a standstill. 'No, Chloe. This has nothing to do with Marissa.' He was standing in front of her now, blocking her path, as white flecks of snow floated onto his shiny black hair. 'I want to ask you to marry me.'

Chloe struggled to breathe as she stared at him and a cyclone of emotions whirled chaotically inside her, stirring all the longing she'd ever felt for him, along with the confusion and pain, the sympathy and tenderness.

For a giddy moment she allowed herself to picture being married to Zac and of course her silly brain zapped straight back to yesterday's lovemaking and she was instantly melting at the thought of a lifetime of fabulous sex.

And she thought about Lucy. The baby was now an inevitable part of the Zac Corrigan package, and Chloe knew she would adore taking care of the little girl and stepping into the role as her mother. And then there was Zac's business which Chloe knew inside out and was almost as passionate about as he was.

For so many reasons his proposal felt right. But, oh, dear heavens, she had to be careful. She had to remember that this gorgeous, kind and generous man was also the playboy she knew all too well. As far as she could tell, Zac had no real concept of being faithful. As for love… for crying out loud, until five minutes ago, he was planning to pick his prospective wife from a spreadsheet.

Chloe shivered inside her warm coat. 'Don't play games,' she said wearily. 'Not today, Zac. Please, don't be silly.'

He gave an angry shake of his head. 'Why do you always assume I'm playing games? I'm absolutely serious. Think about it, Chloe. It makes so much sense.'

'Sense?' Her eyes stung and it wasn't from the cold.

'I thought you liked to be sensible.'

Oh, give me a break, Zac. How many girls want to be sensible about romance?

But the question wasn't worth voicing. 'So why is this so sensible?' she demanded instead. 'Because I tick most of the boxes on your checklist?'

Zac looked surprised. '*Most* of the boxes? Chloe, you tick every single one of them. Actually, I'd have to add extra boxes for you. You're an amazing girl.'

'And I'm so good with Lucy,' she added flatly.

His smile wavered. 'Well, yes,' he said as if this was obvious.

Oh, Lord. Chloe couldn't hold back a heavy, shuddering sigh. *Please, please, don't let me cry.*

Zac stood very still now, watching her with troubled eyes. He wasn't wearing his scarf and she could see the movement of his throat as he swallowed uncomfortably. 'I've stuffed this up, haven't I?' he said quietly.

Fighting tears, Chloe gave a helpless flap of her hands. 'Maybe you got carried away after the luncheon today, when everyone assumed we were married.'

Now, with his hands plunged into his coat pockets, he tipped his head back and stared up at the dark sky. He sighed, releasing his breath in a soft white cloud. 'Give me some credit, Chloe.'

She could feel the weight of the gold bracelet around her wrist, reminding her of their happiness this morning when they went to church together and opened their presents. She hated that this had happened, hated that they were so tense now, on the raw edge of a fight, at the end of this beautiful, perfect day.

'Can I ask you a difficult question, Zac?'

He looked doubtful, but he nodded.

'Are you honestly in love with me?'

'Honestly?' he repeated, looking more worried than ever.

'There's no point in lying,' she said bravely. 'I know we've been pretending to others all day, but I need brutal honesty now.'

There was a long uncomfortable silence as Zac stood staring at her, his silver-grey eyes betraying a haunted uncertainty. He seemed to try for a smile and miss, then he said, 'I told you I don't really believe in "love".' He made air quotes around the word. 'And I'm afraid that's the truth. I think it's a dangerous illusion.'

Lifting his hands, palms up, as if protesting his innocence, he smiled. 'But I really like you, Chloe. As I said before, I think you're amazing. And you can't deny we have fabulous chemistry.'

A sad little laugh escaped her. Here she was in the perfect romantic setting for a marriage proposal, and instead she received a sensible, practical, *logical* proposal without a glimmer of romance.

Zac's eyes were shiny as he watched her. 'So…I take it that's a no then?'

Oh, Zac.

She had an eerie sense of time standing still. She felt so torn. She knew this was her big chance to be reckless and brave and to grab a wonderful opportunity. She had no doubt she could give her heart to Zac and to Lucy, along with her loyalty to ZedCee Management Consultants.

But the big question was—what could she expect from Zac in return? A comfortable, entertaining, possibly exciting lifestyle…until his interest in her waned.

She was far too familiar with the pattern of Zac's love life. When it came to women, he had the attention span of a two-year-old, and if Chloe was ever going to risk love again, she needed certainty. She needed a man who could bring himself to say and mean those dreaded words: *I love you.*

'I'm sorry,' she said, fighting tears. 'I'm still an idealist. A romantic, I guess.'

'So you want an admission of true love *as well as* brutal honesty? *And* you want both from the same man?' Zac shook his head and it was clear he believed she was asking for the impossible.

Inevitably, the day ended on a low note.

There was no reassuring arm around Chloe's shoulders as they went back to the hotel, where they shook out their snowy coats and took the lift upstairs to find Lucy fast asleep and the sitter about to watch the Queen's Christmas message on TV.

So they watched the royal message with the sitter and then she left them with some reluctance, assuring them that she'd had a lovely day.

And Chloe left, too, going next door to remove her make-up and to change out of her red dress. She put the bracelet back in its box, and stowed it in her already packed suitcase. Then she added the dress, carefully folded between sheets of tissue paper.

Although she wanted to cry, she forced herself to be strong as she cleaned her teeth, creamed her face and brushed her hair.

A faint *'waa...'* from next door warned her that Lucy was awake so, although she really didn't want to face Zac again this evening, she went back to his room to help with the evening feed, which was often the most difficult and colicky time.

However, the baby settled quickly, even before Zac and Chloe had drunk their ritual cuppas, but Chloe didn't join Zac in the armchairs for a cosy chat.

'I'll get on with Lucy's packing,' she said, knowing

they would need to head for Heathrow soon after breakfast in the morning.

Taking up space in the middle of the room, Zac managed to look spectacularly manly and helpless. 'Anything
I can do to help?'

'Probably better if I look after it,' Chloe muttered,
ducking around him. 'I have a list.'

He smiled crookedly. 'Of course you do.'

She was so anxious and edgy and sad, she was glad
of an excuse to keep busy, collecting scattered items like
a baby sock from behind a cushion, a bib from beneath
a pillow, and sorting out exactly what they'd need for
Lucy on the journey. She packed a special carry-on bag
with baby bottles, formula, nappies, wipes and several
changes of clothes. Then she double-checked all their
passports and travel documents.

'I've already checked those papers,' Zac said.

'Doesn't hurt to check again.'

Now that she'd rejected his marriage proposal and
their final evening was ruined, she was extra keen to
be on her way. If there was a hitch at the airport tomorrow—anything that meant they couldn't leave the UK—
she was likely to have some kind of breakdown.

She wanted to be home. She needed to be caring for
her boring sweet parents, needed to get her life back
to normal as quickly as possible. Once she was safely
home, she would put this London experience and everything that came with it behind her. Once again she would
be nothing more than Zac Corrigan's highly efficient and
more or less invisible PA. As always, she would co-ordi-
nate his private life as well as his business affairs, while
she secretly turned up her nose at his *Foolish Females*.

CHAPTER TEN

ZAC WAS BEGINNING to suspect that Lucy could pick up on their vibes. Tonight he and Chloe were both as tense as tripwires, and Lucy was fussier than ever after her next feed. It was close to midnight before she settled back to sleep.

'We're going to have a hell of a trip home if she's like this tomorrow night,' Chloe commented tiredly.

'It will help if we make sure we're relaxed.'

'Relaxed?' The word snapped from Chloe like a rifle shot and, out of the corner of his eye, Zac saw the baby flinch.

He sighed. 'Look, I apologise if I've spoiled your Christmas. I know I've upset you.'

'Of course you haven't upset me. I'm fine.' Chloe's eyes were unnaturally wide as she said this and she promptly made an about-turn and headed for the door.

'Where are you going?'

She gave an impatient shrug. 'It's probably best if I sleep in my own room.'

'You really think that's going to help?'

'Help what?' she shot back with a scowling frown.

Was she being deliberately obtuse?

'Help *us*,' Zac said patiently. 'This walking on eggshells tension.' He had visions of a twenty-two-hour flight back to Australia without resolving whatever bugged her.

At least Chloe gave a faint nod, as if she acknowledged this, then she leaned her back against the door and folded her arms over her chest and speared him with her nut-brown gaze. 'So you're saying that you need to talk about our relationship—or rather our lack of a relationship?'

'Well, from my experience, talking things over is usually what girls want.'

She smiled. Damn, even when the smile was glum, she looked incredibly lovely when she smiled. Zac had to work hard to curb his impulse to cross the room and haul her into his arms. He wanted to relight those wild flames again. Taste her lips, her skin, feel her going wild with him. Hell, how could he ever forget that blazing encounter?

How could he forget how much he'd loved having her around on a twenty-four hour basis? He'd never met a girl he felt so comfortable with. Until he'd wrecked things with his clumsy proposal, sharing his personal life with Chloe had felt so unexpectedly *right*...as if their personalities slotted magically together like one of those Chinese puzzles...

'So what do you think we need to talk about?' Chloe asked.

'To be honest, I'm not totally sure, but it sure as hell can't happen if you're on the other side of that wall.'

Now she lifted her hands in a gesture of surrender. 'OK. No big deal. I'll stay here. I'm actually very tired, though.'

'The talk's not mandatory,' he said, feeling ridiculously relieved by this small victory.

Nevertheless, after they both got into their separate beds, he could see, via the faint glow of Lucy's night light, that Chloe remained, as he was, lying on her back with her hands beneath her head, staring up at the ceiling.

It wasn't long before her voice reached him through the darkness. 'So what do you want to talk about?'

There was no mistaking the distrust in her tone.

Zac couldn't help smiling to himself. 'I thought I was supposed to ask that question.'

'But I've already told you. I don't have any issues. I'm perfectly fine.'

This was patently not true. Since they'd arrived back from the park Chloe had been tearing about like a wound-up toy on top speed.

'But I must admit I don't understand *you*,' she said next.

Zac had heard this comment before from women. Had heard it with regular monotony, if he was honest.

'I mean,' Chloe went on in that earnest way of hers, 'I don't understand why you're so convinced that falling in love is nothing but a fairy tale.'

She wasn't going to let go of this. Clearly, it was at the heart of her tension.

'Well, OK,' he said smoothly. 'Convince me otherwise. I'm assuming you have a vast experience of falling in love?'

'I don't know about vast,' she said. 'But I was certainly in love with my fiancé.'

Whack.

Zac's smugness vanished as surprise juddered through

him like a jack-hammer. How had he never known about her fiancé? More importantly, why hadn't Chloe said something about this guy when she so quickly and force-fully rejected his proposal?

Although he'd tried to make light of her rejection, her loud and clear *no* had stung. Zac had felt as if he was standing at the door of Aladdin's Cave, where the glit-tering riches and jewels represented a chance for a life-time's happiness and contentment.

Heaven help him, he'd actually pictured a home with Chloe and Lucy and then, just when this dream was within his reach, the portcullis had slammed down, cut-ting him off from his vision of happiness.

Now, he said, 'I...I didn't realise you were engaged.'

'I'm not any more,' Chloe said softly. 'My fiancé died.'

Another shock. Despite the hotel's perfectly con-trolled heating, Zac was suddenly cold. 'Hell. I'm sorry. I had no idea.'

'I wouldn't expect you to know. It happened before I started working for you.'

'Right.' He swallowed uncomfortably as he absorbed this news.

Lying there in the dark beside her, it occurred to him that his assumptions about his PA had been en-tirely based on the image she presented at the office, but over the past few days that image had been crumbling and now it was blasted clear out of the water. 'Is it OK to ask what happened?'

After a small silence she said, 'Sam was a soldier— a Special Forces soldier. He was killed in Afghanistan.'

Zac swore and then quickly apologised. But this was almost one surprise too many. Special Forces sol-

diers were so damn tough and daring—the most highly
skilled—which meant that Chloe had been about to
marry a real life hero. 'I had no idea,' he said lamely.

'I don't like to talk about it.'

'No, I guess it must be hard.'

From the bed beside him, he heard a heavy sigh.

'I was a complete mess when it happened,' she said.
'That's why I came home to live with my parents. I didn't
want to go out like other young people. I just wanted to
hide away and…and grieve. I guess it wasn't exactly a
healthy reaction.'

'But understandable.'

He heard the rustle of sheets as Chloe rolled to face
him. 'Anyway, for what it's worth, I did love Sam. For
me it was very real, an inescapable emotion. I suppose
it was an attraction of opposites, but it worked for us.
We were very happy and we had big plans for a family
and everything.'

'That's…great…'

Zac had no idea what to say, but thinking about Chloe
and her soldier made him feel inexplicably jealous…
and depressed…

Inadequate, too. He understood now why Chloe had
rejected him. She thought he merely wanted a mother
for Lucy.

Damn it, he should have tried to express his feelings
more truthfully but, chances were, anything he offered
now would be a very poor second best to her true romance with her heroic soldier.

And if he tried to tell her how he really felt, how his
days were always brighter when she was around, how,
even at home in Brisbane, the weekends so often dragged

and he couldn't wait till Monday mornings to see her again, it would sound crazy, as if he was in love...

'Are you asleep, Zac?' Chloe's voice dragged him back from his gloomy musings.

'Sorry. Were you saying something?'

'Now I've spilled my story, I was asking about you. Are you still going to insist that you've never fallen in love?'

His mind flashed to that one time in his past when he'd been young and deeply in love, with his head full of dreams and his heart full of hope. Until...

No. He never talked about that. He'd worked hard to put it all behind him and he wasn't going there now.

Chloe, however, was waiting for his answer.

'Well, yeah, sure I've been in love,' he told her with a joviality he didn't really feel. 'Hundreds of times.'

This was met by silence... It was ages before Chloe spoke and then she said quietly, 'That's exactly the answer I expected from you.'

After that she rolled away with her back to him. 'Goodnight, Zac.'

Her fed-up tone left him with the strong conviction that their conversation hadn't helped either of them and he knew he was going to have trouble getting to sleep.

Damn. The last thing he wanted was to lie awake remembering Rebecca...or what was now far worse—wrestling with regrets about Chloe...

The flight was scheduled for midday and both Chloe and Zac were nervous about how Lucy would behave during the long hours that stretched ahead of them.

To their relief, their fears were unfounded. When Lucy was awake the flight attendants seemed to love fussing over her, and when she slept the droning hum of the plane's engines seemed to soothe her into a deeper slumber.

'She's gorgeous and such a good baby,' several of the female passengers told Chloe. 'You're so lucky.' Chloe could tell from the way their eyes wandered that they considered Zac to be a major component of this luck.

Of course, Chloe thanked them and once again she didn't try to explain that she was neither Lucy's mother nor Zac's wife. But afterwards…she had to try to ignore the gnawing hollowness inside her, the annoying regret and second thoughts that had plagued her ever since she'd turned down Zac's proposal of marriage.

She knew she was going to miss Lucy terribly. In these few short days, she'd lost her heart to the baby. She'd grown to adore her, to love the feel and the smell of her, to love her bright curious eyes and hungry little mouth. When Zac wasn't looking, she'd even given Lucy little baby massages, following the instructions she'd read in one of the magazines.

As for Zac…despite the many strict lectures she'd delivered to herself, she felt desperately miserable whenever she thought about the end of this journey…when they went their separate ways. She'd grown so used to being with him twenty-four hours a day, to sharing meals with him, sharing middle of the night attempts to calm Lucy, listening to him in those quieter moments when he'd felt a need to talk a little more about Liv.

As for making love with him…Chloe's thoughts were seriously undisciplined when it came to *that* subject. She spent far too much time torturing herself by recalling every raunchy detail of going to bed with Zac…before firmly reminding herself it would never happen again.

'A penny for your thoughts.'

Chloe blushed. 'Excuse me?'

Zac leaned closer. 'You had your worried look, Ms Meadows. I wondered what was bothering you.'

She had no idea what to say. 'Um…I wasn't thinking about anything in particular.'

'Lucky you,' Zac murmured, leaning closer still.

'Why am I lucky?'

'You're not being tormented the way I am. I can't stop thinking about how much I want to kiss you.'

'Zac, don't be crazy. You can't start kissing on a plane.' Was he no longer bothered that she'd rejected his proposal?

'Why not?' he asked with that winning smile of his. 'They've dimmed the lights and no one's looking.'

So tempting…

'You want to, don't you?'

'No,' Chloe whispered, but she knew she didn't sound very convincing. No doubt because it wasn't the truth. She wanted nothing more.

When Zac leaned even closer and touched his lips to her cheek, she felt her whole body break into a smile. Instinctively, she closed her eyes and turned to him so her lips and his were almost touching. He needed no further invitation. His mouth brushed over hers in a teasing whisper-soft kiss that sent warm coils of pleasure spiralling deep. Chloe let her lips drift open and she welcomed the slide of his tongue.

'Mmm…' With a soft sound of longing, she moved as close to him as possible, kissing him harder…losing herself in the strength and the taste and the smell of him.

'I love you,' he whispered and wave after wave of happiness welled inside her. Everything was all right after all. It was OK to love Zac. There was no reason to hold back.

She slipped one hand behind his neck to anchor herself and then she nudged her leg against his, as she was seized by a hot and feverish longing to climb into his lap.

'Chloe?'

Zac's questioning voice sounded quite loudly in her ear.

Chloe blinked. Her head was on Zac's shoulder. Her hand was curled around his nape. Her knee was hooked over his thigh. When she pulled back to check his face, he was staring at her with a strangely puzzled smile.

'What happened?' she asked.

'I think you fell asleep.'

Oh, my God. Had she been dreaming?

Cheeks burning with embarrassment, Chloe whipped her hand away and swerved back into her seat. 'I...I'm so sorry. I have no idea how that happened.' With a soft moan she sank her face into her hands.

'Hey, don't worry,' she heard him say. 'I'm already wishing I didn't wake you up.'

Chloe lowered her hands from her face. 'How long was I—?'

'Climbing all over me?'

She cringed. 'Yeah.'

'Only about ten minutes or so. I'd say there were only about a dozen people who walked past.'

She stared at him in horror. 'They saw me?'

But Zac was grinning hard now and she realised he was teasing her. She gave his arm a punch. 'You're a lying rat, Zac Corrigan.'

Her embarrassment lingered, however. Even if half the people in the cabin hadn't seen her draping herself all over Zac, *he* knew all about it. She thanked her lucky stars that he hadn't pushed her for a proper explanation. But what must he be thinking?

They were finally flying over Australian soil, although it would still be several hours before they touched down in Brisbane.

Chloe had just come back from the changing room with Lucy, and Zac was waiting with the heated bottle the flight attendant had delivered.

'Do you want to do the honours?' Chloe asked him.

'Sure.' He held out his arms for the baby and Chloe's heart had a minor meltdown as she watched the tender way he smiled at his niece.

'You know,' he said, as he settled Lucy in his arms and carefully tipped the teat into her eager little mouth, 'I hate to think about trying to do this on my own when I get home. It won't be the same without your help.'

Chloe closed her eyes against the pang of dismay his comment aroused. She was going to miss this, too, more than she could possibly have imagined. When she opened her eyes again, the sight of Zac and Lucy together was beyond gorgeous.

In moments like this, the temptation to retract her rejection of Zac's proposal was huge…until she remembered that he only wanted her because she was good with Lucy…and possibly because their chemistry was undeniably hot. Was she crazy to believe these reasons weren't enough?

She thought about Sam and the way he'd made her feel and the many ways he'd showed her that he cared…just through little things like gifts or a surprise invitation, or the way he held her close. Of course, those gestures weren't all that different from Zac's behaviour, really. And the annoying thing was there were times when she felt even closer to Zac than she ever had with Sam.

Truth to tell, during the two years Chloe had known Sam, he'd spent a good proportion of the time on deployment in Afghanistan. So she was certainly better acquainted with Zac, with his good and bad habits, his strengths, hopes and fears. His belief that love was an illusion...

This thought sobered Chloe. 'You'll find some other woman to help you,' she said.

'Not straight away. That will take time to arrange.'

'Well, yes, I doubt that even you could manage to pull off a wedding inside a week, Zac. You'll need to hire a sitter or a nanny for the interim.'

'And that won't be easy in the week between Christmas and New Year.'

Chloe slid him a sideways glance. 'You'll manage.'

'So you wouldn't consider it?' he asked, trapping her once again with his clear grey gaze.

'Consider what, exactly?'

'Helping me out for a few more days?'

She should have seen this coming, should have been prepared, but she'd thought, after her rejection, that Zac would back right off.

'Chloe?'

'I don't know,' she said. 'I'm thinking.'

'I've plenty of bedrooms,' he went on, offering one of his customary coaxing smiles. 'You could have your own room and we could put Lucy in the room next door to you.'

'Where would you be?'

'Just down the hall a bit.' Now he had the cheek to

grin at her. 'Safely out of your way, but near enough to be on call to help with Lucy.'

If she thought about it rationally, without her silly emotions getting in the way, his request was probably reasonable. As long as this wasn't the thin end of the wedge...

'So what's your plan, Zac? You're still planning to... to...get married, aren't you?'

Chloe saw an unreadable flicker in his eyes, but his face was deadpan. 'I still think that's the preferable option.'

'And Marissa's the preferable candidate?'

'I guess so, yes.' His tone suggested that he still needed to give this serious thought. 'But I know I'll have important groundwork to do before I can convince her. At the moment, I don't even know if she's still available.'

'So it could take some time...'

Zac set the baby's bottle on the tray table while he gently lifted Lucy onto his shoulder to help her to bring up her wind. 'I wouldn't expect you to stay at my place for too long, Chloe. Just for a night or two, till I get my bearings.'

'My parents might—'

'Your parents are welcome to stay on at the hotel, as long as they're enjoying it.'

'Oh, they're enjoying it all right.'

'Then, would you consider it?'

The last thing Chloe needed was more time in Zac's company. What she needed was distance. Time and space to regroup and to clear herself of her tangled thoughts and emotions. But then she looked at Lucy. Zac had shifted her onto his lap and she was curled over his big hand as he gently rubbed her back. She was such a dear little thing and she looked so cute now.

'I wonder if Marissa likes babies,' she found herself saying.

Zac lifted a dark eyebrow. 'I have no idea. I guess that's one of the many things I'll have to ask her.'

Chloe had never been to Zac's penthouse apartment, perched high in an inner city tower block. He'd project-managed its construction and it was a striking piece of architecture with views up and down the Brisbane River—all very shiny and modern with high gloss timber floors, large expanses of glass and a flashy granite and stainless steel kitchen.

By the time they'd emerged from Customs it was too late to try to go shopping for baby gear, so they went straight to Zac's place and made a snug nest for Lucy by pushing two black leather lounge chairs together and then lining the space with a quilt.

'She looks impossibly tiny, doesn't she?' Lucy said as they stood looking down at her.

'Yeah.' Zac reached down and softly stroked Lucy's dark hair. 'Welcome home, tiny girl.'

The love shining in his eyes brought a lump to Chloe's throat. Then he straightened and his eyes were still shiny as he smiled at Chloe.

'There's a restaurant downstairs,' he said. 'I could send down for a takeaway meal.'

'I'm not especially hungry.' She would blame jet lag for her low mood, but from the moment she'd arrived she'd felt on the verge of tears.

'Maybe just one serving to share?' Zac suggested. 'Something light? They do great chilli prawns.'

Which was how they ended up on that first night, sitting on his balcony with a fresh breeze blowing up the river, eating chilli prawns and washing it down with a glass of white wine, while they enjoyed the city lights.

'You must love living here,' Chloe commented as she watched pretty ladders of light stretch across the smooth surface of the river.

'It's been great,' Zac admitted. 'At least it's been very handy for a bachelor.'

'Party Central?'

'At times, yes.' But Zac was frowning. 'I'm not sure I'd like to stay here with Lucy. She'll need a backyard with swings and other kids in her street to play with.'

'That safe suburban life you dream of,' Chloe suggested with a tired smile.

'Exactly.'

'Do you think you'll find it hard to adapt to that kind of life?'

'I guess that depends on who I can convince to come and live with us,' he said quietly and there was just enough light for Chloe to see the way his gaze flashed in her direction.

Without warning, her throat was choked and her eyes were stinging, spilling tears.

'Chloe.'

She threw up her hands. 'It's just jet lag. I need to hit the sack.' Already she was on her feet. 'Thanks for the prawns, Zac. They were delicious.'

'Don't get up when Lucy wakes,' he called after her. 'I'm not too tired. I'll be fine.'

'OK, thanks.' She kept her tear-stained face averted. 'See you in the morning. Goodnight.'

Of course, after that, Chloe took ages to get to sleep. She tossed and turned and agonised about Zac, but when she finally nodded off she slept deeply and soundly. She woke to find bright daylight streaming through the crack between her curtains and from below she could hear the sounds of city traffic.

Feeling guilty about spending an entire night without helping, she sprang out of bed and hurried to the lounge room, but the baby wasn't in her makeshift cot.

Chloe shot a hasty glance to the kitchen. An empty baby's bottle stood on the granite counter, but there was no other sign that Zac had been up and she couldn't hear any sounds from within the apartment. Quickly she dashed back to her room to check the time. It was only just coming up to six o'clock, much earlier than she'd expected, but of course the sun rose super-early in Brisbane in midsummer.

And where was Lucy?

She tiptoed down the hallway towards Zac's room, then stood listening for Lucy's snuffles and snorts.

Nothing.

She knew it was silly to panic, but where Lucy was concerned her imagination leapt into overdrive. Something had happened. Lucy was ill. Zac had rushed with her to a twenty-four-hour medical centre.

Having thoroughly alarmed herself, she dashed into Zac's bedroom. And came to a skidding halt.

He was sound asleep, lying on his back. And Lucy was in the bed beside him, while another empty baby's bottle stood on the bedside table.

Chloe found herself transfixed as she looked down at them—the great big man and the tiny baby girl. Zac had kicked the sheet off and he was only wearing a pair of black silk boxer shorts, which allowed her a perfect opportunity to admire his broad bare chest, his muscular arms and shoulders, the smattering of dark hair narrowing down to the waistband of his shorts.

She couldn't help reliving her amazing experience of being up close and personal with that toned and golden body.

'Morning.'

His deep voice startled her. She'd been so busy ogling him, she hadn't noticed that he'd woken.

'I...I was just checking to see where Lucy was,' she stammered.

Zac grinned sleepily. His eyes were mere silver slits, but she knew he'd caught her checking him out. Then he sat up, scrubbed a hand over his face and blinked at the baby beside him. 'I didn't mean to bring her back here, but with the jet lag and everything...' He frowned as he leaned closer to check the tiny sleeping girl. Her tummy was moving softly up and down as she breathed. 'Thank God I didn't roll on her.'

'When's she due for another feed?' Chloe was eager now to shoulder her share of the duties.

Zac squinted at the bedside clock. 'I'd say in about another hour.'

'You should go back to sleep then. If she wakes I'll deal with her.'

'Sounds great. Thanks.' He was smiling as he flopped back onto the bed.

As she left Zac's room, Chloe hoped he hadn't been keeping tabs on her recent 'lapses'. First there'd been her attempt to climb all over him in the plane, then her tears last night, and now this morning's ogling. Surely these added up to highly inappropriate behaviour from a girl who had flatly rejected him?

* * *

It was a difficult day. They had to drag themselves around while their body clocks readjusted, and between snatches of sleep they made phone calls. Chloe rang her parents and Zac rang Marissa. His phone call took ages. Chloe had no idea what transpired and her curiosity was killing her but Zac chose not to tell her, which was appropriate, of course, now that she was simply his PA again. In the afternoon they went shopping for the necessary baby gear.

They aimed for an early night and fortunately Lucy co-operated. While Chloe put through a load of washing, Zac cooked their dinner, making a fair fist of grilling steaks on the balcony barbecue. He served them with mushrooms and beans and they ate the meal outside again, enjoying the warm evening and the city lights.

'Wow,' said Chloe as she tucked in. 'This is delicious, Zac. You've put lemon and chilli on the beans, haven't you? And some kind of herb on the mushrooms?'

He ducked his head towards the attractive cluster of potted herbs on his balcony. 'I sprinkled a little thyme over them.'

'Hmm.' Chloe speared a succulent mushroom with her fork. 'I think I've uncovered a dark horse, Zachary Corrigan.'

'What makes you say that?'

'You're actually a closet chef.'

He lifted a gorgeous black eyebrow.

'You are, aren't you, Zac?'

This brought an embarrassed smile. 'Closet chef? That's a big statement to make after sampling one hasty meal.'

'Hasty or not, this meal is sensational.' Chloe sliced

off a tender corner of steak. 'But I actually have further evidence. I checked out your pantry and fridge.'

'When?'

'While I was stowing away Lucy's formula.'

'So you've been spying on me?'

'I couldn't resist a little snooping. Sorry, it's a bad habit of mine, but I have a thing about fridges and pantries. You see, they tell so much about a person—in the kitchen, at least. And, well, I noticed you keep a French brand of Parmesan and an Italian brand of risotto, and you have all these bottles of Thai and Vietnamese sauces and about three different types of olive oil...'

'So?'

'Zac, you know very well that only a serious cook would bother.'

'I like to eat.' He shrugged. 'And cooking's actually relaxing...'

Relaxing? This was such a surprise Chloe laughed. 'And here I was, imagining that you ate out every night.'

'No way. Only every second night.'

They smiled at each other across the table. It was a smile of friendship and understanding and...something far deeper...which made Chloe feel all shivery and confused again.

'Do you like to cook?' Zac asked her.

'Well, I usually cook for my parents, but they only like very plain food like shepherd's pie or—' She stopped. This conversation was becoming far too intimate. It was making her feel closer to Zac when she was supposed to be stepping away.

CHAPTER ELEVEN

CHLOE WAS GIVING Lucy her bath when Zac left, shortly after breakfast.

'See you later,' he said, ducking his head around the bathroom doorway.

Unhappily guessing that he was heading off to see Marissa, Chloe forced brightness into her voice. 'You might heighten your luck if you take her flowers and chocolate.'

Zac frowned. 'I guess...'

'Marissa likes Oriental lilies and ginger chocolate.'

'How do you know these things?' he asked, but then he gave a soft humourless laugh. 'Don't tell me. It's all on a spreadsheet.'

'Naturally.' Chloe wished him luck but, as soon as she heard the apartment's front door close behind him, her face crumpled and she was overwhelmed by the most devastating, painful loss.

Zac was gone. She'd thrown away her very last opportunity and this was the end.

She felt cold all over as she scooped the baby out of the water and wrapped her in a fluffy bath towel.

'Oh, God, Lucy,' she whispered. 'You know what I've done, don't you? I've just thrown away the chance to be your mummy. And I've lost my very last opportunity to be with Zac.'

A terrible ache bloomed in her chest as she hugged Lucy to her and breathed in the scent of her clean baby skin. 'Honestly, Luce, I was only trying to be sensible. I can't marry a man who doesn't even know if he loves me.'

But how could I have known that being sensible and letting him go would still break my heart?

Misery washed through her, as cold and bleak as when she'd lost Sam. She carried Lucy through to the spare bedroom, now designated as the baby's nursery, and laid her gently on the new changing table, part of the furniture she and Zac had bought yesterday. Carefully, she patted the baby's skin dry and sprinkled and smoothed talcum powder into her creases. She picked up one of the tiny singlets and slipped it over Lucy's head, before angling her arms through the holes.

Luckily, she'd done this many times now because the entire time she worked her mind was miles away. With Zac. She was picturing his arrival at Marissa's, making his charming apologies or doing whatever was necessary to placate her, and then inviting her out. They would probably go to the beach. Chloe could imagine them walking hand in hand along the sand at the water's edge, or having a drink at a bar overlooking the sea. Zac would be at his alluring best as he explained the sad situation that had left him with Lucy. By the time he'd finished, Marissa would be putty in his hands.

Of course she would want to marry him.

And Chloe couldn't bear it. Couldn't bear to think that Zac would marry a woman he didn't love—and who probably didn't love him, simply to provide a mother for Lucy. How could he be such a fool?

She finished dressing the baby and took her through to the kitchen to collect a bottle of formula from the fridge. As she waited for it to heat, she paced restlessly, agonising over her own foolishness. And Zac's foolishness, too.

Surely he was deceiving himself when he claimed that he didn't believe in love? For heaven's sake, she only had to think back over the past few days to see all kinds of evidence of Zac's love in action.

He'd gone above and beyond the call of mere duty for Liv and for Lucy, but he'd also gone out of his way for Chloe as well. Not just with lovely gifts like the brace-let and the Christmas banquet, although she knew these were more personal and special than the gifts Zac usually bestowed on his women—but, beyond that, he'd also been thoughtful and considerate and kind. And fun.

Both in and out of bed...

Chloe wondered now, too late, if she should have given Zac a chance to explain his vision of the marriage he'd proposed. She'd simply jumped to conclusions and assumed he would continue to play the field.

But if she thought about the past week, when she'd been with him day and night, she couldn't really fault his behaviour. Actually, if anyone had misbehaved, she had. She'd practically thrown herself into his arms on that day they'd made love.

Now, as she went back to the kitchen to collect the heated bottle, she was more depressed than ever. She couldn't believe she'd brought this pain on herself and she'd thrown everything away because she'd needed to hear three stupid words from Zac. Hadn't she known all along that words were easy? Actions carried so much more weight…and Zac's actions had said so much… but now she'd lost him and she had no one to blame but herself.

'I hope I don't weep all over you,' she told Lucy as she settled in an armchair to feed her. 'I don't want to upset you. Don't take any notice of me, will you, darling? I'll try to stop thinking about him.'

It was impossible to turn her thoughts off, of course. She figured that by now Zac would be well on his way to the Gold Coast—too far down the expressway for her to phone him with some weak excuse that would bring him back. She had tried to be sensible one time too many, and as a result she felt as bereft and as heartbroken as she had when she lost Sam.

And Lucy had already finished her bottle.

'Sorry!' Chloe felt all kinds of guilty as she set the bottle aside and lifted Lucy to her shoulder. She hadn't been paying attention and she'd let the baby feed too quickly. Now the poor darling would probably be in pain.

Chloe stood, hoping that a little walking up and down would do the trick, but she was only halfway across the lounge room when the doorbell rang.

'Who on earth could this be?' she complained, sounding scarily like her mother, and as she went to open the door she dashed a hand to her face and hoped it wasn't too obvious that she'd been crying.

A young woman stood on the doorstep—a very pretty young woman with long blonde hair and the kind of slender figure that came from living on lettuce leaves and very little else. She was wearing strong perfume, tight floral jeans and a tiny tight top that revealed a toned and tanned midriff, as well as a silver navel ring.

The girl's jaw dropped when she saw Chloe and Lucy. 'Who are you?' she demanded.

'Are you looking for Zac?' Chloe asked in response.

'Yes. What's happened to him?' The girl looked genuinely worried. 'He just took off and he's been away for the whole of Christmas.'

'There was a family emergency and he had to rush to London.' Chloe felt obliged to explain this, even though she had no idea who this girl was. She certainly wasn't one of Zac's regulars. 'Zac's sister died,' she said.

The girl frowned, clearly struggling to take this in. 'That's sad. So are you a relative then?'

'No, I'm Zac's PA and this is his little niece, Lucy.'

'His PA? I think you rang Zac last week. Yes, it was you, wasn't it? And then he went racing off.'

'Yes, it was all terribly sudden.' Chloe realised this had to be the girl who'd answered Zac's phone on that fateful Wednesday night. She'd pretended to be answering from a Chinese takeaway.

'I'm sorry to hear about his sister,' the girl said.

'It was terrible,' Chloe agreed just as Lucy pulled up her knees and began to wail loudly.

'I take it Zac's not here now?' The girl raised her voice to be heard above Lucy.

'No. I'm not sure when he'll be back.'

'I guess I'll just have to keep trying his mobile then.'

'I'm not sure that's a good idea,' Chloe responded hastily. 'Not today. He's…he's still very busy.'

The girl pouted. 'Well, can you at least tell him that Daisy called?'

'Of course I can, Daisy. I won't forget. Nice to meet you.'

Lucy was distraught as Chloe closed the door. 'Oh,

sweetheart, I'm so sorry.' She began to pace, jiggling the baby gently. 'I'm afraid I know how you feel. I want to wail along with you.'

Back in the lounge room, she tried sitting with Lucy in her lap. Zac had perfected the art of burping her this way and Chloe willed herself to forget about her own woes and to concentrate on comforting the baby. She was rewarded by a massive burp.

'Oh, wow! Good girl. Aren't you clever?' She kissed the baby's downy head and cuddled her close and she sat there for a while, enjoying the warmth and snuggling closeness. But she was close to tears again as she took Lucy back to her brand new cot and tucked her in. She set the teddy bear that Liv had bought where Lucy could see it and then she tiptoed away.

From the doorway she looked back. 'I'm going to miss you so much.'

She waited for an answering wail, but the baby remained silent. When Chloe stole back into the room to double-check, Lucy's eyes were already closed. Chloe went back to the lounge room and collected the empty bottle, took it through to the kitchen…

Now what?

Unfortunately, the answer came almost immediately. Her next task was to write her letter of resignation.

She gave an agonised groan as this thought hit home. But she had no choice. It had to be done. She couldn't continue as Zac's PA now that she'd become so intimately involved in his personal life. She cared too much about Lucy *and* about Zac and she would care too much about the personal choices Zac made in the future.

And how could she pretend that their blazing lovemaking wouldn't always be there between them? A teasing, haunting memory. How could she ever forget that amazing spontaneity and passion? Heavens, if she stayed in Zac's office, she might find herself hoping it could happen again.

For that reason alone, she had no choice but to leave. It would be untenable for her to continue working for Zac after he was married to Marissa.

She hoped he would see that, too.

She should act immediately, draft a resignation now and have it ready for when he returned. She could type it on her phone, could even email it straight to Zac. With luck, he would accept it without too much argument.

It was so hard, though… Chloe felt sick as she started to type.

She began with *Dear Mr Corrigan,* then deleted it and replaced it with *Dear Zac.* Her hands were shaking, her thumbs fumbling on the keys as she forced herself to continue.

It is with deep regret…

Again she stopped and deleted. She had to keep this businesslike.

I wish to advise that I am resigning from my position as Personal Assistant to the Managing Director of ZedCee Management Consultants.

The terms of my contract require two weeks' notice for the termination of employment from either party. I will make myself available to assist in a smooth transition for my replacement.

Chloe pressed her hand against the new ache that flared just beneath her ribs, then she continued to type…

I've enjoyed working at…

She stopped and let out another soft groan. What was the point of telling Zac that? He knew only too well how much she'd loved her job. Better to just ask him for a reference.

Did she want a reference? She supposed she should have one, but she hated the thought of having to hunt for another job…

As she began to type again she heard a noise… Once again, it was coming from the front door…

Another caller?

This time there was the unmistakable sound of a key turning in the lock…

Not another of Zac's girlfriends? Chloe wasn't sure she could face another of Zac's blonde beauties. And it seemed that this one had privileged status and her very own key.

Wincing as she set her half-written letter aside, Chloe got to her feet. Her *bare* feet.

She couldn't remember the last time she'd checked her appearance in a mirror and there was every chance she had baby dribble on her T-shirt, and if this woman had a key she was sure to be at least as glamorous as Daisy. Chloe was madly finger-combing her hair as she heard footsteps coming down the hallway. She braced herself for a vision of sexy high fashion.

She had the words ready. 'I'm sorry, but Zac isn't—'

The figure coming into the lounge room was tall and

dark and exceptionally masculine. Chloe's heart almost stopped.

'Zac?'

'Hi.' He dropped his keys into a pottery dish on the low entertainment unit, and then he set down a pot of bright red double gerberas and a box of chocolates. He looked pale, almost unwell, and deep lines furrowed his brow and the sides of his mouth.

'What happened?' Chloe had visions of a highway smash. 'Is everything all right? Did you get as far as the Gold Coast?'

'No.' Zac stood in the middle of the room with his hands on his hips. His chest expanded as he drew a deep breath.

Something had clearly gone wrong. Had Marissa refused to see him?

'Is there anything I can do? A cup of—'

A faint sad smile briefly tilted a corner of his mouth. 'All I need is for you to listen, Chloe. There's—' his Adam's apple rippled as he swallowed '—there's something I need to tell you.'

The growing knots of anxiety in Chloe's stomach tightened as Zac turned, looked around his lounge room, almost as if he was seeing it for the first time. Then he took a seat in the chair opposite her, and he leaned back against the smooth leather upholstery as if this could somehow help him to relax.

He was wearing jeans and a white shirt, unbuttoned at the collar and with the sleeves rolled back. Despite the crackling tension, Chloe couldn't help admiring the way his dark hair and bronzed skin contrasted so gorgeously with the whiteness of his shirt.

'I hope you haven't had more bad news,' she said gently.

'No, just a painful revelation.' Again, he cracked the faintest glimmer of a smile, before he dropped his gaze and traced the arm of the chair with his fingertips, as if he was testing the texture of the leather.

Chloe tried not to notice how beautiful his hands were, so long-fingered and strong, and she struggled to banish unhelpful memories of his hands touching and caressing her, driving her to rapture.

'I didn't go to the Gold Coast,' he said. 'Actually, I have a confession. Almost as soon as I dialled Marissa's number yesterday, I knew that proposing to her would be a huge mistake, but then I had to spend the next hour coming up with a crazy explanation for why I'd rung her…and then more time trying to wriggle out of seeing her again.' He gave a wry smile as he shook his head. 'It was yet another of my famous stuff-ups.'

Chloe swallowed nervously, unsure what to say.

'I'm sorry I gave you the wrong impression, Chloe. I should have set you straight this morning when you mentioned the flowers, but I wasn't ready to explain.'

'It's not really my business.'

Zac smiled at her then. 'Of course, Ms Meadows.' Then his expression was serious once more as he said, 'Truth is, I've been walking the streets, trying to clear my head and think everything through.'

Chloe nodded. This was understandable. He'd had next to no privacy in the past few days.

'You asked me in London if I've ever been in love,' he said next, somewhat abruptly.

In an instant her skin turned to goosebumps. 'Yes, I did.'

'I said I hadn't, but I lied.'

Oh. Chloe couldn't think what to say, but her heart had begun to pound so loudly now that she was sure Zac must be able to hear it.

'I was in love once, a long time ago,' he went on quietly. 'It was in my first year at university.' His shoulders lifted in a shrug. 'I guess it was first love, or puppy love, or whatever, but it certainly felt real at the time.' He looked away to the far window and its views of the sunny city skyline. 'Her name was Rebecca and I was crazy about her.'

Chloe had no idea why Zac had come back with flowers or why he was telling her this, and she certainly couldn't risk trying to guess, but she was so tense now she thought she might snap in two.

'Of course, I had all these dreams,' he went on. 'Nothing flash. Just the usual—marriage, family, happy ever after...'

The things he no longer believed in.

'Then my parents disappeared,' he said. 'And my life changed overnight. I felt I had to give up university and get a job, and take on the responsibility of looking after Liv. I needed to be home for her on the weekends and in the evenings. I didn't have time for a social life, so I put my dreams on the back burner.'

'And you broke up with Rebecca,' Chloe guessed.

'Yes.' He gave another crookedly cynical smile. 'She soon took up with another guy and within two years she married him.'

Oh, dear.

Chloe could see it all so clearly... Zac's world had been turned upside down when his parents disappeared… He'd sacrificed his dreams, only to be rewarded by heartbreak…

But as she sat there, listening and watching him and not daring to analyse why he was telling her this, she realised something so surprising that she gasped and felt quite giddy…

Surely, Zac's whole playboy persona had been a reaction to this heartbreak? After he'd lost his parents and his first girlfriend—a girl he'd genuinely loved—he'd been desperate to save his little sister. But then Liv had proved rebellious and Zac had responded with his own form of rebellion—his never-ending procession of *Foolish Females*.

Playing the field had been Zac's way of escaping, of protecting himself from ever being hurt again…

Of course it was far safer to never fall in love. Chloe knew this only too well. She'd been doing the same thing in a different way. After Sam's death, she'd avoided a social life, with its accompanying risks and pain, by hiding away and caring for her parents.

Oh, Zac. Her heart ached for him as she watched him now, as he drew another deep, nervous breath and let it out with a sigh.

She wondered if his current dilemma was her fault somehow. Had he realised that Marissa would also expect a declaration of love…and that, for him, it was still a step too far…

'So does this mean…?' she began, but then she stopped, uncertain of how to voice her thoughts diplomatically.

Zac looked across at her, not quite smiling. 'The long-winded point that I'm trying to make is that I do know what it's like to love someone and to lose her.'

'Yes, but that shouldn't—'

Chloe stopped again as the silent message in Zac's eyes made her heart thump so loudly she was sure he must hear it. She was poised on the edge of her seat now and she held her breath, not daring to say anything more, not daring to wonder, even fearfully, where exactly this revelation was heading.

Without warning, Zac launched to his feet again.

'I walked over the bridge and into the city,' he said. 'One of my mates is a real estate agent and I was going to ask him to look out for a place for Lucy and me.'

Chloe nodded miserably. Zac had decided to take responsibility for Lucy after all—without 'using' one of his women. It was an important step forward for him and she knew she should be pleased.

He forced an edgy smile, then turned and picked up the pot of red gerberas. 'I didn't get as far as my mate's office. I walked past a florist's.' The flowers trembled in Zac's hand. He was shaking and Chloe couldn't bear it.

'There were all these lilies in the window. You'd told me to get lilies for Marissa, but I suddenly knew: if I bought flowers for anyone, it had to be for you.'

She could barely hear him now over the ridiculous thundering of her heartbeats and it was almost impossible to see him through her tears.

'But I had no idea which were your favourites,' Zac said. 'I don't have a spreadsheet for you, Chloe.' He gave her another of his gorgeous crooked, sad smiles. 'But these made me think of your red dress and…and I hope you like them. Anyway, I had no choice. I had to bring them back to *you*.'

She was shaking, pressing a hand to her mouth…

'I was hoping to…to have another shot at that pro-posal.'

Now Chloe was on the edge of her seat, so tense she could only bite her lip as tears filled her eyes.

'I…I think I might have given you the impression last time that I only asked you to marry me because you would make a good mother for Lucy. And you would—you'd be perfect, but that's not why I need you, Chloe. That's so, so wrong.'

She swiped at her stupid, blinding tears. She wanted to see him—*needed* to see him. Oh, dear Lord, he looked so worried.

'The truth is,' Zac said, 'I reckon I've probably been in love with you since you first arrived in the office. I guess I just wouldn't let myself admit it, but I love being around you, Chloe. I love seeing you, whether you're serious or happy, or telling me off. I love hearing your voice. I love asking your advice. I even love drinking your damn cups of tea… I know it sounds crazy, but I hurry to work each day, just to see you.'

She thought of all those mornings that she'd looked forward to, too… Zac almost always arrived early, around the same time that she did and they always shared a little harmless light conversation. He would crack a joke, talk about something he'd heard on the news as he was driving to work, share a little gossip about one of their competitors. Drink the tea that she made.

Those mornings, before the rest of the staff arrived, had been her favourite time of day and now she could feel the truth of his claim filling her with light. Golden light was flooding her from the toes up, filling her chest, her arms, her head.

'No, it doesn't sound crazy,' she told him.

Zac swallowed. 'No?'

'I've felt the same about you.'

His eyes widened. 'You have?'

She felt brave enough to tell him now. 'Hopelessly in love from Day One. Probably ever since my job interview.'

For a trembling moment they stared at each other while this astonishing truth sank in. Then Zac set down the flowers and held out his arms and at last—at *last*—Chloe flew to safety.

As she hurled herself against him, his arms came around her, holding her preciously close. 'Oh, Chloe, I do love you. So, so much.'

'I know, I know.' She pressed her face against his shoulder, loving that she now had the right to be there, in his arms, leaning in to his strength.

'But I need to apologise about the way I carried on with the rubbish about romance and delusions,' Zac persisted. 'I was deluding myself. I *know* love's real. It's how I feel about you. Standing outside that florist's, I couldn't breathe when I realised I was losing you. I love you so much.'

He pulled back to look into her eyes. 'You do believe me, don't you?'

'I do, Zac.'

'Honestly?'

'You've already shown me in so many ways.'

'Oh, God, I hope so.'

There were no more tears now as she kissed his jaw, his cheek.

'Oh, Chloe.' Framing her face with his hands, Zac touched his lips to hers and his kiss was so tender and lingering and loving, Chloe thought she might actually swoon with an excess of happiness.

It was some time before their kiss ended and she nestled her head against his shoulder again. 'You were right,' she said. 'We don't need the words.'

He gave a soft laugh. 'But I want to say them now. I'm not scared of them and it feels so good. I'm going to tell you every day that I love you.' With gentle fingers, he traced the line of her cheek. 'Isn't it incredible that we've both been waiting? Why did it take us so damn long to work this out?'

'We're both sticklers for office protocol?'

This brought one of Zac's beautifully devilish grins and, a beat later, he slipped one arm around Chloe's shoulders, then a hand beneath her knees as he literally swept her off her feet. 'Stuff the protocol, Ms Meadows.'

He was already halfway to the bedroom.

EPILOGUE

AT FIRST, WHEN Chloe woke, she forgot what day it was. She lay very still with her eyes closed, enjoying the warm stream of the sunlight that filtered through the poinciana tree outside the bedroom window.

Then she rolled towards Zac, reaching for him…only to find an empty space in the bed. Her eyes flashed open and she saw their bedroom, bright with summer sunlight, saw the little silver tree on the dressing table, the red glass tumblers holding the tea light candles that she'd lit last night. She'd had so much fun decorating the house for Christmas.

Zap. She sat up with a jolt as she remembered. This was it. Christmas morning.

How on earth could she have slept in? She'd been looking forward to this day with an almost childish excitement.

Now there was no time to waste. She had to see if Lucy was awake and she needed to know what Zac was up to.

Throwing off the sheet, she smiled at her new Christmas pyjamas—a red T-shirt teamed with cotton pants decorated with bright green holly and red bows. Although Chloe had always loved Christmas, this year she'd probably gone a trifle overboard, with decorations in every room of the house as well as extra details like special tablecloths and napkins for their Christmas dinner. She'd even bought special festive coffee mugs. Luckily, Zac didn't seem to mind.

Now, she ducked into Lucy's room. 'Merry Christmas, baby g—'

The cot was empty and Chloe felt a stab of disappointment, but she quickly squashed it as the smell of coffee wafted from downstairs…and then, as she descended, she heard the deep rumbling voice that she knew so well…

'And this is a special ornament that Mummy bought last Christmas in Selfridges in London… You were there, too, you know, pumpkin. Such a teensy little thing you were then…and it was wintertime and cold, not sweltering and hot like today… And over here under the tree are all the lovely presents… No, no, hang on. You can't rip them to pieces just yet. We can't open them till Mummy wakes up…'

At the bottom of the stairs now, Chloe caught a glimpse through to the lounge room and she stopped to admire the view of Zac and Lucy together. Zac was balancing Lucy on his hip with the practised ease of an expert and the baby was chuckling and reaching up to grab at a bright decoration. When she couldn't reach, she tried to squeeze his nose instead.

In response, Zac ducked, then playfully pretended to nibble Lucy's hand, which made her squeal with delight.

Chloe grinned. She never tired of seeing these two together. Over the past year they had formed a very special bond that boded very well for the future.

Lucy had grown into such a cute little bundle of mischief. She was a sturdy and determined one-year-old, now, and her hair was a mass of glossy dark curls, her eyes a bright, vivid blue. And she was constantly breaking into the most wonderfully happy smiles.

In Zac's strong arms, however, she still looked small and vulnerable…but safe. So wonderfully safe.

'And up here is something incredibly important,' Zac told the little girl as he pointed to a bunch of greenery in the doorway. 'This is a VIP plant that I have to show your mummy. It's called mistletoe and it's a tradition. Your mum's very fond of tradition…'

Chloe smiled again and felt a flush of pure, unfiltered joy. Soon it would all begin—the exchange of presents, the feasting, and sharing the day with her parents…

It would be quite a simple Christmas compared with last year's cathedral and banquet, but for Chloe this felt like the perfect end to a year that had been wonderful in so many ways—bringing happiness beyond her wildest dreams. At times it had seemed almost too good to be true and she'd had to pinch herself.

Of course, the three hundred and sixty-five days since their Christmas in London hadn't been a total bed of roses. In fact, the year had started off quite busily, and Chloe had spent most of January learning to balance caring for Lucy with helping a new PA to settle into her job.

Zac had been worried that Chloe might be bored with staying at home full-time and so they'd experimented with hiring a babysitter, who minded Lucy for one day a week while Chloe worked on the ZedCee files from her home office. It had worked well. Chloe loved being Lucy's mum, but she also found it rewarding to keep in touch with projects that had nothing to do with nappies or feeding schedules.

Then, in March, they'd moved out of the inner city apartment and into their contemporary two-storey home in the leafy suburb of Kenmore. They'd had a ton of fun house-hunting together, and they loved this house. With Zac's assistance, Chloe's parents were resettled two blocks away, in a lovely cottage in a retirement complex.

Chloe visited them almost every day, often walking there and taking Lucy for an outing in the pram. The little girl loved her Grammy and Gramps, and of course Hettie and Joe Meadows were utterly smitten by the baby, and they were completely shameless about their hero worship of Zac.

The wedding had been in June. Zac and Chloe had chosen a simple ceremony on the beach with a select group of friends and Chloe's misty-eyed parents. Afterwards, Zac and Chloe had flown north to Hamilton Island and, naturally, they'd taken Lucy with them. It was all quite magical.

There'd been tough days too, of course, times when Zac's grief for Liv had caught up with him, but it helped that Chloe had been through her own dark days of grief and she understood.

She'd been worried when Lucy's first birthday drew near, knowing that it coincided with a very sad anniversary. But six days ago the three of them had taken the ferry across to Stradbroke Island and there, while Lucy crawled on the sand and tried to chase tiny crabs, Chloe had watched as Zac paddled alone on a surfboard, out beyond the breakers. He'd taken a bunch of yellow roses and the small urn with Liv's ashes...

Afterwards, they'd stayed on the beach, playing with Lucy and talking quietly, remembering their journey to London...and Zac had shared one or two memories of Liv...

Eventually, Lucy had fallen asleep in Zac's arms and so they'd stayed there, sitting together on the warm sand and watching the distant horizon until the last of the daylight faded into the black of night...and the moon rose, bright and golden and full of new promise...

'I'd like to come here every year,' Zac had said. 'Liv loved this place...and...and I reckon it helps.'

'Yes, it's important,' Chloe had agreed. Somehow, the sea and the wind, the wide open sky and the reassuring crash and thump of the surf seemed to help to soothe Zac's pain. 'We should definitely make it a tradition.'

Now, Zac turned and caught sight of Chloe at the bottom of the stairs.

'Hey,' he cried, his face lighting up. 'Lucy, look who's awake!'

'Mumma!' the baby girl shouted as she held out her chubby arms.

Still holding Lucy, Zac hurried over and slipped an arm around Chloe and kissed her. 'Merry Christmas, my bright-eyed girl.'

'Merry Christmas.' Chloe couldn't resist stroking his lovely bare chest. 'I hear you've been educating Lucy about Christmas traditions.'

'Like mistletoe?'

'Uh-huh.'

His eyes shimmered with secret amusement as he smiled at her. 'If you'd been listening carefully, you

BARBARA HANNAY 187

would know that there are one or two other traditions I'm reserving just for you.'

Chloe grinned. It was a promise she would definitely hold him to.

* * * * *

MILLS & BOON®

Sparkling Christmas sensations!

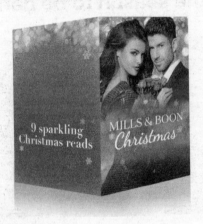

This fantastic Christmas collection is fit to burst with billionaire businessmen, Regency rakes, festive families and smouldering encounters.

Set your pulse racing with this festive bundle of 24 stories, plus get a fantastic 40% OFF!

Visit the Mills & Boon website today to take advantage of this spectacular offer!

www.millsandboon.co.uk/Xmasbundle

ST_4